boiling
a frog

christopher
brookmyre

LITTLE, BROWN AND COMPANY

A *Little, Brown* Book

First published in Great Britain in 2000
by Little, Brown and Company

Copyright © Christopher Brookmyre 2000

The moral right of the author has been asserted.

A CIP catalogue record for this book
is available from the British Library.

HARDBACK ISBN 0 316 85190 6
C FORMAT ISBN 0 316 85191 4

Typeset by Palimpsest Book Production Limited,
Polmont, Stirlingshire
Printed and bound in Great Britain by
Clays Ltd, St Ives plc

Little, Brown and Company (UK)
Brettenham House
Lancaster Place
London WC2E 7EN

For Nicola, who liked Fooaltiye.

Special thanks to Iain Ruxton, who would rather have been no help at all. Thanks also: Marisa for her ministrations, Roger Dubar for his verifications, Perg for pressing motivation, POTZW for therapeutic distraction and SMFC for palpitations.
KTF, FTOF.

author's note

Amphibians are poikilothermic: their body temperatures adapt automatically to changes in their environment, without their noticing. Theoretically, this means that if you were to put a frog in a pan of cold water, then turn up the heat gradually enough, you could cook the poor creature to death before it realised it was in danger.

NB: The title of this novel is a metaphor, not a recipe. The author is not in any way advocating or condoning the boiling of frogs. Not if there's a perfectly healthy cat available, anyway.

Let him who is without sin cast the first stone.

– some sandal-wearing bleeding-heart
who got what was coming to him

what jail is like

'John Lapsley Parlabane. That you stand before this court today will, I am sure, have come as a surprise to many, not least your erstwhile smug and, as it turns out, disastrously complacent self. However, to those with a more rounded experience of your methods and morality, both the beneficiaries and the victims of your self-righteous and self-appointed crusading, it will remain a source of bed-wetting astonishment that it has taken so long for the forces of the law to bring themselves to bear upon your arrogant and devious person.

'You are, in the well-chosen words of our Prime Minister in describing your ilk, an unreconstructed wanker. To that one might add that you have infinitely more to say for yourself than your knowledge or experience could possibly justify, and that I have seldom found myself passing sentence on someone so evidently lacking the benefits of a damn good kicking.

'You have thrust upon us your ill-informed, half-baked, out-dated and, frankly, paranoid theories for a tiresome number of years now, and the wonder of it is that anyone continued to listen long enough for you to persist with the behaviour that has ultimately led to your downfall. I would remind you, Mr Parlabane, that paranoia is often merely the flipside of egotism: both deludedly imagine the world to revolve around oneself.

'While your journalistic exploits have occasionally enjoyed

vindication in the past, it should be evident to anyone remotely cognisant with the facts that your roles in certain notorious events have been grossly exaggerated by both posterity – which is often inexplicably kind to the self-aggrandising – and by your own indulgently biased accounts. No doubt you like to depict yourself as a thorn in the flesh of the establishment, but closer to the truth would be to say that you are merely an irritant, and that the subsequent rashes are far more the result of your unwanted presence than of any defect on the part of those you choose to infect.

'In the case of someone so self-absorbed, it is perhaps plausible that certain developments in the wider world may have escaped your notice; to wit, the inexorable passing of the years and the irrefutable testimony of the calendar, which states, if you would take note, that this is not the 1990s any more. Once upon a time, you found and to your credit exposed corruption and conspiracy among those of whom we expected better. Your problem, it strikes me, was that you did not know what to be about next. You have continued to seek out such nefariousness, but where you have not found it you have instead imagined it – and more insidiously, implied it. If I were you, I might wish to consider whether a man who finds corruption in every place he looks might perhaps be seeing the reflection of what lies within himself.

'In the instance that has brought you before me, you arrogantly pitted yourself against an organisation far more august and enduring than the windmills at which you had tilted before; and though you were but a mosquito attacking an elephant, it cannot be ignored that this mosquito wished the elephant harm, and its bite may have done so had it not been swatted.

2

'In short, Mr Parlabane, there is no place for you here in the future. This is a new Scotland, a new country, with new standards and a new morality. I must not allow it or its institutions – nascent and ancient alike – to be disparaged and prejudiced by the diseased mind of a wee shite like you. For this reason, I order that you be taken from this court, henceforth to a place of confinement, there to dwell in perpetual fear of being chibbed and humped by rabid schemies.

'Take him down.'

Okay, so those weren't the sheriff's precise words, but the import was much the same, and Parlabane wasn't arguing. No grand conspiracy had ensnared him, just his own stubbornness and complacency, in combination with a nihilistic recklessness that was unmistakably borne of wilful self-destruction. He was in the huff with the whole wide world, and indulged the negligent abandon of a wounded fool, heedless of danger because he's convinced nothing can hurt him anymore than he's been hurt already.

The slamming of the cell door shook him out of it and loudly begged to differ.

The sheriff's pronouncement of sentence had failed to deliver such a jolt, Parlabane meekly absorbing it with a masochistic resignation. Go on, do your worst. See if I care. You think I'm scared of pain and misery? Let me tell you about pain and misery, pal. Let me tell you what jail is really like. Loneliness? Isolation? Humiliation? Ostracisation? Tick, tick, tick, tick.

The van, the guards, the handcuffs, the prison building, none of them penetrated the cocoon of symbiotic self-pity and self-loathing. They were all part of a journey, and on journeys it's always easy, if you wish, to blot out all thoughts of what awaits at your destination. Parlabane remembered the supreme acts of will it once took to get him to leave even a diesel-reeking railway carriage at Glasgow Central when only lectures and tutorials lay ahead. Elaborate sexual imaginings and scything ripostes to Old-Firm-biased football pundits were hardly the stuff of profound immersion, but nonetheless most mornings he was willing the train to slow. Whether it be by van, train, car or womb, coping with reality could be suspended until you reached your destination – but only until then.

In truth, it wasn't really the slamming and locking of the reception cell that woke Parlabane from his weeks of absorption, but what happened in the immediate moments following: viz, nothing at all. The jangle of some keys, the muted echoes of shouts from somewhere else in the hall, the departing footsteps of the warder, and after that, only the sound of his own breath.

A few seconds of that and all the things it had seemed so bloody important to be right about suddenly lost their hypnotic allure, finally revealing themselves to be as tarnished and worthless as anyone else could have told him. Or rather, as one particular person had been trying to tell him, if only he'd taken his head out of his arse long enough to hear her.

Sarah. Oh shit.

Yep, he'd really shown her, hadn't he? She'd certainly learn her lesson now. No more stepping out of line for that one, no sirree.

Christ.

Unreconstructed wanker? Total fucking arsehole.

He sat down on the edge of the lower bunk, staring at the door, head sinking to palms, elbows in anticipatory support on his thighs.

Remind me again, he asked himself, why you thought it a constructive course of action to go breaking into the headquarters of the Scottish Catholic Church. Stumped? Too tough? All right, how about an easier one. Run by me one more time why you decided your own pride would keep you company once it had successfully alienated your wife. Maybe you'd like some more time to think about it. No problem. How about six months, minus remission?

'Awwww, fuck.'

He closed his eyes, waiting for tears, but no such comfort came. He was still too numb to feel anything but stupid.

'Haaa! You're gaunny greet, ya fuckin' waaank!'

Fright ripped through Parlabane like an electro-magnetic pulse, as the voice intruded on his confinement from about a foot behind his ear. In his startlement he tried to stand up and smacked his head off the top bunk, consequently collapsing to the floor as his legs buckled beneath him.

'Ah-hahahahahaha – fuckin' waaank!'

He was facing away from the bed, barely able to focus, breathing rapidly through gritted teeth. He clutched both hands to the top of his head, pressing down so hard that if he had been a Striker football figurine, his right foot would have booted the ball off the table and all the way under the fridge, whence never to return. Tears, it did not escape his notice, were no problem now.

Sarah had once explained to him why applying pressure to an injury helps dull the pain: it sends supplementary information along the nerves, effectively taking up some of the brain's sensory-processing capacity that would otherwise be more exclusively applied to acknowledging the fact that you'd just, for example, rattled your head off a metal bedframe. On this occasion, however, Parlabane felt it was more a matter of holding his skull together.

'Ah-hahahahahaha! Fuckin' lyin' burlin'. Ah-hahahaha! Daft cunt.'

He blinked a few times, widened his eyes, shut them, then widened them again, strenuously beseeching the room to behave. In time, the batteries ran out on the stroboscope, and the giant who was shaking the cell like an unopened Christmas parcel finally got bored and put it down on the floor again. Parlabane tentatively lifted his fingers from his scalp, and grimaced at the sensation of stickiness. There couldn't be many parts of the human body which didn't make him queasy upon the secretion of moisture to the touch. Indeed, off-hand the only one he could think of wasn't even on *his* body, but it would be wise to put that from his mind for a while. A long while.

Parlabane examined his fingers. There was blood, but little more than a smear. It would probably be pushing it to ask the warder whether a CT scan might be called for.

He turned his head delicately to look at the bunks. On the bottom, pressed back against the wall and leaning up on one elbow, there lay this wraith of a creature, sneering like an anorexic gargoyle. Parlabane hadn't noticed anyone else in the cell when he was brought in, and though he would admit his own dedicated obliviousness could account for certain observational deficiencies, it nonetheless failed to explain entirely how he could miss the fact that the bed he'd sat down on was already occupied. But then, that was because he was used to people existing in three dimensions. This sliver barely put a ripple in the blanket.

'Fuckin' never saw me there, did ye? Fuckin' daft cunt. Hahahahaha.'

It was initially difficult to make out a face atop what the sliver was attempting to pass off as a body – at least until you knew what you were looking for. The bloke's

6

skin was a bluey-grey colour that would have had any competent physician diving for the intubation kit, and which, by what Parlabane sincerely hoped was coincidence, matched the walls of the cell to within a pantone. When he laughed – which had so far been about sixty percent of the time – he wore an expression that suggested he was simultaneously attempting to pass an agricultural implement, with the subsidiary effect of stretching his skin so tight across his face that there seemed a tangible danger of his cheekbones bursting through the pallid membrane. Fortunately, he didn't appear to *have* any cheekbones. Evolution, Parlabane reflected, could be awful clever that way.

He patted tenderly at his scalp again. It was still seeping, the reverberations continuing to shudder through his head in time with his pulse. He had a look at the ascent required to reach the top bunk and opted to stay crumpled on the floor for a few more minutes' convalescence.

'Fooaltiyeman, that looked fuckin' sair. Hahahahahaha. Fuckin' daft cunt.'

The sliver adjusted his reclining posture, shuffling forwards from the wall, presumably to afford himself a better view of the ongoing daft-cuntery.

'Serve ye fuckin' right, sittin' there when it's ma fuckin' bed.'

With his sleeve having fallen away from it a couple of inches, Parlabane could now more clearly see the grey twiglet of arm that was implausibly supporting Sliver's head. It looked as though all it would take to snap the thing would be for a fly to alight on his nose, but Parlabane knew better than to assume his appearance was any reflection on his ability to look after himself. He certainly wasn't about to put it to the test by telling him to shut the fuck

7

up. Nonetheless, Parlabane felt sure, if Sliver had been in Belsen, his nickname would have been 'Slim'.

'Sorry,' he managed quietly. 'I'll take the top one, shall I?'

'Fuckin' right ye will. Go up there an' greet.'

'In a minute.'

'Fuckin' first time, innit, eh? Fuckin' never been in the jile afore, huv ye? Ahhh, fuckin' shitin' it I bet, fuckinnn. Ahh-haa. Fuckin' . . . Fooaltiyeman, I don't fuckin' like the look o' your fuckin' chances man, ne'er I don't. Fuckin' sideyways for you, pal, mark my fuckin' words. Fuckin' daft cunt. Fooaltiye, I've been inside a few times, man, fuckin' seen it aw afore, man, fuckin' *awyit*, an' fuckin' . . . fuckin' cunts like you, naw, man, hahaha, don't fuckin' fancy ye, altiye. Haha. Fuckin' sideyways. Fuckin' twirly sheets job, man, altiye. Ahh-haaaah. Fuckin' waaank.'

Parlabane, even in his embattled, embittered and em, just-hit-his-head-off-an-iron-bedframe state, retained sufficient presence of mind to appreciate the significance of the moment. As a man who scornfully disapproved of inappropriate superlatives, he could honestly say he was now in the presence of the least charming person he had ever met. Given that he worked in the journalism trade, and that through his wife he had unavoidably met a number of surgeons, this was saying something.

'Fooaltiyeman, I've seen your type afore, many a time. Many. A. Fu. Kin. Time. Fooaltiye, fuckin' easy meat, man, that's you, fuckinnnn ah-haa.'

Parlabane felt an enormous temptation to point at him, narrow his eyes and say: 'Gordonstoun? No, no, no, that's right. Fettes, Fettes.' Resisting was assisted by the thought that he had precipitated the previous torrents merely by being in the same cell. Actually upsetting the cadaverous bastard was, as Sarah might put it, contra-indicated.

He winced at the phrase, the remembered sound of her voice in his head. It was like pouring Tabasco sauce on to his injured scalp. Daft cunt right enough. Fuckin' wank. Ahh-haaa. Fuckinnnn.

Without warning or apparent explanation, something evidently occurred to Sliver (or 'Fooaltiye', as Parlabane was beginning to think of him). He softened his expression and leaned that bit further forward. The effect on his face was to make it look like merely a death-mask, as opposed to an atrophied skull, but the intention was clearly solicitous.

'Nah mate, just kiddin ye oan like n'at, know? Just a fuckin' wee joke, man, fuckinnn. I mean, ye awright like? Ye awright? Banged your heid? Fooaltiye, looked fuckin' sair, man, so it did. Ye awright?'

What, Parlabane wondered, could possibly have caused this impromptu *volte-face* (or volte-skull if he was being pedantic)? What pacific thought could have tamed the rage in this tormented and misunderstood young man's heart?

'Ye any fags?'

That would be it, then.

'Sorry, I don't smoke.'

'Fuck's sake. Aye right. Naw, ne'er ye dae. Fuckinnn. Altiyeman, it's amazin'. Nae cunt smokes in this place, no when ye fuckin' tap them anyway. Fuckinn. Come oan, ya cunt. Just gie's a fag. Just wan. Fuck's sake.'

Parlabane felt an amplified throb in his head as Fooaltiye raised his voice. Despite the distraction of pain, his detective skills had successfully decoded the human skelf's eponymous, punctuatory ejaculation. He had achieved this through the cryptographic technique of comparing its constituent variants: Fooaltiyeman, Fooaltiye, Altiyeman and just plain Altiye. Translated from the primitive and obscure

'Prick' dialect, it meant 'Phew, I'll tell you, man . . .' and heralded an observation of deepest wisdom.

'I don't smoke,' Parlabane repeated, slowly, quietly, every word's resonation giving his napper another twinge.

'Awww, fuck's sake, man. Fuckinnn, come on, man. If I had some I'd gie you wan, 'mon tae fuck. Just fuckin' cough, man, just wan, 'mon.'

Parlabane cradled his head again as the throbbing threatened to resume its previous intensity.

'I don't smoke. I never have.'

'Right.'

There was a flurry of dark and light greys as the bottom bunk's blanket billowed angrily and Fooaltiye emerged from beneath it. He hopped down to the floor and squatted in front of Parlabane, scrawny, pale and sweatily greasy: Smeagol with a habit.

'Fuckin' stop an' search time, ya cunt. An' altiye, if I fuckin' fin' any fags, you're gettin' a fuckin' skelp, man. Alfuckintiye.'

Fooaltiye was in his face, his emaciated and pock-marked limbs seeming to enclose Parlabane. Hands patted him down, a bony knee pressed into his ribs, and from his dental write-off of a mouth there wafted vapours internationally outlawed since the First World War.

Parlabane just sat there, motionless, unresisting, head-bowed, feeling the utter humiliation of his vulnerability. This was what he had brought himself to: being menaced by some junky scrote practically half his age, and being too fucking scared to do anything about it but close his eyes and wait for it to be over.

What the hell *could* he do? On the outside he'd once been a man of boundless (and, when necessary, lawless) resources, all of which could be put to use in compensating for the fact that when it came to physical brutality, he wouldn't last three rounds with Tweety-Pie. He'd always been slight, but with it had come the benefits of a low centre of gravity and a blessed gift in the middle-ear department. Balance and aim came easily, which in his schooldays had made him a fairly nippy winger in the classic Scottish 'irritating wee bastard' mould. In later life they had afforded an unusual (but frequently utilised) facility for negotiating the exteriors of otherwise inaccessible premises; and an even more dubious subsidiary bonus was that they also made him a natural shot. These abilities, together with a connoisseur's eye for subterfuge, had allowed him to evade the malice and vengeance of billionaires, politicians, conspirators, crooks, thugs and professional assassins on two continents.

None of them, however, were any use one-on-one in a Saughton jail-cell, with his brain still reverberating and his sense of self at a record low. Fooaltiye was hardly likely to be the worst of it, either.

The patting-down ceased with a loud tut and a 'fuck's sake'. Fooaltiye got up and returned to his lair on the bottom bunk. Parlabane remained staring at the floor, fearing that if he stood up, he'd find himself less than an inch tall.

'Fuckin' waank. Fuckin' nae use tae nae cunt, fuck's sake.'

Parlabane harboured fleeting thoughts of the Beretta once secreted in his flat in East London Street. Childish. He glanced up at Fooaltiye, his revenge fantasy mutating absurdly. The scrawny bawhair became the Emperor Palpatine, the Beretta sitting on the arm of his chair. 'You want . . . *this* . . . don't you?'

Get over it. Get used to it.

'Fuck's sake, man. Nae fuckin' fags. Aww, fuck, man. I'm fuckin' dyin' man, altiye. Fuckin' nuhin since this mornin'

11

man, fuckin' chronic, man. Altiye, s'gaunny be 'oors afore we get sorted oot here – an' that means fuckin' 'oors afore *I* can get sorted oot, if ye ken whit I mean. Fuckinnn . . . take their time, so they will, the fuckin' screws. You might as well get comfy, ya cunt, 'cause we're gaun naewhere. Aww, s'gaunny be murder, man, fuuuck. Fuckin' need somethin' man. Just a fuckin' fag would dae me the noo.'

This was the closest thing to helpful advice he was likely to get. It would indeed be a while – maybe even overnight, given the hour already – before the powers-that-be decided more specifically what they were going to do with him. He eyed the upper bunk. The brain-rattling exertions of the ascent would be rewarded with the convalescent opportunities of a lie-down, and maybe with a little luck the whole fucking thing might collapse and crush Kate Moss down there to death.

Unfortunately, the solidity suggested by the frame's earlier impact on Parlabane's head was borne out when he stretched himself upon the mattress, itself possibly the only thing in the building skinnier than his cell-mate. Rest was to be found only in the strict, physically immobile sense, as Fooaltiye's garrulousness was not impeded by Parlabane's retreat to bed anymore than it had been by his serial refusal to in any way engage him. Fooaltiye, he gathered, was just a trifle anxious about a certain chemical imbalance which he wished to remedy at the earliest possible juncture, and his forced abstention from even so much as a skinny roll-up was somewhat limiting the scope of his conversational motifs.

'Aww, fuck, man, altiye, I'm fuckin' sufferin' here, man, so I am. Fuckinnn.'

Good, Parlabane thought, before calculating the greater ramifications, principally those affecting the likelihood of

12

the bugger shutting up about it. He wasn't worried about anything more dramatic, having benefited from the dual perspectives on overnight smackhead behaviour offered by Sarah, as an anaesthetist, and their friend Jenny Dalziel, as a cop. In hospital, incapacitated and cut off from their supply, Sarah said they invariably went totally candy-floss, trying to convince the heartless bastard staff that the very demons of hell had been unleashed upon them by their excruciating withdrawal. The goal of these scenery-chewing performances was to elicit any pharmaceuticals the docs might be willing to part with for the sake of a quiet night.

Down at the cells, however, Jenny insisted it was a very different story. They knew they were in for the night, knew there was absolutely no chance of getting anything more exhilarating than a good kick in the balls for their troubles, so they were good as gold, co-operating in any way that would more quickly expedite getting back on the street. *French Connection* 2 reconstructions were very few and far between. They just sat tight, sniffed and sweated, waited for their statutory roll and sausage in the morning, then fucked off as soon as the polis let them.

Fooaltiye wouldn't go nuts, Parlabane knew, but more worryingly, he had a literally captive audience, and very little sensitivity to how his material was going down. He tried holding the pillow to his ears, but it was too flimsy to do more than slightly muffle the interminable soliloquy, and given that Fooaltiye's vocabulary was barely into three figures, nor was there any danger of losing the import through missing some subtle nuance.

The defining aspect of this latterday epic – *The Sweariad*, as Parlabane had begun thinking of it after the first hour or so – was not Fooaltiye's anally detailed odyssey through the Fabled Realms of Skag; nor even his evocative descriptions of tonight's anguished deprivation; but his exemplary employment of Junkie Logic. This was a phenomenon of which he had often heard both Sarah and Jenny talk, in terms of awe and wonder. (The awe was as in 'awe fuck, here he goes again'; the wonder as in 'I wonder if this arsehole really thinks anybody is so fucking stupid as to believe that?')

Junkie logic was tortuously complicated, fashioning elaborately structured equations that required exhausting powers of imagination to construct, and complementarily vast faculties of comprehension to follow. Hawking, it was rumoured, had considered a book on the subject, but shat it when he decided he wasn't sure he could pull it off. However, if like him you found it all too intimidatingly complex, there was always a simple primer, which is that it all ultimately adds up to an exercise in demonstrating how everything that has ever gone wrong in the life of the said junkie was entirely the fault and responsibility of someone else.

'Thae Tamazepams, man,' said Fooaltiye, for instance, 'fuckin' doctors shouldnae be allowed tae gie them oot. Altiyeman, fuckin' mate o' mine lost a fuckin' leg 'cause o' thae fuckin' things, man. Fuckin' lost a leg. Fuckin' injectin' thae jellies, fuckin' clogged up his veins, man. An' fuckin' doctors are giein them oot? Fuckin' disgrace, altiye. Shoulda been fuckin' banned yonks ago, man, if you cannae fuckin' inject the fuckin' things withoot them gummin' up your fuckin' veins. What fuckin' good are they then, man? I mean, whit stupit cunt thought that up – puttin' the stuff in fuckin' jellies? Know fuckin' nothin' these doctor cunts, altiye.'

Parlabane stifled an anguished moan. He remembered

the old joke about a new arrival in hell. The bloke gets shown a door and told, 'You're in there,' by his accompanying imp. When he gets inside, he finds a bunch of men sitting up to their necks in shit, drinking cups of tea. 'This isn't so bad,' he tells himself. 'Get used to the smell and it might even seem quite civilised.' At which point another imp sticks his head round the door and says: 'Right lads, tea-break's over. Back on your heids.'

The difference in Parlabane's case was that right then he'd prefer to be on his head. Just as long as the keech completely insulated his ears.

'Aw here, wait a minute. Wait. A. Wee. Minute. Here. Yessss!'

He couldn't help looking over the side to investigate the creature's sudden discovery, his curiosity engaged by the sheer unlikelihood of anything in any way consumable lying unused and undiscovered in a tiny prison cell. The concept of a stray fag lying unclaimed under the table was about as plausible as a stray tuppence lying unclaimed in Aberdeen.

Fooaltiye, however, was a creature of either deeper faith or greater vision. He hopped from the bed and scuttled a couple of feet across the floor, reinforcing Parlabane's Smeagol comparison.

'Fuckin' beauty, man.'

Fooaltiye placed his prize on the tabletop. Parlabane was, he would admit, a comparative ingenu in the world of serious drug usage, but he felt confident enough in his limited knowledge to be able to identify this treasured object as a teabag. In fact, a retired teabag might be more like it, the shrivelled and dried-out little thing having been pensioned off to a dusty corner of the cell after an arduous and over-long working life. Fooaltiye, to Parlabane's growing incredulity, placed a Rizla next to the teabag before picking the perforated paper open and dumping its contents on to the skin. Or rather, half its contents, as it would clearly be a shocking extravagance to waste the lot on just one roll-up.

Implausibly, the improvised cigarettes did in fact have the desired effect; or at least the effect desired by Parlabane, which was to stop Fooaltiye talking for a while. What they did for wraith-boy he couldn't care less. The smell, predictably, was revolting; Parlabane found it hard to think of descriptive comparisons, but was still sure that if Jilly Goolden got a whiff, she'd be applying it to a new cabernet-blanc varietal within the month.

The reason for Fooaltiye's silence was less the placebo effect of his faux-fags than their stubborn lack of combustibility. The sound of matches being struck and fizzing into light soon established a near-rhythmic regularity, interspersed in syncopation with fevered bouts of sucking and disappointed 'fuck's sake's. The bugger was probably inhaling more sulphur dioxide than whatever insipid fumes could be drawn from the exhausted herbs, and it entertained Parlabane to imagine it turning into oleum somewhere around Fooaltiye's tonsils, then burning through his vocal chords with a smoky hiss.

The sounds of doors slamming and locks turning echoed from beyond the cell, resonantly audible now that Fooaltiye's mouth was otherwise engaged. At first, Parlabane expected each thump and clatter to herald the arrival of the warder who would advise him of his security category and escort him to his more permanent quarters. No-one came, though. The sounds continued, merely the noises of a prison systematically getting on with its business, of which he was now a small and not particularly significant part.

16

Fear and humiliation had given way to banality and tedium, and it was the latter two that truly brought home what he was now stuck with. Not the vulnerability, the indignity or the danger of his situation, but the inexorable onset of its mundanity. He sighed, deeply, doing so before it occurred to him that it might attract Fooaltiye's interest. Fortunately, the sliver wasn't equipped for multi-tasking, so couldn't listen *and* concentrate on keeping his fag lit at the same time.

It was a good time to ask himself what the hell had gone wrong. Not as good, admittedly, as a few weeks back, when technically it was still in his gift *not* to fuck up, but that was by the by. What mattered was the question of what had led him to the course of actions that had in turn led him to this cell; what had caused him to lose his rationality, his perspective and ultimately his freedom; and what had changed him from Jack Parlabane, investigative hack, to Parlabane, John, 46967.

Tricky.

In his guilt-ridden state, it was not a struggle to lay the responsibility on his own pride and his own stupidity. Certainly, if he needed a reminder of the level of self-knowledge attained by blaming society at large for your own shortcomings, he only had to breathe in the whiff of burnt, stale tea permeating the cell. However, despite the curious comforts of self-flagellation, he was wise enough to understand that it was equally useless to divorce what he had done from the circumstances in which he had done it. The whole country, let's face it, had gone a little nuts, and while it wasn't an excuse, it was still part of the equation.

So had he been punished for being the one sane man fighting the cause of reason in a world gone crazy? Or had he been himself infected by the moralistic madness, and

17

lost his sense of judgement as a consequence? The truth, he suspected, lay somewhere in between.

The political climate had altered suddenly and violently, something which, in Parlabane's experience, political climates seldom did. New eras in politics were not precipitous. They didn't dawn, no matter how many fanfares were sounded. They took shape slowly and subtly, and you didn't realise you were in the midst of change until that change was irreversibly underway.

In the natural world, radical climatic change could be precipitated by nothing less than a disaster, such as a meteor strike or a volcanic eruption. The political world was little different, except that its disasters were invariably of the victims' own making. In the case of both, power fell to those already equipped to cope with the new conditions, and to those others who were quickest to adapt.

Parlabane hadn't adapted. This was due to a combination of disbelief and wilful intransigence.

He had been ready for a lot of things about post-devolution Scottish politics. The much-bemoaned sense of anti-climax was, to his mind, inevitable; he didn't remember any party's manifesto promising a Socialist Utopia (Creation of) bill, least of all New Labour's.

The teething troubles, the jostlings, the stumblings and the embarrassments were also inevitable. The new parliament was an infant with much growing to do; it wasn't supposed to spring fully formed from the loins of Zeus.

That Labour Lite™ should continue to fortify its centre-right comfort zone, while cloaking it in nauseatingly touchy-feely rhetoric, was no great surprise. That the SNP should respond with leftist posturing, and that the impression should be less convincing than Alex Salmond in a silk négligé, was no great surprise. That the Tories should continue to exert as much influence as a pissed conscience over a stiff prick, no matter how much tartanry they affected, was also no great surprise. In fact, that this new, allegedly consensual and co-operative era of Scottish politics should very quickly begin to resemble all the old, back-stabbing, eye-gouging eras was pretty much what Parlabane expected.

Cynical as he knew this sounded, he nonetheless did expect that progress would ultimately be made. Change, though, would be incremental, not dramatic. Donald Dewar's first-term agenda was rightly decried as a hyper-cautious and anodyne snooze-fest, but there was also an argument for getting used to the new vehicle with a few slow laps before you tried flooring the accelerator.

And for a while progress *was* being made, though maybe not so much *by* politics than *in* politics, which was arguably even more important. With the excuse of blaming the English now inadmissible (or at least, in the SNP's case, mutated into blaming 'London-controlled Labour'), a clearer sense of political self-identity was beginning to emerge. The agenda was, if not dictated, at least and at last influenced by the issues the Scottish electorate were vocally concerned about, rather than by what effect a *Daily Mail* front page might have on the swithering classes down south.

With comparing themselves and their behaviour to England no longer relevant (if it ever was), the Scots were forced to take a more honest look at who they really were. Racism, for instance, had been their grubby little secret for the best part of a century, from the Church of Scotland's infamous pamphlet on *The Menace of the Irish Race to our Scottish Nationality*, to the revelation that the instance of assault on ethnic minorities was three times the UK average. 'Wha's like us?' myths of a warm-hearted and liberal nation had long been reinforced by head-shaking (but secretly delighted) disapproval as English football thugs laid waste another foreign city. Bereft of such distractions, and perhaps now in possession of sufficient confidence, Scotland was beginning to acknowledge what it didn't like about itself as well as re-evaluating the often suspect worth of what it did. Whether this led to any of it actually getting sorted out was, of course, another matter, but it was undeniably, like a hundred dead spin-doctors, a start.

The whole *thing* was a start. It was the kind of opportunity history seldom afforded: to begin again and do it differently next time. To create something new, and in so doing, purge whatever had corrupted version 1.1. Hence the widespread anxiety that whatever we had created should work, and that it should not repeat the mistakes that necessitated its creation in the first place.

This led to disproportionate public censure of early out-breaks of confrontational, point-scoring exchanges (there-after referred to with gleeful scorn as 'Westminster-style' politics). Equally disproportionate were the appalled reactions of seasoned commentators to the rather rough-and-ready contributions of certain MSPs not schooled in the starchier formalities of public speaking. But all of this was perfectly natural: the creation was in infancy, and to the concerned parent, every minor blemish can look like a potential deformity; every anomaly the onset of fatal disease. In time, though, the wee bugger usually thrives.

The definition of 'thriving' was, of course, entirely sub-jective. It was said that if you had low expectations, you couldn't be disappointed, but in Parlabane's experience of politicians, no matter how low you set the threshold, they could still contrive to come up short. That they hadn't might still say as much about his standards as about their achievements, but nonetheless his impression of post-devolution Scotland had been that it was no better than he'd hoped for and no worse than he'd feared.

There had even been the odd glimpse of something that might, in a certain light, be taken for maturity. The Peter Logan thing, for example. Some regarded the fact that he hung on to his post after *that* as the ultimate dubious testimony to Labour Lite's spin capabilities. However, Parlabane knew they'd never have managed it – never *attempted* it – if they didn't think people's priorities and perspectives had changed. Cabinet careers, it seemed, were no longer going to be in the gift of the tabloids, and if the Churches wanted to talk about morality, they would maybe have to start looking beyond the crotch for a fucking change.

It was a pity the *cause célèbre* had to be that self-satisfied knob-end, but it would have been churlish not to see the bigger picture. Joe Punter certainly had, and that, Parlabane thought, constituted serious grounds for optimism.

But that was months ago. September. Before the meteor-strike. Before the disaster and its relentlessly corrosive fall-out.

paging doctor spin

'Hello?'

'Hello, Andrew?'

'Yes?'

'Oh, thank Christ.'

'Is that? Peter?'

'Yeah. It's me. Andrew, I've got a bit of a problem.'

'Look, Peter, this isn't a very good time—'

'Aye, well it's not a career high for me either, let me assure you. I tried getting hold of Gerry Smith, but his mobile's switched off and I don't have his bleep number.'

'For God's sake, Peter, I'm in the middle of dinner with half the board of Masukita. I'll admit I'm not an expert on Taiwanese table etiquette, but I've yet to encounter a culture that smiles on turning your back and whispering into a bloody mobile. I thought I'd switched the thing off.'

'I'm sorry, Andrew, I swear, but I'm not kidding, I need some help. This is code red.'

'What's the problem?'

'It's sensitive. Very sensitive.'

'Can't you give me a bloody clue?'

'Not on a cellular, mate.'

'Oh for Christ's sake, Peter, knock off the theatrics. What's going on?'

'Not on a cellular, Andrew, I mean it.'

'All right, what do you want me to do? I can't leave here, you know that, and I can't speak much longer either.

Just me answering this call's probably going to cost us a subsidy hike.'

'I need a fixer and I need one fast. Can you get hold of Ewan Dickson for me?'

'Can't you bleep him yourself?'

'All my numbers are . . . look, I'm not at home and I can't *go* home, okay? The only numbers I've got are the ones programmed into my mobile. Can you get Ewan or not?'

'Oh Jesus, the entrées have just arrived. I've got to cut this off, Peter.'

'Andrew, I'm fucking begging you here.'

'Christ. Okay, okay. Look, I don't have Ewan's number on me. Tell you what. Let me get through the main courses here, then I'll get a message through to John Cooper while everybody's ordering dessert, all right?'

'Yeah. All right.'

'You better tell me where you are.'

'Sure. It's 14 Dublin Street. Graham on the buzzer.'

'14 Dublin Street. Graham.'

'Thanks, Andrew. I owe you big-time.'

'Aye, damn right you do.'

. . . J.C. CODE RED . . . J.C. CODE RED . . . PETER L IN BIG BOTHER . . . SAYS IT'S A JOB FOR E.D. . . . REQUESTS E.D. AT 14 DUBLIN ST ASAFP . . . NAME ON BUZZER GRAHAM . . .

'Of course I'm bloody bitter, Ian. So would anyone be. I feel like Debbie Reynolds in *Singing in the Rain*. It's my work behind the scenes that's keeping the show on the road, but it's been made crystal clear they don't want me out in front of the audience.'

Elspeth had another sip of her mineral water. Beadie's

cigar smoke was bothering her throat, and the over-sugary dessert had left a stickiness in her mouth. Midway through the last sentence, it had caused her voice to catch in that phlegmy way that made her sound like Elmer Fudd. She was talking too much, she knew, but with the unaccustomed luxury of an attentive ear before her, it was beyond her will-power not to take advantage. Usually she was the one who had to do all the listening, the taking note, the thinking about other people's problems. And for what, she was increasingly asking herself.

'Och, I suppose I ought to try and be more philosophical about it. The irony's not easy to miss, that's for dead sure: the wages of spin. I've put all my energies into the great New Labour voodoo of politics-by-presentation, making the packaging as important as what's in the box, so I shouldn't be so surprised when they decide I'm not saleable and sexy enough for the front benches.'

'Whoever said you weren't sexy, Elspeth? Tell me, I'll lamp him one.'

'Oh, piss off, Ian, I know what I look like, and I know what you think I look like too. "Thirty-five going on sixty," I overheard you saying once, back when we were at the *Recorder*.'

Beadie blushed a little, which she took to be almost touchingly deferential. In his tabloid days he had regularly said far more vicious things than that, to his underlings' faces, and was not known to be kept awake in later years by remorse. The memory of him firing a pictures editor by screaming at the entire newsroom to 'tell Security to get that spastic-looking cunt out of my sight' was one that never left anyone who witnessed it (and no doubt, knowing Beadie, that was probably the idea).

'And don't get all bashful, it's hardly the worst I've been called. When you're the one designated to muck the press around, they don't hold back in their revenge. In the past year I've been compared to any skinny and austere icon they can dream up, from a half-chewed toothbrush to the Wicked Witch of the West. I've never had any bloody illusions about being a glamour-puss, but it's not even that that's the obstacle. It's not just me that isn't sexy enough – it's my politics.'

'Aye, well I was gaunny say, look at Margaret Grier. She looks like she's no stranger to a deep-fried Mars bar, but it hasnae stopped her climbin' the ranks.'

'Exactly. The problem with me is . . .' Elspeth stopped talking and stared across the table. Having been a hack herself for a long time, she had an in-built suspicion of sympathetic entreaties to unburden oneself. The shoulder offered for you to cry on late at night could by morning be applied to digging your grave. The very fact that Beadie had been so quickly on hand at a time like this had also set a few alarm bells ringing.

Beadie and she had remained friends – or rather had *become* friends now that they had both moved on in their careers and were no longer butting heads on a daily basis – but they enjoyed each other's company more than each other's confidence. There was often a degree of cautious circling about their irregular get-togethers, sparring part-ners who each relished the challenge the other presented. However, mutual respect did not exclude a hint of malice.

'This is all still *seriously* off the record, yeah?'

'Oh come on, Elspeth, I'm not in that game anymore. You can pat me down for dictaphones if you like. And besides – why would I want to stitch you up? You're not important enough, remember? I mean, maybe if you hadnae been overlooked in the reshuffle . . .'

Elspeth threw her napkin at him.

25

'Cheeky bastard.'

Beadie, having been Scottish editor of two tabloids (one red-top and one with delusions of respectability), had bailed out a few years back to start his own PR company. He and Elspeth were alike in many ways, both drawing upon their journalistic backgrounds in order to provide advice on handling (and where possible, manipulating) media coverage. She did it for the Scottish Labour Party, he for whoever paid the retainer. His company, Clamour, handled an ever-widening remit these days, from upscale corporate press liaisons right down to brokering shag-and-tell memoirs for greedy little starfuckers. However, Beadie himself operated on what he liked to call 'the paramilitary wing' of the PR industry.

The underhand nature of this activity, Elspeth had to grudgingly admit, was best summed up by that snidey wee shite Jack Parlabane. In a recent column, he had written that: 'personal contrition is realising you're in the wrong and consequently making amends; corporate contrition is realising you're in the wrong and consequently hiring Ian Beadie.'

There was more than a hint of sour grapes about the remark. Beadie, in fact, was a keenly sought antidote to old-school newshounds like Parlabane. No matter how much information they could glean on your or your company's alleged misdoings, when they presented it at their big 'Ha-ha!' moment, the hacks made the mistake of thinking that was the end of the game. With Beadie at the table, it was only the opening gambit. Whatever you came up with, Beadie could neutralise, or at least dilute it with boundless means of dissemblage and distraction, ensuring that any objective onlooker could not possibly see the wood for the trees. And if that didn't work, well . . . there were rumours about what he did if that didn't work, rumours Elspeth knew him well enough to believe. But the end result was usually that what began the week as a major news story would be, by Thursday, popularly regarded as 'a big fuss over nothing'. Then on Friday, Beadie would take his cheque to the bank.

One of the differences between the two of them was that Beadie, with very few exceptions, was called in once the horse had already bolted (hence Parlabane's contrition gag), whereas a big part of Elspeth's job was making sure nobody left the stable door gaping in the first place. In a time when politicians' off-the-cuff, unscripted single sentences could be dissected and scanned for any nuance that could possibly be interpreted as even slightly diverging from the views of a colleague ('ministers in rift shocker'), or from the party line ('minister in gaffe shocker'), it didn't take much of a gap for Dobbin to slip through. Such banana-skin detection and clearance (or 'minesweeping' as she officially called it) provided the mainstay of her spin responsibilities. However, loath as she'd be to own up to it, she found the task of containment far more exhilarating. Lassooing Dobbin on the loose provided far greater excitement than slamming his door shut, just as long as it was only once in a while. And, of course, out-manoeuvring the would-be horse-thieves was always satisfying, especially when both sides knew they'd be back for more later.

They seldom got the better of her. In the whole of the last year, the closest the SNP had come to scaring up a gaffe story was over the SOL deal, and that was only front-page news because it was summer and the broadsheets couldn't lead with paparazzi shots of topless soap stars on holiday. Scotia OnLine had won the contract to be the new parliament's official Internet Service Provider,

27

supplying connections to all the MSPs, both in Edinburgh and their constituency offices. The stooshie was over the fact that the Scottish Secretary had been the one who signed on the dotted line, rather than the First Minister. This was due to the geographical and photo-op convenience of both the Scottish Secretary and SOL's heid-bummer being in Frankfurt to beat the drum for Silicon Glen at a European computer-biz exhibition. Unfortunately, the SNP's rather deft spin was that this was 'yet another dire example' of Westminster imposing its will on the devolved parliament by signing deals for its facilities over the First Minister's head.

Labour responded with assurances that all the tenders had been solicited, received and assessed in Edinburgh, but the SNP counter-spun that Edinburgh was doing the donkey work while London made the decisions and took the credit. Absolute mince, of course, and both parties knew it, but it was all part of the game, and Elspeth played it better than most.

Perhaps, as Beadie suggested, she actually played it too well.

'I think your problem, Elspeth, could be that you're too good at the job you're in. I've seen it happen. They don't want to move you because you're so bloody useful where you are.'

'Maybe I should jack it in and come work for you then.'

'Maybe you should, aye. An' tell you what, if I made you an offer, they'd promote you in a bloody flash. The thought of you sellin' the goods on that lot to a guy like me would fair grease the wheels.'

But no. Effective as she was, she knew that wasn't the real reason she'd been overlooked.

Elspeth was the eldest daughter of Joseph 'Uncle Joe'

Doyle, who had been a near-totemic figure in Glasgow Labour circles throughout the Sixties and Seventies. He was what the right-wing press liked to refer to as a 'firebrand' socialist, the term being their euphemism for a politician from a working-class background, lacking formal education and having clearly no right whatsoever to be talking to his betters in such a disrespectful manner. Whether it had been his earlier days in local government or latterly as the four-times returned MP for Nettleston and Provanhill, Joe Doyle had been a principled, uncompromising and passionate politician, venerated by his colleagues, feared by his opponents, worshipped by his family. Elspeth, despite also knowing him as a warm and humorous father, had grown up so much in awe of his political stature and achievements that she found the idea of following in his footsteps far too daunting. She chose a career in journalism instead, and resolved to apply the qualities and principles she had inherited from him to that. In doing so she earned her father's pride by garnering a fierce reputation as both a campaigning reporter and an impassioned commentator.

It was only after his death in 1993 that she felt moved to enter the arena he had made his own. She took two months' unpaid leave after the funeral, during which time the idea of carrying on the family name in the Party gradually took root. This epiphany, she believed, was a symbiosis of her deeply felt desire to honour him and the removal of his shadow from that door she'd previously been unable to walk through.

As his nickname suggested, Uncle Joe Doyle was about as 'Old Labour' as 'Old Labour' ever got, but as his death predated the very concept of Old and New in the party, his association had no negative repercussions for Elspeth's career. He had not hung around long enough to become an inconvenient anachronism, so his reputation survived the zeal of the revisionists and thus served his daughter as she was sure he would have wished.

She occasionally had to field jibes from left-wing traditionalists as to what her father would have thought of certain policies she was peddling, but these were cheap shots that reflected most unflatteringly on those who made them. Or at least, they did by the time Elspeth was finished with them. She countered that she knew him a lot better than they ever had, and that it insulted his political intellect to suggest he would apply the values and policies of his heyday to a landscape that had seen quarter-of-a-century of change.

With her father's name and her journalistic reputation behind her, the announcement of her new-found political aspirations was greeted with welcoming enthusiasm by the Party in Scotland. The 'New Generation' card seemed to them an attractive ticket: the traditional past and modern future of Labour conveniently encapsulated. Being the media-savvy New Labour daughter of an Old Labour legend very quickly marked her out for big things.

So why, despite winning the true-blue Glasgow Southwood seat (albeit in May '97's Tory wipe-out) in what was supposed to be a cannon-fodder trial run; despite then successfully standing for the Nettleston and Provanhill seat in the '99 Scottish elections; and despite delivering on everything that had been asked of her, was there still no place for her at the top table?

Quite simply, it was a question of faith.

Elspeth Doyle had grown up in a house where two things were absolutely sacred: the Labour Party and the Catholic Church. There was no point asking in what order, because at the time they had seemed two sides of the same thing.

They were both part of a faith, a philosophy and a way of life, to which she had learned to be wholly dedicated. For a long time in Scotland, the Labour Party had been regarded as the Catholic Party; the Catholic Church the Labour Party at prayer. These were the party and religion of the oppressed minority, the Irish immigrant classes, while the Tories enjoyed the support of the dominant Scottish Prods. With the vote thus divided along sectarian lines, back in the Fifties, for instance, the Conservatives' share of the ballot was higher in Scotland than anywhere else in the UK.

Growing up, Elspeth had witnessed the broadening of Labour's support as the Scottish vote began increasingly to divide along class lines rather than denominational ones. Times, politics and religion gradually changed. Her faith and her loyalties did not.

Given her pedigree, she was also a Tory target for accusations of selling out in endorsing Tony Blair's reforms. She had become yet another New Labour robot, they said, and had betrayed everything her father stood for simply to further her own career. Yeah, sure, and the band played 'Believe it if You Like'. Labour politicians had always been accused of abandoning their principles in pursuit of power, since long before Tony Blair appeared on the scene. It was part of the Tories' time-served pincer-movement strategy: if you took a hard line you were a dangerous lefty out to wreck the economy; if you softened your position, you were an unprincipled chancer who'd do anything for a sniff of power. The Tories knew they'd never face the same charge because they didn't have any principles in the first place. How do you ideologically compromise a stance built on greed, materialism and xenophobia?

Consequently, she didn't mourn Clause Four's passing. Holding on to it was a futile gesture of stubborn and misguided faith, like wearing the medal of some mediaeval saint whose canonisation had been rescinded. It was an anachronism and an impossible dream, but far more damaging, it was also a stick with which their enemies had too often beaten them.

Compromise was always depicted as a political sin by those in the grandstand. Those in the game knew that politics *is* compromise. If you want a party that believes in all the things you do, and with which you disagree on nothing, you'll have to start it yourself, and the membership is extremely unlikely ever to exceed single figures. In binary.

It was much the same as religion. You couldn't pick and choose which parts of Catholicism to believe in, like it was some sort of ideological buffet. Whether it was the Church or the Labour Party, you had to invest your faith and your loyalty in what the greater whole could achieve, and sometimes that meant swallowing things you didn't personally like the taste of.

The crucial difference, however, was that in politics you didn't actually have to *believe* in those things. You only had to say you did, and this was where the problem lay. Elspeth Doyle might be New Labour, but there was no such thing as New Catholic.

There had always been divergences between Church and Party, both being broad enough to accommodate as wide a mix of types as they did a spectrum of opinion. Plenty of Catholics (admittedly the more middle-class ones) were strictly Tory-voting, as they regarded anything further left as the thin end of an atheist-communist wedge. Equally, there had always been those in the Party (again, funnily enough, the more middle-class ones) who disapproved of religion in general, considering it an instrument of oppression.

She remembered her father's weary expression and visible discomfort when his explanations to her could not reconcile the views of both. It was from him that she learned how the tolerance of policies you disapproved of could be a necessary sacrifice for the cause of a greater good. This didn't mean that you were abandoning or betraying your beliefs. It just meant that even when you believed the Party was wrong, you kept your dissent to yourself.

There were those who might, with gravely shaking heads, condemn your silence as a breach of the Faith ('far worse that a good man should do nothing . . .'), but what political options did that leave them? Total abstention (aka copping out) or starting that aforementioned one-member party and voting for it. It was such narrow-mindedness that led to the appearance of one-issue Holy Wullie outfits like the Pro-Life Alliance. Sure, they had Elspeth's sympathies on that subject, but what about everything else?

'So, you've covered abortion and euthanasia, and you've touched a little on human embryo research. Now, on to the economy.'

'Er . . .'

'Unemployment?'

'Er . . .'

'Foreign policy?'

'Er . . .'

Her father had regarded as unquestionable the tenet that the Church was always right, and had taught her that politics, not religion, was the place where compromise could be accommodated. When Church and Party were at odds, you agreed to disagree. It was a matter, he explained, of mutual respect. You respected the Party's need for solidarity and, holding a minority view, you respected the democratic process. The Party, in turn, respected that there were times when your beliefs meant you could not support them, and they did not hold it against you.

Well, that was the theory. Maybe it had been true in her father's time, but things had changed since then. These days, in New Labour, it seemed Catholicism was the faith that dare not speak its name.

Having lived most of her life in the West of Scotland, Elspeth was wise enough to know that it was electoral poison to make a lot of noise about which foot you kicked with. She had never worn her Tim colours on her sleeve, and certainly not around her neck, which was more than could be said for others in the Party – there were Saturdays when you could probably convene a PLP meeting at Celtic Park. But then, that was a Guy Thing, and the irritating truth was that for every bigoted Hun they might be alienating, there were plenty of other Rangers fans who didn't care about religion and would be impressed with their laddish fitba credentials.

So being a Saturday Tim was all right, and being a Sunday Tim was fine too: Cherie was a left-footer, after all, and unlike that Godless Kinnock, Tony did like his minions to be identified with a wee bit of head-bowed Christian solemnity. Being a Tim twenty-four/seven, however, was not on.

It gave off the wrong signals. It had connotations of prudishness, austerity, servility and being 'behind the times'; connotations which were, in the marketing-speak that increasingly substituted for political strategy, 'not sexy'. Sex, of course, being the metaphor's panacea as the most marketable commodity known to man.

34

Elspeth would be the last person to hold up the USA as an exemplary society, but at least in politics over the pond, you could still wear your religion with a bit of pride. Here in the UK, with the phrase 'family values' so degraded by the Tories' abuses of it, being readily identifiable as a Christian was to be singled out as a would-be spoilsport in the materialist classes' sexual playground. For Catholic, double the dose.

She wasn't some bloody *Opus Dei* fundamentalist nutter, though sometimes she thought she might as well have been. No. Her thought-crime had been to repeatedly question a culture in which the values of consumerism were being extended to the bedroom, and in which the perceived 'right' to sexual gratification took precedence over consequence or responsibility.

Nothing was supposed to stand in the way of this so-called 'personal freedom', a freedom that society seemed determined to extend to its subjects at a younger and younger age. We were bombarding them with condoms and safe-sex adverts in the name of 'protection', but woe betide anyone who dared to suggest that bolstering certain aspects of their morality might provide a prophylaxis of its own. After all, disease and pregnancy weren't the only things they needed to be protected against; each other, for a start, and more pressingly, their more experienced elders.

There was no more selfish urge in the human condition than sexual desire, and therefore no urge more capable of compromising all other moral considerations. In a sense, it brought out the little Tory bastard in everyone. It was about me, me, me: ego-driven individualism, id-driven indulgence, and it didn't care who got hurt, neglected or abandoned in the process.

That was why, in her 'unsexy' opinion, what went on

35

in politicians' bedrooms (or indeed lavatory cubicles) *was* a matter of public interest, and their sexual conduct *did* have ramifications for their professional character. There was no greater test of character, in fact. If a politician lacked the self-discipline to deny himself indulgences that breached the contract he had agreed with the person who was supposed to be his closest companion, what did this say about his likely fidelity in other agreements, or even simply about his self-discipline?

These were questions she had committed to print before her career switch, which made her an early port of call for hacks and politicos alike any time one of her Party got caught with his pants down. She knew it was putting a hole in her own canoe, but she felt too strongly about the principle to back down from her previous sentiments. Thus her remarks about the Robin Cook fiasco in '98 – and no doubt her scorn of the self-styled playboy image Peter Logan liked to bask in – had been noted down in New Labour's black book, right next to the entries under 'homophobia'.

She'd once written of her concern that gay sexuality was being 'pitched to impressionable teenagers like it was a fashion statement or a lifestyle choice'. It had been ten years ago, again back in her print days, which had offered her something of an alibi when the thought police came to question her about it. However, Elspeth could not have looked herself in the mirror if she'd backed down. Sex, as she had always argued, was an area where young people were particularly vulnerable, because it was the area where their older counterparts could least trust themselves. Heterosexual males could be predatory enough in that respect, but homosexual males were far more promiscuous and, by their nature, even less inhibited by moral considerations. It made sense that teenage boys – and that's what they were talking about, here: mere boys – be given that bit more protection. This wasn't homophobia, it was genuine concern, and to prove it, Elspeth's suggested solution was to raise the heterosexual age to an equal eighteen, thus not prejudicing anyone.

'Aye,' Beadie said with a sigh. 'It's a sad day when they're sacrificing talents like yours on the altar of political correctness. You'll forgive the religious nature of my imagery, I hope. But it's not just your talents they're undervaluing. I think they're so over-run with arse-bandits, they don't realise the general public – and especially the Scottish public – are a sight closer to *your* views on certain subjects.'

'You could choose your terms more diplomatically, Ian.'

'You know what I mean. There's a lot of concerned parents out there, Elspeth. Me among them. I hate to think of my Cameron havin' his heid filled with ideas he's no' equipped to handle, an' startin' to think he's somethin' he's not just because he's confused. All teenagers are confused. You don't know what the hell's happenin' to your body or your mind at that age.'

'I know, I know. I suppose I could have spun it better if I'd had kids myself. Then I could come across like a concerned mother. As it is, I've just been painted as some frigid, shrewish stick-in-the-mud, and I've been marked down accordingly.'

Beadie's eyes narrowed and he stubbed out his cigar. He had that look about him which suggested he either disagreed or hadn't been listening, and was now ready to lay down whatever he'd been mulling over.

'I know you're too sore the now to see it any other way, but maybe you shouldn't be so sure it's a snub.'

This sounded like another devil's advocate wind-up, something Beadie specialised in. She wasn't in the mood;

though admittedly this was because she was, as he said, too sore.

'Oh come on, Ian. It's not as if they passed me over for the cabinet because they've somethin' bigger in mind.'

'Well, yes and no. Bigger for them, perhaps, not for you. What I meant was, the reason they didnae promote you wasn't necessarily about slappin' you on the wrist. It could have been about keepin' you out of the way. Maybe they've got some policies up their sleeve that they don't want the likes of you meddling with. Have you thought about that?'

Elspeth lifted her glass to her lips. There was barely a sip left in it, but she was really only using it as a prop, a distraction with which to buy a few seconds. This time Beadie really was angling for her to cough something, but angry as she was, it took more than dinner and a sympathetic ear to soften her self-discipline.

'No comment, Mr Beadie.'

Beadie laughed, but there was still business behind the smile.

'You're slippin', Elspeth. You could have just said no, but . . . No comment means there's somethin' to comment on.'

She looked at the glass again. It was empty now. No more procrastinatory mouthfuls to be had. She felt suddenly very vulnerable. It was that shivering dread that woke spin doctors in the middle of the night: the fear of having given something away. Elspeth didn't actually *have* much to give away, but that in itself was what she didn't want known. Beadie was dead right. Something had been brewing and she was out of the loop. Until that point, she'd taken this exclusion to have been merely a portent of her being passed over. Now she realised that she had been passed over to help facilitate such exclusion.

Bee-eep. Bee-eep. Bee-eep.

Her pager's peremptory shrieking was, for once, a welcome intrusion.

'Ah,' said Ian. 'Her Master's Voice. The bugs must have picked up my attempt to squeeze you for some gen. Probably a hidden microphone in the raspberry *mille-feuilles*. What's it say?'

Elspeth watched the message scroll across the grey LCD window.

. . . ELSPETH SOS . . . GOT MESSAGE FROM A.L. . . . PETER LOGAN NEEDS YOU ON SOMETHING URGENTLY . . . REQUESTED YOU BY NAME . . . GO TO 14 DUBLIN ST ASAFP . . . NAME ON BUZZER GRAHAM . . .

'It says God works in mysterious ways.'

containment

Parlabane had lost track of time. He had been staring at the envelope in his hand for, well, could have been two minutes, could have been ten. The screw had opened it and handed it to him, and he had immediately stuffed the pages back inside and returned to the cell. Sarah's handwriting was all he needed to see. Looking at her familiar, barely decipherable doctor-scrawl, an arcane calligraphy taught at medical schools the world over, was like probing the proverbial sore tooth. Actually reading it would be like *Marathon Man*.

It was day six. Various survival mechanisms had kicked in – some subconsciously, some deliberate – to get him through this, get him through the fear, the isolation, the regret, the desperation and the lack of adequate male grooming facilities. But he knew he had nothing in reserve that could contain the damage his wife's letter threatened to unleash.

The first step had been to rationalise what he was afraid of, to disentangle the intimidating morass of fears and see what its constituents amounted to. For a start, there was the sentence itself. He wasn't being locked away forever, just a few months, a period his more experienced fellow inmates would look upon with defiant scorn. 'A Jakey sentence,' someone called it, referring to the comparable stretches winos and down-and-outs tended to get. It was six months, likely to serve three. 'Six moon,' as they put it in here; or more probably 'six moon – canter', in predicting the ease with which they intended to see it out.

'Fuckin' dae it staunin' on ma heid,' he'd regularly heard them boast. Parlabane hoped they restricted such bravado to the inside; there was no shortage of sheriffs out there who might make that a stipulation if you caught them on the wrong day.

Next was the danger of getting shagged in the showers, which the general public's joke-jaundiced impression had suggested was mandatory. It hadn't happened yet, but what with all the overcrowding you read about, perhaps there was a long rota. Parlabane's worst experience there so far had been making a tit of himself, when on his first visit he warned a warder that he'd make sure the media knew all about it if anything bad happened to him.

'Oh, sorry, sir, I didn't realise we had a VIP in our presence,' the screw replied. 'In that case, I'd better ask everybody else in the showers just to concentrate on washin' their hair for a wee change. I mean, normally it's wall-to-wall buggery in there, and us stupit screws are powerless to prevent it, but tell you what, we'll all make a special effort on your behalf. How does that sound?'

However, while there were certain fears that it was healthiest to put from one's mind, the overall threat of physical harm was one Parlabane considered it wise not to discount, especially with a mouth like his. So far he had maintained a strict policy of keeping it shut, augmented by avoiding eye contact with everyone but the screws whenever he was outside his cell. His first trip down to breakfast among the general population had consequently taken place in something of a trance, as he shut out everything but what was in his immediate line of sight. That was until his attention was unavoidably drawn to an incident taking place a few yards to his left.

Thinking logistically, he had previously reckoned that the potential for violence in such public areas must be tempered by the time-limit the screws' intervention would place upon it. What took place that first morning in the canteen taught him just how little time was needed, as well as providing a highly educative demonstration of the difference between a brawl and an assault. Five seconds, five fractures, would be a fair account.

The feeling of vulnerability was almost paralysing. In here, there was no protection and no sanction. If someone wanted to hurt you, he was going to hurt you. After all, what were they going to do to the perp? Throw him in jail?

Parlabane eventually calmed himself with the rationale that this was merely shitty timing: just because he saw this on his first morning didn't mean it happened every morning. Rather unhelpfully, it happened the next morning too, but as the mutterings he overheard suggested the incidents were related, he made a nervous bet with himself that day three wouldn't witness a hat-trick, and was proved right.

Fear would subside (though its baseline would be higher than on the outside). Monotony would replace it. Tedium, indignity and inconvenience were far more tangible torments than personal harm. The time would pass slowly, but nonetheless it would pass. Three months. Canter. 'Fucken Tam o' Shanter 2000-style', as the toilet-wall sages put it.

But with these threads thus disentangled, it was easier to see what was at the morass's core, and understand the hardest, most painful part: that none of his real problems were on the inside: this was merely where his problems had taken him. He couldn't put them right while he was stuck in here, but worse still was the fear that he wouldn't be able to change anything once he got out, either. The fear that being here didn't simply prevent you putting your life back together – being here told you it was already too late.

An old friend of his, Tam McInnes, had served seven years for his part in a string of high-stakes and very high-profile burglaries. Tam had once told him that prison wasn't where you were punished: prison was just where they kept you until your real punishment was ready. The world Tam had left behind was no longer there when he got out again, and he didn't recognise much of what he found. That was why a lot of guys found it so difficult to readjust, and consequently why a lot of them ended up right back inside. It was also why Parlabane was not ready to open that envelope.

He appreciated that he could hardly compare Tam's seven years to his paltry term (fuckin' three moon – Nigel Tranter!), but equally, he had recently been granted a vivid perspective upon just how quickly irreparable damage could be inflicted in this place.

Parlabane and Fooaltiye had been forcibly separated the morning after they met, by the cruel facelessness of a system that refused to recognise the bond that had been forged between them. (Actually, Parlabane did have to concede one benefit to Fooaltiye's endless burbling: like listening to hardcore dance music, you felt fucking great whenever it stopped.)

He was taken from the reception cell to one of the prison's main halls, a structure so Dickensian he could imagine himself growing bushy facial hair the moment he crossed its threshold. He checked his hands to make sure fingerless woollen gloves hadn't materialised upon them.

The only accessory they were currently sporting was a pair of steel cuffs.

The screw led him up two flights of stairs on to an iron gantry, which took him across a mesh-protected drop to the opposite landing. He opened the cell door with an action of near-ceremonial precision: faaaace *door*; raaaise *key*; keeeey *insert*; keeeey *turn*; dooooor *open*. This man liked his job. Parlabane could picture him locking up Action Man dolls as a child.

He removed Parlabane's cuffs and ushered him into the cell, walking exactly two feet inside, to the inch.

'Right, Parlabane. It'll be a couple of days before they decide what they want to do with you, so just make yourself comfortable here for the present.'

With that, he withdrew, locking up again with near-orgasmic exactitude.

Parlabane, having learned from yesterday, checked the lower bunk for occupants. The front and back pages of the *Daily Mail* looked back out at him, gripped by two gnarled and wiry hands. Their owner spoke without lowering his paper.

'I'll tell you two things for dead-sure certain. Wan is you'll have some job makin' yoursel' comfortable in here, an' the other yin is, you're gettin' nae fuckin' present.'

Parlabane said nothing, but remained focused on the newspaper and the bony digits that were supporting it. So far, the physical condition of his fellow inmates was hinting at serious ramifications for the quality and quantity of the establishment's catering. The newspaper dropped a few inches, and a scowling wee punter with thin but angrily ginger hair peered intently over the top of it. The man looked about sixty-ish, much of it probably spent wearing that same expression. He gave Parlabane a thorough once-over, then the scowl twisted slightly into a sneer with optimistic aspirations of a grin.

'First time, innit?'

Oh for fuck's sake. Here we go again. He wondered whether it was perhaps tattooed on his forehead, but Scowl put him straight on that.

'Pure obvious. Face like a well-skelped arse, an' you look like you're aboot tae fill your breeks. Well, you'll no be roon' here long.'

Oh Christ, not the suicide routine again, please.

'They'll have you up tae E Hall in nae time, wi' the rest o' the lassies. Whit you in fur? Tax was it? Fraud?'

'B and E,' Parlabane said. He wanted it to come out confident and knowing, but as he'd barely spoken in twenty-four hours, his voice cracked and it issued in a croaky whisper. He cleared his throat. 'B and E,' he repeated. It was marginally better the second time, in as much as he merely sounded like a nervous wreck, as opposed to a nervous wreck with a tracheotomy.

'First time at that an' all, I bet. Nae wunner you got caught.'

Parlabane felt the stirrings of injured pride, but put the brakes on any defiant response. For one thing, rhyming off the places he'd broken into *without* being caught was not the most discreet course of action in the company of someone who looked no stranger to a police interview room. But mainly he was silenced by a sense of disgust at his own emotions. Christ al-fucking-mighty, what was happening to him? He had started yesterday vowing that he'd use all his inner strength to prevent this place from changing him, yet within less than a day he had already felt an urge to defend his criminal pedigree.

Don't be a prick, he told himself. At this rate, within a

week he'd be planning his next 'job'. A fortnight and he'd have a home-made Rangers tattoo.

Scowl scrutinised him again, closer this time, as Parlabane climbed to the top bunk. The wee man then hopped off his own bed and stood up to get a better look, placing his newspaper open on the cell's rickety table.

'Hing on,' he said. 'I ken who you are. I recognise you.'

Way to go, Sherlock, Parlabane thought. His face was only taking up half of one of the dreary tabloid's pages.

'B and E, eh? Well, I just want you tae know, here an' now, that I'm a Catholic.'

Uh-oh.

'You an Orangeman then, eh?'

Parlabane already knew that this was an argument you couldn't possibly win. Unfortunately, abstention wasn't an option either. Ignoring the bloke might be worse.

'I'm an atheist. What happened was nothing to do with—'

'Atheist, is it? Sounds like a new name for an Orangeman tae me. Whit have you got against Catholics, eh? Notice you werenae breakin' intae any Proddy church heidquarters.'

'I've nothin' against Catholics. I told you, I'm not religious.'

'Aye, that's what you say. It aw adds up tae the same thing as far as I'm concerned. If you're no' wi' us, you're agin us.' Scowl picked up the paper. 'Says here you ca' yoursel' an investigative reporter.'

'That's right. I was tryin' to find out—'

'Naw, naw, listen son. Listen tae me an' you might learn somethin'. Noo, I'll gie you the benefit o' the doubt. That's me aw the way – I'm a fair-minded man.'

Oh Christ. Scowl was warming up a sermon. Time to strap in.

'But I think you've been used, son. They're aw oot tae get

us Catholics, mark my words – an' you've just got caught up in it. If you're lookin' for stories o' injustice an' corruption, then you've got it the wrang way roon. You should be investigatin' the way we get treated in Scotland.'

'It wasn't Catholics I was—'

'Naw, just you haud your wheesht. I'm tryin' tae tell you somethin' here. For example, did you know there's a prejudice against Irish doctors in this country? Eh? Did you know that? They'll no' gie them jobs. The NHS is cryin' oot for doctors, cryin' oot for them so it is. But they'll no' gie them tae the Irish, 'cause they're Catholics, an' 'cause they'll no sign a contract that forces them tae cairry oot abortions.'

Scowl nodded, his minimalist equivalent of a flourish to indicate that he felt he had made an unanswerable point. He paused too, presumably long enough for Parlabane to realise that the sheer irrefutability of Scowl's argument had rendered him speechless, upon which Scowl would resume. Parlabane, over-burdened with reasons not to answer back, decided wisely against a counter-point, even though he knew his cell-mate to be talking utter mince. However, the journalist in him was intrigued by one thing.

'Where did you find this out?'

'It's a well-known fact, son.'

Parlabane swallowed back a sigh. 'Aye, but I mean, where specifically did you hear it?'

'A pamphlet fae the chapel hall. It had aw the details, aw the *facts*. So why's your newspapers no' reportin' it? Tell me that. Because there's a bloody cover-up, that's why. Newspapers are aw written by Orangemen, and don't think we don't know it.'

'Where did the pamphlet come from? The local parish, or was it—'

'Ach, I don't know. But I'll tell you another thing the newspapers *suspiciously* never picked up on. That whole Scottish election was fixed. The vote-countin' was totally rigged, so it was. They never counted votes for the Pro-Life pairty. Didnae want them gettin' any o' thae top-up seats.'

'In the second vote, you mean? I don't remember seeing that name on the ballot paper.'

'Aye, that's the point. They werenae even *on* aw the papers. That's how biased it was.'

'Wasn't that because they only stood in a few of the constituencies?'

'What's that got tae dae wi' it? You should still have been able tae vote for them, an' in fact, that's what we did. Us an' thoosands o' others. The priest says at the sermon that Sunday, vote for Pro-Life. An' if it doesnae say Pro-Life on the paper, you've tae write doon "I am voting for Pro-Life" at the bottom.'

Parlabane could see where this was going. That sigh was becoming harder to contain. So was a grin.

'But do you know what they did? Bloody fix. They refused tae count those votes.'

'Spoiled ballot papers.'

'Aye – so you *did* hear aboot it. Spoiled they said. Absolute rubbish. How could they be spoiled? Aw thae folk had made it clear as day who they were votin' for. Aye, you want tae write aboot corruption, son: there's a story for you. Totally bloody dishonest.'

Parlabane dearly wanted to pick that moment to ask Scowl what he was inside for, but figured anything that antagonised him would only prolong the indignant harangue.

Scowl sat down at the table and picked up his paper again. He turned to one of its picture-byline columns, which he proceeded to read with the occasional sage nod or concurring harumph. This caused Parlabane to revise one of his own preconceptions. Previously, the only thing he had found more frightening than that particular columnist's opinions, was the thought that there was a fat, tattooed white guy out there somewhere who, when he wasn't beating his wife and shagging his own children, actually agreed with them. To that he now had to add a credulously paranoid and extremely bitter old lag.

At least it shut him up for a while. Less happily, Scowl hadn't reached the football section yet, which was certain to provoke another lecture on the unspeakable sufferings of the oppressed Tims in this bigoted and evil land. Parlabane lay back in his bunk and wondered whether the Howard League knew about this kind of torture.

Two days later, in accordance with Cheery Chops's prediction, a screw informed Parlabane that he was being moved to E Hall. It was Hayes, the bloke he'd embarrassed himself in front of at the showers with his fear-inspired outbreak of defensive pomposity.

'Must be all those powerful friends of yours pulling strings,' Hayes took obvious delight in saying. 'Making sure you're being looked after properly. Either that or you've tested negative for classified substances and have also been categorised as low risk where it comes to the likelihood of chibbing the staff. Who knows. I'm going with the VIP angle myself.'

'The drug-free inmates are housed in E Hall?' Parlabane was compelled to ask.

'Yes. Delicious wee irony, I've always thought. Especially the first two or three thousand times it was pointed out to me. After that it got just the slightest bit tired, know what I mean?'

Parlabane felt his cheeks glow. Two conversations with

Hayes, two humiliations, and he'd deserved both of them.

'Right, Parlabane, get your shit together.'

'I don't have any stuff.'

'I wasn't talking about personal possessions.' He smiled malevolently. 'Let's get going.'

Thus Parlabane took his leave of Scowl, or Joseph Donegan 38635 to give him his full title, though not before he had been 'learned a thing or three'. His penance for desecrating a sacred religious institution had, supplementary to that doled out by the sheriff, included a detailed education about the political oppression, financial inequity, ingrained prejudice and indefensible offside decisions that had made a pitiable underclass of the Scottish Catholic population. And if it all came as a revelation to Parlabane, he was pretty sure it would come as an equal surprise to most ordinary Scottish Catholics; apart, maybe, from the bit about Jorge Cadete.

He had also, more valuably, learned the inestimable importance of sealable containers. The quarters he'd shared with Scowl did not have any toilet facilities, in common with every other cell in the block. This was not because the near-fossilised institution had been constructed without them, but because some time in the highly civilised Victorian era, it had been decided that prisoners did not deserve such luxuries, and they had all been ripped out by government order. This led to a necessary practice known by the revoltingly onomatopoeic term of 'slopping out', by which the inmates pissed into any available vessel, then lined up to dispose of it in the morning. Understandably, anything with a tightly closing lid was to be coveted.

Those caught short after hours with more solid matters to contend with were left with little but the illegal option of crapping on to a newspaper and lobbing the resultant package, or 'bomb', out of the window on to the grass below. The unenvied morning duty of removing these was consequently known as 'bomb disposal'.

Hayes took Parlabane to E Hall, a short walk lengthened by dread thoughts of what kind of insufferable arsehole he'd be cooped up with next; this time long-term. An insomniac Tourette's sufferer, perhaps, with dual incontinence and an expectorant case of tuberculosis. When they got there, however, the cell was empty. A wall of pin-ups and a pile of books suggested this was a temporary condition, though the combination was confusing: the spines bore the weighty names of Cervantes, Swift and Rabelais, which Parlabane found hard to equate with the topless females (whose spines were bearing plenty of weight themselves).

'The master of the house isn't home,' Hayes observed. 'Must be off having a work-out. I think he shat this mornin' and there wasnae a muscle in it, so he'll be doin' double-time. Take the top-bunk, and don't touch any of his stuff.'

Parlabane gulped. Hayes smiled wickedly, having got the desired response.

'Right. This is the drug-free hall, as you so wittily observed. Nicer cells, more perks, and a comparatively smaller chance of gettin' your face opened. For the privilege of staying here you'll be obliged to piss into a plastic beaker once a week. Any trace of anythin' stronger than tea an' you're straight back to Butlins. Got that?'

'Absolutely.'

'Good. Oh, and one other thing. Watch you don't catch Mikebriggitis.'

'What's that?'

But Hayes merely withdrew, that smugly knowing smile on his lips.

Half an hour later, the door opened, causing Parlabane

to sit up in his bunk, as though leaping to attention. A huge, lightly sweating man entered, wearing a damp vest, his shaven head glistening in common with his strainingly muscular shoulders. He stared hard at Parlabane, as though unconvinced anyone else should be there. Parlabane thought the look was disturbingly similar to the one Sarah wore when she spotted an insect and was reaching for a flat-heeled shoe.

To pre-empt a similar measure, Parlabane thought he'd better explain.

'I'm, eh, Jack. I mean, I'm your new eh . . . I mean, I was brought here by the—'

'First time, innit?' he stated rhetorically.

Oh, God, not again. Parlabane's heart sank. So, obviously, did his expression. The giant smiled, laughing a little, and extended a hand. 'Mike Briggs,' he said. 'Four years. Dope-smugglin'. Call me Mikey.' His accent was English. There were regional traces, but they were varied and contradictory, a man who had moved around a lot in his years (which Parlabane estimated to number around forty).

Parlabane gripped the hand and shook it.

'Jack Parlabane. Six months. B & E.'

'Jakey sentence.'

'Can o' Fanta,' Parlabane replied, managing a smile.

'You looked like you were shittin' yourself, mate. That bastard Hayes been windin' you up?'

Parlabane nodded.

'Thought as much. Just ignore 'im. He's an arsehole, but at least he's got a sense of humour.' He turned to face the opposite wall. 'Listen, the other bloke just got libbed yesterday, so I haven't had time to clear up. Gimme a hand an' we'll get all this shit off.'

52

'Yeah, sure,' Parlabane said, climbing down from the bed. 'I was wondering about that stuff, actually. Couldnae quite match it up with the high-brow readin' material.'

Mike laughed. 'You obviously ain't read any Rabelais, mate. But nah, you're right, they're all a bit amazonian for my taste.'

'So what draws you to these heavyweights here?'

'They're long. In this place, the appraisal of literature works on a kind of "never mind the quality, feel the width" basis. That's among those few of us who indulge, right enough. The printed matter of choice generally tends to be wank mags and self-help books.'

'Self-help?'

'Well, "help yourself" would be more accurate. "How to do good crime without getting caught." That sort of thing. So, what was Hayes sayin' about me to get you all aquiver?'

Parlabane shrugged, unsure whether his own fears might have been more to blame than Hayes' remarks. One thing stuck out, though.

'Mikebriggitis. What's that?'

Mikey grinned. 'Total and chronic failure to take jail seriously. Beware. It's highly contagious. You might not think so now, mate, but gimme a few days and I'll have you thoroughly infected.'

Parlabane suspected it would take more than a few days to engender anything resembling the legendarily laid-back attitude his cell-mate had to prison. He observed, however, that the period of adjustment to life inside was not as long, and certainly not as arduous, for everyone. Those who'd been in a few times before simply snapped back into their stride in a matter of hours, such as one wee chancer who'd stuck his head round the door during Parlabane's first night in the new cell.

'Heh, Big Man,' he said to Mikey. 'Just got in the day, likes, you know, an' I'm still gettin ma act together, ken? You couldnae gie's a lenny a wee drap milk for ma cornflakes?'

'Yeah, sure mate,' Mikey told him, nodding to the carton. 'Just don't fuck off with the lot, all right?'

'Aye, nae bother, Big Man. You're a star, so ye are. Eh . . . don't suppose there's any danger o' a wee bit sugar as well? I'll bring it back, I promise. You can kick ma cunt in if I don't, eh?'

'On you go, yeah.'

'Aw, cheers. Cheers. Eh . . . I know I'm a cheeky cunt, like, but . . . you couldnae gie's a wee lenny a bowl for ten minutes?'

Mike had already reached for the plastic receptacle and was holding it up. 'Will sir be requiring a spoon also?'

'Aw, what a fuckin' star. This man is a star. Cheers, Big Man. I owe you, massive-style. Thanks a million.'

'Just remember to bring it all back.'

'Nae bother.'

He backed out of the cell, his cadged items clutched to his chest. Parlabane was about to speak, but Mikey put a finger to his lips. 'Wait for it,' he whispered.

They listened.

'Heh, Big Man,' came a voice from the next cell. 'Just got in the day, likes, you know, an' I'm still gettin ma act together, ken? You couldnae spare us some o' your cornflakes?'

For Parlabane, the process of getting into his stride was somewhat more gradual, but it was happening nonetheless. Mikey was a forthcoming (if orotund) and, he guessed, trustworthy source of information (though he was waiting to hear certain slang phrases in independent use before he went parroting them; it wouldn't have been hard to pin the verbal equivalent of a 'Kick Me' sign to the wide-eyed newbie's back).

'"Give Willie a Jimmy and some Billy to jeer a Johnnie full of Charlie and bring it to the Peter,"' Mikey had, for instance, said to him.

'Come again?' Parlabane replied.

Mikey laughed. 'When that sentence makes perfect sense to you, it means you'll have . . . hang on, how long are you in for?'

'Three months, long as I'm good.'

'Hmmm. Probably not enough.'

'It'll be enough for me.'

'You got that right.'

Mikey gave him a crash course in essential prison jargon, beginning crucially with the area of lexicography he referred to esoterically as 'rocket science'.

'You might think this place is full of nutters,' he explained. 'And it is. Floor to ceiling. But that's like sayin' the Arctic Circle's full of snow. Same as the Eskimos, you need words to be able to distinguish between the different kinds of snow, and you'll need to be able to identify each kind of nutter so that you know what you're dealin' with. If you think the bloke in front of you is a bam, but he turns out to be a nugget, for instance, then your tea could be well and truly out.'

Parlabane smiled. It was slightly strange to hear these Scottish slang phrases spoken so sincerely in an English accent; stranger still for the speaker not to sound like a complete dick in the attempt. The sing-song generic Home Counties accent, for instance, was simply not equipped to cope with the word 'shite', but sadly, this didn't stop many of its adherents struggling on regardless. Reciprocally, the word 'beautiful' got such a mauling from Central Belt Scots as to utterly neutralise its complimentary properties, and prefixing it with 'pure' really stuck a cherry on the top.

Distinguishing between different types of nutter had never been a problem for Parlabane, but naturally the local terms of reference would be a great asset, so he listened carefully.

'You've got your nuggets, your zoomers, your screamers, your steamers, your bams and your rockets.

'Nuggets are your bog-standard headcase. None too bright, probably unaware of the stupidity of their actions, or of the retribution they might be booking themselves up for. Nuggets are like the weather: nothing you can do about them, and it ain't personal, so best just to ignore them.

'Zoomers are a more manic breed. They're just as bereft of self-awareness, but their acts of stupidity tend to be more ostentatious and, in my opinion, unconsciously attention-seeking. They appear reckless on the surface, but there's almost somethin' calculated about your zoomer. He wants a reaction. He might not know why, but he knows he wants one. A zoomer, for example, couldn't just sit in a room where a bunch of guys were minding their own business, you know, playing cards or whatever. He'd feel compelled to disrupt the equilibrium, even at the price of a burst nose. Again, wherever possible, just ignore them.

'A screamer is basically your deluxe-model zoomer. More manic, more reckless, and much more noisy. The attention-seeking is totally subconscious. Almost no central-nervous-system activity whatsoever. Needs external stimuli at all times. A screamer couldn't sit in a room with *one* other guy and let the poor bugger read a book or write a letter.

I'd give you the standard "just ignore" advice, but if a screamer latches on to you, resistance is futile. If you get one for a cell-mate, you're gonna end up hangin' yourself or hangin' him. Fortunately, 99.9% of zoomers and screamers are vocational junkies, so unless you get bounced from E Hall, that particular calamity isn't gonna happen.'

'It already did,' said Parlabane. 'First night.'

'You'll be safe now. Well, you'll run into them occasionally, but at least you know there's sanctuary at the end of the day. Anyway, where was I? Oh yeah. Steamers. Steamers are *über*-nuggets. Even more thick, but tending largely towards the violent. A steamer will punch you in the face halfway through what you thought was an amicable conversation. This is because if there is anything he doesn't understand, his default reaction is to perceive it as a slight, triggering the only response he is comfortable with. Recognise, identify, avoid.'

'How do I recognise one?'

'You just will, trust me.'

'Got you.'

'After that we move on to bams. Not to be confused with bampots, which you'll know from the outside is an all-purpose generalisation; like nutters, in here it's too inclusive and therefore meaningless.

'The bam is an interesting creature. If handled correctly, a bam can be a useful ally: fairly intelligent and definitely self-aware, but the crucial thing about bammery is that it's kind of a conscious lifestyle choice, even an aspirational one. Your bam is not only aware that he's a bam; he's frequently quite proud of it. I once heard a bloke say, very fingers-on-chin: "You know, Mikey, I've always considered myself a bit of a bam." On the whole they're not dangerous, unless you piss them off; or unless you fall into any of the

57

other previous categories. Even if you piss them off, bams can sometimes be reasoned with, unlike rockets.'

'Not a term I've ever heard in anger. I must confess I'm intrigued.'

'I kept it till last so that it remains the freshest in your mind. Do not fuck with a rocket. A rocket is a steamer multiplied by a zoomer, to the power of a screamer. Total. Fucking. Nightmare. Malignant, petty, vengeful, sadistic and utterly, utterly unstable. Understandably, it's not a term we apply lightly, and neither is it one you want to be calling anybody to their face – especially not if they *are* a rocket.'

'I don't think I'll be callin' anybody anythin' to their face. I'd rather be swallowin' pride than swallowin' teeth.'

'A wise philosophy for one so new. Such clarity of vision suggests you will be a worthy apprentice.' Mikey placed his palms together and bowed. 'I will therefore teach you the Way of the Kettle.'

This turned out not to be, as Parlabane half expected, a vital method of self-defence against enraged steamers, but the art of maximising one of E Hall's most valuable privileges: in-cell power points. The lower security category inmates were entrusted with access to electricity due to the lesser risk of them dreaming up ways of using it to damage the staff and/or each other. However, as an Aga was not yet considered 'allowable property', necessity had proven the mother of, if not invention, at least improvisation in applying what few utensils were to hand.

Mikey had 'a reliable supply network in place for the purpose of servicing his protein habit', which in practice meant a bloke called Flinty popped by every other day and sold him a box of eggs. These could be boiled in Mikey's kettle, through sustained application of a determined finger to the On switch, but with the unavoidable side-effect of turning the nine-foot-square room into a sauna. No less steamy, but rather more flamboyant, was Mikey's patent method of making the scrambled variation. This was done by whipping up the eggs in an old Pot Noodle container, jamming it into the open kettle, and stirring the mixture with one hand while the other kept the power on.

Either variety made for a welcome supper, especially accompanied by a slice of toast, which was prepared by the expedient if not immediately obvious trick of ironing bread. It didn't sound like much, but when Mikey rustled it up on Parlabane's fourth night inside, it was the first time he truly felt like he was going to get through this.

By day six, he was starting to get a handle on the place, and some sense of familiarity was forming, sufficient to prevent every waking moment from being the tightrope walk it had seemed at first. Get through that first week, get into the next, get into a rhythm and before he knew it he'd be cantering with the best of them.

Then Sarah's letter arrived.

There were footsteps on the landing. Parlabane quickly stuffed the envelope under his pillow, not wanting his new cell-mate to see it. He had known Mikey barely a couple of days, but it was long enough to be sure he wouldn't leave the matter alone once he got a whiff of what it was about.

Mikey gave him a quizzical stare when he entered the cell. Parlabane, in response, tried to look like he hadn't just hidden an envelope under his pillow.

'Who was the letter from, then?' Mikey asked.

'What letter? How did you know I got a letter?'

'Saw you pickin' it up downstairs. What's the problem? Bad news?'

Parlabane retrieved it from his pillow with a resigned sigh. Nobody had mentioned omniscience being an associated symptom of Mikebriggitis.

'It's from my wife. I haven't opened it. Can't face it just now.'

'You mean you haven't spoken to her since you went down?'

'Haven't spoken to anyone – on the outside, I mean. Friends, family, no-one.'

'Yeah. Probably best to bottle it all up and keep the whole business to yourself. I'm sure the psychologists are all gonna change their minds about that any day now.'

'Gie's a break, Mikey. This is all very new to me, remember. I don't know whether it's precedented around here, but I think I'm experiencing something known as shame. You ever hear of that one? Makes you a wee bit reluctant to go phonin' up your nearest and dearest.'

Mikey nodded. 'Yeah, I've heard of that one, mate. You don't feel you want to go trumpetin' your current state of play from the highest rooftops – though in your case, the papers seem to have done it for you.'

'I'm sure they have. There are few things more uplifting in this world than the downfall of a respected colleague.'

Mikey laughed. 'Still, Jack mate, you're gonna have to face them all in the end. Might as well be now. You can say you don't want to do it while you're down here on your knees, but the other way to look at it is that you're not exactly over-burdened with dignity right now anyway. What's one more turd when you're already up to your neck in shit?'

'Hmmm,' he said, unconvinced.

'People'll be worried about you if they don't hear anythin'. Especially your missus. She'll have written that because you haven't called and you haven't sent her a visiting pass; the poor woman'll be scared you're on the verge of throwin' a seven.'

'She knows me better than that.'

'She knows *nothing* about in here.'

Parlabane was surprised by the severity of Mikey's tone. Maybe Mikey was too, as he backed off and looked away, giving him space. Neither spoke for a while. Confused and defensive as he was, Parlabane knew good advice when he heard it, especially as he guessed a bloke like Mikey didn't divert from his trademark flippant bonhomie without damn good reason.

'You're right,' he said, but didn't feel like elaborating.

'You can't go in the huff with the whole world,' Mikey added, more solicitously. 'Specially while you're in here. Not unless you want to try gettin' by on prison wages an' second-hand true crime books. If it helps, don't think of them as friends and family – think of them as suppliers. But whatever, you gotta get in touch, an' it's gotta be her first.'

'I know. Won't be easy, though. For either of us.'

'Things been a bit sticky, then? With a trial hangin' over your head?'

'They were sticky before that.'

'What was the problem?'

'I can't really talk about it just now.'

Mikey put his hands up to gesture that he wasn't going to pursue it.

Parlabane laughed, pointing to his watch. 'No, I mean, I've got a fulfilling day's floor-mopping ahead of me, starting in about ninety seconds.'

'Yeah. New guys get all the best jobs.' Mikey took the envelope from Parlabane's hand and folded it in half. 'Pop

61

that in your shoe and read it on your break. That's an order. Then after that, your arms might be mopping, but your mind'll be sorting out your love-life.'

career opportunities

Elspeth gunned the engine as she turned on to North Bridge, then had to slam on the brakes as the pelican crossing ordered her to stop. A grey camera sat atop the lights, a little automated jobsworth ensuring she complied with the signal. There was nobody waiting to cross; whoever had hit the button must have been and gone and disappeared out of sight. Either that or the poor bugger had died and totally decomposed on the pavement, which was entirely plausible within the timeframe of the little red man turning to green in that part of the Old Town.

She realised she should be grateful for the obstacle. Without it, she might have hit sixty going down towards Princes Street, so curious and eager was she to reach her destination. Being SOS-paged at that time of night by John Cooper, Scottish Labour's fixer-in-chief, wasn't particularly out of the ordinary; it usually meant her news management skills were required to cap an oil fire before the final editions went to press. But this was clearly something else. John was merely the conduit: this was from Peter Logan via Andrew Lowrie. New Labour's young anointed via the bloody Trade and Industry sec.

This, Elspeth appreciated, was what kept her in the game, despite the hours, despite the setbacks, despite the ingratitude, the feuding, the back-stabbing, the cliques and the plotting. The adrenaline rush when the pager said 'drop everything', the nerve-jangling promise of a coffee-fuelled, high-stakes battle when she'd been five minutes from calling it a night, and the constant possibility that even, as now, when it looked like checkmate, something could upset the whole board and scatter all the pieces. One minute she was mourning being shut out of Scottish Labour's inner circle; the next she was being summoned to their aid – and by God she'd come running.

There was barely even the slightest part of her that suggested she should get huffy and tell them they could sort out whatever it was on their own. No matter how bitter she felt, the best way to remind them of her value wasn't to let them struggle through without her, but to demonstrate vividly what they'd have been missing if she hadn't shown up. And besides, in politics, spite was best served wearing a mask of smiling magnanimity. Just because you didn't point it out didn't mean anyone would be missing the irony of the situation, or who had come out of it best.

She turned left on to Princes Street as the smirring rain began to get heavier, drumming the roof and the windscreen in loud syncopation, occasionally intensified by random gusts of wind. The weather was reliably doing its bit to enhance the mood of post-Festival depression that enveloped Edinburgh each September. The pavements were quiet but for a few lonely figures hugging themselves in bus shelters, and one or two more taking temporary refuge in shop doorways on the north side.

Elspeth stopped at another red light, which prompted an emergence on unsteady feet from a Jenners awning. The bloke waved his right hand high in the air, under the drunken impression that she was driving a taxi. Her Mondeo wasn't even black, it was navy blue, but the combination of rain, darkness, alcohol and desperation had clearly caused sufficient confusion.

It happened all the bloody time, but it was something of a trade-off. In her own print days, she'd enjoyed plenty of scoops on the basis of a tipster spotting a certain car outside a certain address. Working in a town as small as Edinburgh, it wasn't wise to drive something ostentatious or recognisable if you didn't fancy any old hack or photographer being able to follow your every move. This went double when you were the person whose job it was to put a lid on something before the press got hold of it. Nobody looked twice at a dull-coloured Mondeo, except blitzed guys on a rainy night after the last bus had departed.

Perhaps that was another reason why she had been overlooked in the reshuffle. She had so effectively made a virtue of inconspicuousness that it might have been difficult for her superiors to imagine her adapting to a more deliberately visible role. The clowns probably feared she had lurked in the shadows so long that she'd bumble around like a pit-pony if she ever emerged into daylight. What they didn't understand was that an operator like her was a safer bet than most, because she appreciated how bright the light got, and how vividly it showed up your flaws. The true political liabilities were the ones who got so used to it, they forgot how closely the world was watching them, a negligent complacency that had occasionally made tabloid-fodder of even the most seasoned veterans.

There were no such worries with Peter Logan, which served to heighten Elspeth's sense of intrigue as to what more meaty issue this rendezvous might be about. His tactic had always been to hide in plain sight, a technique necessary for someone who had made a political currency out of grandstanding. There was no chance of Peter spilling an unintentional titbit to the press, because if you live to show off, then you never forget there's an audience looking on. There were plenty – Elspeth included – who regarded him as a slappably narcissistic self-publicist, but the smarter among them recognised the value that his touch of glamour invested in a project. They also recognised that he was highly regarded and appropriately protected from on high, so where possible it was wisest to bite your tongue and get your money's worth out of whatever endorsement his pretty face might bring.

If Elspeth's dowdy Mondeo was an appropriate vehicle for her necessarily low-key role, then Peter's choice in cars was equally metaphoric. A self-styled 'flash bastard', he was readily identifiable in – and as importantly *with* – his Seven Series BMW. But that was only half the story: he earned Elspeth's cautious respect when she learned that he also owned a dull-as-ditchwater 1997 Rover 200. The Beamie made him as obvious as he wanted to be, and its widely known association effectively gave the Rover a cloaking device. Yes, Peter played to the gallery and revelled in a bit of ostentation, but if you were daft enough to think that was all there was to him, then he'd run rings around you.

Though it was fair to say that he and Elspeth had never seen eye-to-eye, the truth was there had been precious few occasions when their gazes had reason to cross. Peter was on the Party fast-track, seemingly from the off, and had paid scant attention to those he was overtaking, especially not that sour old prude who was so openly disapproving of his love-life. If you wanted to catch Peter's eye, you had to look a lot younger and cuter than Elspeth, and while there was little chance of them fancying each other, there was even less likelihood of them becoming pals, given their mutual antipathy over each other's sexual morality. Even better known than his fast cars were Peter's fast women, something that had occasionally provoked Elspeth to question what sort of example this latter-day roué was setting.

However, such reservations were never going to cut much ice as long as Peter Logan's love-life – or more accurately, night-life – continued to provide such 'happy' copy. During his Westminster years, he was pictured in the press (and not just the tabloids, either) attending functions, premières and parties with a succession of high-profile celebrity females on his arm. A soap actress, a pop-star, a model, two TV presenters and even an Olympic athlete had all been 'linked' to him, to use the red-tops' rather gruesomely interpretable word. He was typically ambiguous about the nature of these relationships, divulging only cursory, coy and frequently innuendo-laden remarks about 'being good friends'. This dubiety was complicated in one instance by whispers that the model, Jade Tressing, was only dating him to help dispel growing rumours of lesbianism, but the fact that he had become such a chosen totem of heterosexuality said it all. Meanwhile, Millbank indulged – nay, endorsed – this lifestyle because this guy put a sexy face on New Labour, far more marketable and enduring than any of that ill-judged Cool Britannia nonsense.

The Tories tried to question whether the mind of this junior minister could be on his day job while he was out every night being 'the playboy of the Westminster world', but like most of their salvos at that time, it came straight back in their faces. For one thing, Peter Logan was as sharp and competent an operator as the government had, but perhaps more importantly, the punters liked him, so anybody who attacked him on that flank ended up looking as square as they did jealous. More than anyone (except perhaps Robin Cook), his conduct served to galvanise the permissive argument that a politician's sex-life had no bearing on his professional conduct and was therefore nobody else's business. The flaw in this logic, of course, was that Peter took such evident delight in *making* his sex-life other people's business.

Elspeth would have found his behaviour more palatable if he had at least acknowledged some kind of relationship with these women, but instead he seemed to flit ficklely hither and yon, flaunting a casualness that had otherwise disappeared with the advent of AIDS, and had at the very least been unfashionable since the Sixties. Indeed, one right-wing tabloid had run a computerised picture morphing Peter's head on to Austin Powers' body. The result was yet another own goal, the paper's arithmetic failing to anticipate the result of multiplying a rather popular figure by an even more popular one. Many women, it seemed, found him charming, stylish and irritatingly fanciable. (Elspeth would have added the proviso 'at least for a politician', except that it would have been both churlish and inaccurate: he'd made the top ten in several magazines' 'Best Dressed Man' polls and been described as 'British politics' first sex symbol', arguably a dreadful slight on Leon Brittan.)

Meanwhile, the laddish element clearly admired the notches on his bedpost and the motor in his garage, earning him high-testosterone credentials that he got infuriating mileage out of in the age-of-consent debate. By putting him at the forefront of the campaign (arguably more visible than any openly gay MP had been), the inference to the lager-and-bum-cleavage set was that if Labour's Mr Virile Heterosexuality On Legs didn't have a problem with poofs, then neither should you.

Elspeth turned right off Queen Street and headed into the New Town. For all its grandeur and Georgian geometry, it struck her as being an awful long way from the neon and flashbulbs that had illuminated Peter Logan's rise to prominence. His decision to resign his Westminster junior-ministerial post in order to stand for election to Holyrood had been a source of enormous surprise, and consequently even greater speculation. Among Labour MPs, the story was that the PM feared the stirrings of an anti-Scottish backlash in the wake of devolution, and grumblings over the high proportion of Scots in the cabinet. Consequently, the rumour went, it wasn't going to play well if yet another Jock was promoted to the main table, so it had been suggested to Logan that he earn some spurs as a big fish in a small pond until the time was right for a return south. The SNP angle was that Logan's move north amounted to a tacit admission of the inevitability of independence (yawn), as Labour's rising star had astutely recognised where the main game was going to be in years to come.

For the full picture, however, you had to remember the Rover 200 as well as the BMW. Though Elspeth often regarded him as the epitome of all she thought was wrong with the Newest aspects of Labour, she did respect the fact that he had always been a dedicated constituency MP. Peter Logan was an Edinburgh boy through and through, embracing all the contradictions that entailed. The son of working-class parents made good, he had been educated at Edinburgh Academy but never forgot he was a born Leither. Consequently, he had been able to straddle the social strata with an ease essential to representing a constituency that took in the highest spheres of banking and the lowest sinks of poverty. He might have been pictured at West End parties and premières, but only if he still had to be in London the next morning. If not, he was on the first shuttle home.

Elspeth drove slowly along Dublin Street, looking for the numbers. She saw the Rover 200 before she saw 14. There was a free space another forty or so yards ahead, the prospective distance on foot lengthened by the worsening downpour. The car's LED clock read 11:51, then disappeared as she cut the ignition.

She got out, attempting to open her brolly with her right hand as she locked the car door with her left. This proved a mistake. The umbrella sprang open when her thumbnail undid the catch, and was promptly ravaged by a sudden gust that turned the thing inside out. She stared at it in disgust as the rain lashed her cheeks. It looked like a cyborg's feather duster. The Scots had invented many things, but she was sure the umbrella wasn't one of them. It had to have originated in some exotic foreign clime where rain fell vertically rather than at forty-five degrees, and was not perpetually accompanied by gales.

Elspeth bowed her head and began to run, dunking the mangled brolly in a lamppost-mounted litterbin as she passed. She splashed obliviously through the fast-growing puddles, more concerned about reaching shelter than about the resultant state of her trousers (Logan would be getting the dry-cleaning bill anyway, make no mistake). However, in the semi-darkness she had no way of seeing that one of the black pools was covering a three-inch depression, so she plonked her right foot straight into it, soaking it to the ankle and sending her to the deck in the process. Her left knee and both hands broke the fall, skinning her palms and ripping her trousers. As she crouched, prostrate, the tails of her jacket flattened themselves against the wet concrete. She hugged her palms against her sleeves to dull the rasping pain, and all the while the rain ran down her face.

That whole adrenaline and excitement thing had very

rapidly lost its lustre. She no longer felt like a shrewd player, moving stealthily to claim a renewed stake in the game. Instead she felt like a mug. She was wet, sore, miserable and not a little humiliated. Here she was, kneeling on a pavement in the rain in the middle of the night, felled while dashing obediently to the assistance of a self-satisfied superior young enough to be her son, for the greater good of the party that had just ratified her second-class status. Journalism had brought her to some low moments, as any hack would attest, but tonight this felt like rock bottom. A very wet rock at that.

Still, she was here now, and she'd be paying for her own new suit if she just got back in the car.

'Graham', the pager had told her. She pressed the buzzer, rain running off her fingers as she did so. Her palms felt raw. She could use some warm water and a big elastoplast.

'Hello?' came a tentative voice.

'Hello. I'm here to see Peter.'

'Peter? And who are you?'

'Elspeth. John Cooper sent me. This is the right flat, isn't it? Graham?'

'Yes, it, I mean, maybe, I . . . Who sent you?'

'John Cooper. He got a message from Andrew Lowrie. Said Peter needed to see me. Look, can we talk about this inside? It's bucketing out here.'

'Hang on.'

'Hang on? What the—'

There was silence from the intercom. Elspeth was left standing in the doorway, the sound of the rain the only noise in the street, as loud as it gets only when you're locked out and alone. She was about one drip down the back of the neck from leaving when she heard footsteps on a stairway inside the close. The door swung open, revealing a rather

71

serious-looking young man in grey jogging bottoms and a plain white T-shirt. Elspeth didn't recognise him. He was early thirties, short blond hair, probably attractive when he didn't look like the world was about to end.

'Sorry. The door-opening thingy's knackered. Come on upstairs.'

He led her inside to a freshly painted close, in which even the banister railings were glintingly free of dust. The smell of gloss hung in the air, as it had all across the New Town throughout the last few years. Time was, when you stood outside one of those townhouse conversions, you never knew what awaited you: pot-plants and parquet flooring, or peeling walls and taped-on student nameplates. These days, every last square inch was being spruced up for possible sale. Elspeth couldn't imagine a single Edinburgh estate agent having voted against devolution.

'I'm sorry, I didn't catch your name,' the young man said in a near-whisper, mindful of the echo-chamber effect those glossy close walls always had.

'Elspeth. Elspeth Doyle.'

'I'm Teddy. Graham. And this Andrew whatsit called you? I'm sorry, I'm not very clued-up on these Party things.'

'Andrew Lowrie got John Cooper to page me. Said it was urgent. Do you know what this is all about?'

Teddy added open discomfort to his look of grave worry. 'It's sensitive. You better wait and talk to Peter.'

'So you're not . . . professionally involved with Peter?' Going into this scenario cold, Elspeth knew she had to start sussing out the angles. Where this guy stood in relation to it all was priority number one.

'Oh no, not at all. Not unless his ticker packs in, anyway. I'm a consultant cardio-thorassic surgeon up at the RVI.'

72

'So you're a friend?'

'Well, a little more than that, obviously.'

Elspeth nodded, disguising the fact that she had no idea what was supposed to be 'obvious'.

They reached the second-floor landing, where Teddy opened the door to his flat.

'Do you mind taking your shoes off?' he asked, indicating their muddy condition.

Elspeth complied, biting back a quid-pro-quo request for a towel. She then followed him along the polished wood floor of the hallway, musing semi-distractedly on whether there was anyone left in Edinburgh who owned such a thing as a carpet. Her right foot squelched with every step, probably making more mess than had it remained shod. They passed a roomy and well-equipped kitchen, in which Elspeth spied two empty white wine bottles on the farmhouse-style pine table, presiding over a mess of abandoned dinner plates and serving dishes.

Teddy stopped in the doorway to the living room, his eye on a closed door opposite, unintentionally indicating where Peter must be. Elspeth was left standing as her host dithered.

'Shall I go into the living room?' she suggested.

'Ehm, perhaps you should . . . yes. Sorry, I'll get out of your way.'

He stepped aside to let her past, but didn't escort her any further, instead remaining intent upon the closed door. Elspeth eyed two plush sofas that she'd have taken great delight in leaving a watermark on, but opted to remain on her feet. When the great one deigned to grant her an audience, she wanted to meet him at eye-level.

Teddy took a step forward and knocked tentatively on the closed door.

'Peter?'

'Yes?'

'The cavalry's arrived.'

'Oh thank Christ. Just a sec.'

Teddy remained hovering in the hall, obscuring Elspeth's view as the door opened. She saw a flash of white towelling and two hairy legs.

Teddy stood aside. Peter saw Elspeth in front of him and yelled 'AAAAAAGHH!', involuntarily jumping a foot backwards in horrified surprise.

Elspeth knew she wasn't looking her best, but this seemed a disproportionate reaction, even for someone as aesthetically discerning as him.

'What the fuck is *she* doing here?' he asked Teddy, who stared back with a combination of sympathetic horror and total incomprehension.

'Eh? She's the cavalry, Peter. She was sent—'

'What the fuck are you doing here?' he then tried of Elspeth. His tone wasn't challenging; there was too much disbelief and sheer terror in it for that.

'What do you mean? You asked for me. Personally. Via Andrew Lowrie. John Cooper paged me about—'

'John Coo—But . . . I didn't . . . I asked for Ewan Dickson. Why the hell would I . . . ? Oh Jesus Christ. This isn't happening. Someone tell me this isn't bloody happening.' Peter slumped back, leaning on the doorframe for support. 'Ewan Dickson,' he moaned. 'E.D. Oh Jesus fucking Christ, Cooper, you fucking idiot.' He put a hand to his forehead and closed his eyes. Whatever was bothering him, it had him going for the full Victorian histrionics.

Ewan Dickson was a former Westminster whip who was now the Party's principal minder/enforcer on the Mound. His remit was containing and sorting out the kind of messes that you couldn't simply spin your way out of. Elspeth couldn't say much more than that, because half of Ewan's battle was making sure no-one ever found out what those messes were.

John Cooper had assumed Andrew Lowrie meant Elspeth Doyle, partly because John was far more used to despatching Elspeth in times of crisis, but mainly because Peter Logan simply didn't *get* into messes, of any kind. Until, it would appear, tonight.

No-one spoke for a few seconds, during which Elspeth was sure she could hear an electric buzzing. She looked at the bathrobe. She'd interrupted his ablutions. It was a strange time of night to be shaving, but a friend of hers had once explained that the downside of electric razors was that they made you look and feel like you shaved eight hours ago, so you had to use them two or three times a day.

'Did you take that stuff?' Teddy asked.

Peter nodded.

'I'll get you a glass of water. You'll have to drink a lot of fluid. You'd better lie down just now.'

'So what's the problem?' Elspeth asked. 'Are you ill?'

Peter glared in response, then shuffled uncomfortably into the living room, where he proceeded to lie down in the foetal position on one of the sofas. This was about as sartorially understated as any fellow-politico had ever seen him. Even when he played charity five-a-sides, he looked as if he was modelling the kit. The bathrobe looked too small for him, probably because it belonged to the foot-shorter Teddy, and that encumbered gait was a far cry from his unmistakable, cocksure stride. Elspeth was curiously reminded of Abraham's sons seeing their father's nakedness, so short was he falling of his normal stature and dignity.

'This is a nightmare,' he muttered. 'This is a total bloody bad-acid nightmare. All I need now is Michael Aspel to pop up with his big red book. This really would be the perfect moment.'

The still ashen-faced Teddy came back in carrying a pint glass of water, which he apprehensively handed to Peter, as though he might throw it back at him.

Elspeth walked further into the room and sat down on the other sofa, which stood at ninety degrees to its partner.

'Well, are you going to tell me what this is all about, or will I just go away again?'

Peter thought about it.

'Ewan Dickson's in London, as far as I know,' she added. 'In case that has any bearing on your decision.'

Peter was sweating. He was starting to look torn as well as terrified.

She could still hear the faint buzzing noise, even though she was well away from the bathroom. Maybe she was imagining it.

'How long does that stuff take to work?' he asked Teddy.

''Bout an hour, forty minutes?'

'*What*? Forty . . . I thought you meant like tomorrow morning. You mean it's going to . . . ? Oh Jesus Christ, Teddy.'

'What stuff? Will someone please tell me what is going on?'

'Don't look at me like that, Peter. I thought you knew. For God's sake it's the same stuff you spiked—'

Peter looked admonishingly towards Elspeth, prompting Teddy to cease.

'I didn't realise it was the same, you just said the name of it. It meant nothing to me; I'm not the bloody doctor.'

Elspeth stood up. 'Right, I don't see any further point in my being here, so if that's all right with you gentlemen, I'm going to take my leave. Surprising as you may find it, I've got better things to do with my time.'

She made it to the doorway before Peter asked her to stop. Teddy shot him a look that questioned whether he was sure of what he was doing.

'She's here now, isn't she? Who else am I going to get at this time? I'm sorry, Elspeth. This is very difficult for all of us. Have a seat. Teddy, get Elspeth a towel and a cuppa or something. Stop standing there like a spare prick.'

Sighing impatiently, Elspeth returned to her seat as Teddy left the room, muttering something about Peter's choice of metaphor. Peter took a few mouthfuls of his water, still not quite ready to divulge whatever the great pigging mystery was all about. Still the buzzing noise persisted.

'Am I going mad,' Elspeth began, keen to break the silence before the merely reticent Peter rendered himself fully catatonic, 'or is something buzzing in here?'

At that point, Teddy walked back in, carrying a towel. He stopped dead upon Elspeth's last words, mouth hanging open, eyes relaying between the two sofas.

Peter closed his eyes. 'Christ,' he groaned. He took a deep breath, above which the buzzing remained faintly audible. It sounded as if he'd lost his Philishave down the back of the couch. 'It's a vibrator,' he said, very slowly, gravely and deliberately, ensuring that he wouldn't have to repeat or confirm this. He looked Elspeth square in the face, possibly for the first time since her arrival. His expression acknowledged that he was wide open here, but there was still a spark of anger to remind her he could be dangerous when cornered, and that he wouldn't always be this vulnerable.

Elspeth looked away, ostensibly in a gesture of sensitivity, her eyes alighting on her damp right foot. She also took in the torn flap in her trousers and felt the tingle in her skint palms, judging in that gleeful moment that all of her discomforts would prove a bargain fee for a ringside seat at this extravaganza. She also knew then and there that she had a decision to make, though not exactly a difficult one. It *was* an option not to help him, or even to stitch him up for all it was worth, but it would be tantamount to resignation. Being the one who bailed him out, however, could make things . . . interesting, to say the least.

She looked up again, her decision made. Teddy, reanimated, handed her the towel, which she dabbed on her wet face and rubbed briefly at her hair. She then folded it a couple of times and pressed it between her skint palms.

'How did it . . . ?'

She knew fine how it . . . but if she was going to help him, she wanted some entertainment value out of it at the very least.

'I slipped getting out of the shower. Bloody stupid of me to leave a lubricated pocket-rocket standing upright on the bathroom floor, but I guess I'll never learn. Jesus Christ. How do you think?'

'Someone gave me it as a joke,' Teddy offered. 'We were a bit tipsy after dinner and we started messing about. It's not something either of us would normally—'

'Yes, Teddy, I think that's as much as Elspeth would care to hear. It doesn't matter. What does matter is that I can't get it out anymore than I can turn the bastarding thing off.'

'And what were you hoping Ewan Dickson could do about it?' Elspeth asked. 'Has he got a big sink-plunger maybe?'

'Oh, very droll. Why don't you stick to the praying and leave the smutty jokes to us godless deviants, eh?'

Elspeth looked to the heavens, as though threatening to take the huff. Peter was instantly contrite.

'I'm sorry. But Christ, this isn't exactly easy for me, so maybe you could try to enjoy it just a little less, huh? Look, I don't know what I thought Ewan could do, but whatever it was, I was holding out for it not involving a trip to the Royal Victoria Infirmary's very public A&E department after the frigging pubs have shut. Understand?'

'That part, yes. There are other aspects that are a trifle hazy. You have to remember that we second-string aparatchicks aren't always kept fully in the picture.'

'Well, I think you can probably fill in most of the blanks yourself, now.'

'But just to make sure I'm clear on the situation, because neither of us can afford mistaken assumptions, you're telling me you're bisexual, right?'

'No.'

'No? So you're saying you were just "experimenting"?'

'No.'

'So, what? Are we back to slipping coming out of the shower?'

'No, Elspeth, though coming out might be an appropriate turn of phrase.'

'Ah.' Elspeth nodded. She looked to Teddy, who responded with a goofily apologetic expression which she took to be some kind of affirmation. She'd have to confess she hadn't instantly arrived at this solution to the equation, what with the flurry of contradictory or merely distracting data that had been factored in.

'But I take it coming out is not on the immediate agenda.'

79

'No, it bloody isn't. And certainly not via the world discovering I've been admitted for an Ann-Summers-ectomy.'

'So, let me get this straight—'

'Another salient expression.'

'Not intentional. But are you saying you've always been gay?'

'Well, apart from feeling up Marianne Clark at an under-fourteens disco, safe to say, yes.'

'And who else in the Party knows?'

'Oh, Christ, everybody *knows*. Well, not everybody, obviously. Need-to-know basis, and a select few did need to know.'

'And why didn't you come out? It's not like you'd be a political rarity.'

'You know, when you put it like that, Elspeth, I really don't know, because it sounds so bloody easy. Hmmm. Why didn't I? Maybe because it was nobody else's fucking business.'

'Oh come off it, Peter. I could maybe accept that from a few people, but you wrote the New Labour book on mixing sex and politics. You were one of the prime movers on the age-of-consent issue, for God's sake.'

'Yeah, and that's another reason I couldn't come out. Christ, I've wanted to, believe me. Many times I've come close, but the timing was never right.'

Teddy ambled across and sat on one arm of the sofa, at the end nearest Peter's head. He rested a hand on Peter's hair, but received a flinch and an angry look in return. Either he wasn't comfortable with any intimacy in front of Elspeth, or Teddy was still in the bad books for being Mr Butter-Fingers.

'The timing?'

'Yeah. Two or three years back I was really thinking about

it, but then all that shit blew up with Mandy, Nick Brown, Ron Davies, and *The Sun* ran those "Gay Mafia" headlines. It was felt I shouldn't go stoking the flames.'

'"It was felt"? You mean this wasn't entirely your decision?'

'Nothing's entirely *your* decision in politics.'

'Are you telling me you let Millbank House decide whether you could come out and declare your sexual preference? God in Govan, man.'

'I didn't let them decide. I just took their advice, that's all.'

'Advice as to whether or not you'd still have a career if you didn't comply.'

'That's not how it was. But it all got complicated after that. I was a strong advocate of equalising the age of consent, maybe one of the strongest, because I know all about living in fear of prejudice. But it was thought that we should have a straight figurehead for the campaign, so that it didn't look like it was being railroaded through by the so-called "gay lobby". I said no at first, but I felt guilty; I felt that I of all people should be doing whatever I could to help.'

'And you were perceived as the Party's Minister for Testosterone.'

'Something like that.'

'So what about all the models and TV stars – they were just an elaborate camouflage?'

'No. Well, yes, but . . .' He sighed loudly, looking as if the necessary explanation would require advanced calculus.

'Keep drinking that water,' Teddy reminded him.

He took another few gulps, then placed the glass back down on the floor. 'I didn't intend it to be that way.

81

Don't think I could have pulled it off if I had. It just sort of happened. I think the first time, I was going to a music-biz reception with Tracy Willets, who was a friend at the time. Still is. I had a rising profile, she was in the charts with one of her first singles, so neither of us were complaining when the papers ran a few snaps of us together. Same thing again with Annabel Greer. We'd known each other for a while through some mutual friends and she invited me to be her partner at a film première. She'd just left that soap she was in, and she hadn't been deluged with new offers, so she needed to get back in the limelight. Her other option was posing in her undies for *FHM*.

'Actually, if memory serves, she did both,' Teddy added. He looked relieved to elicit a small smile from Peter.

'That's how it works. It's all just a big tableau. A 2-D, four-colour world. You throw them a few coy quotes, giving nothing away, and everybody's happy. They – and I'm talking about the public as much as the paparazzi – don't know, don't care whether you're really in a relationship. They just want the picture: me in a flash suit and she in a tight dress, preferably one you can see her nipples through. It's meaningless tittle-tattle.'

'Meaningless tittle-tattle which you encouraged.'

'Why wouldn't I? I enjoyed the attention. I thought it was a great laugh. So did the girls. That's why you never read any tales of acrimonious break-ups.'

'Or "Peter Logan broke my heart" revelations,' added Teddy.

'It was the press that made all the inferences of sexual involvement. I just didn't contradict them. Neither did my implied partners.'

'Especially not Jade Tressing.'

'I think that's Jade's business, Teddy, don't you?'

'Guess that rumour was true, then?' Elspeth enquired. Peter arched his eyebrows in response.

'A result for both of us. That's partly why I kept playing up to the image. With the papers painting me as some kind of star-shagging *über*-swordsman, I felt less like I had to be looking over my shoulder about my relationship with Teddy.'

'Now who's using unfortunate phrases?' Teddy observed.

'Oh shut up.'

'So you two have been together a while?'

'Close on ten years. It's a lot easier to hide in the closet when there's only two of you in there.'

'You're not out either?' she asked Teddy.

'Are you kidding? Talk about career suicide. Medicine's bigoted enough in general, but cardio-thorassic surgery, Jesus. Utterly overrun with macho wankers. I don't mind telling you, I felt a lot less worried being seen with Peter in restaurants on a Saturday night once the world started believing he was God's gift to women.'

'Millbank felt a lot less nervous too – that's why I was never told to knock it on the head. And once I was on board the age-of-consent thing, well . . . What I didn't fully appreciate at the time was that there would be no going back. Christ, think of the anti-gay backlash if I was found out to be some kind of Trojan horse. I mean, obviously it'd be music to *your* ears, but it would undo a lot of important work.'

'What do you mean, music to my ears? Just because I opposed the bill doesn't make me homophobic, Peter.'

'No, Elspeth. It's your homophobia that makes you homophobic.'

'I'm not ho—'

'Yes you are.' Peter was laughing, but there was a sadness and regret in it that Elspeth found sufficiently disarming to cap her indignation. 'You're the worst kind of homophobe, because you don't even realise the ways in which you *are*. The fully fledged gay-bashers are less bother.'

'I opposed the bill because sixteen-year-old males are at a very vulnerable time in their lives, not because I've anything against homosexuals.'

'Sixteen-year-old girls are vulnerable too. But the boys need more protection don't they, because of "what we do"? Well I've got news for you, Elspeth. We don't all do what you think we do, tonight's drunken misadventure notwithstanding. A larger percentage of heterosexuals are into anal sex, so if you're in the sphincter-protection business, maybe you should be more worried about the girls and their lads-mag-reading boyfriends.'

'Peter,' Teddy cautioned, handing him up his glass of water by way of interruption. 'I don't think this is the time to get all Peter Tatchell on us. There are more pressing matters to be addressed. Buzzing matters, even. Finish that up and I'll get you some more.'

Peter shifted delicately on the sofa, causing a minor change in pitch from the constant electric hum. He emptied the glass and handed it to Teddy, who left for the kitchen.

'I'm sorry,' he said. 'You're the last person I should be noising up, under the circumstances.'

'Quite. So what did you have in mind?'

'I need a doctor. Someone sympathetic, who can be relied upon to keep his mouth shut.'

'Isn't that Teddy's field?'

'We told you, Teddy doesn't want anyone finding out he's

gay. He can't go to anyone he knows. Scottish medicine is a very small world.'

'They wouldn't have to know his part in it.'

'Oh for God's sake, it wouldn't be hard for them to guess. A bloke with a vibrator up his arse in *his* flat. "Yes, houseguests can really let you down sometimes." Forget it. I thought Ewan Dickson could set something up – he's got contacts. Anything to avoid being admitted to bloody hospital. Can you help me?'

Elspeth sat up straight and looked him in the eye. 'Possibly,' she said. 'But I think the question ought to be "will you help me?"'

She knew she had to; they both did. It wasn't just his political career that was now hostage to this errant dildo – it was hers too. However, that didn't mean the balance of power hadn't been tilted a little.

'I have to say, Peter, the words "poetic justice" do leap to mind. Should I, having been frozen out for being a prude and an alleged queer-basher, assist the party in covering up the fact that its gay-rights poster boy *is* actually gay?'

Peter opened his mouth, then closed his eyes for a second, swallowing back his initial response. When he opened them again, his expression was calmer, somehow simultaneously resigned and appellant.

'If you're calling me a coward, fair enough, I'll put my hand up. But just remember, Elspeth, it's easy to be brave from the cheap seats.'

They stared at each other for several tense seconds, the silence and gravity of the impasse slightly diminished by the ever-present buzzing.

Teddy returned, carrying another pint glass of water.

'Did you offer our guest anything?' Peter reminded him.

'Oh no, sorry. Bit preoccupied. Elspeth, would you—'

'A cup of tea, please. Milk, one sugar. Thanks.'

She reached into her jacket pocket for her mobile as Teddy exited once again. Peter's eyes remained fixed apprehensively upon her as she dialled.

'Hello there,' she said. 'News desk please.'

Elspeth watched him try – and painfully fail – to spring upright, horror in his eyes. She shook her head and said: 'Just kidding. It's still ringing.'

He flopped down again, a glare indicating that relief had swiftly given way to anger.

Elspeth's call was finally answered. The apprehension returned to Peter's face as he watched her explain the situation, turning once again to relief as it became apparent that she would be getting what she had asked for.

'Who was it?' he asked as she hung up.

'Old schoolfriend of mine, Janice McLaughlan. A GP. She's had to deal with all sorts out where she lives, from delivering babies to farmyard impalements, so if anyone can come up with an on-the-spot solution, it'll be Janice.'

'Out where she lives? How far is she?'

'West Linton, down towards the Borders.'

'The *Borders*?'

'Keep the heid, it'll take her about forty minutes.'

'And can we trust her?'

'Patient confidentiality, remember. Just her. No nurses or theatre orderlies ready to spill their guts for a backhander from the Currant Bun. Calm down.'

Teddy finally brought Elspeth her cup of tea. She wondered whether he'd been waiting outside the door, holding off to see whether she earned it.

'It's all under control, Peter, so I'd advise you just to relax and bide your time.'

He nodded. He looked calmer; he'd manage the biding

his time part, but relaxation was probably asking a bit much. 'Thank you,' he said. Elspeth sipped her tea. It was duff, but drinkable. Peter glugged some more water.

They sat and watched the clock as time silently passed. There didn't seem to be much more to talk about. Well, there were plenty of things Elspeth would have liked to talk about, but she didn't imagine Peter would be very forthcoming. She contented herself with contemplating the evening's revelations, though she reckoned it would take a gallon jug of Alka Seltzer to digest them.

The roads would be deserted at this time of night, especially out in the country. Unless she got an emergency call in the interim, she reckoned Janice would be there in another ten, fifteen minutes.

Still the buzzing continued.

'How long do the batteries last in one of those things?' she asked.

'Christ, I don't know,' Peter said, irritably.

'They're new in,' Teddy offered. 'Duracell.'

'Maybe you could negotiate an endorsement deal,' Elspeth suggested. 'You know, "We fitted five vibrators with ordinary batteries . . ."'

Peter's stony face started to crack. Elspeth could tell he was trying to keep himself from smiling , but it didn't work. Eventually he gave in and began to laugh.

'"And shoved them up the arses of five MSPs . . ."' he added.

Now Elspeth was laughing too, having been unable to prevent herself visualising a specific five.

'"After one hour,"' Peter continued, '"Donald Dewar's is the first to stop, but his stutter improves throughout. After two hours, Tommy Sheridan's packs in, due to high levels of radiation from his sunlamp. After three hours,

Alex Salmond's is pushed back out by Andrew Wilson, complaining he was there first. After four—'

There was a loud gurgling noise from the vicinity of Peter's stomach. He instantly ceased talking, his face suddenly very pale.

'Ooh,' he said, grimacing.

'You okay?' Elspeth asked.

'Yeah, just . . . ooh. No, it's okay. It's passing.'

'*It*'s passing?'

'No, the pain is.'

'Oh, right.'

'It was just a twinge. It's gone. Felt a bit like *oh Jesus God!*' Peter clutched at his stomach as though he'd been shot, bending his head forwards and curling himself into a ball. He started taking frequent, deep breaths, exhaling noisily through pursed lips. After a few more seconds, he lifted his head again.

'Don't feel so good,' he announced redundantly.

'The Picolax must be kicking in,' said Teddy. 'You'd better get to the bathroom.'

'Picolax?' Elspeth enquired, but Teddy was too intent on helping Peter get to his feet. He offered his shoulder for Peter to drape an arm around, muttering "Could you?" to Elspeth, indicating the glass of water.

'Yes, surely.'

They had travelled six feet towards the door when Peter doubled over, his groan not quite drowning out another ominous gurgle. He repeated the fast breathing.

'I'll be okay, I'll be okay,' he assured them, before resuming progress, now in a semi-bent hobble.

'What has he taken?' Elspeth tried again, standing a few feet behind.

'Picolax.'

'And what does it do?'

'OH MY GOD!' Peter bellowed, suddenly breaking away from Teddy and making a despairing forward lunge. As he reached the hall, his legs buckled beneath him and he dropped to the floor, clutching at his middle. Elspeth heard a loud, even angry squelching sound, like the bubbling of a bleeding radiator just as the last of the air is expelled and the water starts to flow through.

But this wasn't water; at least, not entirely.

Peter was lying once again in the foetal position, the dressing gown ridden up around his waist. There was a pool of something wet and unpleasant accumulating steadily on the polished floorboards at his rear.

'Oh shit,' Elspeth felt obliged to observe.

'It's the Picolax,' Teddy said, kneeling down at Peter's side. Peter pushed at him half-heartedly with a feeble arm, groaning as the bursting and spurting noises echoed around the wide hallway.

'They use it to prep the bowels for surgery. It clears everything out. I thought it might help shift the vibrator.'

'Well, it's certainly shifting something.'

'It looks like the more liquefied, er, matter, is getting past the obstruction, but the rest must be building up behind the blockage. That's what's causing the pain, and it's only going to get worse. We've no choice: we need to get him to a hospital.'

'NOOO!' Peter yelled. 'No.' He began puffing away again, as if he was in labour. 'I can hold on for a while. Seriously. Let's give this Janice woman some more time. *Please.*'

Elspeth looked at Teddy to say it was his call. He looked at his watch.

'Five minutes,' he said. 'Max. Then I'm calling an ambulance.'

'Oh Jesus.'

Countdown to the end of two careers.

More groaning, more spluttering, more puffing.

'Maybe we should help move him,' Teddy suggested.

'I'm not going bloody near him.'

Peter's face was now sweat-soaked and beetroot-coloured. Teddy, crouching nearby, looked only slightly less exerted. He shook his head.

'Sorry, Peter, we really better get an ambulance.'

'No, wait, wait. I think . . . I think it might be . . . nnnnnnn . . . Yes. I think I might be able to . . . nnnnnnn.'

Elspeth looked away, wishing she could avert her nose too. Daddy never told her politics could be so fulfilling.

Peter's straining merely resulted in a further gushing outpour, at the end of which he seemed to be in more pain than ever.

Teddy stood up to go for the telephone, which was when the doorbell finally rang. He turned on a sixpence and leapt over the puddle, heading full tilt for the stairs.

'Oh thank Christ,' Peter moaned.

'She's really going to thank me for this one,' Elspeth muttered. 'And let me tell you, Janice might be in the NHS, but you'd bloody better make it worth her while.'

'I'll fill . . . her mouth with gold,' Peter managed. The prospect of assistance seemed to have given him some renewed spark. He pulled himself up to almost a sitting position, and attempted to shuffle backwards away from the pool, in the direction of the bathroom.

'Maybe I could . . . clean myself up.'

He got about four feet before the next attack, which coincided with Teddy and Janice's appearance at the front door. Elspeth watched her do a double take and feared for a second that she'd follow it with a one-eighty, but she merely sighed.

'Whew! The things you see in the city,' she said.

'You have no idea how sorry I am about this,' Elspeth professed.

Janice walked briskly ahead of Teddy down the hall, opening her black doctor's bag as she did so.

'That goes . . . double . . . for me,' added Peter.

'Well, let's wait to see whether I can be of any help before we all start *waaaah*!'

Janice, having divided her gaze between her prospective patient and the contents of her bag, had failed to notice how far down the polished boards the ordurous pool had spread. She skidded with both feet and was sent into the air as though slide-tackled by an invisible centre-half, landing against one wall with a horribly unmistakable snap. By some minute mercy she at least didn't splash down in the pool, but Elspeth reckoned it would be scant consolation.

Janice lay still for a few seconds, dazed; maybe even – Elspeth feared – unconscious. Then she moaned and tried to sit up, the pain etched across her twisted face. Teddy knelt down and told her to stay still.

'I think I've broken my ankle,' she said to him. 'I might have hit my head too. I don't know. It happened so fast.'

'Right,' Teddy decided. 'I'm calling an ambulance.'

'Oh God,' Peter whined.

Teddy stepped over the two bodies, picking his steps with delicate caution, and made his way into the living room.

'Hang on,' Elspeth commanded.

'*What?*'

'One minute.'

It was her last chance to do something. The snafu could

hardly be described as her fault, but failure was still failure. If she was present on the night Peter Logan's career literally turned to shit, it would not be forgotten. Her already failing party stock would be worth wallies by this time tomorrow.

The circumstances could not be changed, she knew that. An ambulance had to be called, no question. Peter Logan *would* be going to the RVI. But those were merely the facts. What those facts meant was still subject to spin.

'We need a woman,' she said.

'Eh?'

'A girlfriend. To accompany Peter to the hospital. A lone male with a vibrator up his bottom equals gay and/or embarrassing. Throw in a girlfriend and it's kinky sex gone wrong.'

'Jesus,' Peter gasped. 'You're a fucking genius.'

'Problem is, who's going to agree to being the girl?' Elspeth mused.

'Well it bloody well isn't going to be me,' shouted Janice. 'I need a bloody ambulance and I need it now.'

'Paula Reid,' Peter said breathlessly. 'She lives five minutes away. Stockbridge. That's if she's not away to London.'

Elspeth knew the name, another of Peter's supposed conquests.

'But she's a children's TV presenter,' Teddy countered. 'It would be career suicide.'

'She hasn't done – oww – kids' TV for ages. She's trying – aaah – to get a more – fffft – raunchy image.'

'Serendipity,' Elspeth muttered with arch irony. She flipped open her mobile and looked at Teddy. 'You call her, I'll call the ambulance.'

Paula Reid arrived with time to spare, Elspeth having

92

banked correctly on the Scottish Ambulance Service not sticking on the blue light for what the dispatcher had described as 'a broken leg and a Bryce-Job'. Elspeth had been less confident about the wearingly bubbly TV star going for it, but Teddy reported that she didn't need to be asked twice.

'She thinks this might help her get *The Big Breakfast*,' he explained.

Teddy, of course, hadn't mentioned to her that there would be complicating aspects which might only be considered 'raunchy' by a nasally debilitated coprophile. Needless to say, Paula was far from impressed.

'There's shit everywhere,' she announced, upon entering the flat. Elspeth had been sent downstairs to collect her while Teddy helped Peter into the bath and turned the shower on, hoping to clean him up a little before the paramedics arrived.

Janice had administered her own analgesia from her black (and, unfortunately, now partially brown) doctor's bag. She sat just inside Teddy's bedroom door, where she had dragged herself to get away from the mess. She had initially refused Teddy's offer to carry her to the living room, as she thought it prudent to wait for the ambulancemen to move her. However, after a few minutes, the eye-watering awfulness provoked a change of mind.

'What the hell happened?' Paula asked. 'Where's Peter?'

'In the bathroom,' Janice replied.

'Teddy gave him something to try and eh, force the issue,' Elspeth explained. 'Picolax, I think he said it was.'

'Picolax?' Janice spluttered. 'What the hell was he thinking? Typical bloody surgeon. They know plenty about their one wee area of expertise, but bugger-all about everything else. And what was a cardio-thorassic surgeon doing with Picolax at home?'

'I don't know,' Elspeth admitted, though she did have a theory. A few years back, Peter had famously stood in at the last minute for his ministerial superior at the STUC conference. He had given a fabulous off-the-cuff speech after his boss went down with acute post-lunch tummy trouble, and had been appropriately lauded within the Party for his on-the-spot thinking and invaluable ability to 'pick up the ball and run with it'.

Hmmmmm.

'Why is it all over the floor?' Paula demanded. 'Is he incontinent? Is he going to do it again? I'm not so sure about this.'

But sure or not, that's when the doorbell rang once more to announce that the ambulance was outside.

Paula looked to Elspeth.

'You're here now, dear,' Elspeth told her.

Paula nodded, understanding. No way out but forwards.

'Right,' Elspeth announced. 'I'll let them in. Places, everyone.'

Upon which Teddy made himself scarce; Paula replaced him at the side of the wet and writhing Peter; and Elspeth descended the staircase, wondering all the while which ring of hell this achievement was ultimately booking her place in.

nicholas soames can't reach to wipe

'So anyway, he tells the screw tae fuck off, perfectly fuckin' reasonably, if you ask me. I mean, the boy's banked the best part ay a month's kit up there, so he's hardly gaunny welcome a cavity search wi' open arms.'

'Open legs, mair like it.'

'Aye. Anyway, next thing you know, him *and* his peter-mate's been carted, straight tae the digger.'

'His petermate as well? Whit fur?'

'Tae fuck wi' oor heids, man. They want tae keep every cunt on edge. You ken whit they're like. Fuckin' bastards.'

Parlabane turned away to hide his smile, concentrating intently upon his mopping. The stair-landing conversants hadn't seemed particularly concerned about the possibility of his eavesdropping, but they would be less sanguine about providing the source of someone else's mirth. It didn't need Mikey to tell him that such indiscretion would be like playing Russian roulette with an automatic.

His amusement was at the textbook demonstration of inmate paranoia, as outlined by his cell-mate the night before. A certain breed of con regarded everything that ever happened within the walls as part of a concerted campaign of mind-manipulation being waged by the screws and the management.

'No-one in the system has the intelligence or the motivation to play these kinds of mind-games,' Mikey insisted. 'But some of them still seem to believe there's a central office of psychological warfare. If the kitchen runs out of tomato soup, it's part of a ploy to grind you down.'

Dunking the mop into his bucket again, Parlabane wondered whether he should be the one laughing. It sounded a lot like the pot was calling the kettle a paranoid conspiracy theorist. He might even say that it was the pursuit of such theories that had led him to this, but that would be to romanticise what he now knew to be a far less poetic hubris.

He felt Sarah's envelope beneath his sole and sighed.

The problem, ironically, was sex.

No, really. There might not seem anything particularly ironic about their marriage taking a hit in that most mine-strewn stretch of water, except that he and Sarah had worked so very hard on their bomb-proofing. Relationships, they both agreed, were often torpedoed by an over-emphasis on the importance of sex; or perhaps more accurately an over-emphasis on its pseudo-sanctified status.

It was a unique result of two diametric opposites – Christian prudery and mass-media liberal permissiveness – combining not to cancel each other out, but rather to multiply each other's effect. Ostensibly, the Christian prudes turned sex into a sacrament by elevating its significance within a relationship, while the permissive mass-media overstated its importance by endlessly banging on about it. However, at the same time, the Christian prudes were overstating sex's importance by endlessly banging on about it, and the permissive mass media were turning it into a sacrament by overstating its significance within a relationship.

The consequence was that sex ended up way too high on everybody's agenda. You might think you were content in that particular aspect of your love-life, but only if you could block out the nagging voices of a million magazines, newspapers and radio phone-ins, asking whether content really means complacent, and whether your partner is actually one faked orgasm away from packing her bags. 'Are you doing it often enough? Are you doing it in enough positions? Are you doing it in enough locations? Are you doing it with enough invention? Are you doing it on top of the washing machine with a quart of crème fraiche, two ice cubes and a cucumber (and have you tried Gary Rhodes's zingy salsa using the same ingredients? See p 94)?'

Christianity's supposed sanctification of the sexual act fooled no-one, as people knew it was merely the churches' compromise stance, due to their preferred option – eradicating sex altogether – having the impractical side-effect of wiping out the entire human race. However, with one side declaiming sex as the ultimate vice, and the other trumpeting it as the ultimate pleasure, it was no surprise that sexual infidelity came to be regarded as the ultimate betrayal.

It wasn't. There were greater betrayals – something he and Sarah had agreed on *before* he found such a demonstrative means of underlining the point. What they had also agreed on was that sometimes, many times, it was not really a betrayal at all; well, maybe a small one, but the betrayal part was massively outweighed by plain weakness and sheer stupidity.

Should a relationship – should a marriage – be sacrificed because of that? Because of one mistake? Neither of them had thought so. They were both in agreement with the argument that an affair was a sign of other things being wrong, but that wasn't what they were talking about (or indeed what they were trying to insure against). Given the right circumstances, the right environment and the right

97

amount of booze, anybody – especially males – could suspend all sense of love, honour and responsibility long enough (like twenty minutes) to facilitate an act of folly which, unless insufficient precautions were taken, would of itself have no practical consequences whatsoever. As to psychological and emotional consequences, well, that was a different story; but crucially all of those were, in the words of Pat Nevin, 'in ma heid, son'.

They were not advocating an 'ignorance is bliss' policy. Neither was naïve enough to argue that such an encounter meant nothing; their position was that it didn't mean everything. They had both known of couples who jettisoned all that they had built together over several years because one party had been 'unfaithful'. In Parlabane and Sarah's book, all that time together constituted plenty of faith, and as such, plenty of reason why it should take more than a stray dick to unravel it.

Some would say that all those years a couple had invested in each other clearly meant nothing to the adulterer at the time of the Great Betrayal, but that was, in fact, the point. Right then those years, that sworn partner, *did* mean nothing, and would continue to mean nothing until about five seconds after orgasm.

Sex was the area in which human beings were most inclined, despite all honourable intentions, to fuck up, and for that reason it was also the area in which they should be most inclined to cut each other some slack. Sarah had been an even stronger advocate of this than he, something which had come as a relief to Parlabane. Not because he had anything to hide, but because he knew, as a male – as a human being – that one day he very plausibly might. He wasn't looking for a get-out-of-jail-free card, just the assurance that if one of them

98

ever did anything stupid, the damage wouldn't be irreparable.

That assurance had been exchanged at about five am one dark and drizzly morning, after Sarah had successfully argued that a person's sexual frailties, tastes or misadventures should not be held against them in other aspects of their lives (unless, obviously, the other aspects of their lives involved trying to prevail upon everybody else's sexual frailties, tastes or misadventures). This late-night/early-morning philosophising was occasioned by her having recently returned from work, where the adjoining theatre had witnessed the extrication of a small, grey and still operational vibrator from Peter Logan's dusky unmentionables.

He had been brought in, perhaps appropriately, in the company of three women. One was Paula Reid, the Scottish rentabimbo who could be relied upon to turn up to the opening of a fridge since she had made the disastrous (but familiar) mistake of thinking greater things awaited once she ditched her Saturday morning kids' TV gig, *Princess of the Zorgons' World*. Her part in the production was not difficult to guess, nor were the true motives behind her selfless act of tagging along to help him face the music. Since splitting from her polyester animatronic dinosaur co-host and shedding the last of the puppy fat, she had done everything but move into Alisteir Crowley's old digs in her efforts to cultivate a more marketable bad-girl image. Kinky sex with the new parliament's White Rod sounded so much like the answer to her prayers that Parlabane had his doubts as to whose idea this particular perversion had been, and whether Paula's over-enthusiasm had been entirely accidental.

Also in tow was a female GP with a broken ankle, reportedly sustained in an attempt to remove the errant phallus on site. Parlabane's mind, as far as he was concerned, never 'boggled', but it did play host to some peculiar imagery involving just how this injury may have come about. Logan face-down, the doctor crouching with one foot planted on his arse-cheeks, one on the carpet and two hands . . . hmmm.

Completing the triumvirate, and thoroughly complicating his speculations, was Elspeth Doyle: New Labour media-manipulator and all-round nippy sweetie, an ascetic and acidic woman who chillingly reminded Parlabane of every soor-faced primary-school teacher ever to terrorise his youth. He could picture Logan bringing her in to try and contain the situation, but beyond that it got fuzzy. Did *she* call the doctor – maybe someone she could rely on to keep quiet? Was she called in after the doctor's efforts went injuriously awry? And most confusingly, why hadn't she chased Reid, who had a conflicting interest in the incident going as public as possible?

Still, such puzzlements aside, Parlabane thought it was Christmas. Unfortunately, Sarah Claus took his toys back before he could play with them.

'You are *not* telling anyone about this,' she dictated flatly, sitting up in their bed.

'Aye, right. I'm sure that was Deep Throat's last words to Bob Woodward as well.'

'I mean it, Jack. It would be unethical.'

'Unethical? It would be unethical for me not to tell. I'm a bloody reporter.'

'And I'm a doctor. There's such a thing as patient confidentiality.'

'But he wasn't your patient.'

'He was the hospital's patient. He was the department's

patient. Strictly speaking, I shouldn't have told you in the first place, except that I knew you'd find out eventually and you'd go in the huff that I didn't.'

'And *how* would I find out? Because some other bugger at the hospital will cough to the tabloids. Sorry, wrong tense. Some other bugger will already have trousered the backhander for coughing to the tabloids.'

'Yes, and if so, the informer will keep his or her anonymity – unlike the patient. Whereas, if *you* went with this story, how hard would it be for anyone to trace the source, tell me that? Two, three seconds maybe?'

'It wouldn't need to have run under my byline.'

'So what, Jack, it's academic now. As you said, the presses will already be rolling. But even if you could have run with it, I don't think you *should* have.'

'Why not?'

'Because it's nobody's business.'

'That's not really an attitude that has ever caught on in the publishing world, Sarah. People have got a singular way of deciding what's their business, especially when it comes to politicians.'

'Come on, Jack, you know what I mean. This isn't some family-values Tory or some Wee Free minister getting caught with his dick out. This is a, a . . .'

'Self-absorbed arsehole who couldnae pass a mirror – or a vibrator, as it turns out.'

'Granted, he's not my favourite politician either, but what public interest would be served by people finding out about this?'

'Same as my interest in findin' out about it: it's fuckin' hilarious.'

Sarah rolled her eyes. 'Well, your mature and sophisticated sense of humour aside, remember that this is not someone who has ever sought to bring his values into other people's bedrooms.'

'True. But he's never done too badly out of flaunting what goes on in his own. There's a poetic justice to this, Sarah.'

'There's an irony to it, Jack, that's all. Whether it's poetic or not, I don't know, but it's certainly not justice. No matter who this guy is, no matter what you or anyone else thinks of him, this still comes down to private acts between consenting adults.'

Parlabane made ready with another juvenile remark, but Sarah saw it coming and pressed on more forcefully.

'We've got no more right to pry into what goes on in his bedroom than what goes on in his bathroom,' she insisted, 'and it's about time a line got drawn before the tabloids move in there too. Because however they dress it up, the angle here is not about politics or public interest, it's about embarrassment. Like bloody primary school. "Ha ha, we all know, Peter Logan puts things up his bum." What's next: "Ha ha, we all know, William Hague has piles"? "Nicholas Soames can't reach to wipe"? "Jack Straw in diarrhoea shocker"?'

'Well, the man-bites-dog peg would be that it was comin' oot his arse.'

'Yes, very witty, but the point is that we could all of us be embarrassed if people knew exactly what we got up to behind closed doors. That's why the bloody doors are closed. Bedroom or bathroom, these are not spectator sports, and neither are they the sites of the most dignified moments in our lives.'

'Oh, I don't know—'

'No, Jack, much as you enjoy having sex, and much as you may want to delude yourself about the quality of your performance, I don't think any of the expressions you make in the process are among those you'd pick for the cover of your autobiography.'

'I was going to say that I once did this jobbie that—'

Whack.

'Ouch.'

'Don't be disgusting. And don't try to change the subject. What I'm getting at is: "Let him who is without sin cast the first stone." We've all got our idiosyncracies and our dirty little secrets, and sometimes they get found out, but fortunately for most of us, nobody suggests we should lose our jobs because of them. If Peter Logan's career goes up in smoke, it should be because he failed in his responsibilities, or he did something dishonest – not because he got a vibrator stuck up his arse. What's that got to do with anything?'

'It's got to do with selling newspapers. I'm not defending it, so don't shoot the messenger, but that's the way it is. It's that unique tabloid symbiosis of the prurient and the puritanical. You can call it hypocrisy, but you'd be wasting your breath.'

'I know, Jack, but it really pisses me off. Why are people made to pay such a heavy price for their sexual misde-meanours when it's the one area where *anybody* can make a mistake?'

'Maybe for the same reason sex offenders get it so bad from the other prisoners. It makes people feel better about themselves if they can condemn someone for a worse crime than their own.'

'Well, I don't feel that way, and I don't think I'm the only one. Isn't there going to come a time when we all grow up and act like adults about this sort of thing?'

The answer, as it astonishingly turned out, was yes.

Sure enough, the story broke in the last edition of one of the morning red-tops, which had even been sharp enough to get a snapper up to the RVI in time to catch Logan and the bimbette coming out after the op. Neither the photographer nor the hack they had dispatched was much grounded in politics, or they might have identified – and sussed the significance of – the gaunt female in the edge of the shot, walking three steps behind. What they were missing was that they were finding out nothing that she didn't want them to find out.

Elspeth Doyle would have had options to prevent this story going to press – the patient confidentiality Sarah mentioned, for one thing – but this was New Labour in action and in essence. Doyle knew the rumour would be loose regardless, and to a spin doctor rumours were more dangerous than bare facts, whatever the bare facts might be. Facts you could control. Rumours had a life of their own, and in common with all other life-forms, a tendency towards exponential growth in their early stages. Left to fester, within a week it could be common 'knowledge' that Logan had actually been in bed with Zorgon, the aforementioned animatronic dinosaur, and that it was the diminutive Reid herself who had been surgically removed from his ringpiece.

The public's interest was as Parlabane had predicted. The public's reaction was not.

The familiar clamour of condemnation and resultant demands for retribution quite noticeably failed to ensue. Everybody read the story, sure. People pissed themselves laughing, and the Saturnalian laying low of a high figure provided maximum entertainment value on an otherwise rainy and miserable week. But apart from some oppor-tunistic bluster from the Tory ranks, and the obligatory histrionics from the yahoos on the mid-market op-ed pages, there was no groundswell of opinion to suggest that Logan should be fired.

There were a number of possible explanations for this. One was, implausible as Parlabane may have thought it, that most people *did* have that grown-up attitude Sarah was talking about, and either simply weren't interested or failed to see any greater moral relevance. Another factor was that perhaps quite a few people took one look at the unfolding furore and said quietly to themselves: 'There but for the grace of God go I.' Which was not to suggest that the nation was harbouring a silent majority of anal-erotic fetishists, but that many honest people felt deeply for the poor man's embarrassment. As Sarah said, these were not the most dignified moments in our lives, but we all had them, whatever form they might take.

An opposite but equally contributory consideration was, astoundingly enough, envy. Logan had always enjoyed an unhealthy degree of respect for his swordsmanship in certain unreconstructed quarters, and the economic necessity of flogging papers had dictated that the tabloids milk the story for titillation as much as for scandal. The tale provided a barely needed excuse for a trawl through the growing archive of Paula Reid's lads-mag photo-shoots – all erect nipples and see-thru tops – as well as prefacing several double-page features about sex-toys and 'kinky love games'. In many eyes, then, it wasn't about a senior MSP being humiliated, but about some jammy bastard *seriously* getting it on with that tidy bit off the telly (and what a dirty little bitch she must be, eh? Phwoaaar).

But undoubtedly, behind all of these conspicuously undamaging responses were the subtle mind-tricks of Elspeth Doyle and the art of the New Labour Spin-Jedi.

Commentators had argued about whether the Party's success was due to an ability to tap into the public mood, or instead due to a more sinister ability to manipulate that mood. In Parlabane's opinion, it was a combination of the two, but their most crucial ability was making the latter look like the former.

The response from the Logan camp and the official Labour ranks was just the right measure of anger at the media's intrusion, mixed with dignified and good-humoured posturing – all of it deftly and precisely orchestrated to give a prescribed and pre-discussed effect. Yes, Peter had been a little silly and was suitably contrite about the embarrassment it had caused those around him. Yes, Peter could see the funny side, wasn't too proud to face a ribbing, even made a few jokes himself when appropriate. But there was a very serious side to this too, let's not forget, and that was about privacy, for the cause of which Peter had uncomplainingly suffered.

From pervert to victim to martyr in two seamless transformations.

Doyle herself was ironically the perfect figure to be backing him, too. Renownedly prudish, starchly asexual and well known to be no fan of Logan, her support lent all the more gravity for its apparent incongruity. If Scottish Labour's answer to Mary Whitehouse was standing by the guy, scowling her disapproval at the press's conduct, then maybe they *had* stepped out of line.

It was inevitably suggested that she was merely selling out her own moral principles upon order from the Party bosses, but those who peddled such a line were merely walking into her trap. Doyle's track record of sticking by those principles in the face of Party dismay – such as over Robin Cook's affair – meant she could all the more

106

convincingly argue that she was *not* compromising now, but rather defending a different principle. She would admit that she did not approve of Logan's lifestyle or his sexual behaviour, but he still had the right to indulge it without reporters' faces pressed against the glass.

This was, Parlabane knew, utter pish: she was contradicting herself and whoring her opinion like any number of other Labour Lite invertebrates. But if truth be told, she was not compromising her true principles, because Elspeth Doyle had only one: own the story. Whatever it takes, own the story. And by Christ, she owned this one.

Still, there was only so much that news management could achieve, and brainwashing wasn't part of it. People had to be receptive to a certain point of view in the first place: otherwise you weren't so much spinning as polishing a jobbie. Instead of Logan, it was his perceived persecutors who incurred the public's backlash, but this wasn't down to Doyle. This was because Joe Punter had become a lot more media-savvy recently, and the watchmen of the press sometimes forgot that he was watching them.

Those who had called for Logan's head were forced back beneath their parapets under heavy fire; including – in the case of the politicos – the reminder that their own dirty laundry might get a public airing if those were the rules they wanted to play by.

The Churches didn't do very well out of it either. They stuck their oars in with wearing predictability – quotes from their respective spokesmen appeared at the tail ends of the longer articles on the subject – but their impact was negligible. The problem was that they were hopelessly unfocused. Everyone else was talking about privacy, politics and personal freedom, while they, well . . . It was sex, and therefore bad, so sheer reflex and a laboured sense of duty dictated that they say *something*, but neither the Rev William McLeod of the Prods nor Fr Francis Shelley of the Tims seemed to know quite what, other than expressing a grouchy and nebulous disapproval.

And having joined in the condemnation, however ineffectually, they had signed up for their share of the backlash too. In their case, it took the form of an increasingly large question mark being raised over their right to stick those oars in in the first place. Yeah, it was a democracy, and everyone was entitled to a say, but how big that say ought to be was coming under scrutiny. Why, some were asking (well, Parlabane actually, but he was hardly out on a limb), were reporters including those quotes in their articles at all? What other minority groups enjoyed such a disproportionate lobby as the Kirk and the Chapel, that their views could be admitted – even invited – into so many influential forums, despite their dwindling numbers?

No Scottish press story about contraception or an STD initiative, for instance, was complete without the requisite bouts of pious nay-saying from Billy and Franky. It was absurd. The issues at stake were health and education, as borne out by the preceding quotes from, funnily enough, health and education practitioners, but there *they* were too, every time, the holy rentagubs. Why? Why not a spokesman from Tesco, seeing as their Clubcard scheme had more members?

However, Billy, Franky and their respective bosses were left contemplating something worse than the backlash they'd received for attempting to interfere, and that was the desperate reality of just how little interfering they had managed. Instead of setting the agenda as they might once have done, they were now left staring at the dismaying and unmistakable sight of their own irrelevance. Here was an instance of the country getting on with a significant (if messy) piece of business – some might even call it growing up – without any meaningful recourse to these dwindling institutions.

It was a new century, new era, new Scotland. A good time to cast off the rusted shackles of tired traditions and obsolete ideologies. A good time to engender new attitudes and fresh perspectives, especially upon old problems. A time, even, when a reasoned and intelligent couple could place the value of their relationship above convention and hysteria, sufficient to share the hypothetical assurance that it would survive an instance of foolish indiscretion.

So what went wrong?

Well, it was kind of complicated, but a very big part of it was that Parlabane had always assumed *he* would be the one who got drunk and screwed someone else.

The mop hit the bottom of the bucket with a squelching thump. Another landing, another tub of disinfectant. He rested the handle against a wall and headed back downstairs to the storeroom. It wasn't the most satisfying day's work he'd ever done, but there was a certain meditative quality to it, as Mikey suggested, and it was definitely educational. As an investigative hack, Parlabane was a ninth-dan blackbelt in the art of earwigging, but he had soon learned there was little need to be surreptitious about it in a place where nobody would ever describe discretion as the better part of valour. Like primate competitors for dominant-male status, each of them preferred to announce to the pack just how much of a bampot (or steamer, or zoomer) he was, perhaps to deter challengers.

'So whit you in for this time, Big Yin?'

'Aw, fuckin' stupit, really. It was aboot six month back,

I got caught tryin' tae cairry an axe intae a pub. But that was when I'd ma auld job. Noo I'm a tree-surgeon, so I've got a fuckin' chainsaw . . .'

Parlabane suspected that that little exchange, in common with one or two others, had been partly for his benefit, and had shrugged it off accordingly. Far more disturbing had been the sighting of what he felt certain he could categorise as his first rocket. He was a stocky wee bloke in his early thirties, sporting a feeble attempt at a moustache and a badly drawn, home-made-looking tattoo of a shamrock (though it could have been a *fleur de lys*, or possibly even one of the Mister Men). The guy looked like he was bristling even just standing still, but it was his conversation that clinched it.

'Fuckin' liberty this, me bein' in here, so it is.'

'How, whit happened?'

'I'll tell you whit happened an' you'll no fuckin' believe me. You'll ca' me a liar tae ma face. Fuckin' no real. Ye ken I've got a wee boay, aye?'

'Aye.'

'Wee Chandler. Well the fuckin' ex wasnae lettin' me see 'im, ken, so me an' Eddie just took 'im out o' school for the day, thought we'd take 'im doon tae Dunbar, tae the seaside like. Anyway, we're in the motor, drivin' doon, an' this cunt fuckin' overtakes us, eh? Fuckin' cheeky bastart. So I says tae Eddie, I'm no fuckin' havin' this, no wi' the wean there, ken? You've got tae set a fuckin' example, in't ye? So I overtook the cunt back, an' waited tae he was right behin' us, then haunbraked 'im.'

'Haunbraked 'im?'

'Aye. You fuckin' slam on the haunbrake so's you slow right doon, but the cunt cannae see any brake-lights, ken, so he shites it an' has tae jump on the anchors. They sometimes turn their motors ower daein' it. Teaches them a fuckin' lesson. Anyway, that's whit happened. Cunt's motor flipped ower an' landed in a fuckin' field, but here, you'll no believe this: they fuckin' dae *me* for reckless drivin'. *Me?* He's the wan that fuckin' overtook *us*, ken, an' it's me that ends up in the fuckin' dock? No' fuckin' real, is it? Nae fuckin' justice. The cunt only broke his collarbone as well, nothin' serious. Big fuckin' fuss aboot fuck all.'

Apollo Twelve, you are cleared for blast-off.

Parlabane returned to his mop bearing another five-litre tub, surveying the row of cell doors and wondering what heartwarming revelations he'd have been party to by the time he reached the other end. He squatted down to prise off the plastic lid, and was about to pour the contents into the bucket when he noticed that the contents weren't what they were supposed to be. A quick sniff and a glance at the crucial resealable lid confirmed it.

'Dirty bastard.'

Grimacing, he closed the container again and stood up with a weary sigh. He'd learned another lesson – always check the contents *before* you lug the pail up three floors – but wished it had been four hours ago when he still had some energy.

It was therefore not the choicest moment for Fooaltiye to slink skinnily into view.

'Awright? Awright ya cunt? Fuckin' moppin', man, eh? Fuckin' swab the decks me hearties, eh, fuckinnn. Altiye man, don't fuckin' miss any bits or we'll be fuckin', hingmy, puttin' in a complaint, ya cunt. Ahhh-haaa. Naw, man, just fuckin' jokin'. Y'any gear, man, eh? Any stuff?'

'No.'

'Aaah-haaa. Fuckin' kiddin' ye again, ya daft wank. You're wan o' thae E Hall cunts, in't ye? Fuckin' nae

111

drugs for us, we're the fuckin' good little boys, innit, eh? Fuckin' waaanks.'

Parlabane took hold of the mop and looked the cypher in the eye. If Fooaltiye wanted to cut up rough, he'd have to get round the wooden handle first, which was at least twice his width.

'Is there anything I can help you with, mate, apart from maybe your vocabulary?'

'Naw, man, if ye've nae fuckin' gear, you're nae fuckin' use, that's the way I see it. Just fuckin', wanted tae see how you were fuckin' gettin' on, like, know? Fuckin' thought you'd have mebbe done yoursel' in by noo. What's the matter? Could you no' make a fuckin' noose oot the quilt or somehin'?'

'Naw. We've all got 13-tog duvets up on E Hall; too thick to tie. We've electric blankets as well, have you no' heard?'

Fooaltiye's dopey smile disappeared. 'Aye, fuckin' hink you're funny, ya cunt, eh? Fooaltiye, you'll fuckin' no be laughin' soon, that's whit I heard. I know who you are. You're that journalist cunt, in't ye? Your fuckin' card's marked, pal, that's what *I* fuckin' heard.'

Parlabane felt a gut-wrenching lurch of anxiety, then remembered Mikey's words of wisdom. Screamers can't bear to see someone keeping himself to himself: they're compelled to illicit a reaction, and will try whatever tack they think might work. Fooaltiye, however, wasn't going to get any joy today.

'Aye, right. Very good.'

'That's the fuckin' word, man. I'm just sayin'. Fuckin' nae need for you tae gie it sideyways. Just bide your fuckin' time an' somedy'll sort it for ye.'

'Thanks, I appreciate the candour.'

112

Fooaltiye looked disappointedly at Parlabane's smile and sussed that he was wasting his time. He turned and began to walk away. Parlabane was squatting to open the fresh tub of disinfectant when something occurred to him. He stood up again and shouted after the departing stick-insect.

'This your floor, then, mate?'

'Aye, whit aboot it?'

'Nothin'. Just checkin'.'

'Aye. Just fuckin' checkin'. Just get on wi' swabbin' the fuckin' decks ya cunt.'

'Will do.'

Parlabane slid the new tub against the wall with his foot, then reached down for the previously discarded one. Whistling cheerfully to himself, he proceeded to mop the length of Fooaltiye's landing with five litres of unadulterated pish.

public interest

'Huuuullo! Hullo! We are the Billy Boys. Hullo! Hullo! You'll know us by our noise.'

The song boomed triumphantly around the stadium, as it had done after every goal Ian Beadie could remember Rangers scoring. Close to fifty thousand pairs of hands punched the air in time with the 'hullo's, satisfied grins masking their relief at seeing a second goal go in before the interval. Hibs had been threatening an equaliser for ten minutes or so, and the last thing anyone wanted was for the visitors to be making a game of it in the second half. Too much tension, it ruined the atmosphere. The second goal would knock the stuffing out of them. Nobody came back from two down at Ibrox. Everyone could enjoy their half-time refreshment and look forward to the Teddy Berrs running up a good score over the second forty-five. That's what it was all about.

'We're up to our knees in Fenian blood, surrender or you'll die!'

He had a bitter smile to himself, looking along the faces on his row of seats. None of them were singing, though not because they weren't delighted. He could see their shoulders automatically moving to the song's rhythm, a conflict etched in their features, ill-disguised by their smiles. It was almost as bad as not being able to shout 'YES!' when the ball hit the back of the net. They wanted to sing. By God, they wanted to sing. The euphoric emotion was flowing through them – and how could it not be amid such a vibrant throng? – but their mouths had to remain closed.

Why?

Because this was the corporate hospitality section of the stadium, where Scotland's captains of business and industry watched their football from literally a higher level. The upside, apart from comfier seats, was that the periods of play were bracketed by generous helpings of Beef Wellington, fine wine and single malt, but the downside was that you couldn't join in belting out the party songs with the punters in the grandstands.

In May 1999, the then club vice-chairman, Donald Finlay QC, had been surreptitiously videotaped singing what the papers called 'a sectarian medley' at a party after the Scottish Cup Final. The scoop hit the streets at about ten pm, and his resignation was on the chairman's desk before the morning edition. Since then, the denizens of the Camel Coat Loyal had learned to be a lot more circumspect of a Saturday afternoon. All it took was one sneaky bastard with a digital video camera and you could be out on your arse by Monday morning.

It was ludicrously disproportionate, of course; political correctness gone insane. In the modern Scotland, it seemed, if you got some tart to shove a dildo up your arse, your job was safe, but if you sang the wrong song at the football, your head would be demanded.

This was a day out at the game, for God's sake. Everyone knew the chants were only a wee bit of fun, all part of the occasion and the atmosphere. Just because you sang the tune didn't mean you believed the words. However, it was how it appeared that mattered. Ian Beadie, of all people, knew that.

'Heart in hand and sword and shield, we'll guard old Derry's walls.'

He had to laugh, though, watching them all stand silently as another anthem rang around the ground. Their lips were still, but if you looked in their eyes, you would probably see a black ball bouncing along the lyrics.

Self-awareness was seldom in spate around Ibrox, but it took a special level of obtuseness to miss the irony of what was going on in the posh seats. Here were dozens of men who never went near a church and probably harboured no religious prejudice, girning in frustration at not being able to join in songs affirming the superiority of the Scottish Protestant; sung in support of a football team which was today fielding three Dutchmen, two Germans, two Italians, two Australians and an American alongside its one token Scot: Neil McCann, who happened to be a Catholic.

The referee blew for half-time. The stadium rose as one in response, loudly applauding what they had seen. In truth, it had been a fairly rotten first half, but with Celtic snapping on Rangers' heels, a two-goal cushion meant the game was comfortably won; only the final margin remained to be settled. Beadie got to his feet and clapped too, but his eyes were not on the pitch. He scanned the stairway leading to the exit, watching the corporate guests file inside for a warming brandy and some petits fours, to fill whatever hole might have opened since lunch finished almost a whole hour ago.

The man he was looking for was easy to spot. Everyone else had their heads up, scanning for familiar faces and nodding their hellos as they did at every game. Don Petrie, however, editor of the *Daily Recorder*, had his eyes on his shoes. It wasn't that he didn't want to talk to anybody: he just didn't want to talk to Beadie. He'd avoided him at lunch, which was easy enough as their tables had been quite far apart, but half-time was more a matter of stand-up mingling, and who you mingled with was a conscious (and sometimes self-conscious) choice.

A lot of business was done over those fifteen-minute breaks, and Beadie *thought* he had done some himself last Saturday, when he fed Petrie an extremely juicy morsel. He had documentary and photographic proof that Nigel Braidwood, Scotland's most vocal and visible environmental campaigner, was not just a tree-hugger, but an uphill gardener as well.

Braidwood was sandal-wearer-in-chief – or whatever 'non-hierarchical' title the organic muesli brigade bestowed upon their heid-bummer – of PlanetScape (Scotland), and had of late been bringing much pressure to bear in opposition to a major new housing development intended by Castle Homes. Castle wanted to flatten some daft wee wood on the outskirts of Perth, but Braidwood's mob had been all over the media, painting the building firm as a bunch of vandals and murderers just because some fucking owl lived there. Christ, the things had wings, hadn't they? It wasn't as though it couldn't find another tree in Perthshire, for God's sake.

But the public weren't seeing it that way, mainly because the public were only being told how to see it by PlanetScape (Scotland). This was where Ian Beadie and Clamour PR came in. People didn't really give a fuck about owls, as Beadie explained to David Castle. They just thought they did, because they read it in the paper or they saw it on the news. You just needed to remind them that they cared more about other things.

Beadie initially advised a line about the creation of jobs (always grabs you a fortified spot on the moral high ground,

117

that one), as well as the usual stuff about the knock-on effect for the area's economy, regeneration of the region, the need for new housing stock, blah blah blah. As was often the case, however, Beadie had only been brought in once the fires were already raging, so though Castle managed to recover some territory in the propaganda battle, the war itself had moved elsewhere. PlanetScape had caused enough of a stink for it to reach the noses of the new parliament, and now the whole development was in danger of being suspended for months while some environment committee pondered it. Braidwood, of course, was lobbying hard for this; indeed would probably prefer it to an instant refusal of planning permission, because this way he and his mob got to keep their faces in the frame for longer.

He was quite a figurehead, Braidwood, the kind of guy a pressure group needed in an age when sheer ideological self-righteousness was no longer enough. He was a media-savvy operator, knew how to sell his angle to the reporters so that his lot always looked like the plucky underdog fighting for justice, rather than the Luddite busybodies standing in the way of progress. Consequently, they enjoyed more coverage than environmental pressure groups who could boast larger memberships, such as Friends of the Earth. There was, however, a trade-off in employing such a figure. The benefit was that it put a very recognisable public face on your message. The drawback was that your group could become a one-man show, and that was where they were vulnerable. Campaigners like that were there to represent a point of view, and their currency was credibility. Without that, they were nothing.

It was at trying times such as this, therefore, when reason, truth and logic had failed Clamour's clients, that Beadie had recourse to that reliably efficacious public relations device known as the hatchet-job.

Hypocrisy was the best angle, so Beadie put out feelers in search of some environmental transgression they could embarrass Braidwood with. Maybe he secretly owned a gas-guzzling car, or he didn't buy recycled lavvy paper, whatever. Unfortunately, they came up with nothing. Braidwood was that thing the dispassionate PR advisor most dreads: a true believer.

This left no other option than the default, which was to get into his private life and find something that, while admittedly not affecting his professional credibility, caused sufficient distraction to keep everybody's attention off the issue at hand. A quick trawl through Beadie's own extensive files came up with a tale from a few years back, and after that it was little more than a formality to procure more up-to-date evidence.

The guy was an arse-bandit. Not as good as him being a paedophile or having shares in McDonalds, but it would do. Or, rather, it would have done if the *Daily Recorder* had run the fucking thing.

Beadie waited until the initial rush was subsiding, then made his way to the toilets, where he stood outside and waited. Petrie emerged from the door after a couple of minutes, annoyance and depression on his face. He knew what was coming.

'No' much worth readin' in your paper this week, Donny,' Beadie opened.

'Zat right?' he said wearily.

'Aye. Bit of a disappointment. I mean, there was me thinkin' you must have no end of juicy stories lined up, for there to be nae room for the one I gave you. But no, quiet old week, it seems.'

'Fuck off, Ian. It didnae run. Live with it.'

'Why not, for fuck's sake? It all checked out.'

'I know it checked out, but that's no' the point. It was inappropriate.'

'Inappropriate? That's a big word for the editor o' *that* shite-rag. Whit was "inappropriate" aboot it?'

'You know fine. If you'd gie'd us a story aboot him cuttin' doon trees in his garden, or shootin' rabbits or somethin', we'd have been sorted. But this business aboot his private life . . .'

Petrie looked tired. He always looked tired these days, distinctly lacking the *joie de vivre* that had made him such a ruthless operator and, let's be honest, a great laugh, in times past.

'It has no bearin' on his job, Ian, or on this campaign. You know that. An' this isnae somethin' he's been cagey about. It's just no somethin' oor readers would be interested in aboot a guy like that.'

'They'd be interested as soon as it was on the page in front of them. *You* know that.'

Petrie shook his head. 'No' these days, Ian. Look at the roastin' the press got over Mandelson. There was no angle, no conflict of interest. Makin' a big deal aboot him bein' gay just looked liked queer-bashin'.'

'Yeah, and . . .'

'Whit d'ye mean "yeah, and"? We're supposed to be the right-on New Labour tabloid, remember?'

'Oh come off it, Don. Right-on? There's nae paper been a mair reliable queer-basher in Scotland doon the years than the *Daily Recorder*. It's the *real* man's paper. A family paper. Folk expect it to stick to its guns.'

'*You* come off it. Family, Ian? Aye, that's you all the way. 'Why didn't you try floggin' this rubbish to *The Sun*?'

Beadie looked upwards. No point in lying about it; Petrie knew the answer.

'You went to them first, ya bastard, didn't you, an' they KBed you as well.'

Beadie shrugged. Both men knew there were no loyalties in this business.

'Don't know what the newspaper business is comin' to, Don, I really don't. I'd never have bet on you goin' all PC an' self-righteous on us.'

'It's no' a matter of me goin' self-righteous. You know the score. Do you not think I lie awake some nights wishin' it was the mid-Nineties again? Do you not think I wish we *could* be runnin' this stuff? But the fact is that we cannae. The public won't wear it, especially after that carry-on with Peter Logan. We took a right kickin' over that, all of us. And we cannae say it's just tomorrow's chip-wrappers and be done with it. There's pressure from upstairs too. You've got to go with the mood, Ian, or you lose readers. That's always how it's been.'

'Aye, I know, but the mood's never been like this.'

'Tell me aboot it. I'm as baffled as you. I mean, *anybody* gettin' a vibrator stuck up their arse is a good tale, but a fuckin' government minister? With the TV star half the nation's teens are wankin' themselves to sleep over? It should have been manna from heaven. But naw, all we hear aboot is press intrusion, an' "it doesnae have any bearing on the guy's job, it's his business, his private life, blah blah fuckin' blah." The suits upstairs are sayin' this sort of thing is turnin' off the readers.'

'Like fuck it is. The readers are lappin' it up. They just *say* they disapprove, but they still read the story, every word. Same as it ever was.'

'Aye. You know that, an' I know that, but it's no' just

about readers any more, is it? There's advertisers to consider, proprietors tryin' tae keep sweet wi' New Labour, pressure groups jumpin' doon your throat aw the time. An' tae be honest, the public *have* changed. They might still be interested in this stuff, but you cannae kid them on that it's *relevant*. It's no' exposin' hypocrisy an' decadence, it's just peerin' in other people's steamy windaes.'

'And what is relevant? Donald Finlay singin' "The Sash" at a party? Ten-year-old photos of John Grieg wi' a flute band?'

'Well, I'd have thought you'd be applaudin' those stories, given who *you*'re workin' for these days. Ian Beadie, blessed PR advisor to the Scottish Catholic Church.'

Beadie glared. He hadn't known Petrie was aware of that rather clandestine account, but in Scottish media circles, little stayed secret for long.

'Aye, why no' say it a bit louder, Don. Maybe you can get us both a doin'.'

'Naw, naw, you're forgettin'. Nae bigotry among the Ibrox faithful these days. Nobody wants to be revealed in our newspaper as a bigot, remember.'

'Aye, you're a bunch of true moral crusaders, Don.'

'It's no' my fault the game's changed, Ian, but it has. The golden age is past. Deal with it.'

Deal with it.

Aye, right.

Beadie sat down as the teams kicked off for the second half. Rangers soon added a third, through Jorg Albertz, but it did little to lift his spirits. His eyes were taking in the action, but his mind was far from the game. These were very dark times.

'We cannae kid them on that it's relevant.'

'It doesnae have any bearing on the guy's job, it's his business, his private life, blah blah fuckin' blah.'

Yes, that certainly was the constant, pompous, whining refrain these days. People's private lives were nobody's business but their own, and it didn't mean anything to anyone else what they got up to behind closed doors.

Bollocks it didn't.

If it meant nothing, then nobody would be interested, and in Beadie's experience, *everybody* was interested. There was no use them all complaining about it; he didn't make the world that way, but that, without doubt *was* the way of the world. He knew, because he'd learned it first-hand. He'd lost the only woman he ever loved, and witnessed his son growing up only in limited dispatches, all due to foolish, impetuous lust.

It happened fourteen years ago, when he was in London, working as a night news editor at the Voss papers' Deptford HQ. The Compound, as they called it, was an interconnected complex of Victorian warehouses, refurbished in the Seventies, at minimum expense, to house offices and presses on the one site. Cameron had not long been born, and Beadie wasn't getting to see much of Karen because of the shifts he was on. Karen was always too exhausted or too busy with the baby anyway, so that she didn't have much time or energy left for him when he was around. On the odd occasions they were both home and awake at the same time, Karen seemed so besotted and consumed by the wee one that Beadie could barely engage her in a decent conversation, and there were times when it felt like she'd lost interest in him.

He was lonely. He'd never have admitted something so soft to himself at the time, but that was the truth. He was lonely and feeling neglected, which was what made him receptive – maybe vulnerable was the word – when one of the nightshift copytakers started paying him some attention. Her name was Linzi, a cheerfully flirty cockney who'd been born in a mini-skirt and about whom tales and rumours were legion. They played daft wee games with each other, the flirting becoming more overt, but with Beadie not expecting it to lead to anything, perhaps because he so badly wanted it to.

Eventually, they ended up shagging downstairs in the morgue at about eleven on a slow Sunday night. It started off as the prototypical knee-trembler against one of the massive archives. It was a slide-action system, like a giant accordion that opened an access channel to the section you wanted, while compressing all the others to make space. It was also an unnervingly shoogly big bugger, and Beadie was terrified they'd collapse the thing, so he suggested a change of position. Linzi shoved a microfiche reader to one side and sat up on a table, her back to the wall, whereupon they recommenced with renewed and increased vigour.

The table was a narrow but sturdy affair, its legs squeaking rhythmically off the floortiles in time with Linzi's exponentially passionate sounds, like Raleigh's mistress up against the tree: sweessir, swasser, sweessir, swasser. Or in Linzi's case, harderIan, harderIan, harderIan, until Beadie thrusted sufficiently hard for the cheapshit gyproc partition wall to collapse at her back, and the pair of them to crash through it, bringing down a section of equally cheapshit ceiling tiles on top.

They were pinned there for nearly an hour, still engaged, their torsos stacked in the picture-sales filing room, and Beadie's bare arse partially visible from the morgue. There was a now very senior Fleet Street editor who, he knew, still kept a photo of it in his desk drawer.

124

It was an utter, unmitigated catastrophe. Everybody in the Compound knew about it by eight the next morning, and it took little more time in spreading beyond. Linzi was fired outright, but Beadie's recognised potential saw his punishment commuted to banishment. He was sent back whence he came, to a post on one of the Scottish regional editions, but his wife and child did not join him on the flit.

He tried to explain how sorry he was, how it didn't mean anything, how pointless it would be to throw their whole marriage away over one act of stupidity . . . all the things people said when they got caught with their trousers down; all the things they would still be saying in a thousand years' time; all the things that cut no ice with a wronged woman, and certainly not with Karen. She left him and filed for divorce.

No stray shag is meaningless. A betrayal is a betrayal, like a pregnancy is a pregnancy. People know that full well when they're ripping off each other's knickers, no matter what pseudo-psychological shite they come up with. Their justifications are simply an exercise in lying to themselves, and once you've started lying to yourself, who's supposed to trust you after that? Your spouse? Your boss? The public?

Fuck off.

Meaningless. Aye, right. It means bloody plenty, and one of the things it means is that there's a price to pay. Beadie had been made to pay it in full, to lose what he loved and to be treated by his peers like the lowest, basest, amoral, dirty wee lech. He was therefore buggered if some other self-righteous, self-important bastard was going to get away without the same just because he was rich, or he was famous, or he was well-connected.

Beadie knew what shame felt like, and just as importantly, he knew how much it scared people. Growing up, it had been easy to see how the herd instinct could be manipulated, how the fear of being isolated could be a powerful weapon. Whenever some wee prick was getting ideas above his station, you only had to remind your classmates how he peed himself that time in Primary Six, or that he got a 'stauner' in the boys' showers in First Year PE.

Laughter itself derived from ostracisation. Pack animals drove out the weak liabilities among their number by joining in howls of communal derision. Human beings were no different. The fear of it was far more effective than duress when it came to keeping society in line, and the scandal sheets played a crucial part in protecting people from transgressions. Those who resented the tabloids were shooting the messenger, like crooks resenting the police. Neither made the rules: the police merely enforced the law of the land, while the tabloids enforced its morality. If you had done nothing wrong, then you had nothing to hide.

Except that *everybody* has something to hide.

That was why, even once he had left the print game, he was still sought out by reporters with stories to sell; names, dates, quotes, pictures, hotel bills, *billets doux*. Stories about nobodies who might one day be somebodies; stories about nobodies who were causing problems for somebodies; stories about somebodies procured in a manner that precluded publication. Data, information that would be filed away and might never see the light of day, unless . . .

He had it all in files now at home, the details and cross-referencing stored on his PC, which he had appropriately nicknamed 'Hoover'. All he had to do was key a name into the database, and it was amazing how often the machine

126

paid out. Scotland was a very small place; Scottish society (at least the parts that mattered) even smaller.

Until recently it had served him – and his clients – very well. Lately, however, some extremely damaging precedents were being set. Elspeth Doyle had spun the Logan débâcle quite brilliantly, fly old bird that she was, but the papers had been on the back foot over these 'public interest' issues for a while. And now Petrie's burial of the Braidwood story suggested the retreat was in danger of being permanent.

'The golden age is past,' he'd said, but not without visible regret.

'Do you not think I lie awake some nights wishin' it was the mid-Nineties again?'

Would that it could be, Beadie reflected. All this Blairite touchy-feely shite, coupled with so much conciliatory relativism, was proving exceedingly bad for business. What was needed was a good dose of moral certainty, to stiffen a few spines and give guys like Petrie their balls back. What was needed was religion.

If the tabloids were society's moral thermostat, then religion was the pilot light that kept the fire going, even when fuel was low. Unfortunately, the Scottish Churches' flames were flickering in the wind themselves.

Beadie wasn't religious himself, so had been very surprised by Frank Shelley's approach for his services. However, he did harbour a certain admiration for the Catholic Church. The various mainstream Prod factions – the Church of Scotland, the Episcopalians, etc – had all become a bit too mealy-mouthed in recent decades, but the Tims had retained an uncompromising fire-and-brimstone streak, particularly in the area of sexual values. To be fair, there was an even harsher fundamentalism to be found in the

127

Wee Frees, but the problem was that they were just too screamingly fucking mad for anyone to take them seriously. The prospect of making them seem credible to society at large was far beyond even his PR abilities.

If anyone was worth bolstering, it was the Jungle Jims. Even before Ian got involved, it was already Shelley or his boss the Cardinal who the press went to first for a moral angle; unless it was a specifically C of S story, you'd always find the Reverend McLeod's tuppenceworth much further down the columns.

He knew Petrie was right: the tabloids couldn't set the mood, they could only reflect it. However, it was expected of the Churches that they should pontificate, offering a moral lead regardless of the moral climate. Nobody was following that lead these days, but people could be fickle that way. Just because they had swung in one direction didn't mean they couldn't swing back again, given the right signals and the right circumstances. Those circumstances could be a long time coming around, of course, but that was only if you were waiting for them to happen by themselves.

Maybe, he mused, it was possible to make them come around. Or simpler still, given his particular talents, maybe you just had to make people *believe* they had.

Albertz lined up a free kick from about twenty-five yards out, eyeing the Hibs wall with a contemptuous flaring of his nostrils. The big German then burnt the ball straight into the top corner at about a hundred miles an hour.

Beadie leapt to his feet and cheered, a great surge of energy coursing through his whole body. All around him was a vast sea of smiles. Things were definitely looking brighter.

holy shit

'His Eminence will see you now, Father.'

Father Francis Shelley put down his half-drunk cup of half-drinkable tea and climbed to his feet, probably not quite fast enough for the liking of Monsignor Toale, the Cardinal's highly protective secretary, personal assistant and dedicated bum-licker. Toale's eyebrows furrowed in mild impatience as Shelley bent to pick up his coat and briefcase; it didn't do to keep a man as important as the Cardinal waiting, even if your own hesitancy was induced by sitting in the ante-room for the best part of an hour and a half, during which you could slip into a state of trance-like contemplation and forget why it was you were actually there.

Toale would have had that look on his face anyway, narrowed eyes and lips like a camel's arse in a sandstorm. This was because Toale knew he'd be getting his marching orders once the visitor was inside, Shelley being one of the few people whose business with Cardinal Doollan the self-important secretary was not always party to.

'And how did the, ehm, meeting go?' Toale asked, trying to pretend he was halfway in on what Shelley was there to talk about.

'I'm afraid I can't discuss it, Monsignor Toale. I'm sure you understand. It will be at His Eminence's discretion to keep you informed.'

Might as well rub it in, Shelley thought, perfectly aware

that His Eminence was going to tell the Monsignor precisely hee-haw. Let the bugger sulk. He'd be a sight more peeved if he did know what was going on, ignorance being bliss and all that.

Toale opened the door with his usual action suggestive of ceremonial flourish, as though, just inside, six liveried heralds were about to give it laldy in accompaniment. It was another of the habitual ways he was constantly underlining the importance of the man he served; and by extrapolation, the importance of the man chosen to do the serving.

Shelley walked into the room, where the seated Cardinal Doollan, upon pensively looking up from a Bible, met his expectant eyes. Sometimes it was an effort not to then roll them. This was the Cardinal's official greeting posture, and presumably he forgot – or didn't care – that Shelley had seen the routine at least three dozen times before. It was no wonder His Eminence had so taken to Ian Beadie, despite his initial reservations. The PR guru was always going to be catnip to a man so concerned about his public image that he sent his gofer out to retrieve his guests while he composed his regular wee tableau of 'The Holy Man in Solemn Contemplation'.

'Your Eminence, Father Shelley is here to see you,' Toale announced.

Pretending to return from whatever higher plane of theological meditation he had ascended to, Cardinal Doollan made his familiar play of remembering himself, delicately closing his Bible, placing it on the table and standing up to receive his visitor, upon whom a practisedly beatific beam would now be trained.

Shelley guessed he wouldn't be smiling in a minute.

'Father Shelley,' he greeted with a robust geniality, something else that was imminently about to dry up.

130

'Your Eminence,' Shelley replied, the warmth of his own tone at deliberate variance with the look in his eye, which economically communicated that the news was bad and that His Eminence should dispatch Laughing Boy forthwith.

'Monsignor Toale . . .' was all the Cardinal had to say.

'Yes, Your Eminence,' he stated, backing obediently out of the room like some sycophantic courtier.

Doollan sat down again in a chair that seemed to get more worryingly throne-like every time Shelley saw it; either that or the man's posture was becoming less self-consciously regal. He gestured to a small carver in the corner, which Shelley lifted across and set down a minimum respectful distance of four feet away. It was in such stressful moments that Shelley found himself least tolerant of the Cardinal's affectations. There was little doubt that he was a remarkable man, in many eyes the greatest Catholic leader Scotland ever had, but he often gave the impression that his life was one long, barely tolerable inconvenience of waiting for his papacy to commence.

John Paul I had controversially eschewed the pomp and privilege of his tenure, refusing, for instance, to be carried in a sedan chair. Admire the Cardinal as he did, Shelley couldn't really see Pakky Doollan following suit if he ever got the gig.

'You look troubled, Father Shelley. Went the meeting well? Or is that rather a redundant question?'

'It went well in as much as its participants were all of one mind, Your Eminence. Unfortunately, they were all of one mind about how large a challenge we may be about to face.'

Doollan gave his intendedly reassuring faith-will-conquer-all smile, radiating the legendarily inspirational charisma that could often make you believe any problem had a solution. Unfortunately for Shelley, in this case a solution had already come to light, and it was that which was bothering him a sight more than the problem.

The problem, the 'challenge' as he had more euphemistically put it, was nothing all that new, when you stood back from it. It was merely another – albeit major – battle in an on-going war; defeat would not be decisive, but the losses could be heavy and the fight extremely bloody. Shelley, bearing the Catholic Church's flag in the unforgiving theatre of the Scottish media, was a veteran of many such doomed, one-sided campaigns, and was unfazed if hardly overjoyed by the prospect. What was giving him far more pause was the tantalising possibility of an alternative.

You could call it a secret weapon, or perhaps a bloodless coup. No, secret weapon, definitely. Untried, untested, unpredictable, potentially devastating, it could completely neutralise their enemies, or possibly its impact would be so widespread that both sides would be forced to adapt to the altered landscape, but only one would have notice to prepare.

Like any such new and powerful device, the morality of its use was tortuously ambiguous, and what was truly worrying was the thought that there was no precedent for anyone coming through that ideological maze and then choosing *not* to deploy. Nobel might have later given his name and his fortune to peace, but when it came to make-your-mind-up time, he didn't chuck his chemistry set in the bin, did he? So perhaps the most unsettling thing was not that he had a decision to make, but the suspicion that he'd already made it. Perhaps the doubt he felt wasn't over what *could* happen, but whether he was ready for what was unavoidably about to.

Needs must when the Devil drives, they said. Well, Auld Nick had sure been burning rubber in Scotland of late. The struggle for souls had always been what his father would have called 'a sair fecht', and the fecht had become a lot sairer in the past thirty years. Different generations would, understandably, recall their own eras as having witnessed the worst of struggles, but even the oldest priests among them were agreed that an unprecedented rot had set in during the last third of the Twentieth Century. There was also fairly unanimous concord over the source, if not the nature.

Vatican II. 1968. Humanae Vitae.

The conservative traditionalists blamed it for weakening the Church's will and authority, as a needless sop to the transient whims of a frivolous time that was crying out for discipline, not indulgence. People would have less respect for a church that bent like a straw in the wind, they said; it should stand tall and rigid like a great oak. The modernist liberals, for their part, argued that the wind was only going to blow a lot harder, and that there was a greater chance of the more flexible straw being left standing at the end of it. Their complaint was that it didn't bend enough.

Despite his own instincts, Father Shelley had to concede that the liberal point of view more plausibly explained the difficulties the Church had faced since, even if their suggested solutions sounded more like surrenders. It all, rather depressingly, came down to sex, and more specifically contraception. The liberals argued that many Catholics' fervent expectations of Vatican II were of a modernisation that would acknowledge that the planet had become a little more populous since the Bronze Age, and that the need to go forth and multiply was no longer quite so pressing. They felt the teachings of their religion were increasingly at odds

133

with a world in which the pace of change – in science, in communication, in technology and in attitudes – was accelerating by the day. But basically, let's be honest, they just wanted to have consequence-free sex.

They hoped that Humanae Vitae would allow them to reconcile the lives they wanted to live (or were already living and feeling guilty about) with the Church they believed in. Instead it drew a line in the sand between those things. Disappointingly but (the liberals argued) predictably, they crossed to the materialistic side in their multitudes. Many still went to mass, still tried to be faithful in other ways, but such duality could not be sustained. Alienation was inevitable.

In some cases, Catholics could not bear the knowledge of their condemnation, so stayed away from its source. The liberals said they were driven away, but that was a little simplistic, and ignored the fact that as beings of free will, it was still their choice.

Far more destructive, many others, having begun by questioning their Church's teaching on birth control, found themselves less intimidated about questioning other of its tenets. Apostasy soon followed, and worse, such lapsed Catholics usually reneged on their marital vows and failed to pass the faith on to their children.

As a consequence, since the 1970s, congregations had been shrinking exponentially. Falling numbers meant falling influence. The voice of a faith is not the voice of its leaders; the leaders may supply the words, but those words are only truly heard as they are echoed by the flock. With fewer people living by the Church's teachings – or indeed by any Christian teachings – there were fewer to stand up to the increasing secularisation of society, and thus a vicious circle spun. Not only were there fewer Catholics, fewer Christians, but religious faith itself was frequently under attack; constantly subject to disrespect, irreverence and even ridicule.

None of this was particularly new. From their role as warm-up act at the Coliseum onwards, Catholics were used to being abused for the entertainment of a moronic public. What they were not used to was being painted as the oppressors. Again, it all tediously came down to sex. They were oppressing homosexuals, oppressing women, oppressing over-populated third-world countries, oppressing single mothers, oppressing teenagers. And how had the Church carried out this widespread and despicable wickedness? Simply by opposing the recently and inexplicably validated 'right' of an individual to use sexual intercourse for selfish, recreational purposes.

Not only did this alienate even more people, but it made still others uncomfortable about being associated with such a demonised ideology. This was otherwise known as the sin of being 'uncool'. Unfortunately, it never seemed to occur to certain people that Hell was not known to be particularly cool either. The liberals' analysis might be accurate, but sometimes they forgot that the dilutions of pragmatism could leave you with a very watery brew.

Many argued that it was well past time the Church 're-addressed' these issues, by which they really meant changed its mind. Contraception, homosexuality, women priests, married priests . . . they had their prescribed wish-list of ways the faith could make itself more palatable to a public that increasingly regarded it as insensitive, mean-spirited, out of touch and, dare they whisper it, irrelevant.

However, Catholics were well used to holding unpopular beliefs, beliefs that challenged their adherents as well as the society around them. Centuries of experience had taught them that just because the majority thought something different didn't mean the majority were right. Yes, they could change to make their faith 'easier', but easy wasn't the object, and besides, what would that leave? There had been many times before in Scotland and the world abroad when their religion was under threat and their numbers decimated, but as long as the faith itself endured, history taught that it would wax strong again in time.

That faith endured because it had been forged by God and had remained uncompromised, its integrity unbreached. They couldn't alter it to suit society's whims, taking out a component here and an element there, replacing them with feeble, man-made materials. If they did they would be left with something brittle and worthless, a fragile plastic bauble where once they had an indestructible gem.

As Shelley saw it, this would gain nothing anyway, even in the short term. What the self-styled progressives forgot was that the people who left the Church weren't outside chapping at the door, waiting to be invited back in as soon as all those nasty crucifixes had been replaced with trendy fish icons. The fall-out from Humanae Vitae was irreversible. They couldn't turn the clock back to 1968, so there was no point in adulterating their principles for the benefit of people who wouldn't be caring anyway.

Defending the faith of those who remained true was a more worthy objective. That, in fact, was one of the reasons he remained resolutely against the idea of allowing priests to marry. It might be a cliché, but that didn't make it any less true: a Catholic priest was married to the Church. The would-be reformers and modernisers meant well, and they might even think they had the priests' best interests at heart, but they forgot that priests' best interests were not selfish ones. The practical truth was that to have two spouses

136

would be to serve both equally poorly. Both a wife and a congregation expected – no, *deserved* – exclusive dedication.

There were plenty of priests who disagreed with him, he knew: young, idealistic, energetic and perhaps egotistical enough to think that the Church should bend to accommodate them. In the end, they usually left. They fell in love with a parishioner, suffered the intolerable strain of being pulled in two directions, and eventually gave up their ministry – effectively proving Shelley's point. He wouldn't wish such suffering on anyone, which was why he believed in absolute fidelity to the Church. It was there for priests' protection: if they were totally committed to their priesthood, they would blot out such temptations, the way a committed, faithful husband should.

It annoyed him to hear the media commentators say that priests were in no position to moralise about people's sexual desires simply because they were celibate. Priests knew plenty about such yearnings; indeed had endured them more testingly than most. They also, however, knew the value of self-discipline, and what strengths it could bring to other areas of your life at the expense of denial of just one. Not caving in to every human want didn't make you less human.

Shelley was fed up with being perceived as some airy-fairy simpleton just because he wore a dog collar. He often wished he'd been born in another era, a few hundred years back: when the Church wielded true power, when priests could be men of action, dynamic agents of Rome, rather than the meek and cowed creatures they were perceived to be these days. In the war for eternal souls, he was fed-up having to be a lily-livered pacifist. As a military man once put it, 'Get them by the balls, and their hearts and minds will follow.'

In this day and age, however, the Church's interests were no longer defended in parliaments, at royal courts or on muddy fields, though the intrigue, espionage, deception, betrayal and blood-letting remained. Today's battles were fought in the media, which made Francis Shelley, as press spokesman, general of the Scottish Catholic Church's forces. Well, to call them battles would be an undeserved glorification. In the current climate it was more like guerrilla warfare against a vastly superior enemy: making small strikes where and when your resources allowed, engaging in limited skirmishes then disappearing into cover to assess the damage, both inflicted and sustained.

The presence of Cardinal Patrick Doollan added what he might most diplomatically refer to as an element of challenge. That he was an inspirational, charismatic and formidable figure was in no doubt, any more than the impact he had in raising the Church's public profile. However, when you're the one charged with the responsibility of managing that profile, a man like Doollan could be as much a liability as an asset.

The problem was that the needs of the Cardinal's ambitions were not always at one with the needs of the Scottish Church at large, something of which His Eminence seemed to have very little appreciation. Since long before his investiture as Cardinal, Pakky Doollan had always kept one eye on how his actions were playing in Rome. Sometimes Shelley suspected it was two, as he was the one left to field the domestic response. The Cardinal would come up with schemes and statements that he clearly hoped would attract the attention of the Vatican to his vision, dynamism and impact. Available evidence even suggested that it worked, but sometimes with the unfortunate side-effect of hanging his press officer out to dry. Hardline pronouncements –

such as calling abortion 'a holocaust' or saying that a woman's greatest aspiration should be to bear a son who becomes a priest – might go down a storm at St Peter's Basilica, but back in Glasgow they merely served to further erode his popular credibility.

In common with the senior powers in Rome whom he sought to impress, Doollan's world began and ended with Catholicism. Consequently, it was only the impact of his activities within that world that concerned him, or indeed that he was even aware of. Shelley's remit, on the other hand, was in the words of Burns, 'tae see oursels as ithers see us'.

There had seldom been much danger of the Cardinal experiencing such a perspective, not as long as he moved in such exclusively Catholic circles and was permanently attended by arse-kissers like Toale. Someone once said that the Queen thought the whole world smelled like fresh paint, because everywhere she went had always been newly decorated just before she got there. Cardinal Doollan was similarly insulated from his Church's true standing in Scottish society because everywhere he went he met numerous, faithful, uncomplaining Tims. Last week, for instance, Toale had even made sure all the blokes who came to fit the residence's new kitchen were devout left-footers.

It had been for this reason that Shelley made the radical (and, he would admit, fairly desperate) suggestion that they bring in a professional PR consultant. Not just any PR consultant, either, but Ian Beadie: if you were going to dabble in the black arts, might as well go straight to Satan rather than settle for a minor demon. No-one knew the Scottish media like him, and no-one knew the Scottish public like him.

He did have one tricky disadvantage, however.

'The man is a non-Catholic, Father Shelley.'

Convincing the Cardinal to countenance the move was never going to be easy. That Beadie was expensive and that much of what he did was morally reprehensible were really only minor fences – being a Prod was Becher's Brook.

Doollan had first wanted to know what Beadie's track record was, and had been predictably unimpressed to learn about his tenures as journalist and editor on various tabloid newspapers. Shelley explained the invaluable use Beadie was now making of that experience with his PR firm, and how the Church could immeasurably benefit from harnessing his gifts.

'It sounds like you want to bring us down to operating at the level of our enemies, Father. I'm not sure this wouldn't be in itself a form of defeat.'

'Your Eminence, the sad truth is that our enemies have already brought the battle down to that level, and it's a place where we are inexperienced and most vulnerable. This man can show us how to fight there. I would urge you most sincerely to at least meet with the man and see what he has to say.'

The Cardinal sighed, like a father who knows his child won't stop nagging until he caves in.

'Very well, I'll grant him an audience. Who's his parish priest?'

Which was when the bombshell unavoidably had to drop. Shelley, however, had been ready for it.

'In a way, Your Eminence, it is vital, even essential, that this man is *not* a Catholic, because his job would be to consider how our Church looks from the outside, not from within.'

'Hmmmm,' Doollan replied sternly, clearly not convinced. 'I understand your point, Father,' he added, 'but you are effectively talking about entrusting the public image of the Church in Scotland to someone who is not of the faith.'

'Your Eminence, even if he bore us animosity – which I am sure he does not – it would not be in the wider interests of his business to do anything less than his best job.'

'Granted, Father, but there have been many in the past who would sacrifice their own success for an opportunity to do us ill.'

Give me strength, Shelley thought.

'Mr Beadie isn't interested in religion,' he argued, then remembered that it probably wasn't the wisest angle in present company. 'What I mean is, I am sure we can trust him. This is not unprecedented. Remember, back in the early Nineties, there was a non-Catholic appointed editor of the *Celtic View*.'

'Yes, I do remember hearing about this. How did it happen? Did he mislead them?'

'No, Your Eminence, I think they merely forgot to ask. They just assumed . . . Anyway, there were no problems, and the young man did a fine job. He was, in a sense, entrusted with the public face of the football club, just as you're saying Mr Beadie would be of the Church.'

'What was his name?'

'Ehm, Cowey, I think it was.'

'Yes, hmmm. And can you tell me how many trophies Celtic won while this . . . *Cowey* was in charge of the club newspaper?'

'He wasn't in charge of the team, Your Eminence.'

'How many, Father?'

Christ almighty.

'None.'

'None, Father Shelley,' the Cardinal underlined, but he

141

was smiling. 'Just a bit of fun,' he added, chuckling. 'Your choice of metaphor amused me. Perhaps you would have been better mentioning some of the non-Catholics who *were* in charge of the team. Jock Stein, for instance.'

Shelley nodded, relief helping soothe the fury and frustration. 'I can assure you, Your Eminence, that this is the Jock Stein of public relations.'

'In that case, I wonder why Celtic never hired him while that rather volatile McCann fellow was in charge.'

Shelley opted not to proffer an answer. Telling him that it was because the other lot beat them to it might set the whole thing back to square one. Anyway, he knew he only had to get Doollan to agree to a meeting, then Beadie would do the rest. Making a good impression was, after all, what the man did for a living.

Shelley had only met Beadie a couple of times, but had known *of* him for years, as had anyone working with the Scottish media. He had taken a particular interest in the man's progress, as he saw certain parallels between the two of them. Beadie had come from a very working-class background and had brought something of the wee hard man to his career. He knew that his counterparts on the broadsheets had always regarded him as an uncultured oik, but he knew also that they respected – or should that be *feared* – his abilities, his news sense and his sheer nerve. They could look down their noses at him if it made them feel better, but they knew to underestimate him at their peril.

Shelley, for his part, had his origins in a similarly insalubrious part of town, which prepared him for the job he was doing a lot better than a university degree or a post-grad qualification in media studies (both of which, incidentally, he also had). Because he was a priest, there was an infuriating tendency on the part of reporters to regard him as being naïve, out of touch and unworldly. This assumption was corrected very swiftly. Francis Shelley had come from one of the toughest schemes in Glasgow, and while he'd never aspire to being 'trendy', he was a sight more streetwise than most of them would ever be.

Beadie, as expected, won the Cardinal's approval in no time. His manner was assuring without giving the impression that he was trying to promise you the earth. He sounded pragmatic and analytical, which Shelley observed was also a front for his very subtle methods of flattery.

The Cardinal liked to be flattered, subtly or otherwise.

'I regard you, or rather your position, as the greatest asset here, Your Eminence,' Beadie had said. 'From what I've seen, not enough play has been made of Scotland having such a senior figure in the world's biggest religious organisation.'

'Well, that is a result of a certain necessity, Mr Beadie. One is supposed to wear one's rank without ostentation.'

Shelley had almost choked.

'I appreciate your modesty, Your Eminence, but equally, as the Bible says, you shouldn't hide your light under a bushel. It's not enough simply to *be* such an important figure. You also have to *behave* like one for the public eye. I'd recommend you grant some interviews to the broadsheet Sundays – the supplements, not the news sections. These would be profiles as much as interviews. Let's get some big colour photographs out there. Let Scotland see you in your pomp.'

Sold!

From that moment on, Beadie was Doollan's new best friend, and Shelley, as planned, had to worry a lot less about cleaning up after him. Beadie helped maximise the Cardinal's visibility, while at the same time acting as a buffer against potentially damaging gaffes. The Cardinal actually listened to the PR man and heeded his advice, something he had seldom done with Shelley, but then Shelley had never put him on the cover of *Saltire on Sunday*'s colour magazine section.

But Doollan wasn't the only one benefiting from Beadie's expertise. The consultations Shelley had with him gave a fresh and invigorated impetus to his entire job. His suggestions weren't radical or revolutionary, merely changes in tack and important shiftings of perspective.

'You have to be pro-active,' Beadie told him. 'Right now you're only *re*active. Other people are setting the agenda and you are giving the Church's official response. That's fair enough, that's what you're there for, but that doesn't have to be *all* you're there for. Remember that you can set the agenda too, you can make the stories.'

When Beadie visited him at the archdiocese's offices, one of the first things he had done was pick up a leaflet from his desk. Shelley couldn't remember where it had come from – the Church was rife with what might be politely described as pamphleteers, less politely as nutters – but it was bemoaning the plight of Catholic doctors in the NHS, who were apparently being denied jobs because they wouldn't carry out abortions.

'Did you produce this?' Beadie asked.

'Eh, no,' he replied uncomfortably, aware that the content was utter, paranoid rubbish. 'This office is, however, partly responsible for its distribution, so I suppose the buck should stop with me.'

'It's mince, isn't it? What it's saying, I mean.'

'Well, there is a certain amount of pressure brought by the NHS—'

'You don't have to defend it to *me*, Father. I understand

why it's out there. A danger from the outside has a very cohesive effect. This sort of thing helps feed the old persecution complex, and that's something that has served your Church well for a long time.'

'Tell me about it. People tend to stick that bit closer together if they feel they're under threat. I wouldn't admit it outside this room, but there's plenty of times I could have kissed referees for giving Rangers penalties.'

Beadie laughed. 'I know exactly what you mean. But it's tired. It's reductive. It makes you the victim, and victims don't wield power. Remember: pro-active, not reactive. You need to do more to paint yourselves as a vibrant force within the country, in all walks of life. How many Catholics are there in Scotland, incidentally?'

Shelley rolled his eyes. 'Good question. If you're talking bums on pews, then the figure alters radically depending on whether you're taking your snapshot on a wet Sunday in February or on Good Friday. On average, mass attendance is around 200,000, including kids. I mean, obviously there's a lot more *nominal* Catholics than—'

'That's what I'm looking for. You mean baptised, Catholic-educated, that sort of thing?'

'Yes.'

'So how many of those?'

'Ehm, I'd have to ask around, but I think it's probably in the region of 700,000.'

'There you are, then. That's your figure. Well, actually, 700,000 – might as well say three quarters of a million. And if you're saying three quarters of a million, might as well round it up to 800,000.'

'Well, I suppose so.'

'Don't suppose. It's now a fact. And it's a fact you have to reiterate as often as possible. When you refer to Cardinal

Doollan, call him the leader of Scotland's 800,000 Catholics. Any time you're talking to the press, get it in there, get it in there until it becomes like one word: "Scotland's-eight-hundred-thousand-Catholics". You remember the Tories and "the economic miracle" of the Eighties?'

'Yes.'

'Do you remember an economic miracle taking place in the Eighties?'

'Eh, no, not really. Far from it, in fact.'

'Exactly. They got the phrase into the press and into the public mind. And even smarter, they did it in the past tense, they did it after the fact. They referred so often to something as having happened that everyone began to believe it had. Boom. Word association: Eighties, Thatcher, Economic Miracle. It replaced Eighties, Thatcher, Unemployment. See what I'm saying?'

Indeed he did.

'Scotland's 800,000 Catholics, Father. That's who you're representing – that's the mandate you have when you're dealing with the media. Not just 800,000 Catholics, but 800,000 Catholics with a political voice and a political will. A unified, dynamic and motivated force of opinion.'

Exciting and empowering as it sounded, Shelley still had his doubts that it could be that simple. Nonetheless, he followed Beadie's advice conscientiously, dropping the phrase into any and every discussion he had with a journalist. He didn't give it any fanfare; as the PR man told him, 'talk about it naturally, as though the number has been common knowledge for as long as anyone can remember'. As predicted, no-one challenged it, no-one questioned it. They just wrote it down and in it went. Within a couple of months, the phrase was beginning to appear without his prompting: any articles mentioning

146

Catholicism in Scotland faithfully parroted the numbers, regardless of whether they had sought his office out for a quote.

Being what Beadie had called 'pro-active' proved a far more difficult proposition. Aside from the conspicuous and orchestrated raising of the Cardinal's profile, the reality was, 800,000 Scottish Catholics or not, Shelley's role as Church spokesman remained mostly limited to response and defence rather than 'setting the agenda'. Upon Beadie's suggestion, he had attempted to draw press attention to the Church's role in charity campaigns – what he called 'positive involvement' – to create a balance with its role in protest movements such as Pro-Life. The latter, he said, were also important 'presences', but they gave off negative signals which had to be compensated elsewhere. However, positive or negative, none of it was setting the heather alight, and two paragraphs about raising money for famine victims hardly patched up the damage done by two *pages* elsewhere about the Church's 'institutional' sexism or homophobia.

The agenda was quite immovably being set elsewhere, and there was nothing he, the Cardinal or Ian Beadie could do to change that. Worse, every so often there would come an event that underlined just how lowly their position was on that agenda, such as the Peter Logan fiasco. Not only were their opinions being drowned out amid the populist clamour, but the right of the Churches to voice them at all was being called into question, possibly the most dangerous development in all of Shelley's tenure. He had been banging on about the beliefs of 800,000 people (nervously resisting Beadie's hints that he should start nudging it up to 'close to a million'), but now, perhaps inevitably, his bluff was being called.

'Who do the Churches really represent?' was the question that was being more and more frequently asked, and by which the questioners really meant 'how many'. Scotland was, they argued, a secular society, and the Christian lobby, in all its factions, could no longer lay claim to the voice or the influence it enjoyed in the past.

It wasn't only atheist agitators who were saying it, either. During the hideous and unedifying mess that passed for a debate on the issue of multi-cultural prayers at parliament, the contribution that made the biggest splash was that of Richard Holloway, Episcopal Bishop of Edinburgh, who argued that there should be *no* form of worship, and that religion had no place in the workings of the new political assembly.

Scotland was moving into a new era, of this there could be no doubt, and that there would be a place in it for religion was also assured. Unfortunately it was beginning to look as though that place would be somewhere between yoga and feng shui, tucked away under 'minority leisure-time pursuits' and accorded comparable significance.

The portents were grave enough for even the Cardinal to have noticed, and when Beadie suggested that an emergency meeting be convened, Doollan even sanctioned Shelley to invite his counterpart at the Church of Scotland, the Reverend William McLeod. A united front was required to face this threat, and there could be no greater indication of how seriously Doollan was taking it than to be co-operating with the Prods.

The Cardinal kept what he liked to describe as an open mind on the issue of ecumenism, by which he meant his mind was perfectly open to all the other Christian sects renouncing their damnable heresies and re-embracing the One True Church. However, there were times when heretical help was better than no help at all. Doollan gave McLeod the thumbs up, but would not attend the meeting himself, and insisted that all attending parties keep it the utmost secret. This was an unnecessary request, as Beadie had already stated just such a prerequisite.

All attending parties turned out to be Shelley, McLeod, Beadie and the MSP Elspeth Doyle, this last at the insistence of the PR man. She was one of the most senior Catholics in the Scottish executive, and was reportedly concerned at some of the turns her Party and indeed the country had taken of late. That she had found herself forced to assist in certain of them must have been preying all the harder on her conscience.

They gathered, each unaccompanied, at Beadie's house in Eaglesham, the objective being to discuss the unprecedented threat that their religions were facing. However, it was only once their host had completed his overture that Shelley fully appreciated how vast that threat was.

'If you are merely worried, it means you haven't been paying attention,' he warned. 'If you have, and you are scared, then the reason you are not utterly *terrified* is that you are not yet fully informed. Allow me to correct that.'

They were seated around Beadie's dining table at the improbable hour of eight o'clock in the morning. They were all drinking from mugs of tea apart from their host, who restricted himself to a glass of water.

'What you are about to hear, you cannot take out of this room, except in the case of Father Shelley to confide in Cardinal Doollan, if you so choose. You cannot respond to it, and you most certainly cannot do anything in an attempt to pre-empt it. This is information that has come from sources within the upper echelons of the Scottish executive, and not only must I protect my source, but we must all protect Miss Doyle here, whose religious beliefs would have her erroneously fingered for the leak if either of you two gentlemen was so rash as to open his mouth. The information concerns what Labour Party insiders are referring to as the "Life Raft".'

At this, Doyle shot Beadie a dismayed and disbelieving look.

'How the hell did you— ?'

'Sorry, Elspeth. Trade secrets. I long ago gave up trying to tap you for this sort of stuff. Elspeth here knows what I'm talking about, but for the benefit of the assembled clergy, I'll provide a brief summary of the salient points. The Life Raft is so called because it comprises a raft of proposed legislation – and in some cases, merely proposals – intended to breathe belated life into the Scottish parliament's first administration. Among the intended legislation is the legal recognition of same-sex marriages within Scots Law.'

McLeod and Shelley both took involuntary breaths. Doyle simply stared at the table. She knew all of what was coming and knew also that they weren't going to like it much.

'This', Beadie went on, 'would allow the Scottish executive to look radical and forward-thinking in an international context, leading the way in Britain and taking its place among the more "progressive" of its European partners. And, as radical legislation goes, its implementation would also be extremely cheap, so you can be damn sure the coalition will have every desire to make it happen.

'Another proposal is the establishment of a Royal Commission to consider the decriminalisation of cannabis. This is New Labour using Scotland as a side door: it allows them to respond to what most of the country privately believes, but without letting the tabloids point the finger at Downing Street when the "soft on drugs" jibes start flying. If it works out, it's more progressive thinking. If it doesn't, Blair can wash his hands and blame it on those rogue Jocks. I know that both of your Churches have given public backing to the Scotland Against Drugs campaign, so without an ungainly and undignified *volte face*, you're going to find yourselves once again in the No corner, and my prediction is that the No corner is going to lose.

'On top of that, there is a will within the coalition to sound out the possible public reaction to the abolition of separate denominational schools.'

'Holy Mary, Mother of God,' Shelley gasped.

'Now, don't be misled: this is not legislation; it's not even a formal proposal. But I warn you, they are planning to test the water on it. As Miss Doyle here can vouch, New Labour are masters of making an idea seem palatable and even popular once they've decided it's winnable – and they think this one might be. Not for this term, and maybe not even for the next manifesto, but make no mistake, you can consider a long-term campaign to have begun.

'I appreciate that perhaps the Reverend McLeod may consider this less of a concern to *his* Church, but once denominational schools have gone, the next target will be whether religion should be taught in schools at all.'

'No, no, absolutely,' said McLeod. 'It's the thin end of a very insidious wedge.'

'Well, as I said, it's just something they're toying with, but I thought you ought to have the full picture of where things are likely to go. Of greater immediate concern are the more formal proposals. You may find these ideas no more or no less objectionable than many you have been faced with and campaigned against before. However, the stake here is not in whether they are adopted. They *will* be.

'The Bible may have taught you that there is a certain

151

dignity about being the lone voice crying in the wilderness, but I'm afraid it doesn't work that way in politics. Every time you go out there and fight a losing campaign, you chip away a wee bit more of your credibility in the eyes of the public and the eyes of the politicians. You become discountable. In the past it might have been simply another case of licking your wounds and preparing for the next gruelling fight, but not this time.'

Shelley opened his mouth to protest, but Beadie rounded on him immediately.

'Understand me, Father, the Life Raft will float. You can't expect the opposition to stand in the way, because the SNP have been playing "leftier-than-thou" for so long that they'll have no options. New Labour will get their proposals through, and they will do so on a tide of public support. In the event that that public support fails to materialise, they will simply create the *impression* of public support. This is going to be the most high-profile legislation of the first administration in a parliament Scotland has worked and waited a long time to see. If you oppose it – as oppose it you must – your defeat will be resounding. Your irrelevance to Scottish politics, and by extension, Scottish public life, will be confirmed.'

The Cardinal's practised look of serene calm did not survive Shelley's account of the meeting. He seemed to shrink in his chair, like a child being told to get his coat because he was being taken to the dentist. The chasm between his tunnel-vision perception and the panoramic reality had finally opened before him, and he looked like he might be physically afraid of falling in.

Ever the figurehead, he recovered and composed himself.

'The Lord sends these things to try us,' he said, his voice wavering a little at first. 'We've faced worse and recovered, Father. Trust in that. A lot worse, in fact – the abortion bill in '67, for instance. If the government wants to send itself to hell in a handbasket, then we have to stand firm and light the way for those souls who decide they wish to return.'

Shaken up as he was, Doollan still wasn't quite getting it.

'Your Eminence, it isn't the proposals themselves that present the gravest worry. It's the fact that we are powerless to stop them.'

'We are not powerless to protest.'

'No, we are not, but the rub is that our protests would harm us more than they would hinder the legislation. We are being ignored, Your Eminence, and the worst of it is that they can afford to ignore us – they know that. What we are looking at here is the end of the Church as a serious political force.'

This time Doollan did get it, though as a man of faith, he was slow to give up looking for options.

'The voices of 800,000 Catholics can still make a powerful sound, Father Shelley.'

He couldn't help but sigh, knowing they had bottomed out if the Cardinal had started believing Shelley's own press releases.

'I don't doubt it, Your Eminence. If you can tell me where I might find 800,000 Catholics, I'll give it a go.'

'What?'

'Come on, Cardinal, you know what I mean.'

It was Doollan's turn to sigh. He did know.

'So,' he said, getting up from his chair. This was usually body language for 'give me good news or get out'. 'Did anyone at this meeting have anything constructive to offer?'

Should he tell him? How could he not? He'd like to spare him a share of the burden, but there were ways in which it was impossibly heavy for just one man. Shelley knew in his heart that he couldn't go ahead without Doollan's blessing, and in his head that neither could he proceed without his money. Spiriting forty grand away from the archdiocese would not go unnoticed.

It had seemed half an hour ago as though Beadie's plan was merely the sane choice in an insane world. Now that he was faced with relating it to someone – not just someone, but Cardinal Doollan, for God's sake – it was starting to feel like a whole new brand of insanity in itself. Nonetheless, it was the only option they had, so he at least had to tell him *something* of it.

'There is . . . a possibility, Your Eminence,' he began, quietly. 'A suggestion of Mr Beadie.'

'Yes?'

'It is . . . not the most morally clear path, I have to say. Perhaps you should take your seat again, Cardinal.'

He talked, very vaguely outlining Beadie's intentions, which had been vague enough to him in the first place, the man not prepared to give away the fine details of his plan unless Shelley was fully on board. He spoke as flatly and neutrally as he could, not wishing to pre-empt which direction Doollan might jump. Doollan listened attentively, never interrupting, a sign Shelley could not read: either he was lapping it up or was going to post him to a parish in the Arctic Circle as soon as he finished speaking.

When he did finish, the Cardinal still said nothing, his mind clearly very much engaged. The moment tarried uncomfortably. Shelley couldn't stand it.

'As I'm sure you appreciate,' he resumed, nervously, 'we are faced with difficult choices, Your Eminence.'

Doollan put a hand up, finally ready to speak.

'Unfortunately, I would have to say that it is you, and not we, who must make this choice, Father Shelley. We, after all, did not have this conversation.' Shelley nodded. 'But such considerations aside, it would be you who would have to take this task upon himself, so it is not a decision I would feel right or comfortable about making *for* you. I would recommend, therefore, that you take the time to contemplate it over many hours and much solemn prayer, and only after that should you come to a decision. Then, once you have made that decision, if you have chosen to act upon Mr Beadie's advice, so be it.'

Shelley nodded again, but the Cardinal wasn't finished.

'If, however, you have not,' he added, 'then I'm afraid the *Daily Recorder* might have to find out about that wee piece you've been seeing in Bishopbriggs.

'That is all I have to say. Go now, and God bless you, Father.'

send and receive

Elspeth sat and stared at the email on her monitor. The screen-saver had kicked in at twenty-minute intervals to remind her of the steady passing of time as she sat there, unmoving, paralysed by the sheer power of what lay one mouse-click away.

Digital destiny.

All she had to do was press Send and the face of Scottish politics would be altered beyond recognition. Maybe the right word was disfigured.

Could it really be that simple? Well, yes, it could, she knew, because she had helped make it so. When you reduce politics to a level of superficial perception, you leave yourself vulnerable to the deceptive arts of the illusionist. And when it came to political illusion, Ian Beadie was the master. He was Siegfried, Roy and David Copperfield rolled into one, but without the plastic surgery.

He had asked to see each of them alone after the meeting, which was when he made his proposal. This was because he knew that if he spoke to them one at a time, they'd be less concerned about how they looked to one another. Ask the three of them around the table and they'd all have been trying to outdo each other in their displays of outraged refusal; ask them individually and their thoughts would be more concentrated on what he was offering.

Elspeth was last, on Beadie's request. The two clerics had departed, given plenty to consider and twenty-four hours to decide. Beadie invited her through to the lounge, where he offered her a comfier seat and another cup of tea.

'What's with all the drama, Ian?' she asked. 'I mean, I know this stuff has ramifications for the Churches, but I thought you were over-egging the pudding a wee bit. They can't really get any less influential than they are already, so I don't quite buy the notion that there's going to be anything conclusive about the country ignoring them one more time.'

'You're right,' Beadie said, settling into an armchair. 'I'll admit I was putting the wind up them, but it was necessary. There's a tendency among men of the cloth, no matter what realities they're faced with, to believe everything will just carry on as normal and will work out fine in the end.'

'Yes, it's called faith.'

'It's called sleepwalking, Elspeth. They needed a rude awakening before it was too late.'

'Too late for what?'

Beadie didn't answer.

'So who told you about the Life Raft?' she asked, not expecting an answer.

Beadie laughed. There was an edge of contempt to it that she didn't like. 'The Life Raft? It's been Scottish Labour's worst-kept secret for months. Bloody everybody knows about it, Elspeth. Sorry to shatter your illusions, hen, but it's time *you* woke up as well. I mean, I'm sure they gave you the impression that you were being entrusted with this top-secret information because you were now back in the inner circle, a reward for your amazing recovery job on Logan and that daft tart off the telly. But the truth is, they'd have told you anyway, soon enough.

'As far as they're concerned, Elspeth, it wasnae a case of you ridin' to the rescue and them learnin' some appreciation of your true worth. To them it was just proof that you were on-side, and you'd do whatever duty asked of you – includin' swallowin' your principles to bail out a guy you couldnae stand. They're just pattin' you on the heid an' sayin' "well done, good girl, run along". Christ, I knew about the Life Raft months back. They've only finally told you *now* because they reckon they can trust you to do what you're told.'

Beadie stared hard at her, looking for a response. She now knew that he wanted something. This was how he went about it: he didn't flatter you or try to butter you up. He put you on edge, made you insecure, so that you'd think you needed something from *him*. Unfortunately, it usually worked.

He was right, too. He'd forced her to appreciate what the Logan affair must have looked like from the Party bosses' point of view. They'd cut her out of the loop and kept her in the dark about what they were planning because they were afraid she'd try to put a spoke in it. But then, having found herself serendipitously on the spot when her enemy's throat was laid bare, she had drawn her sword to defend him, not finish him off. They knew then that she was fully on-message when it really counted, abandoning her beliefs for the sake of the Party and thus the sake of her career.

There'd been plenty of nod-and-wink intimations to suggest 'we'll see you all right when the time comes', but Elspeth had been in this game long enough to know when she was being patronised. The time would never come. Her heroics would be forgotten about and it would be business as usual, because they knew Elspeth Doyle could be trusted to behave herself no matter how much you arsed her about. That was why her only tangible reward was to get a few slaps on the back and then be told about the Life Raft. It wasn't because they knew she was hot – it was because they knew she was bought.

In one respect, it had been her finest hour. She'd taken a disastrous situation and turned it around one-hundred-and-eighty degrees, until it was the press who were on the defensive. The hardest thing, though, was catching a glimpse of what her abilities could achieve, but realising they were always going to be prostituted, sometimes to ends that made her utterly ashamed of herself.

During the Logan incident, she felt as though she was running on reflex and adrenaline: the ideological conse-quences of what she was doing seemed so insignificant, relegated to the far distance by the automatic needs of the immediate situation. The desire to get a result, to do her job as best she could, had suspended her emotions and beliefs, as if she was a Jewish surgeon working intently to save the life of a white supremacist. The difference, however, was that the surgeon had a duty to suspend those other considerations. As a supposedly conscientious person, Elspeth should have had a duty not to.

She was becoming like a mob goon for the Party: go in, get the job done, no matter how messy, get out again and don't think about it. Never think about it.

Afterwards had come the internal attempts to justify her actions, also known as kidding yourself. It was when you started believing *that* crap that you really knew you were damned, because it was almost the same line she had peddled to the press. She told herself she was only protecting the man's dignity, something anyone deserved. But what she had really done was protect his hypocrisy.

It was scant consolation that most people thought she had fought a worthy fight, a principled battle for privacy, some might even say human rights. But that was because most people didn't know what scandal story she had really covered up that night.

No doubt Logan was also trying to kid himself, and by all evidence making a more successful job of it. He could perhaps believe that he was a victim of circumstance, rather than a deceitful coward. He could believe that he had become impossibly trapped by the sequence of events that had led to him having to live a charade and keep the truth hidden away behind it. But if he had any honesty left in him, he must surely know that he had done this to himself. Every time a decision had needed to be made, he had chosen the option that would best benefit his career, never the option that would allow him to be true.

Elspeth understood this because she was now guilty of the same sin.

She didn't respond to Beadie's jibes, knowing it to be futile. He knew her too well for there to be any point in denying how she felt. However, she also knew him well enough to predict how he intended to use it. Whatever he wanted, it would involve betraying her colleagues, an act he reckoned she'd be feeling thoroughly disposed towards.

'What is it you're after, Ian?' she asked flatly.

'It's not what I'm after, Elspeth, it's what I can offer.'

'Sure, Ian, that's you through and through. Ian "Altruism" Beadie. Infinite in your beneficence. D'you think I came up the Clyde in a banana boat? You want me to stab my Party in the back – you just haven't spelled it out yet.'

'I want to help you, but only if you're prepared to help yourself.'

'You mean only if I'm prepared to help you.'

'That would be a subsidiary benefit of this, yes, but you're the one who stands to gain the most.'

160

'From stopping the Life Raft? I don't think so. You might have put the wind up Father Shelley and his china, but I'm not quaking. For one thing, it's still months away from going public. By that time, I'd be surprised if there was anything contentious left in it. There'll be a resounding crash of bottles, then they'll water it all down and say "let's wait till after the next election before we do anything hasty". Then after the next election they'll say "let's just keep things steady for a while". It's the same old story, especially with cannabis. The time is never right.'

'The time has never been better, Elspeth, for all of it. Sex, drugs, religion: three things everybody in politics is usually too wise or too cowardly to mess with; and not because of the public's reaction, but because of the press's reaction. Except that right now, the press is on the run, and the British public has never had so small an appetite for prudish moralising. They know they can float this thing. They got away with a member of the Scottish executive having a dildo jammed up his bahookie by a piece of telegenic jail-bait. What do you think could scare them after that?'

'Maybe you should be asking what scares me, Ian. Who do you think I am? Eh? Some miserable, homophobic old bat, like Logan thought? Well, I'm not. What do I care if gays want to get married? I'm the one that's against promiscuity, remember? And as for cannabis, yeah, I care about that one. I'm bloody delighted about the idea of a Royal Commission, because it would be proof that politicians can act like adults and evaluate the evidence, instead of letting bloody Fleet Street be the arbiter of public health, ethics and law and order for the rest of our lives.

'As a Catholic, I'll admit I'm not thrilled at the idea of Scottish Labour turning its back on its roots and abolishing denominational schools, but so what? That's a battle that hasn't even started, never mind finished, and I'd rather fight it from within my party, to make sure it does the right thing, thank you very much.'

Beadie was smiling patiently by the end of her rant. Disarmingly, nothing she said had surprised him.

'That's exactly what I'm offering you the chance to do,' he said. 'Fight that battle and win it. Fight *all* your party battles and win them. The time is right for the Life Raft because the climate is right for a certain kind of idea and a certain kind of politician. But that climate can change.'

'Aye, over about ten years at the quickest. What are you on about, Ian, eh? Spare me the moustache-twirling stuff and cut to the evil master-plan.'

Beadie shrugged, as though he was thinking of going in the huff but had decided magnanimously to tolerate her bluster. 'What if that climate could be changed instantly, Elspeth? What if the political environment became censorious to the point of volatile, and any whiff of sexual misconduct was career suicide and electoral poison? Wouldn't the Labour Party want to heighten the profile of someone with a spotless reputation in that department; someone, in fact, who had already been identified in the public eye as a hammer of things permissive and licentious?'

'Yes, I'm sure it would, and suddenly I'd be the dog's bollocks. I get the picture. So what mephistophelean miracle have you got in mind to achieve this, and what would *I* need to do? Go down on Satan, maybe? Go down on *you*?'

'Well, you can do that if you like, but it wouldnae actually be necessary. All you'd have to do is send one email.'

He held up a 3.5-inch computer disc, produced from his pocket with exaggerated nonchalance, like it was the cure for cancer and he was thinking of just chucking it in the fire.

It was a deliberately paradoxical means of emphasising its significance, and for that, very Beadie.

'All right, I'll bite,' she said. 'What's on the disc, and who would I be sending it to? Oh, and why would I be sending it, and not you?'

'Questions, questions,' he said, unbearably. It was the familiar but irritating self-indulgence of a once-and-for-all newsman. He loved knowing what you didn't, but you never remained ignorant for long, because the one thing he loved more was telling.

'There's an executable file on this disc, disguised as a simple *Word* document, the content of which you can alter as appropriate so that it looks like a genuine memo. The recipient double-clicks to read the file, and while he does, the exe discreetly installs a few things elsewhere on his computer. I need you to send it to a select number of prominent MSPs, and the reason I need you to do it is that when they see your name as the sender, they'll be less inclined to subject it to security scans before opening it.'

'And what are the few things it installs?'

'That's not something you need to know. Best for you that you don't, in fact.'

'Fair enough.'

Elspeth looked deliberately blank, trying to counter his bluff. He knew there was no way she would agree to something like this without knowing all the facts, and he was also dying to tell her, but the bugger wanted her to beg for it. It was childish and futile. Feigning indifference was equally childish and futile, but she wanted him to know that she was giving back whatever she got.

'All right, I want you to hear me through on this, Elspeth. Don't freak out and don't saddle up your high horse until you've let this digest.'

Beadie sat forward in his chair. Elspeth didn't know whether he was trying to look more conspiratorial or whether he just couldn't help it in the excitement of revelation. Even in the most hard-edged and formidable of men, the wee boy could be seen not far below the surface if you knew when to look.

'The executable will install images of child pornography to the—'

'*Child pornography*?' Elspeth couldn't help herself. She'd imagined at the worst he would be talking about some dodgy surveillance software that might be used to snoop on the MSPs' computers.

'I told you to keep the heid. It's nothing diabolical. In fact, the stuff's legal in some countries. It's naturist material, just naked pictures of girls on beaches or at campsites and what-have-you. But the point is, they're all under-age: fourteen, thirteen, maybe less. So strictly speaking, it's child porn, and you don't need to be speaking strictly about that, as far as the press and the great British public's concerned.'

'As far as I'm concerned, too. And you want *me* to—'

'I said hear me through. The exe installs this stuff to the recipient's newsgroup cache on the hard disc. That's the place the computer stores files and information about what you've downloaded from internet newsgroups. Even if you erase the files from your News folder, there's still copies in there unless you go in and empty it. Most people don't know that, which is why it's the first place the vice squad look if they impound your machine. The programme also creates subscriptions to innocuous-sounding newsgroups, which are, in fact, the original sources of these same illegal images. It doubles up the proof. They can say they knew nothing about the files, but their news browser will say otherwise. And these being private PCs no-one else had access to, they cannae claim a big boy done it and ran away. Are you gettin' the picture yet?'

Elspeth was, and it didn't look pretty.

'You want me to frame my own colleagues, creating a scandal that's going to shatter our new parliament and ruin my Party. Just out of interest, this is going to help me how?'

'*Some* of your own colleagues, Elspeth. We'll be throwing a Lib Dem and an SNP body on to the pyre as well, in the interests of balance. Then it won't be a Party issue. It'll be a morality issue. Allan Gilford, Charles Letham, Murdo McDonald, and your old friend, Peter Logan. Four high-profile MSPs, all readily associated with permissive attitudes and liberal values concernin' homosexuality, contraception, sex education and recreational drug use. They're discovered to have a shared, secret penchant for kiddie porn, demonstratin' where those attitudes and values ultimately lead, as well as suggestin' what might have motivated them.

'Sex will be the bogeyman of Scottish politics in no time, and within about a week, we'll be seein' the dawn of a new age of puritanism – somethin' we Scots have always been a lot more comfortable with. The parliament will be rocked, though not shattered; same goes for your Party. They *will* both survive, and they'll need somebody to lead the salvage operation; as I said, somebody trusted by the public as a no-nonsense figure. Someone utterly untainted by scandal and unlikely to be tainted by it in the future, because believe you me, the sexual morality of politicians will be right back on the agenda.

'You'll have one of the strongest hands at the Scottish political table, Elspeth, and the Churches are gaunny be dealt right back into the game as well. Their trump card'll be "we told you so". And all it needs is for you to send one wee email.'

Elspeth was reeling, she wasn't sure whether from the insanity or from the plausibility. Nonetheless, she wasn't too dazed to ask the obvious.

'What's in it for you?'

'Money. Plain and simple. If the Churches want this to happen, they'll have to pay for it.'

'Bollocks.'

Beadie laughed, his bluff called once again.

'They *will* have to pay for it; there'll be certain expenses to meet, and I'll be looking for a wee commission on the top. But what's in it for me is the same as is in it for you and is in it for them: power.

'In my experience, I've always found the fear of shame to be a great motivator. I might not be with the tabloids anymore, but I still need them, and I need them to be at their most potent. This none-of-our-business, each-to-his-own attitude prevalent at the moment is provin' to be a right pain in the arse, frankly.'

'You mean protecting your clients' interests by black-mailing people to keep their mouths shut isn't as easy as it used to be.'

'I would never call it blackmail. More a matter of remindin' those who live in glass houses that they shouldnae go lobbin' boulders aboot the place. Let he who is without sin, and all that. I'm doin' my Christian duty, if you like, sharin' a wee bit of humility around to maintain peace and harmony.'

'Aye right, very good. What did you tell Shelley and McLeod? Did you say I was in on this?'

'Calm down, Elspeth. You know a sight more than they do, and no I didn't tell them your intended role.'

166

'Intended by you, maybe.'

'I told them that I could effect something of a coup in their favour, but that it would be illegal and immoral, though the latter is . . . contentious. I said it would involve a scandal and I made it clear that the fall guys would be innocent; at least, innocent of this. However, they're all, in the eyes of the Churches, men who have got away with other "moral transgressions", so I suggested that there would still be a sense of justice about it.

'I didn't tell them the mechanics. They both went off under the impression that all three of you would be made the same offer. I also told them that it would only go ahead if all parties agreed, confidentially; if all three didn't, no-one else would know who said no or indeed whether anyone said yes. But the best of it is, if one of them did say no, we could still go ahead because he'd then think the game was off, and wouldnae know for sure the child-porn scandal was actually manufactured.'

'So what did they say?'

'I didnae ask for an immediate answer. They've got twenty-four hours. So have you.'

Elspeth stood up. 'I don't need twenty-four hours. I don't want any part of this. Christ, I don't know why I've even sat listening to it. You could be bloody taping this conversation to set me up. It would make more sense than what you're suggesting.'

'Oh, for God's sake. What good would a tape of me makin' you an offer be? It's not a crime to be tempted. Jesus was tempted, remember?'

'Yes, and in the end he said "Get thee behind me, Satan".'

'I thought in the end, they nailed him to a tree.'

'No, Ian, in the end, he rose again.'

'You won't, though, hen. Not without this.' He held out the disc. 'Take it away for one night, that's all I'm askin'. If your answer's the same tomorrow, bring it right back.'

She'd taken it just to get out of the house, and had to stop herself from flinging it at his window once she was outside in the drive. It didn't do to upset Ian Beadie. It did worse to let him see *you* were upset.

He'd been devious and disingenuous as always. He fed you just enough truth amid his lies to keep you interested and complicate your decisions, but dogshit interspersed with Cadbury's flake was no more appetising.

It was about power, he'd admitted, but not just the power of the tabloids or the power of moral blackmail. It was about his power over her, his power over government, his power over the Churches.

No matter what he said, he didn't need her to send that email. He could send it himself and they'd still open it; they all knew his name and none of them would be suspicious of what would be, after all, disguised as a harmless note. Neither did he need the Churches to play a pre-ordained role, as proven by the fact that he had a contingency for them turning him down. Once the scandal broke, they'd do their part automatically, raining down opprobrium and taking back their once-fortified positions on the moral high ground. They didn't need to know about it, and neither did she. If Beadie's plan was going to work, then it would work just the same without anyone else's help.

The reason he wanted all of them in on it was so that he would own them ever after. They might each use the situation to further their careers beyond what currently appeared possible, but they'd always know who they owed everything to, and in time he'd collect the debt with punitive interest.

No chance.

There might be a battle going on for the heart and soul of the Labour party, but this was no way to win it. What would her father have thought, for God's sake? He had brought her up to have stronger values – one of which was honesty. Another was loyalty. Betraying her colleagues, sullying the name of her Party and bringing down innocent men in the name of her own career? Who did Ian Beadie think she was, a bloody Tory? Besides, she only had to look back at the Roland Voss affair of '96 to see where such blinkered ambition had led *them*.

Joseph Doyle's daughter was better than that.

She got into her dowdymobile and began driving home. Calmed by her resolve, the anger and confusion in her head gave way to more reasoned contemplation. Now that she knew she was having nothing to do with it, she could analyse Beadie's plan objectively and conclude that it wasn't viable anyway.

Except that it was. You had to hand him that much. He always knew how these things would play, right down to the subtle psychology of going with the mildest form of child porn rather than something more extreme. It made the whole thing seem more plausible, and anyway, people would imagine there must be worse material hidden away deeper. Furthermore, it would serve to illustrate where a vital line was drawn, how easy it was for certain people to step over it, and how you didn't have to step over it very far to be damned.

Yes, Beadie's plan might well work, but it wasn't going to work if she didn't let it, which was his only real oversight. Little as he might have told them, Shelley and McLeod would surely say no too. Beadie wasn't going to own them, and if he wanted to protect his PR clients' interests in future, he was going to have to start working for a living.

The next day, Elspeth got up, had a shower and headed over to Beadie's house before even having a morning coffee. Breakfast would taste better once this nonsense was over and done with.

Beadie answered the door in his dressing gown. She held up the disc and smiled.

'Forget it,' she said.

Beadie took it from her hand and shrugged, which she wasn't expecting. Maybe the other two had already torpedoed it also.

'Come on in,' he invited.

'I've got to go.'

'There's something you should see, Elspeth, believe me.'

An edge to his tone told her she was being threatened, or was about to be. Leaving, she was sure, would fully incite whatever it was.

He led her through the hallway towards where his study door was lying open.

'Want a wee coffee, cup of tea maybe?' he asked with incongruous politeness.

'No thanks, Ian. Just show me whatever you have to and let's get it over with. What is it today? Planting a bestiality video on Tony Blair?'

Beadie laughed. There was a calm, businesslike air about him that was making her more nervous by the second.

They entered his study, a very ordered little room housing a desk, a computer and two shelved walls bearing an impossibly neat collection of folders: hundreds of them. Beadie had always been a compulsively tidy person –

the obsessive control freak made manifest – even back in the hot-metal days. The advent of DTP and the 'paperless office' must have been what he'd always been waiting for. However, offices could never be paperless as long as there were certain things that couldn't be stored on a computer, and Elspeth had a worrying idea of what they were likely to be in Beadie's case. Even more worrying was that one of the files was already sitting on the desk when they walked in. He picked it up and handed it to her.

'Have a wee look.'

Elspeth began thumbing through the file, a sense of trepidation not dulled by the knowledge that she was sure she had nothing to hide; at least, nothing the likes of Beadie could use against her. Several of the sheets were ancient, purple-ink Roneo copies of hand-written documents, dated in and around July 1964. She scanned a few paragraphs, individual lines involuntarily drawing her attention.

'. . . into my bedroom again the next night. I was crying but he told me . . .'

'. . . with a leather belt. After that I let him do what he . . .'

She looked up from the folder to where Beadie was waiting for a reaction.

'What is it?' she asked, her stomach knotting, her mind simultaneously constructing and blotting out possibilities.

'Transcripts of testimony by former residents of Saint Saviour's Children's Home, Nettleston. Several of them were abused, sexually and physically, over a number of years by a priest who worked there. Assaulted, raped, sodomised, beaten, a tragically familiar catalogue in these revelatory days, when the past keeps giving up its nasty wee secrets. The thing is, though, these nasty wee secrets were given up a long time before now. There was an

171

inquiry, of sorts. And to cut a long story short . . . well, funnily enough, that's exactly what your father did. Councillor Joseph Doyle cut a long story short.

'He covered up the abuse to protect his beloved Church. Oh, I'm not saying he did nothing. He got assurances from the priest's superiors that he'd be sent away, and there is anecdotal evidence that he administered his own form of justice to the man, round the back of the home. But the truth was suppressed, and the victims were both leaned on and paid off to stay silent. You know the sort of thing. Father Innes had been a bad man, and he'd been punished and sent away for what he'd done, but what had happened was just between them and God now. Here's twenty quid to keep your mouth shut.'

Elspeth could barely speak. 'You're saying . . . you're saying my father did that?'

'Not the leaning and silencing bit. That was done by other priests. But it was his call to take it to the authorities, and instead he let the Church quietly sweep up their own mess.'

It felt like the room was expanding, or else she was shrinking.

'What happened to the victims?'

'One of them committed suicide. Another is serving life for raping and murdering a nine-year-old boy. You know the deal: vicious cycle of abused turning abuser. But there are other survivors, and they're suing the Catholic Church. Their lawyers know the Church covered up what was going on at the home. Right now they don't know who helped. Nor do they have to.'

He held out the disc.

'How do you know this if—'

'I don't think that's what should be concerning you right now, Elspeth.'

172

She swallowed and closed her eyes. He was still staring expectantly at her when she opened them.

'You fucking bastard.'

He shrugged again, a slightly regretful expression on his chubby face, as though he was saying he was sorry it had to come to this but . . .

'And have you got something on the clerics too? Eh? Are you blackmailing them as well?'

Beadie sniffed out a tiny, contemptuous laugh. 'Well, do you think I'd have hung my balls out there and told you all about this plan if I couldnae guarantee you'd each say yes? What am I, a fuckin' idiot?'

'I've no idea what you are.'

'Look, Elspeth, you needed a helpin' hand to make the right choice. Just take the disc, send the email, reap the reward. And don't sit there all tearful, doin' it for the sake of your deid father's reputation. Do it for yourself. If you really want to honour the man in his grave, think how honoured he'll be in a few years when his daughter's First Minister.'

How did he know? How could he know?

How did he ever know. How did he always know. Ian Beadie was Scotland's answer to J Edgar Hoover. Throughout his tabloid days, he had personally amassed bog-fulls of shit on everybody who was (or was ever likely to be) anybody, often by methods so underhand that he could not publish the material for the risk of exposing his own practices. However, this information wasn't always intended for publication. Some of it was there as leverage, some was there for insurance, and some was just there, laid down like a fine wine in preparation for the day, years hence, when it would be ready to uncork.

It didn't matter how he found out. It only mattered that no-one else did. She couldn't let her father be judged by the values and attitudes of today for something that happened more than thirty years ago. She wouldn't defend what he had done – or rather what he hadn't – but she at least knew he would have acted in what he thought was everyone's best interests. She'd never known someone who cared for children more.

Nobody looked very photogenic through the wide-angle lens of the retrospectoscope. If her father had enjoyed the perspective on child abuse that we all did now, there was no doubt he would have done things differently. He hadn't tried to protect the priest, only the Church, which was a sensitive target back then, with any blows it sustained being felt throughout the Glasgow Catholic community at large. Their religion was a far bigger part of their identity at that time, and if their Church was disgraced, then so were they; if their Church was weakened, so were they.

His posthumous disgrace would be unfairly dispro-portionate to his crime. However, Beadie's alternative prom-ised the same evil. The sense of proportion would again be hysterically skewed, the victims' reputations obliterated beyond any redemption. Stains such as deception, dis-honesty, infidelity, theft and violence might all wash out in time's great Zanussi, as certain careers had undoubt-edly proven; political parties believed in redemption and rehabilitation even if the electorate tended to be a little less convinced. But 'kiddie porn' was a sin for which there was no earthly forgiveness. These men would be marked for life by a stigma of paedophilia, which in this day and age was blacker than murder. Being out of politics would be the least of their worries. They'd be lucky if they ever worked again, for who the hell would employ them?

Elspeth could tell herself, as Beadie had told the church-men, that the four named recipients had all done something to deserve their fate, but what was inescapable was that they hadn't done *this*. Logan was at worst a coward and a hypocrite, hardly hanging offences in politics, let's be honest. What was worse was that since the 'incident', she knew he wasn't even guilty of the irresponsible promiscuity she had condemned him for before. She had to admit it, he and Teddy were about as faithful a couple as she had met, especially among politicos, and had made more sacrifices than most to protect what they had together.

Accusations of homophobia had always bounced off Elspeth before, because she thought they were unfair and ill-informed, but Peter's words that night had haunted her.

'You're the worst kind of homophobe, because you don't even realise the ways in which you *are*.'

She looked at their names, lined up in the addressees panel, separated by semi-colons. That little white box was like a digital gas chamber: anyone she put inside it was finished. But then, if she didn't hit the Send button, so was she. On top of the hurt the revelations would cause her family, there was the fall-out that would unavoidably contaminate her own career. Even if she went public with Beadie's plan (in the unlikely event that he hadn't taken steps to make his role unprovable), it wouldn't stop the vengeful revelations about her father, and all the pain they would bring. She wouldn't be tainted by his sin, only by his shame, but it would be enough; enough to restrict her to her familiar behind-the-scenes, unsung-hero role for the rest of her political life.

So, here she was again: faced with an option to protect colleagues who cared little for her and valued her even less;

an option that came at enormous cost to herself, with little prospect of reward for her efforts or her sacrifice. Another chance to prove to the Party that she was their slavish minion, unfailingly loyal, eternally taken for granted.

Or she could press Send.

after the meteor

'Hello?'

'Hello, Sarah?'

'Jack! Jesus. Thank God it's you, I've been so worried. I didn't know what to think and you didn't phone and then I was on call and I thought maybe you might have phoned then but I was out but then the next night there was nothing and I wasn't sure whether you were safe or whether you'd had some kind of breakdown or been hurt and I couldn't sleep so I wrote to you and then I—'

'Sarah.'

'Sorry. Sorry. God, I needed to hear your voice, Jack. I really needed to hear you.'

'Sarah.'

'What?'

'I've decided to stop being an arsehole. Will you come and see me?'

It was only a one-night stand. Wasn't that what the guy was supposed to say? Guys can't keep it in their pants, you have to cut them some slack. It didn't mean anything, really. He was drunk. The girl shouldn't have led him on; she knew he was married; she should have backed off and not encouraged him; she took advantage of the situation. Yep, no shortage of understanding excuses when a bloke gets, shall we say, carried away with the moment. The woman tended to enjoy a less sympathetic hearing.

It was an age of sexual equality. It said so in *Marie Claire*. Unfortunately this did not extend as far as acknowledging a parity of weakness as well as appetite; stupidity as well as desire. Instead of female emancipation we had 'gel-pah': lager-chugging ladettes exercising their equal right to behave like characters in a wank-mag short story. So when it came to infidelity and indiscretion, it was still always the woman's fault.

It happened at the surgical registrars' Christmas party; occasion of sin and season of slack knickers; the most embarrassingly clichéd night of the year for an illicit and mutually mortifying dalliance. Yuletide. The holly, the ivy, the making merry, the good cheer, the Slade record, the mistletoe and, inevitably, the Dickens: in photocopier rooms, store cupboards, back offices or, in Sarah's case, an airport hotel room.

The surgical registrars' Christmas party was always held at the Airport Excelsior, ostensibly because it was cheaper than any of the hotels in town, but really because it provided a plausible excuse for revellers to book a room for the night rather than get a taxi home. The twelve-quid cab fare was, the more pedantic observer might note, a far smaller outlay than the sixty notes it cost for a double room (including, perhaps ironically, a single-occupancy supplement), but there were more issues at play than mere economics. Convenience, for one thing, and the likelihood of getting a cab at that time of night on the last weekend before Christmas for another. But the principal issue was of keeping one's options open; without, crucially, admitting to oneself (or indeed one's other half) what certain of those options might be.

Of course, there were plenty who weren't remotely coy about it: either hoping to try their hand in the saturnalian lucky dip, or already engaged in a mutually knowing conspiracy of flirting, footsie and ward-round eye contact since mid-November. The former category was frequently filled by the younger female registrar: skirting thirty, with the tick of that biological clock telling her she's dedicated her best years to a career that doesn't love her back. The latter was more the preserve of the pre-forty male consultant, who having striven ruthlessly to reach this stage in his life, realises he forgot to ask himself what would be left after that. He's got the wife, the kids, the Volvo and those horrible shoes that only consultants wear, and it's suddenly striking him that this is it. So Santa brings his kids Dreamcast and Barbie, brings his wife a négligé she'll never wear, and still has room on the sleigh for a nurse half his age who'll make him feel paradoxically virile by effortlessly fucking him into a state of limb-aching exhaustion.

Sarah hadn't booked a room that night, though if she had, it wouldn't have signalled any intent (mind you, wasn't that just the self-denying beauty of it for everybody?). Her co-adulterer had booked a room, but as he was ticketed on a morning shuttle to London to catch up with the wife and eleven-month-old for Chrimbo with the in-laws, it could be reasonably argued that he had set out with no such intentions either. His name was Ross Quinn, a third-year specialist registrar, and that rarity in his profession: a surgeon Sarah didn't instinctively want to bludgeon to death within minutes of his entering theatre.

They had developed a friendly and co-operative working relationship (another rarity where the slice-and-dice fraternity was concerned) as she gassed for his operating lists, but it was in the area of industrial relations that their comradeship truly developed. Ross headed the

Trust's junior doctors' committee, of which Sarah was also a member, and they had both been closely involved in an on-going dispute regarding unpaid overtime. Ross was a selfless, shrewd and articulate operator, but what most earned Sarah's admiration was that he remained militant in the face of the pressure from senior staff that normally reined in such troublemakers. Registrar politicos were frequently full of piss and vinegar until they saw their consultant accreditation looming on the horizon, and heard the discreet whispers from clinical directors suggesting that certain posts might soon be available for the more, shall we say, accommodating candidate.

Officially, Ross had been campaigning to get the Trust to fully implement the government's new agreement on junior doctors' pay and hours; unofficially, Ross said their objective was to at least get the bastards to stop laughing at it. The most recent gambit had been to force the Trust's recognition of overtime outwith Additional Duty Hours. Their contracts paid them on a nine-to-five basis, with on-call remunerated at the ADH rate. However, most doctors had to show up at eight am or before, and were frequently still working past seven in the evening. In the case of the anaesthetists, pre-operative assessments had to be carried out the night before each surgical list, adding extra time each day and an unacknowledged attendance every Sunday evening. It was estimated that the Trust was getting up to twenty hours' free labour a week out of its junior medical staff.

The Midlothian NHS Trust remained indelibly tainted by the Stephen Lime scandal of 1995, a chain of events that had begun for Sarah with the murder of her former husband, and ended rather neatly by setting her up with a new one. In between there had been the not-quite-so-neat matter of

180

the Trust's spectacularly corrupt chief executive conspiring in the murders of close to thirty geriatric patients. The arch-Thatcherite throwback had followed his free-market principles to the extreme and reasoned that the George Romanes Hospital would best serve the Trust if it were shut down, bulldozed and its site sold for a hotel development. An obstacle to this ingenious example of fiscal lateral thinking was that geriatrics are notoriously hard to shift, hence Mr Lime's resorting to rather direct methods. Jack and she had eventually uncovered the grisly truth, but not before Lime attempted to add both of them to the massive bodycount.

With a past administration like that to live down, the Trust was therefore just a tad vulnerable to any campaign fought in the field of public relations, and as Christmas approached that year, it had been looking like they would have no option but to cough up. Ross and Sarah had therefore been in celebratory mood. Add to that the seasonal air of abandonment and the pervading atmosphere of horny pairing-off. Add to that the confused emotions of two people who had been driven together by arduous work towards a common goal. Add to that the fact that she had rather fancied him since medical school and he looked bloody good in a tux. Then douse the whole thing liberally with alcohol.

So, to excuses. She and Jack had been going through a sticky spell round about then. That was a good one. Unfortunately it wasn't true. She and Jack had been absolutely hunky-dory. Maybe both a little tied up with work lately, but no more than had been the case a dozen times before.

It just happened. Really, really, really, it just happened.

Out of excuses, there was always mitigation. It was over in moments, a drunken blur that she could barely remember, unsure whether she might even have dreamt the whole thing. Unfortunately, that wasn't true either. Nor could she say she didn't enjoy it, and as for the inevitable question of whether Ross was, well, bigger, she just hoped that Jack wasn't insecure enough to ask. (Staying with this honesty jag, she would now have to say that size did make a difference, but the jury was still out on whether it 'mattered'. Ross's lovemaking did suffer from a certain consequent complacency, though admittedly no-one is at their most imaginative after three courses and two bottles of wine. The one thing she did know for sure, though, was that she'd been right all along about male surgeons' egotism being inversely proportionate. You never saw Ross Quinn stamping his feet and throwing tantrums . . .)

She'd always imagined that if something like this happened, one or both parties would run tearfully from the room shortly after one or both parties had come. In practice, the sin was willingly compounded, then compounded again in the shower, and then compounded once more amidst a pile of towels on the bathroom floor just to make damn sure. Whether this was down to their both still being drunk, or an unspoken understanding that the guilt was in the post and they might as well be hung for a sheep as a lamb, remained as unexplained as it was irrelevant.

There had been glimpses of consequence amid the limb-tangling and irresistibly eager clumsiness, moments when she involuntarily envisaged how this was going to look and feel in the morning. However, the most effective way of blotting them out was to concentrate on the here and now, something which at the time had seemed very much its own reward.

So there it was. She did it. She did it and she enjoyed it. And did she regret it? Yes. Did she very soon wish it had never happened? Yes. Did she feel wretchedly guilty? Yes. Did she deserve to be punished? Yes, but only she, and only by herself.

The fates didn't see it that way, however.

Ross came into the anaesthetic room on his first day back, something he and any other surgeon who valued his balls never dared. She didn't have a patient in there, but she knew it still had to be something serious for him to have risked the interruption. He said they had to talk, which immediately bothered her, as they had agreed on a Stalinist purge of the incident from history and memory. She just hoped he wasn't going to turn all mushy on her, or worse, say he couldn't live with the lie and was going to have to tell his missus (in which case she'd have told him the lie was like a new puppy: give it time and get used to living with it, because it wasn't just for bloody Christmas).

What he had to talk about was a little more serious. Ross had been approached as he got out of his car by a man carrying an umbrella and a manila folder. The man had called out his name and said he had something to show him. He held the umbrella over Ross's head as he handed him the folder and told him to open it, sheltering the contents from the smirring morning rain. There were photographs of him and Sarah going into and leaving the hotel room, as well as handwritten depositions from hotel staff and an unnamed colleague who had seen them leave the function suite together.

Ross, knocked sideways by the revelation and its means, nonetheless regained sufficient composure to claim that it proved nothing. It was a twin room, Sarah couldn't get a cab home, whatever.

'We've got the condom wrappers, Dr Quinn, and the bedsheets. We can have them analysed if you force us

183

to. They can tell, oh, everything. Saliva traces, condom lubricant, vaginal fluid. From the locations of these we can prove pretty specifically what you got up to, even what positions you were in. It could get very technical, but, as I said, only if you force it.'

'Who was he? Who's this "we"?' Sarah asked.

'I don't know who he was, but I know who he's working for. The Trust. We have to back off from the campaign, accept the next offer on the table or he takes this to the papers.'

'The papers? But why would they publish? It's not as though you're a public figure. Who would be interested?'

'Well, my wife, for one. And I don't know how long it's been since you read the tabloids, Sarah, but you don't have to be bloody famous, you just have to be caught. "Doctors' rights campaigner is love-cheat". Get the picture?'

She did. In CMYK.

'But how did they know? How could they find out?'

'Probably had someone following me for weeks, looking for dirt. Raking through my past, raking through my bins. I was clean, though. Until the party. Makes sense they'd put a tail on me at a debaucherama like that, I suppose, and unfortunately I didn't disappoint. They must have thought it was, well, Christmas.'

'So what are you going to do?'

'What can I do? I can't let this get out, Sarah. It was just a daft mistake, and I can't let it ruin my whole life. Bad enough for Yvonne to find out, but if she found out like this. Christ. The humiliation. It would destroy her. It would destroy me. Marriage would be over, instant broken home for wee Callum . . . fuck, what a mess. Can't see it doing much for you and Jack either. And all for one stupid . . .' He sighed, shaking his head. 'I can't let this happen.'

184

'No, you can't,' she agreed, vastly relieved that this was his position. No doubt someone in the back row might mutter about selling out their colleagues, but even if Ross had been so stubbornly defiant as to make such a vast sacrifice, she knew it would be for nothing. The campaign had been fought in the field of public relations, where credibility is all, and theirs had just taken a mortal blow. Adding insult to that injury was the fact that they couldn't expose what methods the Trust had stooped to. Defeat was total, and all for a drunken fuck.

Ross didn't give them exactly what they wanted, however; rather than wait around to agree a fudged deal, he resigned from the committee. It had much the same effect, as his successor was as inexperienced as he was unprepared, but it did spare Ross the humiliation of bowing before his enemies. No-one could grudge him that.

For Sarah, outrage and disgust having given way briefly to relief, there remained the self-inflicted penance of harbouring her guilty secret, mingled with the tormenting fear of discovery. It felt like such a heavy burden to carry alone, and it weighed all the more because the one person she normally shared her worries with was the last person she could turn to. She thought many times of coming clean because she didn't think she could cope with the pressure and the tension, always watching what she said in case a stray remark somehow gave her away. However, the self-flagellatory part of her conscience told her that would be an easy way out, asking for forgiveness's get-out-of-jail card instead of doing her time. Besides, she suspected it might be an exemplary instance of a problem shared being a problem doubled. Jack might forgive her, in time, but they'd both be carrying it around with them ever after.

It might have been a daft mistake, a drunken one-night

stand, but the one thing it most definitely hadn't proven was 'meaningless'. Precisely what it meant, and why it meant so bloody much, she still didn't know. Sarah had done nothing before or since to suggest she loved Jack any less than she ever had, and she had meant him no harm on that night; in fact, so far had he been from her thoughts that in her less accusatory moments, she regarded her sin as merely forgetting him. But nonetheless, she knew it had been her duty to remember.

There were ways to rationalise it, ways to quantify it, ways to understand it, deconstruct it, analyse it, reduce it. There was just no way to change what all of the above concluded: it *was* a betrayal. She accepted that. It was a sin. It did mean something, and if it didn't, she wouldn't be sitting up at night worrying about what its revelation would do to the man she loved. But what was far more difficult to accept was how easy that sin had been to commit; not just for her, but for every other guilty person lying awake in the darkness worrying about the same thing.

We were weak, we were stupid, we were foolish. But did we have to pay such a heavy price for it? Well, according to the evidence, yes, we did. There were doctors still working the best part of an unpaid extra week a month at the Royal Victoria Infirmary as the cost of what she and Ross had done together.

The question for society was *should* we? And the answer, rather ficklely, depended upon when you asked it. When circumstances finally, inevitably asked it for Sarah, it was not long after the MSP child-porn scandal, which was, all things considered, probably not the ideal time.

It didn't seem like a scandal in the beginning, more a mystery. The initial reports had been so litigation-consciously tentative that the entire story seemed to have quote marks around it for the first couple of days. Lots of 'police have said only's and 'sources would not confirm's. When at last it was clarified that four MSPs' computers had been confiscated by police investigating allegations of child pornography, there was still a reluctance to conclude – and in Sarah's case to believe – that it truly meant what it appeared to. Even when the police announced that the alleged files had indeed been found on the impounded PCs, it was evident from most reporters' dispatches that they expected the real meat of this story would lie in discovering how they happened to get there. There must have been some kind of security breach on The Mound, allowing mischievous or possibly malicious access to senior MSPs' private computers, and clearly this had massive ramifications for the Scottish Executive. What sensitive information might have been disclosed, and more importantly, who had been behind it?

The police, however, were starting to make some worrying noises, mainly about having found nothing to substantiate the claims that someone else could have installed the illegal material. Furthermore, their email archives showed that the four had exchanged messages directing each other to websites and newsgroups hosting the same images as had been found in their hard-disc caches.

The financial consequences of getting something as explosive as this wrong meant that the media handled the story like the potential booby trap it was, and for a rare change, the four MSPs' innocence was presumed until proven guilty. Upon advice from their lawyers (and more importantly their Parties), the four accused declined to speak publicly about the situation, which, however understandable, did not look good. The difference between the public's perception of a dignified silence and a guilty silence is merely a matter of time.

Aware of the speculation that would naturally fill such a void, a spokesperson for the four reiterated their innocence, and stated that though the police hadn't found evidence of outside involvement *yet*, they were nonetheless confident that such evidence would be uncovered eventually. Besides, all that existed currently were files on computers, which in themselves proved nothing: as far as they were concerned, it was incumbent upon the police to prove that the accused put them there, not upon the accused to prove that it was someone else.

At that point, Sarah had expected the story would begin to peter out. Bearing in mind the astronomical consequences of a failed prosecution, the police would sensibly buy the security breach angle and concentrate their subsequent investigations thus. It would turn out to be computer hackers, or maybe something more colourful, like a disgruntled Tory who wanted to discredit this devolved legislature, the creation of which he had ineffectively opposed.

The next night, however, all news programmes, regional and national, led with the arrests of Allan Gilford, Charles Letham, Murdo McDonald and Peter Logan. The ensuing press conference looked sufficiently well organised to suggest that weighty decisions had been taken much earlier in the day, and careful preparation had been made in light of all that would be unleashed.

In his best don't-fuck-with-me voice, the plod in charge read a statement revealing that the new parliament's internet service provider had, upon sequestration, released log files indelibly and indisputably recording the on-line activities of the four suspects. Not only did the logs confirm downloads from the aforementioned newsgroups and websites, but the dates and times coincided with more innocuous web-browsing and work-related email exchanges. This provided proof that it was the suspects, and no-one else, who were using the computers at all of the incriminating times.

Given the nature of these crimes, the public reaction was always going to be severe, but it was given an extra whiplash-sting by the public's anger at having given them the benefit of the doubt. Not only had the bastards done it, but they had tried to spin their way out of it, and had clung on through political muscle and judicial hair-splitting until finally they were snared by a piece of solid, objective evidence that they hadn't anticipated. It was Lolicia Aitken's BA itinerary all over again, except the stakes were a little higher than undeclared perks.

Child porn, for God's sake. It was so much the bogeyman of the digital age that its very odiousness had played an ironic part in her and Jack's initial incredulity. The press, having this new phantom to seek, assumed the role of the boy who cried kiddie porn, tending to find it a little too often for plausibility, just like they had 'found' dozens of cases of 'the flesh-eating bug' necrotising fasciitis during its fifteen minutes in the early Nineties (and not a one since).

No hack, it seemed, could write a paragraph about the internet without mentioning child porn, until the words practically became synonyms, like 'sex and violence' in the Seventies (thanks to the National Viewers and Listeners Association, with whose bedroom habits, one had to surmise, something must have been well wrong). Once upon a time, the word 'porn' would have been enough, but attitudes and definitions had since got a little too complicated for the tabloid mindset to cope with. Now the word 'child' was automatically appended, restoring that power to create a stain that never washed out, a stigma that branded instantly by accusation. If someone was fired for having dirty pictures on their office hard disc, the press could call it child porn to create a bit of what they called 'top spin', without much fear of legal redress if it turned out only to have been jpegs from the ubiquitous Pam and Tommy video. The bloke wouldn't be in much of a position to sue for libel, not having any reputation left to defend.

This time, however, it was the real deal.

The word 'scandal' had been grossly overused in the sensationalist simple-speak of the era, being the 'double-plus bad' of the political lexicon. When every minor indiscretion or financial irregularity was seized upon, and hair-splitting semantics could turn a chance remark into a melodrama, it took something like this to remind everybody of what 'scandal' truly meant. Granted, it wasn't in the same league as the Dutroux abominations in Belgium – for one thing, nobody was dead – but neither was it some prurient matter of dubious public relevance. These were men whom the Scottish electorate had entrusted with power and responsibility, men to whom we supposedly looked for leadership and example, and it turned out they were getting their jollies collecting naked images of under-age girls.

The police, aware that some semblance of perspective would have to be maintained amid the obligatory hysteria, had released a little more information about the nature of the offending files. There were no hard-core images on any of the PCs, or indeed on the subscribed newsgroups (if there had been, the ISP would have been in deep Portillo for hosting them). However, this naturally led to speculation as to what kind of depraved material might still lie hidden, or have been surreptitiously erased since the initial bust. It was noted that all four in the ring, though members of three different parties, also served as Westminster MPs as well as in the new assembly. How long had it been going on, people were asking. And who else might have been part of their sick little circle?

Perhaps most damaging, however, was that another thing all four had in common was a liberal track record on sexual issues. Damaging because where there is scandal, there must be cause: a greater, deeper blame beyond the sins of the principals.

What was to blame? – What have you got?

All the usual chestnuts. This was where permissiveness led. It started with promiscuity, then before you knew it, homosexuality was supposed to be acceptable too. Stands to reason the next thing they'd be telling us was that paedophilia was all right as well, and we shouldn't be prejudiced against them either. This started in the Sixties, mark my words. We've been going down a slippery slope ever since.

Yawn.

Thus the affair quickly became the Day of Vindication for every repressed sad-case with an axe to grind: proof that their demon of choice was finally being unmasked as the source of unmitigated evil they had always professed. Sarah's personal favourite had been overheard in a super-market queue in Canonmills.

'This aw goes back tae the English, Tam.'

'Aye, you're tootin' there, Alec.'

'Bloody right I am. They've ayeways hud looser morals than us, it's a known fact, but we end up gettin' polluted. I mean, when did you ever hear o' a poof in Scotland afore aboot twenty year ago?'

'Cannae think o' wan.'

'Exactly. But doon there, they've been up tae aw sorts for centuries. Sure there was that Edward the Second pansy, back in bloody mediaeval times. Ayeways been obsessed wi' sex, the English. It starts doon there an' it seeps in.'

Sarah had to admit that it made sense. What with the Scots inventing everything of positive and practical use in the world, it had to be left to someone else to devise all its pestilences, so at least that left some kind of achievement for her own people to claim.

But, of course, when it came to saying 'I told you so', no voice sounded louder or smugger than the religious lobby. Repressed sad case with an axe to grind? 'Hey, they're playing our hymn.' The media having gleefully rediscovered its receptivity to pious whining, the Churches didn't miss any opportunity to stick the boot in; and with Logan part of the package, it must have been sweet payback for both groups, given the hammerings they had each taken over the flamboyant young minister's recent misadventure.

In fact, the third and fourth estates were very much at one in their analyses of the situation, objectively and independently reaching the same, only ever-so-slightly self-serving conclusion, that it underlined their right – no, their *duty* – to go sticking their noses into other people's private matters (and the more important the person, the more pressing the obligation). All this wishy-washy nonsense about it having no bearing on their professional capacities had been shown up as a worthless smokescreen, behind which goodness knew what they were getting up to. What this sorry affair had proven, beyond all shadow of a doubt, was that the public had a right to know what kind of people their would-be leaders were.

Et après, le déluge . . .

It was like the early Nineties revisited. Every public-figure sex story that had been languishing in a tabloid editor's desk drawer throughout this dry spell of 'grown-up politics' got dusted down and splashed on page one.

The last such feeding frenzy had been precipitated by John Major's clumsy and rather desperate attempt to fashion a political agenda for an ideologically exhausted government. Poor bastard, what happened wasn't his fault or his intention, but if he had any knowledge of his own party's natural instincts, he should have foreseen how easily and eagerly the notion would be hijacked. (This, after all, was a political organisation that gave Dr Adrian Rogers a platform, when what the man clearly needed was a straitjacket and tranquillisers, or maybe just a blow-job.)

'Back to Basics' left the Conservatives hopelessly exposed to charges of sexual hypocrisy, and made it open season on their MPs' private lives, regardless of the members' own individual pronouncements. The season (and the media's justification) finally ended when the Tories got horsed in the general election, but the papers had been champing at the bit ever since. Now they had a mandate to go after anyone, whatever their party, whatever their philosophy, and this time the hunting licence had no fixed expiry date.

Every Sunday brought new exclusives, leaving the rest of the week to rake through the debris. Resignations were demanded, and with all parties now terrified of being perceived as tolerating licentious conduct, resignations were swiftly forthcoming; Tuesday proving the most popular choice for looking out the revolver and whisky, after a couple of long nights to mull over the lack of options. There were no evasive spins, no wives and kids at garden gates, just quiet clearings of desks in Edinburgh, London and Cardiff.

The hysteria would burn itself out, Sarah knew – there was only a finite number of such stories to be unearthed

– but the damage would be permanent, and the political landscape would be altered irrevocably.

Not all politicians suffered, mind you. With sex suddenly the new leprosy, there was cachet to be had in ratified prudish credentials. Frump chic was in. Down south, for instance, the neo-Fifties morality proved another boon to the thus-far inexplicable rise of Anne Widdecombe. The Tories had long been besotted by her – perhaps because she reminded them of Matron at whichever public school mater and pater had packed them off to in lieu of a childhood – and this emotion-memory transfer of affections seemingly blinded them to the fact that she clearly terrified the shit out of voters.

Meanwhile, in Scotland, Labour had very quickly made a paragon of the previously underwhelming Elspeth Doyle, or 'the Wraith', as Jack referred to her. In the wake of 'Moundgate', there hadn't so much been a cabinet reshuffle as a complete dismantling and a hasty delivery of flatpacks. This had left the Wraith officially in charge of Home Affairs, mainly because she'd never had any, and unofficially in charge of a whole lot more besides.

The criteria for credibility had changed, and it wasn't only certain elected members who found themselves newly empowered. The respective spokesmen of the Kirk and the Chapel progressed almost overnight from glorified press secretaries to 'opinion makers', prompting more than one commentator to record approvingly that the Moundgate affair had breathed new political life into the Churches.

In truth, it would be more accurate to say that it had merely reanimated a corpse. The media might be paying Father Francis Shelley and the Reverend William McLeod a lot more attention, but it didn't mean that the public had started flocking back to their folds. The pews were as empty as ever, but as long as someone was sticking microphones in their faces, they were going to take full advantage. They played the silent (i.e. non-existent) majority card in support of their sermonising, which very quickly graduated to full-on lobbying. The social agenda had been in their firm control for centuries before being impudently wrested away throughout these abhorrent times, but now it was up for grabs once again.

Astutely picking the right fight for the right time, they had sought to tackle 'the very root of the problem' by launching a cross-denominational campaign to revise the current methods of sex education in our schools. This, they argued, must be couched in moral rather than crudely physiological terms. If we taught children about sex in a graphic and mechanical manner, then it was no wonder our society had such an unhealthy attitude to it.

In the preceding months, health education thinking had been gravitating towards the Dutch and Danish models, the frankest and most technically explicit in Europe, and which also favoured the earliest introduction. Both these countries recorded teenage pregnancy rates at less than a seventh of Scotland's, and it had been suggested that these statistics were probably not a coincidence. This, however, cut little ice with Father Shelley. 'Abstinence,' he pointed out, 'is the most reliable form of contraception,' bringing himself neatly around to his other major agenda.

It wasn't only in the realm of soundbites that they were now able to command column inches. The activities of Church-backed pressure groups were being spun as evidence of a groundswell of popular feeling, even when they only amounted to twenty arseholes holding placards outside an abortion clinic, or, more topically, a high-street chemist.

195

Prior to Moundgate, the Greencross chain had co-operated with the Health Education Board for Scotland in an incentive to offer advice on sexually related issues to teenagers who might, for any number of reasons, be wary of approaching the family GP. Within days of the venture being announced, a pressure group had been formed, calling itself Families for Innocence, urging 'concerned' (read 'Catholic') parents to boycott the company, which was 'only interested in exploiting our children to make more profit from contraceptives'.

Families for Innocence initially picketed for a few days, throughout which all they had to show for it was a few paragraphs – included by obligation in the interests of 'balance' – at the ends of stories more concerned with the initiative's projected benefits. Sarah had little doubt, however, that if the scheme hadn't already been up and running before the scandal broke, it would have been quietly shelved. As it was, post-Moundgate, the picketing restarted, but this time it was reported more prominently as evidence of 'strong public opinion'. That opinion got particularly strong on the day a Greencross pharmacist had her nose broken on her way into work at the flagship Glasgow city-centre premises; stronger still when an advisor at an Edinburgh branch had acid thrown in her face.

Having long contested the disproportionate say such minority organisations enjoyed in Scottish public affairs, Jack remained unconvinced of how four men looking at dirty pictures had done anything to alter that. He began to ask searching questions, in print and in person, about the source of this relentlessly bandied '800,000 Catholics' statistic, questions which Father Shelley's office refused to answer. Did the figure, he enquired, include anyone and everyone who had been baptised or Catholic-educated?

Did it therefore include people who no longer took any interest in – or paid any heed to – religion? Did it by further extension also include people, such as Jack's own father, who had not only given up their religion, but now utterly objected to everything the Catholic Church stood for? And was it then, perhaps, just the teensy-weensiest bit disingenuous to suggest that Father Shelley or his boss Cardinal Doollan spoke for all those people?

Searching further, Jack asked whether Shelley and McLeod's intemperate rhetoric might have contributed to the hysteria that had recently spilled into violence against Greencross Chemist staff. This tricky contention came in a piece he had penned after going undercover (if wearing a bad jumper and slacks counted as subterfuge) on one of the Families for Innocence pickets.

He knew he was up against a rising tide, but being a life member of the Scottish press's Awkward Squad, Contrary Bastard Division (Unreconstructed Wanker Class One), he willingly assumed the Canute role. 'Religion', he wrote, 'might yet turn out to be a virus sent by some malevolent alien civilisation with an extremely busy colonisation pro-gramme. They know they're not going to get around to invading your planet for a few thousand years, so in the meantime they introduce religion, to slow down your evolution in order that you'll still be weak and primitive when they finally turn up in the mothership.'

Despite their shared anger, Sarah could tell that part of Jack was perversely enjoying the whole thing. The past few years had been very frustrating for him, career-wise. The New Labour politics of stealthily manufactured consensus and straitjacketed news management left slim pickings for the professional shit-stirrer; meanwhile, many of his investigative efforts in the private sector had foundered on the rocks of spin and bare-faced deceit. Big business's smoke-and-mirrors merchants were nothing new, of course, but Jack's problem was that he could no longer rely on his previous methods of circumventing them, such as burglary, theft, hacking, espionage and the occasional resort to small-arms fire. Sarah had agreed to marry him on the condition that he begin to behave like a responsible human being, and as far as remaining within the law was concerned, he had been true to his word.

Possibly, in light of the universal outrage over the child-porn scandal, he was relishing the opportunity to fly in the face of all that was being widely regarded as decent and good. (Psychologists would no doubt have much sport with the fact that Jack had been an only child.) He even submitted a mischievous think-piece – mercifully spiked – arguing that it was natural for men to be titillated by nude images of girls under sixteen, but that this didn't mean they would necessarily want to act upon it. 'You'd have given a million quid to see under your classmate's blouse when you were fourteen. Your tastes mature, your conscience hopefully matures, but your eyes don't ask for a birth certificate before they decide they like what they see.'

Even without that sample of gratuitous provocation, his efforts had been enough to solicit his first hate-mail since two years ago, when *The Saltire*'s sports editor rather recklessly commissioned him to go incognito among the fans throughout the twenty-four hours surrounding an Old Firm game.

He had a delighted, little-boy grin when the first poison-pen letters arrived. It was the last smile Sarah got from him.

Maybe it was a slow day on the shag-rags. Maybe it was that Jack had raised his head too far above the parapet by scornfully suggesting in a column that the tabloids were full of kiss-and-tell drivel because finding a more substantial news story was beyond their capabilities (certainly the phrase 'what other people get up to in their bedrooms is of no relevance to me' would very soon come back to haunt him). Sarah didn't know, and it didn't matter. But the bottom line was that one of the above-maligned tabloids ran the now almost year-old story about her and Ross Quinn.

They phoned her up the day before, so at least Jack didn't have to find out the same way as everybody else. The wanker at the other end sounded so matter-of-fact, it was as though he was offering her double glazing. What he did offer her was two grand to 'tell all' and pose for some accompanying pictures. Three grand if she'd take her top off. Her voice trembling and her eyes filling up as she realised the enormity and unstoppable nature of what was in motion, she nonetheless managed to reply.

'What did you say your name was, again?' she asked, struggling to keep her voice from breaking up.

'Kevin. Kevin Simpson.'

'You ever cheated on anybody, Kevin?'

He just laughed. She put the phone down at that, because she knew her next words would not be anything she'd like quoted. The hack, as it turned out, had a Plan B anyway: some nurse Ross had gone out with before he met Yvonne, who played the role of technical advisor on the subject of his prowess between the sheets and, of course, the measure of the man.

Sarah had not truly understood what humiliation was until that paper was published, and worse, she knew there were three other people sharing it. Everyone who knew them, everyone who worked with them, everyone they had ever known would get to see this, and instantly. Bad news travels fast, but embarrassing news moves at maximum warp. It would be all over the Edinburgh hospitals before lunchtime, and lapped up in every newsroom in the country.

Perhaps it was slightly easier for Ross and Yvonne, as they were able to offer each other a bit of mutual support. It turned out he had confessed the one-night stand around about the time he resigned from the junior doctors' committee. He'd made sacrifices to spare his wife this nightmare, and though it turned out to have been merely postponed, at least they were able to face it as a couple.

Sarah had never summoned the nerve to confess; had, in fact, convinced herself that she'd never need to, never ought to, for both their sakes. There was always the risk he'd find out on his own, but she thought she'd cross that bridge when she came to it. How was she to know that the bridge would dwarf Golden Gate, and that it still wouldn't be wide enough to span the gap that opened up between them?

She had taken comfort from those conversations about their relationship being strong enough to cope with precisely such a stupid mistake, at the same time worrying he'd suspect she was softening him up for a revelation, as she kept returning to the theme. Jack, however, suspected nothing, which probably made it easier for him to agree with her hypothesising.

In practice, he was a little less philosophical, but she could hardly blame him. It was one thing hoping your husband would love you enough to play the magnanimous cuckold, but quite another when you followed up the truth of your misdeeds with the information that the whole country was

200

going to read all about it within twenty-four hours. Most wronged spouses only had to cope with the betrayal, and they had the option of coping with it fairly privately. Jack had to get up the next day and face a world that knew his wife had gone behind his back for a 'steamy night' with Dr Schlong ('He's insatiable – and he's REALLY got it where it counts, says ex-lover Gemma').

In fact, what he did was get up the next day, go out to a pub where no-one knew him, and proceed to get miserably wasted, after which he didn't come home. Instead, he staggered the short distance from the boozer to their friend Jenny Dalziel's flat, where he sat on the stairs in her close – intermittently dozing and sobbing – until she came home from her shift about ten at night. Jenny, having seen the paper, didn't have to ask what he was doing, which was just as well, as he wasn't in any state to answer. She put him to bed and called Sarah to let her know where he was, and to offer a few words of support.

Jack was so ill the next day that he only moved from Jenny's couch to be sick or to refill the pint-glass of water she had left for him. He was still there when she got home again, hiding under a duvet like it was the last refuge in the world where the news hadn't reached. She coaxed him out and made him eat something, then told him he was being booted back around the corner in the morning.

'Sarah's going through this shit as much as you,' Jenny had told him, 'and she must need you right now like she's never needed you before. Wound-licking time is over.'

Jack offered predictable resistance along the lines of Sarah having been the one who dropped them in the said shit, but he was in no condition, physically or psychologically, to butt heads with Jenny, especially as it was her flat. He was home the following afternoon when Sarah woke up.

She was sleeping by day because she had just started working the five-until-nine overnight shift in the Intensive Therapy Unit. ITU was the part of the anaesthetics rota she most detested, and the runs of nights were the worst again within that, but it did have the consolation that she didn't see much of anyone she knew, other than at hand-over, and that was strictly business. No awkward looks, no jokes and, thank God, no pity.

However, though Jack was home, it didn't mean he was ready to talk. In fact, he didn't speak a word to her for more than a week. With her working all night and sleeping all day, there wasn't actually much time for uncomfortable silences, but that didn't make it any easier. He was all she could think about throughout those endless, knackering nights; the lack of any communication – even if it was only abuse – making her feel like the loneliest person on earth.

It couldn't last, of course. In time, they did start speaking again; they just didn't speak about the thing they really needed to. They shared a chilly politeness at first, which thawed out into something an onlooker might understandably confuse with conversation, but they were both just acting roles. The people they used to be to each other would remain behind those masks until they dealt with what lay between them, and Jack wasn't ready for that to happen. Even when she tried to apologise, he seemed to close off and wouldn't let her look him in the eye. It was as though he wasn't prepared to hear her say sorry, because it reminded him of what she was saying sorry for.

Some would call what had opened between them a rift or a gap. Sarah thought of it as a wound, and knew that wounds fester if you leave them untreated. Jack was not dealing with this, and she began to worry what it might lead to. An infidelity of his own seemed a conceivable recourse, maybe even an apt one, and sure enough, he soon granted himself recompense.

Unfortunately, it didn't take the predicted form of a retaliatory fuck.

blackmail is such an ugly word

The fires of the Moundgate scandal had been burning for a while before David Sanderson came to the uncomfortable realisation that he had helped start them; still longer before he began to appreciate the full ramifications. His part in the crime – and he now understood just how large a crime – had been smaller than others', but he knew he had been complicit all the same. Someone else might have lit the fuse, but he had built the incendiary device.

He'd been under no illusions about the fact that he was assisting Beadie in fucking somebody over – his pockets were five grand the heavier, and people seldom punted you for your part in an act of benevolence – but at the time he had had no idea who; or how far-reaching the consequences would be.

His involvement had started a fortnight or so after that business in the papers about the MSP who got a vibrator stuck up his arse. Previously, David wouldn't have naturally chosen that as his chronological marker, but the connection with subsequent events now inescapably underlined its significance.

He remembered he'd been indoors, eating a dodgy donner pizza from the three-in-one take-away place; there was nothing on telly that night, and he'd started watching *Leon* on the video again. It had just got to the good bit when the phone rang.

He didn't recognise the voice.

'Hello, is that Mr David Sanderson?'

'Yes,' he said tiredly. 'But I don't want a new fucking fitted kitchen.'

'Oh, that's not what I'm ringing about. I'm not selling, Mr Sanderson, I'm buying.'

'Buying what? Who is this?'

'Meet me at the main entrance to the Burrell Collection tomorrow at ten and I'll tell you all you need to know.'

'Gimme a fuckin' break. The Burrell Collection. Who is this?'

'I told you, meet me—'

'I heard what you said. Go and wind somebody else up, ya sad bastard.'

'Oh, I don't think I'm the one who would be considered a sad bastard. Not by the Pattaya police, anyway. Ten o'clock. Be there.'

David had been left holding on to the phone, trembling like a fucking Parkinson's sufferer. Those two words had reached straight into his abdomen, grabbed his guts and squeezed.

Pattaya police.

Who was this guy? How could he know? And more to the point, what did he want?

David didn't sleep a second that night. In fact, he was doing well to breathe. He'd buried all that stuff so far down in his mind that he'd almost convinced himself it happened to somebody else. But all it took was two words to exhume the lot.

She was fourteen. Fourteen was old enough in some countries. Twelve in others. Anyway, he hadn't known – how could he? Christ, she'd looked twice that if she was a day. They all did, and the fucking Thai cops knew it. That was why he got off with a fine. It was all in the past,

205

though. All left behind, thousands of miles away, never to reach these shores.

Until now.

David met the guy as directed. Ian Beadie, his name was. They sat on a bench outside in Pollok Park and he handed David a folder. Inside was a copy of the arrest report, his mugshots, a picture of the girl. Enough to ruin his whole life in no time if it got out.

Beadie told him what he wanted, flat out, bang bang bang. He had it all planned, knew exactly what he needed and he also knew David could deliver. He'd give him five grand for doing it, and his silence afterwards would ensure Beadie's silence about other matters.

Talk about an offer you couldn't refuse.

It took less than a day to write the exe. Beadie gave him the emails, presumably having composed them himself, but it was up to David to find the porn, and to make sure the newsgroups he sourced were directly available to Scotia OnLine users. That stipulation was to facilitate part two, his doctoring the SOL server logs to corroborate the other evidence. However, all David needed to know for that task was the usernames, and as he hadn't read the emails, he didn't know precisely whom he was stitching up. Neither did he want to, which was why he didn't bother to look up the username details, figuring the less he knew, the better. Besides that, he hadn't expected the names to mean anything to him anyway.

They sure did now. To everyone in the UK and beyond.

The scale, the ambition and the sheer audacity of it was staggering. A political scandal so spectacularly odious that they had probably read about this shit over their tinnies in Australia – and it was all a fake. A fake that had wrecked careers and shaken the whole government. A fake that had altered the country's entire moral climate to a temperature Ian Beadie presumably found more conducive to his own prosperity. A fake that had been constructed by *him*, here in his bedroom in Langside. And a fake for which he had been paid what, under the circumstances, was beginning to look like a very measly sum.

When he first heard about the allegations on the news, he had taken them at face value, looking on with the same mixture of curiosity and *Schadenfreude* as everyone else. But then, as the details began to emerge, the truth hit him like a steamhammer to the guts. He had to take a couple of days off sick because he was worse than useless with worry, and had even seriously considered bundling up the cash Beadie had given him and leaving the country, maybe getting some work in Europe. Then as it became plain that the cops were biting, his fear quickly turned to anger, and with no convenient outlet, his anger was forced to turn into something more constructively rational.

Public morality was not the only place where the balance of power had shifted. Ian Beadie still had that file to hold over him, but David was just beginning to appreciate what he could hold over Ian Beadie. In the original breakdown, he had been paid cash for the job, and their silences traded equally on top. Now it looked like his silence was worth a shitload more than Beadie's, and it was definitely worth more than five grand.

He would have to plan this very carefully, though, and choose his moment well. Beadie was definitely not the kind of guy you crossed lightly, and he was clearly a lot more experienced at this sort of face-off. Now was not the right time, for sure. The scandal was months old, and there had been a lot of sludge under the press's bridge since. It was old news, and Beadie would be feeling robustly secure about having got away with it.

However, there would come a time when he might be feeling a little more vulnerable about the dangers and consequences of discovery, such as when the four MSPs went to court. The trial would light up the whole thing again, and their inevitable punishment – custodial sentences were being vocally demanded – would increase the stakes were the true perpetrators ever to be unveiled. David, more than most, knew how frightening the prospect of prison could be. When he was arrested and facing those Thai cops across that table, he'd have given anything in his possession to avoid it.

Yeah, he thought. Let's see what Beadie would give.

who cares

Sarah stood in the waiting area, feeling conspicuously out of place without any Old Firm leisurewear. Nobody had spoken to her, nobody had even looked at her, but she felt self-conscious anyway. It looked like casualty on a Saturday night; in fact, she even recognised one fellow visitor from having gassed her a few months back. The girl was hard to forget, right enough. She had four piercings in each ear, a stud through her nose, a ring through one eyebrow, and a Red Hand of Ulster tattoo on her right shoulder, but had insisted on a general rather than local anaesthetic because 'I dinnae like needles'. Problem was, Sarah didn't have the white coat or theatre greens to distinguish herself today. She was a prisoner's missus, just like all the other women here, so she could knock off the snobbery for a start. It didn't prevent her feeling intimidated though, or the more worrying realisation that Jack was stuck inside this place with all of their provenly *not* better halves.

Time seeped away. Five, seven, ten minutes after the appointed visiting time, and she didn't imagine they'd be allowed to make it up at the other end. Still, maybe she shouldn't complain; it could be a mercy. The sum of all the meaningful discussions they'd had in the past month could be comfortably accommodated in the twenty minutes remaining.

There was a quiet murmur around the room, as those who had come accompanied carried on their conversations in lowered tones, as though afraid of being eavesdropped. Maybe with good reason, she mused.

A warder entered and told them that they could now follow him though to the visiting area. Sarah let the others file out first, then sheepishly joined the back of the line, head bowed, guts churning. She looked at her feet as she walked, and only knew she was approaching the visiting room from the sound of chairlegs squeaking on floortiles. When she glanced up, she saw a room partitioned by a zig-zag arrangement of tables and barriers, entirely cutting the prisoners' side off from that of the visitors.

The prisoners were already seated at their chosen tables, all of them focused on the door as the visitors entered in single file. They scanned the arriving faces one by one, each bearing the same hardened, neutral countenance, finally breaking into a smile when their visitor was spotted. Jack was no different, except that when he broke into a smile, Sarah didn't return it because she didn't at first realise who she was looking at.

Jack Parlabane had entered her life by sneaking up behind her in a darkened close as she completed her highly illegal trespass of a police-sealed crime scene. It was an unquestionable testament to his effortless air of cocksure charm that she didn't smash his face in for it. Since then she'd learned to recognise a number of people in his different faces. She'd witnessed his malicious delight (often bordering on slappable self-satisfaction) as his machiavellian manoeuvrings triggered the downfall of his journalistic prey. She'd seen him shoving a shotgun into Stephen Lime's mouth, rage sparking like a static aura, all the while belying a calculated control deep beneath the surface. She'd seen the calmest serenity in his captivated gaze as he looked across at her from a honeymoon sunlounger, staring like that for who knows how long as she lay there reading. The face before her now, however, was a complete stranger.

He looked cowed and submissive, his smile one of vanquished apology. His eyes, normally a restless gauge of untrustworthy activity, were wide and supplicant. Christ, what had they done to him? What had *she* done to him?

He held out a hand. Sarah took it and pulled him to herself across the table. They held each other until they became aware of all other eyes in the room being trained on their extrapolated embrace, and even then hung on for a few more precious seconds.

'I'm so sorry, Jack,' she said, tears already running down her face.

Jack's eyes were moist too. 'I'm the one who's sorry, Sarah. I did this.'

'We both did this.'

'No, we didn't. It took an arsehole of historical magnitude to pull this off, and I'm afraid you just don't fit the suspect's description.'

They both sat down.

'So how are you?' Sarah couldn't keep the worry from her voice. She was trying to sound bright and conversational, but they knew each other's tones and nuances too well. Jack smiled in recognition of her concern, then shook his head gently to ward it away.

'I'm fine, Sarah. I'm . . . learning a lesson. Don't worry. Mind and body are still together. To be honest, having châteaubriand every night is starting to grind me down a wee bit, but, you know, you're not here to enjoy yourself.'

'Seriously, Jack.'

'Seriously, I'm okay. And I don't mean okay as in I don't want to talk about it. I mean okay as in I'm gaunny get through this. It's a kick in the arse I was big enough to earn for myself, so I'm big enough to take it. And I really have learned some lessons: about what's valuable; about what matters.

'You matter, Sarah. We matter. Nothing else.'

They clasped hands across the table.

'It's only a few weeks, really. This'll all be over before you know it, and then we can get back to what we had before I fucked it all up.'

'Promise me you'll be careful, Jack, you'll keep your head down and not do anything . . .'

He smiled again, that apologetic, beaten smile.

'You don't need to worry. I've learned a new respect for the dignity of silence, and it's no' as though there's a prison newspaper for me to be runnin' an exposé of Mr Big. Anyway, the real bampots are too busy with each other. Nobody cares aboot a wee scrote like me.'

'I care.'

others who care

'I want that Parlabane bastard taken care of,' said Stephen Lime.

'Who's he, then?' Fulton asked.

'He's the bloody reason I'm in here, that's who he is. Irritating, self-righteous little fucker. It was his unappointed crusading that got me condemned, his endless self-seeking quest to demonstrate how fucking clever he is that led to me being banged up at Her Majesty's pleasure.'

'I think all those murders may have played a part too, Stephen. Might be best to keep them in perspective. Help you get in touch with your anger and all that.'

'Oh very bloody funny. Anyway, it's stretching a point to call them murders. Mercy killings. What were they deprived of? Another couple of years of drooling incontinence? Bollocks. Euthanasia, mate, that's what it was.'

'I think it was the involuntary aspect the authorities objected to. Can't blame that on this Parlabane bloke.'

'I'd be a millionaire by now if he hadn't stuck his trunk in – I fucking well blame him for that. And believe me, you don't know this man. Five minutes in a room with him and you'd be contemplating very foul deeds, I guarantee it. Look at this.'

Lime removed the plate from his palate and bared what was left of his own teeth.

'The bastard jammed a shotgun into my mouth. Knocked

out half my ivories, and I thought my brains were going to follow them.'

'Well, you did order a hit on him, if memory serves. People can be touchy about things like that.'

'Touchy? He was a fucking maniac. An absolute psychotic. *He*'s the one who was a danger to society, and I can't believe it's taken them until now to put him out of circulation.'

Lime would never forget the moment Parlabane shattered everything he'd so painstakingly constructed, and would never forgive because of what came next. The smug, smart-mouthed little prick had eased off on the trigger, but the relief only lasted until Parlabane accurately outlined the awaiting alternative. Life imprisonment, with all the dread imagined horrors that entailed.

'Don't think of it as rape – think of it as their way of "touching base".'

Fucking vicious little shit. And the worst of it was, he'd been right. Stephen Lime's introduction to the Scottish prison system was everything he'd been afraid of and more, as it turned out half the bloody Saughton population had a grandparent who'd snuffed it at the George Romanes Hospital – including the screws. He wore two scars on his face as a permanent reminder of his first weeks in prison, but there were deeper marks on the inside, from the constant terror and the repeated humiliations. In truth, *it* only happened twice (only!), both occasions inside the first fortnight, but it was like the golfer conceding a handicap of ten strokes to his opponent in exchange for two 'gotchas'. Just as the better player tees off at the first, he gets a club between his legs from behind: 'Gotcha!' It ruins his shot, but he points out that his opponent can only do it once more.

'Yes, but you'll never know when.'

Lime had been fast turning into a quivering wreck, and

feared he was going to end up either committing suicide or going out of his mind. The possibility of the latter provided some inspiration, and he began to pretend that he was going doolally in the twin hopes that the animals would leave him alone and the authorities would ship him out. Unfortunately, it transpired that this had become a popular prison pastime since Ernest Saunders's infamously temporary debilitation, and Lime's own attempt fell far short of convincing anybody. All it did achieve was to have him placed on suicide-watch, which unfortunately closed off his other contemplated escape route.

However, salvation was fortuitously close at hand, in the unlikely form of ageing gangster Malky Gray. Malky had obviously watched *The Shawshank Redemption* a few times too many, and having heard Lime used to be the chief executive of an NHS trust, reckoned he could usefully harness his business knowledge. Lime then came under Malky's protection, which meant the violence and intimidation stopped, in exchange for Lime's expert advice on managing his inside operations and investing his outside capital.

Lime quickly proved that prison and adversity had not robbed him of his touch. He transformed Malky's portfolio, getting his money out of the nascent internet stocks he'd previously been nudged towards (a nine-day wonder if ever Lime saw one) and sunk the lot into the South-East Asian markets instead. Within less than a year, he had reduced the value of the gangster's legitimate assets by more than sixty percent.

Malky would undoubtedly have killed him if the news hadn't killed Malky. The silly old sod had a myocardial infarction and was dead on arrival at the RVI, leaving Lime without a patron, but also the unexpected recipient of much gratitude from the screws. Malky had been running the biggest drugs, protection and contraband operations in Saughton for years, and they'd been almost powerless to rein him in, as he was always one remove from the crimes and *nobody* would ever dare testify against him.

Lime's activities on Malky's behalf didn't all turn out so badly, at least not for Lime. He got a vivid grounding in the prison's economic system, much of which revolved around Malky's own variation of the supply and demand principle. This worked on the simple basis of Malky demanding something and it very swiftly being supplied, unless the demandee didn't particularly value his bollocks. With Malky gone, though, there were vacuums to be filled.

Prison had taught Lime, perhaps for the first time in his life, to be honest with himself. Out there in the world, he had benefited from the invaluable assistance afforded by connections: family connections, political connections, education (ahem) connections, masonic connections. Now that he was locked in a world where the old school tie would be useful only for hanging yourself, he had to come to terms with the fact that he had no-one but himself to rely on, and it gave him a shocking perspective upon the dependency of his past. He might have been able to pretend otherwise at the time, but now he could see that his career had not been built on who he was, but on who he knew. Granted, there had still been times when it took a bit of nous to capitalise fully upon such advantage, but for the most part he had been protected from his own limitations by an insulating layer of nepotistic influence. His first senior appointment had been on the board of his father's own company, and his last had been largely down to his generosity in lining Conservative Party pockets throughout the intervening years.

He had relied too much on other people, and ultimately it had brought about his downfall, when he hired a lumbering cretin of a hitman to do his dirty work. From here on in, he'd learned, if he wanted to better his limited lot, he would have to start relying on himself.

He had picked up enough about the running of Malky's little scams to grab a slice of the action when niches appeared in the market following the superannuated psychopath's untimely demise. Obviously, drugs were a no-no, as Lime didn't have the muscle or the connections for what would be a perilously competitive field. The protection racket could also be ruled out on similar grounds.

Those markets were quickly gobbled up by bigger fish; guys like Jimmy 'Corpus' Christie, a heavyweight thug with a rather incongruous passion for his religion (or perhaps more accurately, a passionate hatred for everyone else's). He attended mass every Sunday at the prison chapel, but had a more *laissez-faire* attitude to the other nine Commandments, which he tended to regard as guidelines rather than rules.

However, the lower-profile commerce of proper supply and demand offered opportunities for a man with a bit of business knowledge (or at least more business knowledge than any other bugger in here). Tobacco, phone cards, alcohol, pornography – there were many little luxuries that could make the days pass more pleasantly in a place like this, and very soon he was becoming known as a reliable source for all of them.

Naturally, this attracted the attention of the money-with-menaces chancers, to which Lime applied a satisfyingly free-market solution: he simply paid a bigger thug to knock seven bells out of the ones who were trying to shake him down. The bigger thug, 'Arnie', knew when he was on to a good thing, and offered his long-term services.

Nonetheless, Lime already knew better than to be too reliant on someone else's brawn or reputation – doubly so in an environment such as this – and set about some important personal changes. He began working out, losing the gut and replacing it with muscle. Then he got Arnie to teach him some pugilistic principles that would have had the Marquis of Queensberry retching in the spit-bucket.

Aware that reputation was everything, he waited patiently and took care in the choice of both his victim and his moment. Bob 'Big Boabby' Renwick was widely known to have 'boabbied' Lime (among many others) when he was first incarcerated, and indeed made frequent reminding jibes about it whenever there was company around to laugh. Choosing him was the perfect combination of the personal and the expedient.

Lime attacked him in the recreation area. Boabby was sitting watching two guys playing pool when Lime kicked the chair from beneath him and slammed his head off the table. He then proceeded to mash Boabby's blubbery face into a slippery, bloody pulp using the net-clamp he'd purposefully removed from the nearby tennis table a few moments earlier.

He lost remisssion (ha! what remission?) and got a period in the digger for it, but he'd known that would be part of the price. The purpose of the exercise was to make sure everybody saw it, and by God, everybody did. What they hadn't seen was Lime slipping a mickey into Boabby's tea half-an-hour earlier, but even if they had, reputations weren't about fighting fair. They were about winning.

He still kept Arnie on his payroll, but the incident ensured that if and when the big man was ever not around, Stephen

Lime – and Stephen Lime's business – was not to be fucked with. It was an insurance more than a necessity. On the whole, he was a popular bloke, as is anyone who can get you what you want. The screws tolerated him too: some on the 'devil you know' basis, in case someone more troublesome sprang up in his place; and others, notably Fulton, because he kept them in backhanders.

For the first time in his life he was in charge of a successful business, and for the first time in his life he owed none of it to anyone else. Well, maybe something was owed to Jack Parlabane for getting him started, and now that fate had delivered the little shit into his hands, he intended to deliver payment in full.

'Won't this guy be watching out for you?' Fulton asked.

'Doesn't have a clue. I've walked right past him twice and got nothing. He'll remember a fat little bloke with a bushy beard, not this.'

'So why haven't you had a pop at him?'

'I'm not planning to just punch him on the nose, Fulton.'

The prison officer put down his tea and quickly swallowed his contraband chocolate Hob-Nob. 'Now, wait a minute, Stephen. I think you should keep the heid here. If this guy gets a going-over, yeah, what the hell, but if you're talkin' about puttin' a price on him . . . forget it. It's a non-starter. There'd be a major investigation, and it would lead back to you. It would lead back to me too, even if you hadn't bloody come right out and told me.'

'Do you think I'm a fucking idiot? Of course I'm not putting a contract on him. Where's the fun in that? This is personal, Fulton. And you don't need to worry about fall-out. What I've got in mind, he's not going to be in a big hurry to report, if you know what I mean.'

'Got you. So what do you want from me?'

'A window of opportunity, that's all. The bastard's out of reach at the moment. Never strays far from E Hall, and his work duties tend to keep him out of harm's way too. Can you oblige?'

'We're here to serve, Mr Lime.'

'I want that Parlabane bastard taken care of,' said Jimmy Christie.

'Who?'

'Thon wee orange cunt that broke intae the Glesga arch-diocese, that's who. Bigoted wee bastart was slaggin' aff the Church in the papers, an noo he thinks it's fuckin' Watergate – except he's fuckin' Nixon.'

'Oh aye, him. The journalist. The wan Joe Donegan was talkin' aboot?'

'Aye. Wee orange cunt.'

'You're takin' it a bit personal, but, Jimmy, are you no'?'

'Personal? Fuckin' right it's personal, Gerry boy. 'Cause this is the same interferin' wee shite that got my brother-in-law a twelve-stretch in Peterheid, an' fucked up oor whole network at the same time.'

'You mean your Michael? That was runnin' the coach trips tae Lourdes an' bringin' gear back fae France?'

'Aye. An' it was sweet as a fuckin' nut, I'm tellin' you. Naebody' gaunny search a bus full o' spastics, are they? Aw, man, it was beautiful. D'you know pure heroin just dissolves, totally clear? Nae cookin', nae broon sludge, just intae water an' whoosh – disappears. They were bringin' over gallons o' it dissolved in bottles o' holy water, then distillin' it back tae powder at this end. We'd holy pictures dipped in acid, tae. It was perfect. The spastics got their trip tae Lourdes aw paid for – hotels an' everythin' – an' we got oor gear. Fair do's, I thought. But then this wee cunt comes along an' blabs it aw tae the papers.'

'How did he fin' oot?'

'Fuck knows. Some eejit probably opened their mooth, an' he did the rest. Fuckin' investigative reporter? I'll gie him a fuckin' investigation.'

'He's been in a wee while, but, Jimmy. Mair than a month it must be. I thought you'd have sorted him oot by noo.'

'Aye, so did I. It's no been easy, but. He's petermates wi' Mike Briggs, an' he's hardly oot his sight.'

'Ach, come on. There's plenty o' blokes in here could take Mike Briggs.'

'Sure, but they'd rather no' have tae, gied the choice, know what I mean?'

'Aye, I suppose so. So whit's changed?'

'Wan o' the screws says he's gaunny be workin' in the spraypainters fae next week.'

'Ah. Spraypainters. I hear ye.'

'Put the word oot, Gerry boy. This cunt needs tae be taught some respect, an' I'll be generous wi' my gratitude tae whoever administers the lesson.'

'I want that Parlabane bastard taken care of,' said Ian Beadie.

'I thought we already had,' Shelley replied. 'You gave the papers that story about his wife.'

'No. That was just to get him riled up so he'd take the bait. Now we need to reel him in.'

'Reel him in? What more do we need to do? The bloke's got no credibility left. He's the laughing stock of the whole Scottish press.'

'Do you know who Jack Parlabane *is*, Frank?'

'What's to know? He's a journalist with a bee in his bonnet.'

'Right. That's what I suspected.'

'What? Is there something I should know?'

'To say the least, yes. I don't have time to give you his full CV, but here's a crash course. You remember that scandal through in Edinburgh with the hospital trust boss a few years back?'

'Shocking business, yes.'

'Guess who blew the lid off the story.'

'Oh.'

'And the Roland Voss murders? Alastair Dalgleish and Michael Swan? Small matter of a homicidal conspiracy at the highest levels of government? That ring a bell?'

'I'm getting the picture.'

'I hope so, because Jack Parlabane is the last bloke in the world you want takin' an interest in your affairs, especially given what your affairs have illicitly involved in recent times. He's already started sniffin' around you and the Cardinal, so I'd advise you to listen when I tell you we need him out of the picture well before Logan and co get their day in court.'

'What do you have in mind?'

Beadie couldn't help having a soft spot for Jack Parlabane. Any old-fashioned newsman would, except maybe his editor, poor bastard, who probably wanted to kill him half the time. They were alike in many ways, searching out and exposing the unpleasant little truths that people would rather were kept hidden from view. Both of them knew that the world was full of hypocrites, and that those hypocrites would do absolutely anything in their power to prevent their duplicities from being exposed. Consequently, both of them understood that when the system is complicit in protecting such duplicity, sometimes you have to resort to nefarious methods to circumvent it.

He was aware that as a PR consultant he was now a determined part of the system Parlabane was up against, but that didn't mean he wasn't sympathetic. Beadie knew what it was like to see your catch squirming its way off the hook, especially in this day and age, but he couldn't afford to let sentiment get in the way when the stakes were so high. Whether or not Parlabane might uncover anything was moot; the issue was that if anyone could uncover it, it would be him, and that wasn't a risk Beadie was prepared to live with. Shelley's newly raised profile had piqued the interest of the irrepressible wee bastard, and as the priest was so negligently underestimating the threat, Beadie had taken it upon himself to see whether he couldn't repress the bugger after all.

When he fed Parlabane's name into his database, it had led him instantly to the man's wife, Dr Sarah Slaughter, and a fling she'd had with a colleague. That one had been a tail-job he'd assigned to a hack when Midlothian NHS Trust retained his services. It was the colleague he was after – bloke was being a right royal fly in the Trust's ointment – and they came up trumps at some Christmas bash (always the happiest time of year in the Beadie household). The mere threat had been enough to do the job in that case, and the story had gone back into storage until fate dictated that he'd be getting double his money's worth out of it.

He had never expected it would get Parlabane off the Churches' back, despite its impact on the man's credibility. What he had expected was that it might make the bloke a little less conservative in his conduct, which in recent years had failed to live up to his reputation.

Recent intelligence suggested that it had worked, with reliable sources reporting that he was fit to be tied. The poor dear was undoubtedly in desperate need of something to pour his raging energies into, and Beadie was ready to oblige.

'He calls your office now and again, doesn't he?' Beadie said to Shelley.

'Now and again? He calls all the bloody time. I'm never available, though.'

'You will be the next time.'

'I will?'

'Yes. And this is what you're going to say . . .'

faust reads the small print

Elspeth felt ill. Her hands were trembling, her insides were imploding and her brain seemed to be running at minimum capacity. It was always the same when she had to make a speech in the chamber. Points of order were okay, proper argument was okay: natural instinct and a near-primal taste for the cut-and-thrust took over, and she really quite enjoyed it. In open debate, she would be concentrating too hard on the issues and the logic to worry about how she was coming across; whereas with a prepared statement, the issues and logic were already dealt with, so the only thing left to worry about was whether she looked to everyone else how she looked to herself: a fraud.

Her father had been a commanding orator. He had a personality that filled any room, and a confident projection in his register, learned in meetings on the shop floor where the sounds of heavy machinery would drown a lesser voice. When he spoke, he never worried whether his audience was listening; he knew he could damn well make them.

Another thing he was sure of was that he had earned the right to speak, that he was addressing the floor because he had something to say, and not merely through the formalities of a position. When Elspeth had contributed from the benches, she had always done so with the confidence and conviction of someone carrying out what she had been democratically elected to do. However, when the Speaker called the Home Affairs minister to address the chamber, she was always half-expecting someone else to get to their feet.

She barely heard – and certainly never remembered – anything of the debates that preceded her ministerial speeches, so concentrated was she upon preparing herself for the ordeal ahead. Then, when the moment unavoidably arrived, she always felt as though her personality drained out through the effort of rising to her feet. Gone went the impassioned and shrewd combatant, to be replaced by a lumbering automaton, seemingly incapable of anything more rudimentary than delivering the words on the page in front of her.

At first she'd told herself that this crippling anxiety was simply down to her being new to the role, and that in time she would get used to it, like no doubt many had done before her. But as the weeks passed and the symptoms proved chronic, she was forced to look for other explanations. The first to come to mind was a long-harboured suspicion that the game of politics was made for those not cursed with self-awareness. If a charisma-vacuum like John Major could become Prime Minister, then surely she could grow a thicker skin and just get on with it.

However, what she was starting to understand was that no skin could ever be thick enough to hide the lies from herself. The inescapable truth was that she would never feel comfortable in her position while she knew she had no right to be there.

She was a liar and a fraud, and every time she stood up to address the chamber, she felt as though everyone could see her guilt.

In the first days of the scandal, her greatest concern had been over the seeming inevitability that the scheme would be discovered, and of the shame and punishment that would ensue. She had been sure that the email device was too simple, that some clever techie would reveal the whole thing to have been a malicious hoax and then unravel the threads until they led back to the sender: edoyle@sol.co.uk. Beadie's programme had been more sophisticated, though, installing false emails to the recipients' Deleted Items folders so that the evidence consisted of more than just illegal images. However, whether they be emails or images, they were all merely files on a PC, and there was bound to be a way of proving that their source was not as it seemed. Certainly, that was the buzz theory around the parliament, where the closing of ranks transcended party affiliations.

Elspeth had faithfully voiced her scepticism that the allegations could possibly be true, all the time feeling as if she was throwing more logs on the pile beneath the stake where she'd very soon be burnt. But then this outside evidence appeared, and all doubt was blown away. Beadie had never given her the full picture, but it was easy enough to fill in the blanks. He had nobbled an insider at Scotia OnLine, maybe even the same person who'd coded the email programme, and the server logs duly corresponded with the rest of the evidence.

Discovery, then, was not forthcoming, but the shame and punishment ensued nonetheless. When the Moundgate affair went from a computer mystery to a fully fledged child porn scandal, it heralded one of the ugliest periods in the history of Scottish politics, and throughout all of its hideousness, Elspeth was stuck at the eye of the hurricane, her wretchedness compounded by the knowledge that she had played an invaluable role in bringing it about.

As Beadie predicted, in the aftermath of the scandal she had been called upon as a totem of trustworthy stuffiness, and given some semblance of responsibility at long last, but only because she was one of the MSPs least likely to feature on the next Sunday's *News of the World* front page. In the past, it had always stung her that her political abilities were being overlooked; now it seemed her inabilities were equally irrelevant. It didn't matter that she didn't make a very good parliamentarian any more than it had mattered that she made an excellent media advisor.

And adding injury to compounded insult was that after so long on the fringes, frustrated by never getting the chance to pursue her true political ideals, she was finally allowed a hand on the helm at a time when all ambition and ideology had been jettisoned for fear it sank the ship. Forget the Life Raft. Forget 'education, education, education'. Forget health. Forget housing. Damage limitation was the only item on the agenda.

The parliament might as well have been in recession. Nobody was paying any attention to what it was trying to do, only what its members might be doing, saying, smoking, drinking, exchanging or masturbating over in their spare time. And anyone who *had* been paying attention would have been worthy of congratulation for perseverance in the face of such anodyne business. It was very difficult to get constructive legislation off the ground amid such an atmosphere of siege, harder still when you weren't sure whether your colleagues would still be in their positions the same time next week.

If Elspeth had been disillusioned in the past that her party was prioritising presentation over content, then it now seemed like a lost golden age of radicalism. Anything with a whiff of potential controversy was being replaced with legislative placebos, with the mollification of leader-writers taking precedence over whether an idea would actually help the nation the parliament was there to serve.

228

'The time just isn't right,' had replaced 'All together now' as the latest New Labour slogan.

Teenage pregnancies were the highest in Europe, but they were burying their sex education proposals.

'The time just isn't right.'

Drug deaths were at a record high, but nobody suggested we listen to the police when they said they might be able to do more about it if 85% of their time and resources weren't taken up with cannabis offences.

'The time just isn't right.'

Computer-literacy was going to be as vital to our children's futures as the three Rs, but plans to put internet PCs in schools were being quietly suspended because the words 'computer', 'child' and 'parliament' did not have the healthiest connotations these days.

'The time just isn't right.'

'It would be like channeling a river of filth directly into our classrooms,' was how one 'columnist and concerned parent' put it.

The only thing the time was right for was Ian Beadie and his ilk, snooping with impunity and self-importantly trumpeting each new item of worthless gossip like it was the scoop of the decade.

She looked down at the 'approved draft' in front of her. More bland and chary piffle, the political equivalent of treading water. A crackdown on car burglaries. Whoop-di-do. Gaun yersel. By now there had to be more stolen car stereos in circulation than there were cars, for God's sake. Sheer market economics would reduce the rates soon enough; this crap wasn't going to make a difference either way. To shame, remorse and regret she could also add embarrassment. All it would take was a ringing endorsement of the policy from the *Daily Express* and she would be sticking her head in the oven over the weekend.

Elspeth had campaigned for the establishment of this parliament for as long as she could remember: as a journalist, as an activist, as a politician, as an MP. She remembered the half-hearted fiasco of '79; the gauntlet-sting of Thatcher; a growing anger rekindling the flame while that creature tightened her claw; the vigil on Calton Hill; the growing sense of destiny; the vengeful wipeout of the Tories in '97; the referendum a few months later; and then finally in 1999, the reconvening after nearly three centuries. Elspeth had been there every step of the way, and now that the parliament was a reality at last, she had tainted it indelibly with an undeserved disgrace.

Worse than that, she had cut its newly formed balls off.

zen and the art of floor-polishing

Parlabane and Mikey were standing with Jocky Bruar and Dan Cuffe at the door to Robbie Linnegan's cell, watching its inhabitant perform a masterclass demonstration of buffing technique. His shoulders rotated smoothly, like a cultured golf swing, while his legs remained straight and motionless, like an upside-down version of the Riverdance. The buffing machine, boasting a jealously coveted new finishing pad, glided effortlessly across the lino under his expert guidance, bringing up a near-shimmering and flawlessly consistent finish. Heads nodded in reverently admiring approval, accompanied by utterances of vicariously shared satisfaction. This was magnificent work.

'You look like Evel Kneivel there, Robbie,' observed Parlabane, 'the way you're grippin' those handlebars.'

'Aye, you're takin' me back noo, Jackie lad,' he replied, impressively able to converse without detracting from the precision of his buffing. 'See, when I was daein' a four-stretch in here aboot ten year ago, I wance cleared twelve prostrate armed robbers on wan o' these things. I'd tae soup it up a bit mind, turbo-charger an' fuel-injection, an' I'd tae start the run-up fae A-Hall, slalomin' screws aw the way. But I hold the record tae this day.'

Cell cleanliness, Mikey had explained, contributed brownie points towards the hall's 'enhancement procedure', the ulti-mate goal of which was a cell to yourself upstairs, with all its attendant benefits (ie your own telly and nobody threatening you with dismemberment if you didn't stop playing the Afghan Whigs). Neatness was given some regard, but due to the limitations on allowable property, was never considered much of an achievement, even accounting for the corresponding limitations on storage space. Your floor, however, was the area where you could quite literally shine.

On this particular evening, a rumour had filtered through E Hall about a spate of impromptu inspections being planned for the next morning, with the predictable result that the polishing apparatus was in competitive demand. A rota had been drawn up, in fact; a rota Parlabane and Mikey were not on because they had each assumed the other to have staked a claim. The buffing machine was going to be otherwise engaged until lights-out (complete with that new pad the screws had finally relented to supply), so they had settled for some vigorous mopping, followed by the sheer entertainment value of watching the others work.

As Parlabane had soon learned, one bloke getting busy with the buffer did not constitute a legitimate, quorate polishing sesh. For that you needed three or four guys hanging round the door, keenly scrutinising the procedure and offering constructive criticism, such as, 'Aye, no' bad, but if you really want to bring that up, you'll need to strip it right back and start again.' This was in reference to the quite vicious chemical stripper one could use to dissolve all the previous layers of polish, right down to the Kirkcaldy lino.

'It's the only way to deal with a problem floor,' he'd heard said in all sincerity by an eighteen-stone former Hell's Angel who was in for dousing and igniting four rival gang members. ('The judge halved the sentence 'cause I used unleaded.')

Nobody was offering criticism of Robbie, of course. They

were there to learn, even Dan, who might be Robbie's cell-mate, but would one day have to wield the thing himself once Robbie had secured his higher status. It was such a privilege to witness that they all must have felt a little death when he reached for the plug-socket and thereby ended the lesson.

Mikey and Parlabane ambled back to their cell, where the floor would now be dry, but would look depressingly tarnished and dull by comparison. Still, there would be toast and scrambled eggs to revive their spirits. Mikey pushed open the cell door, then put a hand out to stop Parlabane walking in.

'What?' he asked.

'That,' Mikey replied, indicating the floor, where two words were legible on the lino. 'Some fucker's written that with stripper.'

'But how? We were two doors along. I didnae see anybody.'

'Could have been any time in the past two days. It only showed up once we'd wet it and mopped the polish away.'

They both stared at it for a few seconds. It said:

YOUR
DEED

'"Your deed",' Mikey mused. 'What deed? And what about it? I don't know, maybe he's gonna sneak back another time and complete it.'

'I think he means deid as in broon breid,' Parlabane mused. 'He's missing an E.'

'Well, what d'you expect in this place. Full of fucking thieves. You leave Es lying around the place, someone's

233

bound to help themselves. The only wonder is they didn't take the other two.'

'Bastards took the apostrophe as well.'

'Yeah, well, you see, they can sharpen apostrophes an' use them as shivs. They're not very effective, though.'

'Why not?'

'Well, how many fuckers in here do you think know how to use an apostrophe?'

They both laughed, each, he suspected, pretending for the other's benefit that it was nothing to worry about, which was in itself acknowledgement of the opposite. Parlabane waited until they were sitting down to their tea and toast to voice his concern.

'Have you upset somebody, Mikey?' he asked. 'I mean, more than usual?'

Mikey's refusal to take jail seriously extended to all of its inmates as well as the system itself. He reserved particular scorn and irreverence for its would-be big men, an attitude afforded by his physique and protected by his overall affability. No matter how much he pissed off some of the gangsters, the ones brave enough to have a go at him also had to consider how many other hardcases thought he was a great guy, and might therefore be inclined to avenge any assault. However, there were still plenty of people in here who were too mad or too stupid to let any such calculated reasoning stand in the way of their base desires.

'Not that I can think of, mate. Have you?'

Parlabane thought he was joking again.

Parlabane didn't know what he had done right to finally get himself assigned to duties in the sheds, but he figured he was due a break on the work front anyway. So far he had been restricted to what were euphemistically referred to as 'custodial tasks', to the extent that he could probably now mop for Scotland in both the prescribed-stroke and freestyle categories. He'd started to wonder whether it was part of a concerted establishment plan to break his spirit by wearing him down with the tedious and mundane. If so, they were sorely mistaken. He'd once read a whole John Grisham novel. He could take anything.

The spraypainters wasn't exactly a blank canvas upon which to express his frustrated creativity, but it was at least a change of scene, and it didn't involve the detergent version of Russian roulette, whereby one in six tubs could be full of maturing con-urine.

He'd actually been quite buoyed up at the prospect, a feeling simultaneously undermined and exacerbated by Mikey fussing over him like he was his mother and it was the first day of an apprenticeship. Mikey had, as ever, given him an advance crash course in conduct, technique and etiquette, but Parlabane suspected he was setting him up for a fall when he insisted on giving him a large potato to take along. It was a shapely and well-scrubbed tuber, grown with care by the man himself in the prison gardens, and presented to Parlabane with obvious pride.

'What the fuck do I want with a potato?' Parlabane asked, extremely ungraciously.

'You'll want a potato once you've been there a while, believe me.'

Mikey could be insufferable this way. They were both aware of how much Parlabane relied upon him for advice, but the downside was that he occasionally threw in utterly erroneous and potentially embarrassing information as well. The challenge for the novice was to spot the bogus stuff, but Mikey deliberately made it harder by being coy and circumlocutory about genuine matters too. Wrongly

235

calling his bluff was a point to Mikey, so Parlabane had learned to take a certain amount of things on faith, and to conceal his doubts about the rest until independent verification was obtainable. In this case, he left the cell with the potato, but stashed it in a store-press as soon as he was out of sight.

The spraypainters was where prisoners were put to work painting items for in- and out-of-prison use, everything from post office trolleys to fence posts. The system was based around an overhead track, from which hung the various items to be painted. They moved around from station to station, where cons worked on different stages of the process, and part of this included a fifteen-minute spell in the shop's enormous drying oven.

About mid-morning on the first day, several inmates produced potatoes from their pockets and attached them to the track. In time, they made their way back around to their point of origin, perfectly baked.

'Fuck,' Parlabane muttered to himself.

The learning curve for prison work skills was necessarily short and gentle, due to the wilful incapability of some inmates, and the sheer, incurable stupidity of others. He was therefore well into the swing of things by the second morning, but his new-kid status meant he wasn't surprised to be assigned fetch-and-carry tasks by the screw in charge.

'Parlabane,' the warder barked.

'Yes, sir.'

'We're out of mustard yellow on bench two. Grab some from the storeroom.'

'Certainly, Mr Fulton.'

The storeroom was through the back of the spraypainters, via a short passageway. With its high ceilings and rows of multi-shelved metal storage racks, it was the type of place he expected to be dark, ramshackle and cluttered, but in fact the two large skylights brightly illuminated a neat and well-ordered facility. Even the floor looked recently swept; nothing Robbie Linnegan would have put his name to, but clean enough all the same. The only link to jumbled chaos was the chemical smell, which comfortingly reminded Parlabane of his grandad's garden shed when he was a wean.

The door from the access channel opened to face the wall, the body of the kirk to the left as you entered. Parlabane wandered in, taking a lungful of the smell. Probably carcinogenic, but the olfactory was the sense most closely linked to memory, so it was worth it for the nostalgia hit. He'd been in earlier that morning, maybe about an hour ago, and was sure he'd seen the mustard yellow close to the back, on the right-hand side.

Parlabane proceeded down the passage between the two rows of shelving units, then stopped with a loud intake of breath as someone stepped out in front of him. He laughed at himself, placing a hand to his chest. The man smiled back.

'The fright you gave me,' Parlabane said. 'I didn't know there was anybody else here.'

'Oh, there is,' the man replied; rather redundantly Parlabane thought, until he realised it was supposed to sound portentous.

He heard the door close, and turned around to see a crop-headed bear shutting off his exit. He recognised him immediately as Big Arnie, a formally classified Heavy Steamer with a lethargic streak, whereby he seldom went to the effort of dispensing violence unless there was a profit in it. Arnie began moving towards him, balling his giant hands into presumably pre-contracted fists. Parlabane felt his insides dissolve. It didn't even occur to him to look around for a weapon. Paralysis was imminently setting in, and within five minutes it might be rendered permanent.

As Arnie came almost within swinging distance, the transfixation suddenly cleared, and either reflex or sheer survival instinct took over. He waited for the steamer's next step, then dropped to a crouch between two of the units, shooting out his right leg as he did so. Arnie's own leg thumped into it, much as a baseball bat would a twig. He stopped where he stood and looked down, frowning. Then he connected a left-handed punch to the right side of Parlabane's head, knocking him into a dazed sprawl.

He felt Arnie's hands on his shoulders, picking him up, while behind him the smaller bloke was clearing paint cans from a shelf. The big man bent Parlabane's head forward so that it would go under the shelf above, at the same time slamming his midriff into the one below. The smaller man moved around to the other side and brought his face up close.

'You don't remember me, do you, Mr Parlabane?'

The accent was one of the more pompous Home Counties varietals, shot through with upper-middle-class self-importance. It wasn't one you heard a lot of in Saughton, but Parlabane was still at a loss, thinking he didn't remember upsetting any other inmates, and certainly not one who sounded like a Sixties BBC newsreader in a bad mood.

'Well, perhaps it's vain of me to hope so. A crusading hero like yourself can't be expected to remember every wicked villain he brings to justice, can he?'

Arnie pulled him back a few inches, then slammed his stomach into the shelf again, knocking out whatever last few molecules of air might be left inside Parlabane's lungs.

That was when he made the connection and realised who he was looking at. It wasn't the face or the voice, or even the matinée-serial baddie's attempt at sounding masterful. It was the scenario of a nasty wee wank paying a lumbering goon to help him out with his dirty work.

'Stephen Lime,' Parlabane managed to splutter.

'Oh, we are honoured,' Lime replied. 'It remembers.'

'I remember what happened to your last henchman. Have you told Arnie about your employee safety record?'

Lime spat viciously into Parlabane's face.

'Well perhaps your memory will also recall what you said to me the last time we met, along the lines of what happens to people who get sent to jail. Arnie, change sides. I'll be taking the rear.'

Lime put his arms around Parlabane's neck and pulled his head downwards so that he couldn't move while Arnie came around from the other side of the shelves. Lime produced a rag from his pocket and stuffed it into Parlabane's mouth.

'You've no idea how long I've wanted to do that,' said Lime. 'Even longer than I've wanted to do what's coming next, you arrogant little prick.'

'What happened to this bloke he's talkin' aboot, then?' Arnie asked.

'Shut up and grab him,' Lime snapped.

Arnie gripped Parlabane's shoulders and pressed down, pinning him rigidly to the spot. Lime walked round to the other side and punched him powerfully in the kidneys. Parlabane felt pain pulse through him, but his resulting howl was absorbed almost fully by the rag. Lime punched him twice more in the same place. He could feel tears running down his cheeks, mucus bursting from his nostrils in time with the blows.

Then Lime reached down and undid Parlabane's trousers.

A masochistic part of him reflected with resignation that he was thoroughly due this; indeed, that it was a miracle it had taken so long in coming around. Meanwhile, the told-you-so part of his conscience was muttering something about how his wife getting tipsy and screwing someone else was maybe not worth making such a big deal about after all. Certainly, there were worse things in life.

He closed his eyes as he heard the sound of Lime undoing his fly, then opened them again when it was followed very swiftly by the clatter of the door being flung open. All three of them looked up to see who the intruder was, Parlabane thinking Mikey Mikey Mikey Mikey Mikey.

'Whit's the fuckin' score here?' the intruder demanded.

It wasn't Mikey. Instead, it was what Mikey had conscientiously taught Parlabane to recognise and avoid, a certified and definitely certifiable rocket: Chico Chalmers, life, murder (partial beheading with a machete) and attempted murder (partial disembowelment with a claw-hammer). Parlabane, even in this straw-clutching predicament, was doubtful that he constituted the cavalry.

'What does it fuckin' look like?' Arnie replied. 'Fuck off an' shut the door.'

'Aye, that'll be shinin' bright. I'm on a purse fae Corpus tae gie this cunt some steel. You're no' fuckin' nabbin' it.'

'Pipe down,' said Lime. 'You can have him when I'm finished.'

'No he fuckin' cannae,' Arnie objected. 'That purse is up for grabs, Chico. First come, first served.'

'What?' Lime asked.

'I thought you knew, Lime-o. Jimmy Christie's wantin'

240

him sortet oot. I thought we could kill two birds wi' wan stane.'

'But you just forgot to mention that part to me, did you?'

'Well, it's no' as though *you*'d be daein' it, is it?'

'Yes, but it's me it could get back to, isn't it?'

'Never fuckin' mind that,' Chico interjected, aware he was in danger of being sidelined. 'I fuckin' paid Fulton for the nod on when I could take this cunt. He's fuckin' mine, aw right?'

'*You* paid Fulton?'

'Aye.'

'Cheeky two-timing bastard. We paid him first. Why do you think we were in here waiting? Why do you think he got moved to the sheds?'

'I don't gie a fuck. Fuckin' hand him ower or I'll fuckin' rip the pair o' yous.'

Chico produced a blade from up his sleeve in a swift, smooth motion. He probably sat up at night practising it. Either that or he had a de Niro curtain-rail job inside his overalls. It looked like an ordinary table-knife that had been patiently honed over many a long evening, until it had a fine cutting edge and a tapered point.

Arnie let go of Parlabane and drew a similarly concealed weapon from his person. It was a toothbrush, the plastic melted at one end to secure the two razor-blades that were embedded into it. He turned to face Chico, stepping into the narrow passage as he did so.

Chico immediately lunged at him, while Arnie, in response, dropped his centre of gravity slightly and bent forward. He met his onrushing opponent in the chest with his head and lifted him off the ground. Chico clung on to Arnie with one arm around his neck and began stabbing at his back with

241

the other. Arnie, meanwhile, was slashing wildly with his own implement, trying to find purchase on his squirming and flailing burden. The blood-spurting, two-headed and multi-limbed creature tumbled against a shelf unit, which rocked back for a precarious second, then toppled over when Chico's legs kicked out at the wall behind. It crashed into the next unit, beginning a domino effect, with the two-headed octopus flailing at its base, squirting red-ink at imaginary enemies on all sides.

Lime had leaned on Parlabane's back as soon as Arnie turned to face Chico, clearly confident that normal service would soon be resumed. The outcome didn't look a cert from where Parlabane was watching (in fact it was only possible to tell which arm was whose according to the weapon it held), but Lime, having waited his years and with nothing to lose, was not going to be denied.

Bent forward as he was, Parlabane could see – and more importantly reach – a spray-gun resting on the knee-height shelf below him. Stretching his left arm down, he took hold of it by the trigger, then passed it to his right hand. He needed Lime to get closer, so he tried to arch his back, as though attempting to struggle free. It elicited the desired response. Lime leaned forward to press more weight upon him, which was when Parlabane closed his eyes, lifted the gun to head-height, and with the nozzle facing himself, pushed the trigger with both thumbs.

Lime screamed and jumped off him, crashing into the shelves behind as he did so. Parlabane sprang up and turned round. Lime was bent double, covering his face with both hands, howling in agony. He was also blocking the way.

'My eyes, my fucking eyes.'

The octopus was dividing itself. Chico had struggled to

the top, Arnie evidently weakening below him. The rocket cast a glance in Parlabane's direction.

'Where d'you think you're fuckin' gaun?'

Parlabane took hold of Lime by the hair and kicked him in the face with everything he had, feeling his foot connect with fingers and bone. Lime collapsed into the passageway, blood streaming from his broken nose. Parlabane allowed himself one stomp to Lime's groin, then made his escape, Chico's knife swishing the air behind his head as he lunged past.

Chico was fully extricated from Arnie by the time Parlabane reached the door. He placed a sweat-slippery palm to the handle, feeling his guts liquefy again in the micro-second before it opened. He slammed it shut at his back and ran down the connecting corridor.

He could hear Chico's footfalls behind him and glanced over his shoulder as he burst through the second door into the spraypainters. The rocket was, reassuringly, three or four yards back. However, the price of that reassurance was that Parlabane neglected to notice the wastebin almost directly in front, and was consequently up-ended when he caught it a glancing blow at thigh-level.

Everyone in the room turned to see what was going on as Parlabane tumbled unballetically to the deck. It was quite an entrance, but it was soon bettered. He twisted himself on to his back in time to see Chico explode through the door, his bloodied face and overalls looking like he'd spilled Edward Scissorhands' pint.

Chico stopped where he was upon seeing Parlabane sprawled before him. All of the assembled inmates seemed frozen to the spot, transfixed by the tension of whatever might be about to happen next. Only Fulton made a move, but unfortunately for Parlabane, it was out the door. Given the exchange he'd heard in the storeroom, the most charitable interpretation was that he had gone to get reinforcements.

'Right, ya wee cunt,' Chico bellowed. He took one purposeful step forward before bellyflopping indelicately to the ground, as the partially recovered Arnie smashed suddenly into him from behind.

The crowd in the shed then began to move in for a better view as the steamer and the rocket resumed their bloody entanglement. Heads butted, arms swung, blades gouged and slashed.

Parlabane climbed to his feet and let the gathering audience pass him to encircle the fight. He stood just a few feet back from the cheering mob, feeling sore, tired, relieved and not a little dazed.

'Fuckinn . . . spawny break there, eh?'

It was Fooaltiye, standing next to him with a dopey grin, eyes not quite focusing as usual. He looked like he'd lost weight.

'Fuckinnn . . . every cunt wants big Corpus's purse. Fuckin' jammy as fuck. Cannae fuckin' believe it.'

'Yeah, maybe my luck's changin'.'

Fooaltiye put a hand on Parlabane's back and moved closer.

'I didnae mean you,' he said.

Parlabane felt Fooaltiye punch him in the stomach, then became aware of a deeper, colder sensation, something that he immediately knew wasn't going to fade. Fooaltiye whispered in his ear, his hand remaining on Parlabane's back as he bent over from the blow.

'Fuckin' nothin' personal, pal. There's a fuckin' prize goin', ye know? Got fuckin' overheids, man. See ya.'

Fooaltiye moved away, leaving Parlabane to look down

at his middle. Sticking out of his stomach was a steel ruler, tapered diagonally and sharpened along one edge, with a piece of blue cloth wrapped several times around it to form a grip. He could still read the measurements. There was four inches of it inside him. Or ten centimetres, if you prefer, as it had metric markings too.

Parlabane saw Fooaltiye walk briskly out of the shop just as six screws came running in. The shouts of the crowd and the screams of the combatants got louder and seemed to swirl about him, before merging into one great, roaring, rushing sound in his head as he collapsed.

He found himself fading in and out of consciousness, only catching glimpses of what was happening, as though seeing it on TV while an attention-deficient channel-surfer had control of the remote.

It had taken a while for anyone to notice his condition. With the crowd intent upon the screws' attempts to conclude the steamer-rocket interfederation championship bout, it was only once his blood had seeped among their feet that one of them was distracted enough to investigate.

After that, he remembered more shouting, faces peering down, more screws, a stretcher, an ambulance. There were two screws in the back with him, trying unsuccessfully not to get in the way of the paramedics. One of them was Hayes; the other Parlabane didn't recognise. The paramedics were asking questions, some to him, some to the screws. Sometimes he answered, sometimes he tried to answer but seemed to lose the ability to speak, and other times he could only make out voices, not what was being said.

'Any idea what this was all about?' the nameless screw asked at one more lucid point.

'Until we get the measure of it, I don't think we can rule

245

anythin' out at this stage,' Hayes replied. 'In fact, it might be best just to draw a line under the whole thing. You know, you give these guys an inch . . .'

'I'm . . . go . . . gaunny . . . fuckin' . . . kill you,' Parlabane spluttered.

On the other channel, they were showing highlights of Parlabane's past, which was worrying the hell out of him, given what that was said to mean. However, it wasn't so much his life that was flashing before him, as all the many insanely reckless ways in which he had already come very close to ending it.

For years he'd conducted his version of investigative journalism with scant regard for the laws of the land, and only marginally more for the laws of gravity. When the evidence of what he already knew but couldn't prove was locked away behind corporate walls, there had been two options: ask politely, or find a way inside. To be fair, he never resorted to the second before trying the first, but these days, manners just weren't what they used to be. In his experience, Please only got you so far. A glass-cutter and a climbing harness took you all the way.

There was more to it than that, of course. Alarms to circumvent, surveillance systems to evade. Death by ravenous doberman to avoid. Dogs were usually pretty lax in their duties after a generous helping of *boeuf à la sleeping-tablet*, while the other obstacles could always be overcome as long as you did your homework and came prepared. At the Midlothian NHS Trust, it had been as simple as placing a photograph of the office he was screwing in front of the camera that would otherwise have been monitoring it. At the more high-tech Gable Pharmaceuticals in Los Angeles, he'd called the electricity supplier and reported smoke and sparks coming from a nearby substation. They shut down the local power for an hour while they investigated. Parlabane had only needed twenty-eight minutes.

Once he got what he was after, his favoured method of explanation of how he came by it was to claim it had been leaked by an anonymous source, whom ethics prevented him from revealing. The people he had stolen from usually knew fine who his source was – they just couldn't legally do anything about it. But that wasn't to say they did nothing, which was where the real risk factor came in.

Someone had once talked about 'death's great seduction', but from this evidence, Parlabane hadn't exactly played hard to get. Right enough, to extend the analogy, there had also been times when he'd been a bit of a prick-tease (as well as the times when he'd just been a bit of a prick). Death had turned up and started putting on the moves, only for him to slap its face and say he wasn't that type of girl. He'd survived several highly motivated and often professional attempts on his life: a hit-man, patiently sitting in his kitchen with a silenced nine-mil, like he was waiting to sell him insurance; that shellsuited genetic accident Lime had hired; ski-masked mercenaries breaking into his flat in the dead of night.

It would therefore be depressingly meaningless if, having seen off that lot, he succumbed to a dig from some skinny ned just trying to keep himself in kit. Meaningless, but perhaps appropriately so.

All those risks, all those stunts, all those crusades: they had all been *about* something. Exposing corruption, unmasking the bad guy, proving the innocence of the framed. But what did he end up in jail for? Trying to prove the Scottish Catholic Church was exaggerating its congregation.

Well, stop the presses and hold the fucking front page.

'Church tries to exaggerate its influence.' Hell of a scoop, Jack. What was he planning to follow it up with? 'God in non-existence shocker', perhaps, or 'Revealed: religion full of shit'.

Not exactly man bites dog, was it?

He'd phoned up Father Francis Fucking Shelley for the umpteenth time and, perhaps through the attrition of bloody-minded persistence or perhaps through a telecommunications error, he was actually put through.

'What is it you're really trying to find out, Mr Parlabane?' the priest had asked. 'I mean, I've read some of your reporting and to me it just amounts to a non-specific disgruntlement. You disagree with our beliefs – that's your prerogative – but what are we supposed to have done so wrong that you're bombarding this office with phone calls?'

'You're claiming to represent 800,000 people, Father Shelley. That suggests a considerable amount of clout in a democracy. I'd just like to know what the source is for that figure.'

'I'm afraid we don't have the resources to go door-to-door in a census, Mr Parlabane. However, we do have our registers of baptised Catholics, and that can be corroborated with the figures for those educated at Catholic schools.'

'I don't doubt that. What I'm less convinced about is how many of those people still subscribe to the creed and morality you're espousing on all of their behalves.'

'Well, while I can appreciate the issues you're touching upon, I don't know how either of us would go about reliably determining those numbers. But the morality I "espouse", as you put it, is one that is subscribed to by many people who are *not* Catholics, and how are we to count them? These are complicated matters, and they're not as simple as how many people might have gone to mass on a given Sunday.'

'But how many people do, Father Shelley? How many people went to mass in Scotland *last* Sunday?'

'We don't keep gate receipts, Mr Parlabane. I mean, we did have a snapshot survey carried out, but snapshots are like opinion polls: highly volatile, and never the same from one week to the next. A snapshot on Good Friday afternoon, for example, would be a sight different from a torrential Sunday morning in February.'

'What did it show? What week was it, and how many people did it record?'

'It was an ordinary Sunday. Autumn. But what it showed, as I've just explained, would be meaningless in determining the figure *you*'re disputing.'

'So it was a bit less than 800,000 then.'

'You'd be surprised, Mr Parlabane.'

'So surprise me.'

'Faith and belief are deeper matters than attendance figures. This is not Ibrox Park, or the Roxy on a Saturday night. This survey was carried out for our own internal purposes, not for justifying our existence to journalists.'

'When was it carried out, Father Shelley? Who conducted it?'

'It was carried out last year, and it was conducted by lay parishioners, so I'll spare you the bother of pestering all the market research companies. The only place you'd find a copy of it is in this office, and as I said, its purpose was not public, so that's where it's going to stay.'

He was wheeled into casualty on a trolley, more faces appearing above his own. Nurses, doctors, Sarah. He could see her but he couldn't speak to her. She was in theatre scrubs, word having travelled to wherever she was working. She looked scared. He could tell she was crying. She said something to him but he couldn't make it out. He might have managed a word in reply, he couldn't be sure.

For what it was worth, the word he intended was 'sorry'.

She had been what this was really all about, not religion or politics or whatever else he might have convinced himself of. The only sexual morality at issue had been Sarah's, not society's.

He did it to punish her; no greater motive. He did it to teach her a lesson because she had cheated on him. Before they got married, he promised no more recklessness, no more illegality, no more tilting at windmills; but then, she'd made promises too. She had broken her vow, so he was due a wee badness of his own, wasn't that the logic?

Well, no, actually. Deep down – and maybe not even very deep down – he knew the truth was worse. It wasn't about an indulgence or a reparation: it was about hurting her, and the way to do that wasn't simply to revert to his forsworn ways.

The way to do that was to get caught.

He could tell himself it had been down to complacency (some bunch of bead-rattlers with their heads in the clouds, it would be like taking candy from a baby), or that he'd been rusty and out of shape after three years of being a good boy, and maybe both of those things were true. But what was also true was that the easiest way to hurt someone who loves you is to hurt yourself. In his pitiful spiral of masochistic self-loathing, a big part of him had wanted to get fingered, because then *she*'d be sorry. She who had betrayed him; she who had humiliated him; she who had been terrified her husband would end up in prison, or worse.

Well, he'd really shown her, hadn't he? Prison *and* worse. Wanker among wankers, dickhead among dickheads.

The whole job had been half-arsed. He hadn't even brought his proper gear, so what did that say about his unadmitted motivations? Did he really think he could break into a place like that, undetected, with a fucking screwdriver and a gentle tiptoe, just because it was the HQ of a Church and not the HQ of a business? Probably not, but then he'd been playing stupid games with himself about what he was really up to, hadn't he. He had driven through to Glasgow telling himself he was just checking out the archdiocese building *in case* he decided to take things further; but he wouldn't be taking things further, would he? Course not. Certainly not that day, anyway. No sirree.

All that shit. The kind of thing Sarah probably told herself when she was flirting with *him*.

He'd gone in a back window – classy – from an L-shaped alley that ran between the buildings. It was a damp and knackered-looking thing, the frame conveniently warped enough to let him slip the screwdriver through a gap just under the rusted catch. He'd checked for alarm trips, but hadn't seen any; nor did he expect to. These guys had God looking after them, didn't they? What did they need with a burglar alarm. Accordingly, he heard nothing when he opened the window: no bells, no lights, no thumping of feet. Nor was there any response as he made his way through the building until he located Shelley's office. This was probably because he had obliviously tripped several photo-diode sensors, triggering a silent system that eschewed the scare-the-bugger-off approach in favour of automatically notifying the local police, who had made their way swiftly and forthwith.

He was rooting methodically through Shelley's desk –

failing to locate the report he was after, and failing also in his other speculative quest: to uncover evidence that might directly connect Shelley with Families for Innocence – when the room began pulsating with blue and red light. With a cold, hollow sensation, he quickly sussed that it wasn't due to any celestial presence. A glance out of the window confirmed two police cars in the street below. Huckling shortly ensued.

He confessed all and pleaded guilty, partly out of the aforementioned masochistic self-loathing, and partly because nothing pissed off a sheriff more than some prick who so obviously 'did it' but insisted on forcing the whole apparatus to go through the motions. He *was* guilty. He did it, and there was no-one else to blame.

The sheriff was right: 'A man who finds corruption in every place he looks might perhaps be seeing the reflection of what lies within himself.' There were no ruthless bad guys behind the scenes, no earth-shattering secrets to be uncovered, no murderous conspiracies to be unveiled.

Not anymore. Not this time.

They were trundling the trolley along a corridor, footsteps around him on all sides. He thought he heard the word 'theatre'. Someone was telling the screws to back off, they couldn't come in. Then he recognised another face peering down at him: it was Ross Quinn, in scrubs and a green plastic hat, ready to operate. The agony was complete. Even if he made it through this, the bastard who screwed Sarah was going to be the person to whom he owed his life.

'Nnn . . . oh,' he gasped.

'Don't worry, Mr Parlabane,' Quinn said sincerely. 'You're going to be taken care of.'

252

ruthless bad guy hatches murderous conspiracy to cover up earth-shattering secret

'Hello, Ian Beadie speaking.'

'Hello?'

'Yes, hello there, who's speaking?'

'It's ehm, David. David Sanderson.'

'David. You didn't sound sure for a minute. What can I do for you?'

'Ehm, well, the thing is . . . I've been thinking.'

'Thinking, David? I thought you had computers to do that for you.'

'Yeah, I do, but the trouble is, their conclusions aren't as reliable as everybody assumes. Not that I need to tell *you* that, Mr Beadie. If you know what I'm getting at.'

'What do you want, David?'

'Like I said, I've been thinking. It's been a dramatic few months in the old politics game, hasn't it?'

'To say the least.'

'I mean, shamed to admit it, I don't keep up to date on current affairs that much, but even *I* noticed that business with the MSPs and the child pornography. Quite a story. Doesn't get any less shocking the second time around, especially in court.'

'Look, stop dicking me around, David. Get to the fucking point.'

'The fucking point is that you didn't tell me what I was into. You gave me no clue what this was really all about.'

'Oh, bollocks I didn't. I gave you the emails to include in the exe, for God's sake. All the names were on them.'

'I included them, I didn't fucking read them. And as for the server logs, all you gave me was a bunch of usernames: plog, agilf, cleth. They could have been anybody. If I'd known who they were, Jesus Christ.'

'Which is why I thought it best for both of us if I didn't tell you.'

'I had a right to know. This was practically a fucking coup. I had no idea what I was involved in.'

'Well, it's over now, so I don't see what you're getting your knickers in a twist about. Nobody knows what you did.'

'No, you're right. Nobody knows. It doesn't have to stay that way, though.'

'Well, I'm not going to go shooting my mouth off, if that's what you're worried about.'

'Actually, it's *my* mouth you should be worried about, after what happened in court today. What was it? Six months apiece? Heavy going just for a few wee gifs and jpegs. But then, who could have known what a big storm was gaunny blow up out of this thing? So now that all the facts have become apparent, it strikes me that five grand was a hellish cheap price for what I provided.'

'If memory serves, David, the price was five grand plus your employers, friends and extended family not finding out about the twelve-year-old prostitute in Pattaya.'

'She was fourteen, and she looked twice that. *I* can say I didnae know. What are *you* gaunny say, Mr Beadie? "Oops, I seem to have slipped and accidentally framed half the fucking government. Sorry, Your Honour, I'll be more careful in future"? See, the way it looks to me, you'd be in a fuck's sight more trouble than I would. Especially

254

if I turn Queen's witness. I'd cut a deal. You'd be the one who went down.'

'I'll hang you out to dry, you cheeky wee bastard. You'll be on the fuckin' paedophile register in a flash, with Mags Hainey an' the angry-mother mob breakin' doon your fuckin' door.'

'I don't doubt it, Mr Beadie. I believe it's called mutually assured destruction. But it doesnae have to be like that, does it? We can come to an arrangement.'

'Cut to the fuckin' car-chase. What do you want?'

'Fifty grand.'

'Fif . . .? Get tae—'

'Per annum.'

'*What?*'

'You heard. I think, given the scale of what you've pulled off, you should consider this a realistic expense. I mean, let's face it, you didn't do this for a laugh, did you? You and whoever you're in cahoots with must stand to gain plenty from this – and not just in the short-term, either. You couldnae have done it without me, so I want my fair share.

'And anyway, I'm just tryin' to be up-front about this. I mean, I could say gimme fifty K and I promise you'll never hear from me again, but you're not stupid enough to believe that, are you? That's the problem with computers. Things are so easy to copy. If I gave you a disc with the evidence, you'd have no guarantee I hadnae backed it up and wouldnae be in your face again later, askin' for another sub. At least this way, it'll be structured. You'll have plenty of notice when the next payment's due. And as long as you keep payin', nobody needs to know how the face of Scottish politics was *really* changed.'

'I'll change your fuckin' face, you wee prick.'

'It's not nice being blackmailed, is it Mr Beadie? Let's see how you fuckin' like it. You've got a week, or it's gaunny be your mug on the front page for a change.'

Beadie didn't need a week. He didn't even need until the end of the phone call. There was no way he was shelling out a penny to this fucking chancer. Even if he did, the wee wank had made it perfectly plain that he wasn't to be trusted, and Beadie couldn't afford to have such a person holding that kind of leverage over him. Cheeky wee shite. Who did he think Beadie was? Some fucking amateur? He didn't need anybody else telling him about the scale of this thing, or the stakes, and he hadn't come up with it for fun; the bastard got that much right. When he devised this scheme, he had done so with absolute, calculated awareness of all the possible consequences and ramifications, including his potential for exposure to double-crossing wee wanks like David Sanderson.

Sanderson had, until now, been a good little boy. At the time, he suspected that the geek might not appreciate (or particularly care) exactly who he was helping set up, and had anticipated an element of panic when it finally dawned, but so far there hadn't even been that. The silence, he had assumed, was down to the dependable effect of a conspirator – reluctant or not – realising how much shit he'd be in if the truth got out, and consequently feeling no pressing urge to unburden himself. Unfortunately, there was always the danger that fear could graduate from an obstacle to a spur, and this was something you had to be prepared for from the kick-off.

Beadie was prepared. Well prepared.

Before he put any part of his plan into motion, he had first asked himself just how far he was ready to go to protect his position, if the worst came to the absolute worst. If he hadn't been one hundred percent sure of the answer, he'd never have embarked upon any of it. When it came to games like this, you played for keeps or you didn't play at all.

He unlocked his desk's bottom drawer and lifted out a pack of copier paper, dropping it to the floor with a thump. Then he reached in again and removed the spotless steel presentation case, placing it on his desk, unlocking it and easing it open with delicate care. It was a gift from Virgil Matthews, a former NRA press spokesman Beadie had brought in as a consultant when the British gun lobby hired Clamour PR to help take some heat off themselves in the wake of Dunblane. Inside, nestling snugly in the precisely shaped blue foam padding, was a Sternmeyer P-35 11mm pistol, complete with laser-sighting, along with two full magazines.

Beadie picked up the telephone on his desk and dialled a number.

'Hello, Craggan Moor Hotel.'

'Oh, hello there, Donald. It's Ian Beadie here.'

'Mr Beadie. Always a pleasure. And what can we do for you today?'

'I was wondering whether you might have two rooms spare on Thursday, for dinner, bed and breakfast.'

'Let me see. Ehm, no, I'm afraid we're fully booked on Thursday. I don't suppose Wednesday would suit?'

'Wednesday would be fine. Wednesday would be just fine. And I'd like ground floor rooms, if that's possible.'

'Going to be that sort of night, is it?'

'It certainly is. Which reminds me, can I just check something with your sommelier?'

'Well, he's not in just now, but perhaps I can help.'

'Yes, perhaps you can. I've been bumming to my intended

companion about one of your wines, and I'd just like to make sure it's in plentiful supply. It's the 1993 Château Musar.'

'We took delivery of a case of twelve only this morning, Mr Beadie.'

'That's exactly what I needed to hear.'

Beadie had been under no illusions about what might be required once this business was in motion. Hence, there would be no hasty improvisations; nothing impetuous and half-baked leaving a trail of bloody footprints back to his own door. He had worked out his contingency down to the finest detail: a swift and decisive solution that would leave no margin for future doubt. The only weakness was that it needed two men, but even that, in his expert hands, could be turned into a strength, especially as one of them was going to be a priest.

Guilt and innocence were, like everything else in this world, entirely about perception. Thus, getting away with murder was just another PR job.

white collar crime

Shelley stood at the car-hire reception desk and did his best not to look like he was holding on to the thing. He had to catch a grip of himself. If this was how he was feeling now, what would he be like tomorrow night, when the real show started?

He'd felt almost reconciled to it this morning, a million years ago in the land of faith and hypothesis, before he committed the overt act of walking through the Europcar door and thereby took his first, deliberate steps towards implementing the plan. Before that, he'd been able to stand back and rationalise, despite the churning nausea that had made him puke up his breakfast. It was about taking responsibility, he'd managed to convince himself. It was about standing up to be counted for the good of his religion, as priests had done for centuries before him. To refuse the burden would be to abandon the Scottish Church to a catastrophic fate, and like God's first priest on this Earth, he knew he could not ask that the chalice be taken from his lips.

Aye, right.

Now, standing by that desk, he only had desperate hopes to cling to; and when those failed, there was always denial. It wasn't real until it was real, he kept telling himself. At this stage he was only hiring a car, they were only going for a drive. It wasn't real until it was real. For goodness sake, the whole thing could be Beadie's idea of a joke, or even a test, pushing him to see how far he'd go along with it. It wasn't real until it was real. There was still a day or so for the situation to change. Anything could happen in that time. Until then, he was just going through the motions. None of it was real until a trigger got pulled.

'Do you wish any additional drivers to be added, sir?' the girl behind the desk was asking. Shelley wasn't listening, though. He was staring out of the window at the Lexus, inside which Beadie sat with his back to the office.

He'd appeared at nearly twelve, just when Shelley was about to go to his bed, and though he only stayed an hour, it might as well have been all night, as there would be no sleep after what Beadie had to say.

It was simply unthinkable.

He was a priest, a man of God. 'Thou shall not kill' left no leeway for interpretation, even in these relativistic times. There was no way he could even consider this.

'For God's sake, man,' he said, 'you're talking about . . . *murder*. You're asking me . . . I can't believe I'm even hearing it.'

'Well, have you got any better ideas, Father? Or have you maybe got a spare fifty large burnin' a hole in your pocket?'

'What happened to the forty thousand we gave you?'

'Who the fuck do you think that was for? It was to pay him for his services and his silence. But now the greedy wee bastard wants more, so unless you can organise a fast sale of holy relics, then I'm afraid this is the only way out.'

'No,' Shelley told him, as firmly as he could manage. 'I won't countenance such a thing. I don't have the stomach for this, Mr Beadie.'

'Have you the stomach for ten years in the jail? That's what we could be lookin' at here, Franky boy. We fucked

260

with the whole democratic process of a parliament people waited three hundred years for – they're no' gaunny let us off with a stern lecture. And have you the stomach for watchin' your precious Church get turned into a discredited nonentity? Because that's what's gaunny happen while you're rottin' away behind bars. Everythin' that's changed in recent months will be changed right back; all the things you detest will be totally exonerated. And whatever poor bastard gets *your* job next had better have thon stigmata, because he's gaunny get fuckin' crucified every time he opens his mouth. The Catholic Church's influence in Scottish society will rank somewhere between the Save the Midge campaign and the Geoff Hurst Fan Club.'

Beadie wasn't exaggerating, Shelley knew that much. The scenarios for what would happen should their deceit be revealed had been playing in cinemascope since the whole thing began. Though every day that passed decreased the likelihood of suspicion being raised, at the same time, every benefit it brought increased the stakes of what they stood to lose. He didn't need it spelt out. The higher they climbed on these stolen wings, the deeper the crater if they fell to earth; and these days they were soaring.

The word from Rome was that the odds were shortening by the week on Cardinal Doollan getting a shot at the world title. Scotland was once again being regarded in the Vatican as a country where the Church was strong and dynamic, rather than another post-modernist secular lost cause. Parliament was running scared, ditching proposals that only a year ago they would have steamrolled through, and it was widely felt the time had never been so ripe to demand that abortion be made a devolved issue. Progress that had once been the stuff of dreams and prayers was turning into a tangible possibility. It felt as if it was in touching distance.

A Scottish repeal of the 1967 act would be a victory the like of which the Church had not enjoyed for generations, and they'd be measuring Shelley for a mitre at the very least.

But the whole thing had always been contingent upon the truth remaining secret. He'd known from the beginning that this eventuality might one day need to be faced, and he had also known that there was but one option for damage limitation: he could call the shame and anger down upon his own head. Martyrdom bestowed a divine dignity that could endure any such earthly humiliations.

'I can take the fall for it myself, Mr Beadie. I always knew I might have to. The Church will be blameless.'

'Aye, that will be fuckin' right. Listen, if I go down, I'm goin' down in flames, an' I'm burnin' everythin' I touch on the way. I'll testify that Doollan knew all about this. There's not gaunny be any "one bad apple" shite. This went right to the top, and all three of us know it.'

'It would be your word against his.'

'No, it would be his word against the recording I've got of me tellin' him about your wee girlfriend in Bishopbriggs, in case you needed a shove.'

'You swine.'

'Yeah, yeah. Save your temper for Sanderson. He's the reason we're in the shit here, not me. And I wouldnae get all conscience-stricken aboot it: the guy's scum. He's a fucking paedophile. Who did you think was the source of the child porn?'

'But vengeance is mine, says the Lord.'

'The Lord has options, Father. You don't. Not if you want to do his bidding, anyway. Christ, you priests used to knock people off all the time, on orders from the fuckin' Pope.'

'That was a long, long way back in the Church's history, Mr Beadie.'

'Aye, and look at what's happened to it since they stopped. It's time for guys like you to grow their balls back, Frank. Otherwise you're gaunny be extinct.'

'Our faith has endured sterner tests than this, for two thousand years.'

'Oh, knock the piety on the head for five minutes, will you? You're foolin' nobody. You're a bunch of fuckin' hypocrites, and I'm gaunny make sure everybody knows it unless you get your act together and get on board.'

'I'd rather be a hypocrite than a murderer.'

Beadie grinned, which was most unsettling. It was the grin of someone who knows his hand beats yours, and would rather crow than bluff.

'Interesting comparison, *Father*. Because goin' by your precious faith's definitions, you're a hypocrite *and* a murderer.'

Shelley was speechless with dread. He suddenly felt the floor drop from beneath him. He wanted to ask what Beadie was talking about, but it was sickeningly obvious that they both knew the answer.

'Glasgow Royal Infirmary. March 22nd, 1997. Bernadette Dunn, of 14 Brae Road, Bishopbriggs. Referred by her GP, Dr Angela Cole. Termination carried out by Dr Michael Lewis. Stop me if I'm missing anything out.'

Shelley gasped like a landed fish. How did he know? How could he *possibly* know?

'You . . . you b—' he stumbled. 'You . . .'

'Oops. Careful now, Father, your halo's slippin'. You almost said a swearie-word there.'

Shelley struggled to control his rage, feeling as though the room was spinning around him. He thought all of this had been buried; certainly his feelings about it had. Now they were violently unearthed, and all the turmoil, all the conflict, all the confusion was once again unleashed. He swallowed and looked Beadie in the eye.

'How dare you judge me,' he said, his voice a hoarse growl. 'You don't know anything about it.'

'I know enough about it. I know the parts that matter, the parts people will be interested in. Priest, girlfriend, love-child, abortion.'

The memories were crashing against him like waves in winter. The burst condom, the weeks of uncertainty. The dreaded confirmation. The fear, the distress of an impossible situation that neither of them was equipped to deal with.

'It wasn't my decision. It was hers.'

'So it was *her* right to choose, is that what you're sayin'?'

'Well I couldn't force her, not without everybody finding out. And either way, I didn't want to put the poor woman through what the papers would do to her.'

'That's very selfless of you. Very understanding, too. Women *can* sometimes find themselves in these difficult situations, wouldn't you agree, Father? And what they need then is understanding. Just a shame your faith tends not to see it that way.'

'God forgive you, Beadie. You're an evil, evil man.'

'I don't think you're exactly towerin' above me on the morality ladder here. I don't *want* to reveal this stuff, but I'm fucked if I'm goin' down because you wouldn't help me.'

'Wouldn't help you murder somebody?'

'Oh, get off the high horse, ya pompous prick. I think we've just proven it wouldnae be the first time somebody had to die to spare you and your Church some embarrassment. Look on the bright side, at least this time it won't be your own flesh and blood.'

Shelley felt his fury well to the surface in an uncontainable surge. He lunged at Beadie across the coffee table, intent on throttling him. Beadie, however, knew it was coming and effortlessly evaded the attack. Shelley crashed into an empty armchair, and in a twinkling Beadie was upon him from behind. He punched Shelley in the kidneys and dragged him to the carpet, where he rolled him over and knelt on his chest.

Beadie brought his face down until their noses were almost touching.

'That's it, Father,' he said, his eyes cold steel. 'Wee bit of anger's what we need. Now, try and think of how angry you'll feel when everybody knows about Bernadette's wee appointment. Think of how angry you'll feel when the pro-choice mob have got all this to play with, on top of the Church's part in the Moundgate affair. Then think how angry you'll feel when you realise you had the chance to stop it.'

Shelley swallowed.

Bernadette had been like a sister to him. He had enjoyed a companionship with her like nothing he had known before in his life. She was a good woman, a truly good woman, and it meant everything to him to be the one who made her happy. The physical side of it had never been his intention, but it was impossible to prevent it spilling over when there was such closeness, such affection between two people. He could have withstood the sacrifice of going without, but she needed that affection, needed it manifest. She was only human. They both were.

She would be destroyed if this got out, if Beadie dragged her name through the tabloid mire. She taught in a Catholic primary school, for goodness sake. They would all be destroyed: Doollan, himself, the whole Scottish Church. But the difference was that Bernadette had done nothing

265

to deserve it. She hadn't done a deal with the devil; she hadn't subverted the nation's democracy to further her own ambitions.

She had done nothing.

'Do yourself a fuckin' favour.'

Beadie stood up. He could tell the discussion was over from what he must have seen in Shelley's eyes.

'There's a hire car booked in your name.'

'*My* name?'

'Don't argue. You're collectin' it tomorrow. I'll pick you up and drive you over there at three.'

'Mr Shelley? Sir? Mr Shelley?'

Shelley barely recognised his own name without the 'Father' prefix, but either way, it would still have taken a while to bring him back from the gloomy depths of his thoughts.

'Sorry, pet. I was miles away.'

'Do you want any additional drivers added to the documentation?'

'Eh, no, just me,' he replied automatically. The car was in his name, the rooms in Beadie's. A fair balance, Beadie had said. Mutual assurance. Aye, right. They weren't going to be driving the fucking hotel rooms to Glasgow, though, were they? He eyed the Lexus again with venom.

'Actually, on second thoughts . . .'

Shelley glanced again in the rearview mirror, where the squat lozenge of Beadie's fatcatmobile loomed in funereal black, dogging him like depression. His own vehicle was a bottle-green Vauxhall Vectra, the kind of car, he hoped, nobody would look twice at. With the tricky issue of free will removed from the equation by Beadie's threat to tell

266

all, his worries had transferred from the morality of doing it, to simply whether they would get away with it. The PR man was supremely confident, but it hadn't rubbed off. This might have been because he hadn't filled Shelley in on all the details, giving him instead only what he needed to know at each stage. It might have been another of the power games the bugger was so fond of, but the more likely explanation was that he didn't trust Shelley not to be looking for a way of deliberately messing it up before it came to the big moment.

The skies had been blackening all the way up the road. This was in accordance with Beadie's wish that it be dark when they reached Craggan, but it was easy to imagine that it was actually because the evil so-and-so had commanded it, with a wave of his hand and a booming, maniacal laugh. With a full cover of clouds above, it was pitch by the time he passed Pitlochry.

The turn-off for the village of Craggan was signposted fifteen miles further north. As soon as they passed the sign, Beadie pulled out and overtook, then powered his way ahead as planned. Shelley watched the Lexus indicate as it approached the slip road. He had a brief image of himself flooring the accelerator and just blazing on up the A9, but where was he going to go? The *best* he could hope for was Sanderson surviving to carry out his threat, with everything that would bring down upon Bernadette, the Cardinal and the whole shooting match.

He winced at his choice of phrase as he turned on to the B road, the Lexus' lights visible in the growing distance.

Turn right at the war monument, had been the instruction, then park in front of the long, low terrace of houses. He made the turn and passed the Lexus, parked close to the junction on the left-hand side, lights off, Beadie in the driver's seat pretending to examine a roadmap. There were two people on the pavement on the opposite side, walking away from the monument, newsprint-wrapped parcels in their hands from the chippy on the main street. Shelley therefore kept on driving, again as instructed, before heading out of town and making a second circuit.

He was back at the war monument in less than three minutes, and this time the street was empty. The Lexus' lights flashed once as he passed it, confirming that this time was go. The last car in front of the terrace was an ancient-looking Volvo estate. After that there was a dozen empty yards before the pavement ended and the road ran into the countryside. He pulled over in front of the Volvo and killed the engine, by which time Beadie's car was already crawling along at his back, lights off.

It stopped alongside. Shelley yanked the lever by his right foot to open the Vectra's boot, then got out and stood up. Beadie walked around the back of the hire car and placed a briefcase inside. He closed the boot firmly, then returned to his own vehicle. Shelley locked the Vectra and climbed into the passenger seat of the Lexus, which began moving away before he had closed the door.

They got back to Glasgow before midnight, despite Beadie keeping it under sixty all the way down the road, for fear of attracting any police interest. The first either of them spoke was outside Shelley's house in Lenzie.

'Get some sleep, Frank,' Beadie said, with a tone of sincerity that sounded almost solicitous.

'I'll try,' he replied, and meant it. He may as well grab it while he still could. After tomorrow, chances were he'd never sleep again.

murder and ribena

Beadie looked at the items on his bed and ran through his mental checklist once more, unable to shake the unsettling fear that he had forgotten something, but equally unable to think what it might be. It was probably just nerves. He sometimes got this way when he was flying abroad, sure that when he reached the check-in desk he would find he was missing his passport or flight tickets, even though he'd checked them a dozen times. Everything was present and correct. The Sternmeyer, in its case. The mobile. The small polythene bag of charlie. The four Château Musar bottles, each with a blue plastic stopper. The four red plastic stoppers. The gloves. The change of clothes. He'd checked that his window opened easily, and called next door to make sure Shelley's did too.

No, that was definitely everything.

He walked to the window and looked out at the view down to the river, over the row of parked cars on the hotel's gravel drive. The Lexus was sitting nearest the front door, in deliberate view of reception. Sticking it in plain sight had an extra motive this evening, where normally it was merely a habit borne of having the stereo stolen and the paintwork keyed on too many nights out in town. It struck him, as it always did at such times, to wonder whether he'd remembered to set the alarm, which of course he had. Then he realised *that* was what was wrong: he had meant to leave it disabled. All it would take was a bloody crow landing on the roof in the middle of the night and they'd be ringing his room to switch it off, something he absolutely could not afford.

He took a wander outside and aimed the infra-red, eliciting the reassuring double-flash, an electronic placebo if ever there was one. After that he opened and closed the door, just to make sure.

Now he was ready.

Beadie pulled the stiff white plastic bag a little nearer as the smiling waitress approached, leather-bound menus in hand. He had requested his favourite table by the window, but had been beaten to it by two honeymooners. With good grace he refused the next table along, saying the young lovers wouldn't want two old farts cramping their style, but really because he needed one next to a wall, where the bag would be less conspicuous. As well as the four bottles, it contained several laminated A4 display cards, some of which he had ostentatiously passed to Shelley when they sat down, for his brief perusal and return. The cards displayed nothing but meaningless charts and statistics; their dual purposes were to provide a plausible explanation for his bringing the bag down to the dining room, and to prevent the bottles from clinking together as he carried the thing.

'Would you like to see the wine list, sir?'

'Ehm, no need. We know exactly what we want,' he replied with a friendly laugh.

The girl smiled again. 'What would you like, sir?'

'We would like a bottle of the 1993 Château Musar, please.'

'Château Musar. Certainly, sir.'

Beadie opened the menu and allowed himself a moment to savour the descriptions. There was a second – maybe less

– when the atmosphere, the smells and the clink of cutlery made him forget the real reason he was there, and when it had passed he found himself regretting that this wasn't purely a recreational visit. Still, it might be the last time he got to come here if he didn't take care of tonight's business, a thought that put fire back in his now mouth-wateringly hungry belly.

'"Pan-fried pigeon breast with crispy leeks and raspberry vinaigrette,"' he read aloud. '"Guinea fowl on a bed of puy lentils, with beetroot and a red wine sauce. Salmon fillet with plum tomato compôte, parma ham and pesto." Ahhh, decisions, decisions. I'll tell you this, Frank, if you're gaunny do a thing, do it in style, eh?'

Shelley glared back at him from over his own menu. 'I don't think I'll be able to eat a bite,' he said. 'I don't share your appetites, Mr Beadie. For anything.'

Beadie returned the glare with a deliberately warm smile, lapping up the self-righteous bastard's discomfort. Shelley was turning the piety up full, in compensation for what he was involved with, and it had started to get on Beadie's nerves. That was the downside of his dealings with the Tims: their moral rectitude had its uses, but they thought they were so fucking superior all the time. He was going to enjoy dragging this one down off the high ground. Let's see if he can still look smug and aloof when Sanderson's brains are splattered around his shoes.

'You know, Franky,' he said bouyantly, 'I'd think about cheerin' up and tryin' to relax if I was you. It's part of your alibi, remember.'

The waitress took their order, then returned shortly afterwards with the wine. She opened it at the table and poured Beadie a small splash, which he sniffed and approved before placing a hand over the glass to prevent her filling it.

'We'll pour our own, thanks,' he told her.

Beadie waited until she had disappeared off to the kitchen, then lifted the bottle with his left hand, holding it above his lap and looking down as though examining the label. His right hand, meanwhile, was reaching into the bag, where he gripped an identical bottle by the neck and flipped off the blue stopper with his thumb. He pulled the original bottle down to his lap out of sight, meanwhile resting the second on the spiralled metal stand on the table in front of him. Then he reached into his trouser pocket for a red stopper and plugged it into the top of the original bottle, before placing it gently into the bag.

'Wine, Francis?' he asked, pouring both of them a large glass of dilute Ribena.

Beadie lifted his glass. 'Cheers,' he announced loudly. Shelley grudgingly held up his glass and knocked back a mouthful.

Beadie ordered another bottle when the waitress came to take away their starter plates, then carefully repeated the switch, glancing down to make sure the replacement had a blue stopper. However, for two dining companions already on to their second bottle, the conversation was not flowing as quickly as the Ribena.

'I'm serious about this cheering up business,' he said quietly as they commenced their main courses. 'If we don't start lookin' like we're havin' a good time knockin' this stuff back, they're gaunny think we're a pair of alcoholics.'

Shelley took another mouthful and gave him a sarcastic smile. 'All right, *Ian*,' he said acidly. 'I'll tell you a wee story. Would that be more cordial?'

'I think we're well-sorted for cordial, but fire away.'

'Fine. Okay, there's these three boy scouts get lost on a camping trip. They come across this old cottage just as night falls, and a bloke answers the door. He takes them in out of the rain, and is about to serve them some supper when something occurs to him, and he asks them all what religion they are. Two of them say they're Protestants, and the third one says he's a Catholic. At this, the bloke tells the two wee Prods to go into the living room, where they sit in front of a roaring fire eating hot soup and sandwiches. The Catholic, meanwhile, has to sit in the cold hall with just stale bread and water.

'The next morning, when they all wake up, he asks them whether they had any dreams. One of the Prods says he dreamt he was in Heaven. "What was it like?" The host asks. The wee punter says: "It was just like here. All warm and cosy, with nice food and good company." The other wee Prod says he dreamt the same thing.

'Then he asks the Catholic what he dreamt, and he says he dreamt he was in Hell. "What was it like?" the bloke asks. "Well, it was just like here," the wee fella says. "You couldnae get near the fire for Protestants."'

Beadie laughed, an exaggeratedly hearty, shoulder-shaking affair, all the while fixing Shelley with a look that acknowledged and returned the priest's seething contempt.

'That's a stoater, Frank, it really is. But I've got one for you too. What's the difference between acne and a Catholic priest?'

'I don't know,' Shelley replied, smiling through the hatred in his eyes.

'Acne waits until you're in your teens before it comes all over your face.'

They both laughed again, each trying to outdo the other's volume. It occurred to Beadie that it was a good thing they had someone else lined up to kill tonight, and a good thing they were drinking Ribena, otherwise they might end up stabbing each other with their steak-knives. Nonetheless, it had the desired effect, as they traded sectarian jokes well past dessert and into their third bottle.

The photographer arrived shortly before they opened the fourth. Beadie saw him hovering by the door, and told Shelley to get ready with his best pissed-looking smile. The snapper was a freelance covering the Highlands and northern Perthshire, and had been commissioned by a friend of Beadie's on one of the Sundays. The picture would run in the glossy supplement's 'diary' photo-spread, Beadie having told his pal it was to heighten Shelley's profile in a 'more glam, less churchy kind of way – show him out having a good time somewhere classy'. The caption, of course, would put both of them more than a hundred miles away on the night of Sanderson's murder, an article of photographic evidence to add to the dozen witnesses who had seen them drink themselves incapable in the Craggan Moor Hotel restaurant.

They took coffees in the drawing room as the clock ticked towards eleven, Beadie having gone there via his room, to drop off the bag. Donald, the proprietor, popped in briefly to offer them malts on the house, but Beadie politely declined.

'I know it's . . . a bit kinda late to start showin' restraint, Donald,' he slurred. 'But I think we'd better . . . call it a night, you know? The Château Musar was, exce, excellent. All four bottles of it.'

Beadie finished the last of his coffee and yawned, climbing unsteadily to his feet. Shelley followed his lead, making great show of emphasising his full stomach.

'We won't be expecting you gentlemen for breakfast at seven-thirty, then?' said Donald.

'How late do you serve?'

'Until nine-thirty.'

'Hmm. What time do we need to check out? I think that would be more relevant.'

'Midday.'

'Book us both an alarm call for 11:55, then. And not a minute earlier.'

Beadie lay in the dark, letting his eyes grow accustomed, listening out for the sound of Donald locking the storm doors. It was a family-run wee place, so there were no night staff to worry about. Once it was closed for the night, it was closed for the night.

He waited ten minutes after he heard the bolts slam, then knocked on the wall to give Shelley the green light. Sticking the charlie in his pocket, he pulled on his gloves and eased open the window. Shelley appeared there a few seconds later. Beadie handed him the presentation case and climbed out on to the grass.

They took the long way around to the other side of the hotel, avoiding the gravel drive, then cut through some trees and out on to the main road.

The hotel was quarter of a mile outside the village. They walked on the other side of a low hedgerow separating the road from the fields, so that they could stay out of sight if a car passed them. None did. The Vectra was soon in view, still sitting in front of that ancient Volvo.

Shelley opened the driver's door and got behind the wheel. Beadie put his presentation case into the passenger-side footwell and climbed into the seat.

'Go,' he ordered.

Shelley turned the key, put the car in gear and pulled

away, switching on the lights after a hundred yards.

'You know, you drive pretty well, considering how much you drank.'

Shelley laughed. Beadie could tell he'd tried not to, but couldn't help it. Probably the tension.

'Well, I do have to say, Ian. The food was excellent, but the wine was pish.'

'Thirty quid a bottle, as well.'

'Thir— that's a hundred and twenty quid for Ribena?'

'Cheaper than fifty grand, Father, that's the way I'm lookin' at it.'

Beadie's remark killed the levity. They didn't speak again until Pollokshaws.

'What if he's not in?' Shelley asked, the indistinguishable tones of hope and desperation betraying that the thought had only just occurred to him.

Beadie flatly put him straight. 'He will be. He's expecting me. I told him I'd be along tonight and I'd be bringing him eighteen grand.'

'Eighteen? But he's expecting fifty.'

'Basic psychology. If I said I was gaunny front up with the full whack just like that, he'd be a tube not to get suspicious. I've told him it's all I could scrape together at short notice. I also played the hard-bastard negotiator a wee bit, reminded him that any future instalments were contingent upon nobody else discoverin' what this is all about. He's a fuckin' amateur, just a wee wank that doesnae have a clue what he's doin' – an' he knows it. Me takin' him so seriously had him creamin' his troosers. He was all "yes, Mr Beadie, that sounds fine." He'll do anythin' if he thinks he's really gaunny get this money.'

Shelley parked the Vectra fifty yards past Sanderson's close on Dundrennan Road, switching off the lights and the engine. Beadie flipped open his mobile and speed-dialled. Sanderson answered immediately.

'Beadie?'

'Yes.'

'Where the fuck have you been? It's after two.'

'I know what time it is, David. I don't like wandering about Glasgow in broad daylight with a briefcase full of money.'

'Where are you?'

'I'm right outside.' Beadie looked up to the second floor, where he then saw the curtains pulled back, Sanderson's silhouette against the glow of the room. He told Shelley to flash his headlights.

'Who's with you?' Sanderson asked. 'I can see two people.'

'You've been eating your carrots, then. That is Father Francis Shelley, of the Scottish Catholic Church, to whom you should be very polite because he is sponsoring the best part of this little transaction.'

'Okay. Come on up. Only you, though.'

'Not okay. You come down. And bring your car keys.'

'Fuck off. Just bring me up the money and get it over with. You're forgettin' who holds the cards, here.'

'And you're forgettin' that this is a transaction, not a fucking gift. We're buyin' somethin' from you with this money: goodwill, if you like. So you better start showin' some. If we get the impression you're just gaunny fuck us around, then we can get that for free.'

'I'm not fuckin' anyone around. You're the one that's fuckin' me around. Just bring the money up the stairs now.'

'I'm not prepared to be seen walkin' into your place, David. This is all about our wee connection remainin' a secret.'

'Oh, for Christ's sake, who's gaunny see you?'

'I don't know. That's the point. And it's a point you should bear in mind, too. If our relationship goes public, you won't be gettin' any money.'

There was a pause. Beadie's heart was thumping, no doubt Shelley's too, each hoping for opposite outcomes. This part was the weakest link in the chain.

'All right,' he said. 'I'm coming.'

Beadie covered the mouthpiece and sighed. Shelley closed his eyes.

'Bring your car keys.'

'I heard you.'

'Good, so you'll hear this too. Get in your car and follow us.'

'Where are we goin'?'

'Just somewhere we can give you the money and you can check it without any pryin' eyes takin' notice.'

'Right. Okay.'

Beadie disconnected the call. 'He's on his way,' he told Shelley.

Sanderson emerged a couple of minutes later. Shelley waited until they heard his engine start, then pulled away.

'Stay below the limit,' Beadie instructed. 'And amber means stop.'

It started to rain as they wound their way through the streets of the south side, past the Tollbooth roundabout and on to the dual carriageway, heading for Auchenlea. He'd chosen the venue for its proximity to Paisley, where drug-related violence was rife enough to plausibly explain any random killing.

Beadie hadn't told Shelley where they were going, so was giving him directions junction by junction, checking the mirror every few seconds to make sure Sanderson's

Hyundai was still following. It was, faithfully, like any little kid expecting a treat when he reaches his destination.

'He's going to turn back,' Shelley said. 'He must be getting suspicious.'

'You wish. What's he got to be suspicious of? You're a priest, for God's sake. Trust me, even if he is suspicious, he's still no' gaunny turn back until he's sure there's no money, and right now he sincerely wants to believe that there will be. Take this next left.'

Shelley obeyed. It was a single-track leading into a disused quarry. Beadie glanced in the mirror again. The Hyundai's headlights remained at their back all the way.

They reached the wide horseshoe of stone, hewn out of the surrounding braes.

'Okay, stop here.'

The rain was getting heavier, drumming the roof of the car in heavy drops, like the fingers of an impatient ogre. The Hyundai stopped too, then reversed a few yards, keeping some distance.

Beadie lifted the presentation case to his lap and opened the lid. He removed the gun from the foam padding and clicked a magazine into the breach, then took hold of the slide and chambered a round. The red point of the laser-sight danced around the dashboard, hypnotising Shelley's gaze.

Beadie tucked the gun into his belt at the back, under his jacket, then reached for the doorhandle, but Shelley put a restraining hand on his arm.

'Ian, for the love of God, let's not do this. This is insanity.'

He let go of the handle and turned back to face Shelley.

'You're right,' he said. 'Let's not.'

The priest sighed loudly, the relief releasing like steam from a pressure-cooker.

'Let's go to jail instead,' Beadie added. 'And let's add conspiracy to murder to the charge-sheet, because that's what's gaunny happen if we let this fucker go. What conclusion do you think he's gaunny come to if we drag him all the way oot here and then say fuck off, there's nae money? Get a fuckin' grip, Shelley. I'm no' goin' to jail. Did you no' hear what happened to Jack Parlabane in there? Sharpened steel ruler through the guts? No fuckin' way. Let's get this done. Gimme the keys.'

'What keys?'

Beadie leaned over and pulled the car keys from the steering column.

'I'm not havin' you drivin' off or anythin' stupit like that. Now open the boot.'

Shelley pulled the release lever as Beadie climbed out of the car, Sanderson's headlights trained on him in the now pouring rain. He took a few quick, deep breaths as nervousness threatened to flood his insides. His hands were trembling.

'For the love of God, let's not do this.'

He heard Shelley's appeal repeating in his head, and for a moment it offered comfort and shelter, like getting back into the car out of this rain. Then he thought of Parlabane. 'Filleted', was the word that had been used.

Fuck that.

This wasn't murder, it was self-defence.

He pulled open the boot and lifted the briefcase, then quickly trotted across the ten yards or so to where the Hyundai was sitting, engine idling, wipers flapping back and forth. Sanderson was watching him carefully, seatbelt still on. Beadie knocked on the driver's side window.

'Open up,' he said, holding up the case for the occupant to see.

280

Sanderson opened his door and Beadie passed him the case, placing it on his lap with both hands.

He spoke loudly above the sound of the rain.

'Now don't go fuckin' depositin' this lot in your local bank in the mornin', okay? Remember: anythin' that gives me away takes the money with it.'

Beadie reached behind his back with his right hand, easing the gun from his belt.

'I'm not an idiot, Mr Beadie.'

'Good. Are you gaunny check this, then?'

'I trust you.'

'Well, I don't trust you. I'm not payin' you for nothin' – I'm payin' you for peace of mind, so I want to hear you acknowledge that there is eighteen grand in that case. Then you'll get the rest if your mouth stays shut.'

Beadie's thumb released the safety catch as Sanderson's thumbs released the locks. He felt a wave pass through his body, a near-deafening sound of blood rushing in his ears. The wave was like a creeping paralysis. It started in his feet and lower legs, then he could feel it climbing apace with the swinging arc of the opening lid.

Sanderson looked at the pile of folded newspapers inside, then turned to look at Beadie, who had managed to draw the gun before the wave reached his arms. There was the briefest, most fleeting pulse behind Sanderson's eyes, and in it Beadie could see that he understood everything. They stared at each other for one more heartbeat, during which the wave took hold of Beadie's hands, the moment locking the two men together in suspended animation.

Sanderson, suddenly reanimated, breathed in sharply, then in one movement, stuck the car into gear and hit the accelerator. The motion also reanimated the wave, finally causing it to pass.

Beadie pulled the trigger as the car lurched forward. The shot blew Sanderson's head in half and continued through the windscreen, its sound swallowed by the rain, the engine and the darkness. The car rolled on, door open, listing to the right and missing the Vectra by a couple of yards, before the knee-high weeds sapped its momentum and brought it to a halt. Beadie stood still and stared at it for a few seconds, as though afraid it would rear up into movement again, like some wounded but savage beast.

He looked at the Vectra, Shelley's silhouette within. The quarry walls rose up around him, giving the sensation that the earth was swallowing him down. It felt as if the last minute had taken place somewhere else, in some dark dimension that only contained himself, the ground and the Hyundai. Now a world was being built up around it, like theatrical scenery, a world he was going to have to live the rest of his life in.

There was rain running down his neck. An impulse told him he had to get inside where it was dry, and from that impulse, logic once again began to flow. He pushed the wet hair back from his face and took some more quick, deep breaths.

'Right,' he said, his voice breaking, his mouth dry.

He put the safety catch back on the gun, then started out towards the Hyundai, reaching into his pocket for the cocaine as he did so. The first thing he could see was the windscreen, black with blood and other matter. Moving closer, he saw Sanderson slumped over to his left by the impact of the shot, his body twisted around like he was turning to kiss a girlfriend in the passenger seat. Beadie was grateful to be spared the sight of his face, whatever might be left of it. The case was still open, trapped at

282

an awkward angle between Sanderson's knees and his dangling right arm.

Beadie stuck the gun back in his belt, needing two hands to get the strip-sealed plastic bag open. His fingers were shaking, his skintight leather gloves wet outside and in. In the end, he had to take his gloves off with his teeth and hold them between his knees while his bare fingers finally got the bag open. He pulled the gloves back on and proceeded to sprinkle some cocaine inside the case, then opened the boot and spilled a little on the grey felt inside.

He closed the boot with a thump and walked back to the hire-car. When he tried the handle, it was locked. Looking inside, he could see Shelley staring back out, tears on his cheeks, head shaking. Beadie rolled his eyes. The idiot had forgotten he had the keys, either that or it was just a pointless but symbolic gesture, something his lot were famously fond of. He unlocked the door and climbed in, tossing the keys to the priest as he did so.

'Drive,' he said.

'God forgive you,' Shelley spluttered.

'He might, but I *know* the polis won't, so get a fuckin' shift on. *MOVE.*'

Beadie sat with his face in his hands, concentrating on breathing, concentrating on not throwing up. His head was swimming. There wasn't enough oxygen. The gunshot kept repeating, a muffled clap in the rain. He saw Sanderson's head split in half, the image multiplied as though bounced eternally between two mirrors. He saw the car roll away, the door flapping, the windscreen awash, then back to the muzzle flash like a tape-loop.

He'd played a version of it in his head over the past two days, preparing himself for the moment; as though anything could have prepared him for the moment. In that version, everything was ordered, neat, calculated, controlled. He walked up to the car. The weather was dry, the night clear, a bomber's moon illuminating the quarry like floodlights. Sanderson unlocked the door. He handed him the case. Sanderson opened it. He shot him in the temple. The shell-case tinkled on the dry stone at his feet. Sanderson died. Blood oozed from the neat, circular drill-hole while Beadie sprinkled coke in the case. Then he bent down, picked up the spent shell and walked away.

'Oh fuck.'

The spent shell. He'd forgotten to lift it; Christ, even if he'd remembered, he might still be there looking for the bloody thing, amid the rain and puddles and rocks.

Calm down, he told himself. No matter how careful you were, no matter how meticulous in your planning, there was no way you could pull off something like this without making a mistake; he'd known that all along. And the time you were most likely to screw up was directly around the deed itself: calculation and preparation went out the window at a moment like that, and it all came down to reflex and instinct. There were worse things that could have gone wrong. A discarded shell-case was not a disaster. If he'd had to pick one fuck-up beforehand and live with it, he'd have settled for that. Might even add to the plausibility: the Paisley neds probably weren't professional enough to remove such evidence.

After all, nobody knew about the gun.

'Just don't go registering it, whatever you do,' Virgil had said, back in the days when at least owning the thing would still have been legal.

'Why not?'

'Because there can't be more than about five of these

things in this whole piss-ant country. You shoot somebody with it, and there'd be a real short list of suspects.'

Beadie lifted his head and looked out of the car's windows. The streets were empty but for minicabs ferrying drunk people home. Everything looked normal. Everything looked the same as it had half an hour ago, except wetter. They were at Cowglen, waiting for the lights to change before they joined the M77, which would take them in turn to the M8, M9, A9 and ultimately Craggan. It was going to be fine. They were going to get clean away.

Then he noticed a flash of blue in the wing-mirror, and turned around to see a police car approaching from the Pollok roundabout.

'Oh Christ.'

He and Shelley looked at each other. The lights were still red.

Beadie felt a lurching sensation, an angry voice asking how the fuck he could have been so stupid as to think he'd get away with this.

The police car came right up behind them and gave its siren a quick blast. Both of them turned around. The cop at the wheel gestured angrily to them to pull into the side.

'You utter, utter, idiot,' Shelley hissed, giving him a full blast of that told-you-so look that priests were presumably required to master at seminary.

Beadie felt the wave return, faster this time, stiffening him where he sat. Shelley indicated and pulled the car slowly over to the white-chevroned verge at the edge of the slip road.

The police car immediately spun off through the gap they had opened, heading at full-tilt on to the motorway, blue lights still twinkling away on top.

The pair of them looked at each other again and let out

enormous sighs. Shelley's contempt, however, remained undissipated.

The feeling of relief did not last. In that moment, in fact, Beadie had been given a sickeningly vivid glimpse of what getting caught would feel like, rendering the possibility real to the point of inevitable. He saw the shell-case being lifted on the end of a pencil by a forensic scientist, bagged in cellophane, analysed. He heard the police driver rhyme off the hire-car's registration and the time they had passed it, within three miles of the murder scene. He saw a fire alarm going off at the Craggan Moor Hotel, all the guests outside in their dressing gowns, Donald and the other resident staff carrying out a head-count and finding that two of their guests were missing.

The miles passed beneath the car: Stirling, Dunblane, Gleneagles, Perth. The landscape changed, the rain cleared, and the incident at the quarry could have been another night, another country, but still he expected the blue lights to flash behind them at any moment. He saw malfunctioning speed cameras photographing the car, stating time and date, the registration plate reading GU1 LTY. He heard all-points bulletins on police radio, tracing their movements the whole way north.

'I need to pee,' Shelley announced.

'What?'

'I need to pee. It's all that Ribena. I'm bursting.'

'Oh come on, we're nearly to Pitlochry. You can hold on for another half an hour.'

'I bloody can't. My back teeth have been floatin' since Cumbernauld. It's been about five hours, for goodness sake.'

'I don't care. You are not stopping this car. What if the polis pass by and decide to pull over and ask if we need any assistance? First thing they'll do is radio in our registration – before they even get out their car.'

'Oh give us a break. We've hardly seen a car since Perth, never mind the polis. I have *got* to stop.'

Shelley indicated and began slowing down as they approached a lay-by.

'No,' Beadie insisted. 'Look, there's a fucking truck in it, for Christ's sake.'

Shelley grunted angrily and cancelled the indicator.

'I'm stopping in Pitlochry then. I've got to find a loo.'

'Are you mad? Why not just pull up to a garage and engage the fuckin' attendant in conversation while you're at it?'

'Listen, I'm gaunny piss in my troosers in about thirty seconds. I *need* to stop.'

'Christ,' Beadie muttered, before it occurred to him that he needed to go too. His mind had been too crowded with other voices to hear his bladder telling him it was bursting. 'Hang on,' he said. 'Can you make it another five minutes?'

'It'll be close.'

'There's a picnic spot just after Pitlochry, near Killiecrankie. It's off the road, secluded. There's toilets there.'

Shelley put his foot down and accelerated to eighty.

'Keep the speed doon, for fuck's sake.'

'Oh, gimme a break here.'

'Do you want to go to jail for the sake of thirty seconds?'

'I don't know – I could pee there, at least.'

Beadie directed him to the picnic area. It was off a minor road almost parallel to where the A9 ran fifty feet above, over the bridge that took it across Loch Faskally. The headlights picked out trestle tables and parking spaces in a clearing surrounded by tall pines, the toilets housed in a low timber hut. Shelley drove the car right up to the hut and braked sharply before leaping out. Beadie got out too and walked around to the ladies' side, but it was locked, the words 'Out of order' and yesterday's date chalked on the door. He shrugged, unzipped and peed against a nearby tree, then returned to the car and leaned on the bonnet, glad of the air. Shelley hadn't been kidding about his greater need. It sounded like he was filling a swimming pool.

The splashing had finally begun to tail off when Beadie saw headlights flickering through the trees.

'Oh no no no no no no no no no.'

Keep going, pal, keep going. The guy was just passing, heading along the wee B road, had to be.

The lights swung around until they were pointing directly at him, the car making its way into the picnic spot at an ambling pace.

'Oh fuck.'

It slowed further as it approached, then pulled into a space alongside the Vectra, which was when Beadie noticed that it was a Vectra too.

The driver got out. He looked early forties, business suit, no tie. Sales rep *en route*, probably. Beadie tried to keep the eye contact brief without avoiding it completely, which he thought would seem more suspicious.

Please don't talk. Please don't talk. Please don't talk.

'Rush hour, eh?' the rep said brightly. 'This the queue?'

'Fraid so,' Beadie replied, hoping Shelley got the fuck out of there forthwith.

'I see you're saddled with the same heap of shit as me. Fucking Vauxhalls, eh? Is there some rule about company cars having to be crap? They've a nerve calling it a taxable benefit, if you ask me.'

288

Beadie tried to give a small chuckle by way of polite reply, but only managed to make himself sound nervous. 'Aye,' he added.

Christ. The guy had noticed the car. Make and model. Christ. Christ. Christ. And when Shelley came out he'd have seen both occupants.

The toilet door opened and Shelley stepped into view.

'On you go, mate,' Beadie said. 'I was just waitin' for him.'

'Oh, cheers.'

The man walked towards the toilet as Shelley emerged, then stopped in the priest's path. 'Excuse me, don't I know you?'

Beadie felt the lurch again, same as when the police car had come up behind them. You have got to be fucking kidding, he said to himself.

'I don't think so,' Shelley replied.

Keep your head down, Beadie was thinking, but Shelley was like a deer in the headlights, looking the bloke straight in the face.

'You look familiar. I'm Tom Heron. Manning Tools. That doesn't ring any?'

Shelley shook his head.

Get away from there, Beadie thought.

'I'm sure I know your face. What's your name?'

John Smith. John Smith. John Smith.

'Ehh, Father . . .ing. John . . . Fathering.'

'What's your line?'

Jesus fucking Christ.

'Eh, office . . . supplies.'

'Oh, who are you with?'

Make it up. Make it up. Don't go with a name you know.

'Eh, Canon.'

Fuck.

'Do you cover Edinburgh? Maybe I've seen you at our head office. I definitely know your face.'

The lurching was getting worse and worse, his stomach feeling like his ma's old twin-tub. He could hear the guy giving his statement, the descriptions, the vehicle, the location. He could hear the detective explain to his partner how you could easily get from Craggan to Glasgow and back in five hours, with time for a toilet stop at Killiecrankie.

'Eh, yes,' Shelley stumbled. 'That's maybe it.'

'Well, maybe see you there again. Here's my card, by the way. Have you got one?'

'Eh, no. Not on me.'

'I've got one,' Beadie said, opening the car door and beckoning Heron to come over. He leaned in and picked up the Sternmeyer. This time there was no wave, no rushing sound, just the knowledge of what he had to do.

Beadie turned around just as the rep reached him, put the gun to the middle of his forehead and pulled the trigger. The man fell straight backwards like a felled tree.

Shelley stood, mouth open, staring incredulously at what he'd seen.

'Holy Mary, mother of God. What the hell did you do that for?'

'What the hell did I do that for? Did you not fuckin' hear him? He knew your face.'

'Well, so what? He couldn't place me. He'd have forgotten it by the time he finished his pish.'

'Your face is in the papers every week these days. It might just be a one-column headshot, but it's there, and it'll be there again. He was drivin' the same model of car, as well. He'd remember bloody plenty if the polis asked.'

290

'What were they gaunny ask, ya numpty? When there's a murder in Paisley, they don't go on *Crimewatch* and ask if anybody saw anythin' suspicious in bloomin' Killiecrankie.'

'We cannae afford any risks.'

'And what the hell do you call this?'

'Coverin' our tracks.'

'Coverin' our tracks? Oh, absolute crime genius you are, Beadie. So could you maybe explain how killin' a second person with the same weapon on the same night helps divert attention from our activities in Auchenlea?'

Shelley's words were a kick in the stomach that made the twin-tub sensation feel like minor indigestion.

'There can't be more than about five of these things in this whole piss-ant country.'

He had just drawn a line from that quarry to this picnic site. Instead of looking for Paisley neds, they'd be opening up a country-wide murder hunt. They'd be examining all the tapes from motorway cameras, knowing where to look and when, because they'd know the two times of death and deduce roughly when the killer would have been in transit between. The two police officers at Cowglen would remember they saw two men in a Vectra around the time of the first murder. The tapes would get them the registration. The registration would get them Europcar, and Europcar would give them the name of Francis Shelley.

'We are jiggered,' Shelley said. 'Jiggered beyond salvation. Oh no wait, though, I'm forgettin'. We've got mister PR guru here. Maybe you could just sort it all out by puttin' a positive spin on the whole thing.'

Beadie eyed the body, lying flat on the ground, blood pulsing from the crevice in its forehead. He thought of Sanderson down the road, his brains all over the windscreen.

291

'Actually,' he said, 'maybe I could.'

He had drawn a line from one victim to another, so it followed that what he must do was erase it again.

'Could you maybe explain how killin' a second person with the same weapon on the same night helps divert attention from our activities in Auchenlea?'

No, but a very different kind of murder certainly would.

'What?' Shelley asked.

'He said he worked for Manning Tools, didn't he?'

'Aye.'

'Right. Leave this to me. I want you to find the shell I just fired. We can*not* afford to leave here without it.'

'What are you gaunny do?'

'A bit of PR.'

Beadie got his gloves out of the Vectra and put them on, then knelt over the body, looking for the car keys. In the inside jacket pocket he found a wallet and a packet of three. Typical dirty bastard rep, looking to get his end away while he was far from the wife and weans. However, it did give him an extra idea.

The keys were in his trousers. Beadie opened the other Vectra's boot. It contained a canvas holdall full of toiletries and dirty underwear, and next to it, a demonstration selection of Manning Tools' finest hardware – including, he was pleased to see, a hacksaw.

'What are you planning to do with that?' Shelley asked.

'Relegate a drug-related shooting to "other news".'

'Oh Jesus, Mary and Joseph.'

'Shut up. Have you got that shell yet?'

Shelley held it up.

'Good.' Beadie tossed him the packet of three. 'Get this guy's jukes off and put one of those on his dick.'

'*What?*'

'You heard. One on his dick, then one on your finger to stick another one up his arse.'

'Get lost. I'm not touchin' him.'

'Well would you rather swap for the task of sawin' his heid aff?'

'You're surely not gaunny . . .'

'Yes, I fuckin' am. Headless corpse in gay horror murder. The papers'll think it's Christmas, an' the polis'll be lookin' for some lone pervert. Come on. It'll be by with quicker if we share the work.'

Shelley looked to the heavens. 'It's at times like this I wish I was an atheist.'

Shelley checked carefully for any traffic before rejoining the dual carriageway. There were no headlights to be seen, no engines to be heard. He sped away quickly, he and Beadie both checking the rear-view as they approached the bridge. There was nothing at the back, but a car was coming from the opposite direction. Beadie told him to slow, so that it would be past by the time they reached the centre. Shelley made sure the other car was out of sight, then stopped. Beadie jumped out and lobbed the holdall over the side, taking Mr Heron's underwear, Mr Heron's tools, and Mr Heron's head to the bottom of the loch.

They made it to Craggan less than half an hour later, parking the car in the same spot in front of the old Volvo, then walked briskly back to the hotel, dawn beginning to break in the skies above. Beadie checked his watch. It was ten past seven.

They tiptoed past the kitchen, from where they could hear the clink of crockery and the voices of the staff getting breakfast ready. It drowned the sounds of their footfalls on

293

the gravel and the rattle of their windows sliding open. This was the finish line, and they'd crossed it just in time.

Beadie shut his window with a thump, then went straight to the bathroom, where he was noisily and voluminously sick.

It was purple.

going straight

Parlabane adjusted the pillows one more time, still searching for that optimum configuration of all four that would
afford unparalleled comfort as he made his way through a
pile of Sunday papers. Comfort, Ross Quinn had stressed
to the screws at the prison infirmary, was vital to his
recovery; so much so that they should not even consider
returning him to the general population for anything less
than a month.

Sometimes somebody else's guilty conscience could be a
bounteous provider.

Not that Parlabane would be seeing out the month Quinn
had prescribed, however. His lawyer, Nicole Carrow, had
secured an interim release while a suit was prepared against
the Scottish Office, seeking full remission (for starters) over
the matter of a bent warder being complicit in Parlabane's
skewering.

He'd been there for a fortnight now, though for the first
week or so, comfort had been more a matter of pharmaceutical – rather than pillow – combinations. Quinn had
removed part of his colon; or, more accurately, Fooaltiye
had removed it, and Quinn had merely tidied up afterwards. The tidying up part had been fairly crucial, right
enough, seeing as the seepage of bowel content all round
your internal organs made you just the slightest bit inclined
to potentially fatal infection. For that reason, Quinn had
ended up reopening the incision when he was almost on his

last suture, because, as he explained to the anaesthetist, he was sure he could still smell faecal matter and had to check that he hadn't missed another leak. Sarah had later learned that this was actually due to the anaesthetist having farted and been too embarrassed to own up at the time. Still, best to be sure.

The end result was satisfactory, though Parlabane had subsequently been forced to endure a string of remarks about 'not being quite so full of shit anymore'. Ha ha fucking ha. At least he was alive to endure them, had been his philosophy.

The papers were still fixated by the headless punter at Killiecrankie, with the phrase 'gay serial killer' littering the columns, despite the fact that even the shortest serials had to comprise more than one episode. Sounded like gleeful optimism on the part of the hacks, a few of whom even seemed to have their hearts set on being next. Three red-tops (so far) had come up with the 'exclusive' ploy of hanging around secluded highland public conveniences all night, in the hope of running into the headhunter, or at least some would-be cottager they could accuse. Parlabane wondered whether it had struck the daft bastards what might actually happen if they did meet the man concerned. He couldn't see a dictaphone and a Nikon being much cop in fending off a chainsaw or whatever else the bugger was wielding.

One paper had managed to get exclusive access to the poor widow, who'd no doubt gone through the familiar process of telling them all to fuck off, then ultimately growing so siege-weary that she signed a deal with one lot because they'd at least protect her from the rest. 'I knew nothing of headless husband's secret double-life – by widow of gay murder victim'.

The rest of the tabloids were all concentrating their collective braincell on investigating what one headline intriguingly described as the 'seedy gay underworld of rural roadside honeypots'. This, rather disappointingly, turned out not to feature any sado-masochistic fetishes involving burly men in beekeeping outfits with strategic holes cut in the crotch. Instead it amounted to little more than a collection of photographs of toilet-wall graffiti, illustrating how these 'roadside prowlers' advertised their desires and availability. 'I give handjob's – here every Tues, 10-ish – Travelling Man'. 'I'll suck you – you suck me. Discretion assured – I'm married too! Here most Mons 9-11. Password Sammy.'

The cumulative effect was bound to be a lot of crossed legs on long journeys in the coming weeks, as drivers opted to hold it in rather than risk being propositioned, murdered or arrested if they stopped for a quick single-fish.

Crimewatch UK would be interesting that month, anyway. 'Did *you* see anything? Were you perhaps cottaging in the area that night, and might have noticed something suspicious?' He couldn't picture the public queuing up to help out on this one. Still, he thought, flicking through the pages of another rag, at least the profile of the case might help get a result, unlike the poor bastard who got his brains blown out in Auchenlea the same night. Another squalid drug-war shooting – yawn, who gives a fuck. It had spawned a couple of why-oh-why analysis pieces in the serious papers, about Paisley's on-going drugs-and-guns problem, but in the bigger picture it was dog bites man. Murder wasn't front-page news anymore unless it gave someone a hard-on.

In an otherwise slow week for sex scandals, the Killiecrankie thing must have seemed like manna from heaven to the news desks. Sex, murder and decapitation – could anything beat that? Yes. *Gay* sex, murder and decapitation. Parlabane wondered whether the still-baffled cops might consider a theory he had: that it was actually the work of a desperate news editor. He could give them a list of names, if they wanted to check it out.

Hmm. Maybe not. Upsetting high-echelon hacks was no longer in his affordable luxuries column, as he didn't know who he might end up begging in front of once he got out of here. He could tell himself he would once again be freelance, but it was more realistic to say he would be unemployed. Not only had he been very curtly given his jotters from *The Saltire* – where he had taken a full-time contract as part of his undercover research into the behaviour of normal, responsible adults – but apart from a few Rangers fanzines, there wouldn't be many publications keen on accepting contributions from a man who'd served time for burgling the offices of the Glasgow Catholic archdiocese. He might be sneering at the tabloids today, but in a few months he could be wishing he was the one staking out rural cludgies, because at least it was for a paycheck.

He picked up one of the glossy supplements and had just opened it at the dismal diary spread – minor tartan celebs and would-be movers and shakers on nights out, pretending they weren't utterly fucking delighted to see a photographer – when he heard a noise from the corridor. He closed it with a slap and dropped it on to the pile; he'd suffered enough indignities recently without being caught reading that shite.

He could hear several feet clumping along the polished tiles (buffed without love by the infirmary passman; you always save your best for the cell), and looked up to see a party of three come through the door: a prisoner and two screws. The screws he didn't recognise, but there was no mistaking the con. It was the Right Dishonourable Peter Logan, ex MP, ex MSP, and now probably regretting that prayer in which he asked God that he be remembered for something *other* than getting a vibrator stuck up his bum.

McGinlay, the screw on infirmary duty, walked up to the new arrivals, precipitating a brief discussion, intentionally too quiet for any of the inmates to hear. McGinlay nodded towards Parlabane, at which both of the visiting warders surveyed the room's four beds, then grabbed themselves seats near the door.

McGinlay and Logan walked across to Parlabane's bed.

'Ya fuckin' pervert,' shouted the previously catatonic con in the bed opposite. 'Fuckin' filthy cunt.'

'Oh, we're feeling better are we?' McGinlay said, spinning on one heel. 'Back to O Hall for you then, Kavanagh, eh?' Whereupon Kavanagh broke into a hopelessly unconvincing fit of coughing. McGinlay turned back around to Parlabane.

'Right, Parlabane. Visitor for you. Logan, 47251. You've got ten minutes.'

McGinlay walked away as Logan pulled over a chair and sat down.

'This must be part of the convalescence treatment,' Parlabane said. 'The Scottish Prison Service have managed to get hold of somebody even less popular than me, just to make me feel better. In't that nice.'

'Yeah, very witty, Mr Parlabane. Would you like to make a vibrator gag as well, while you're at it, just to save time later?'

'No thanks. The insertion of foreign objects into the

human body isn't something I find very amusing these days.'

'I can well imagine. So can the SPS. That's why I've got the permanent escort, and not just when I'm outside my own hall. It wouldn't look good on them if something happened to me, and my situation makes me a fucking stab-magnet.'

'Your situation? Do you mean being a public figure or being a sex-offender?'

'Both, Mr Parlabane, and thank you for your delicacy.'

'Oh, I'm sorry. Is there maybe a cosier New Labour term for it that I should have used?'

'Well, yes, there is, as a matter of fact. How about "innocent"? How about "stitched-up"?'

Parlabane laughed. 'Stop it. The surgeon said it could burst my sutures.'

'I'm not here to amuse you, Parlabane. I'm serious. The only naked children I've ever seen pictures of were my niece and nephew when they were about two months old. This whole thing was a set-up.'

'A set-up?' Parlabane responded, feigning astonishment. He'd have sat up straighter, but it would have meant reconstruction work on the pillows afterwards. 'You're telling me you were framed?'

'That's exactly what I'm telling you. A fucking child-porn ring with me and Charles Letham and Murdo McDonald? I've barely even spoken to either of them, even at Westminster. Of course I was framed.'

'Well boo fucking hoo for you. What a dreadful injustice. I wish you all the best with your campaign. Maybe they'll make a film aboot you all one day: In the Name of the Wankers.'

'Listen. The four of us were convicted principally on the

strength of one poxy piece of evidence, a server log – log being the right word, because it was a piece of shit.'

'You mean the log that rather inconveniently recorded all your internet activities.'

'I don't know what the fuck it recorded, but it didn't record me accessing those news groups. It was a piece of paper, for Christ's sake, nothing more. But just because it was computer-generated, everybody goes "woo, can't argue with that". Who's to say the computer that generated it wasn't tampered with?'

'Well, as far as I remember, Scotia OnLine seemed pretty strong on that point, and it *was* their server.'

'For God's sake, listen, I—'

'No, you fuckin' listen, Logan. I've no' been in here long, but I've been in long enough, and if there's one thing I've learned, it's that no bugger in this entire place is guilty. *Everybody* was framed, all right? Especially if they can find some gullible sucker to listen to their sob story. After a while they even start believin' it themselves. Well I'm not that sucker, an' I wasnae framed. I did it, all right? I'm dealin' with it, an' I suggest you try the same.'

'You didn't suggest Tam McInnes should try the same when nobody believed him.'

'That's ancient history. I don't *do* conspiracies anymore.'

'Maybe if I sent you a cryptic message encoded in an old song lyric, would that intrigue you further?'

Now Parlabane did sit up straight, blood pressure shooting skywards also.

'Look, do I fuckin' owe you somethin' pal? I don't think so. So don't give me any shite about what you *think* happened in the past. A friend of mine was murdered over that business, remember?'

'I'm sorry. You're right, you owe me nothing. But I'd say

you owe it to yourself to at least look into this, because whatever's behind it must be one hell of a story.'

Parlabane laughed again, bitterly this time. 'Jesus. You know, I'm tryin' to work out here just how fuckin' desperate you must be, eh? I mean, this really has to be the last throw of the fuckin' dice. Your spin doctors couldnae save you, your lawyers couldnae clear you, so you're doon to this washed-up, disgraced and discredited hack you wouldnae have given the steam aff your shite three months ago, hopin' he's gaunny be the rough diamond that turns oot to be your salvation. Does that mean I'll be in the film?'

Logan sighed, but it was stoical. He wasn't for giving up. Denial died hard, especially in politicians.

'I came to you because you're getting out of here tomorrow, on this interim release ticket.'

'Aye. Also known as "Please don't sue the SPS over the bent screw that helped set you up for a stabbing".'

Logan leaned forward. 'All I'm asking is that you listen to what I've got to say.'

'I told you. I don't do conspiracies anymore.'

'You know, for a journalist, you don't pay much attention to what's going on in the papers.'

'What, are you gaunny tell me the gay headhunter set you up? Or maybe the victim had unwittingly uncovered the truth and was bumped off to keep him silent? No, wait, I've got it: they made it look like a sex-killing to disguise the true motive for the murder.'

Logan sat back again and folded his arms. 'When you're finished being hilarious, you might want to read up a bit on the other bloke who died that night. The shooting victim near Paisley.'

'What about him?'

'What did he do for a living?'

302

'I didnae notice. I think it was what he did in his spare time that was most pertinent, in the end.'

'You reckon? Well, heads up, pal. His name was David Sanderson, and he was a senior software engineer for Scotia OnLine. Now tell me you don't do conspiracies anymore.'

Fucking politicians. Most of them were just self-importance in a suit, dreary personality-deficits happily trading their pittance of individuality for the reflected glory of being servile parts of a greater whole. You could ignore them like you'd ignore the bloke you found yourself next to at a dinner party once he told you he was a Hearts fan and predictably started whining about how St Mirren sold Celtic the title in '86. But some of them – the most success-ful ones, logically – had an infuriating talent for getting you interested despite yourself. Logan's supposed char-isma had always at best left Parlabane cold; his Blairesque 'Hey, I'm one of the guys' seemed laughable when it wasn't making you want to smack him in the teeth. How-ever, the bastard still knew how to get your attention, and there was no question that he had a flair for the dramatic.

No matter what else ought to be on his mind that day – getting out the next morning, for instance – Logan's little piece of showmanship had refused to fade out. Despite a scepticism bordering on complete antipathy, he could sense the seed of the idea taking hold, deep in that part of the brain he'd sealed off as condemned and dangerous. There was no mistaking it, the buzz was back: the possibility that trusted faces were merely masks, respected edifices were but façades, and behind all of it, someone was being a very naughty little boy.

No. Get thee behind me, Logan.

This time, it didn't add up. If he was going to enter-
tain outlandish theories, he might as well hypothesise
that Logan and his kiddie-porn chums had been behind
this Sanderson bloke's murder, as it would lend credence
to their claims of innocence. All they'd need was some
credulous crusader to take the bait. Someone like himself,
for instance.

The problem with Logan's own theory was that there
was no suspect and no motive. The Moundgate scandal
had been the proverbial jobbie sandwich for the whole of
Scottish politics, with everybody at the table being forced
to take a bite. Nobody benefited from it. Logan, Gilford,
Letham and McDonald: two Labour, one Lib Dem and a
Nat. It had been a parliament-wide catastrophe, so there
could be no partisan plot behind the scenes. All right, there
wasn't a Tory among the four, but they hadn't attempted
to score any party-political points from the affair, and they
were so thin on the ground as to be an irrelevance. It was
impossible to imagine them having the initiative to come
up with something like this anyway. Since the wipe-out
in '97, their status in Scottish politics had been like that
of the Vichy regime after World War Two. They'd been
the minority collaborators with the occupying force, and
post-liberation they had learned the wisdom of keeping
their heads down and their mouths shut. Their campaign
for the Scottish elections in '99 had been accented so much
on apology that their official poster slogan was the hardly
ebullient 'You talked. We listened'. Or, 'We're shite and we
know we are' as Parlabane translated it.

It was difficult to see how the scandal had served any
scheming enterprise on the government benches either. The
resulting atmosphere of mistrust and neo-puritanism had
made the public suspicious of politicians in general, and

304

anyone who appeared too thrusting in their ambitions was nominating themselves to be next for the tabloid bin-raking and telephoto-lens treatment. The one person who enjoyed preferment as a result – Elspeth Doyle – had it suddenly foisted upon her, and the woman consequently seemed far from comfortable in the limelight, thus vividly explaining why she'd never been placed centre stage before.

The only winners out of the whole ugly mess had been the media and the Churches, the onlookers and commentators up there in the grandstand. Down on the field of play, nobody had scored.

But still, but still, but still . . .

'Police in Paisley have launched a murder inquiry after the body of a man was found in his car in a quarry outside Auchenlea. The man had been shot once in the head in what detectives described as an "execution-style" killing.'

'Heads up, pal. His name was David Sanderson. He was a senior software engineer with Scotia OnLine.'

Just when I think I got out, they drag me back in.

There was no-one waiting for Parlabane when he was released. It wasn't like he was expecting Ellwood Blues to show up in a decommissioned police cruiser, but there was a strangeness about simply walking out of the gates and on to a street where cars and buses were passing, where the world was obliviously getting on with itself. He'd been inside less than two months – hardly a lifetime – but his existence had been so tightly contained that it had been long enough to get used to the idea of the outside being a faraway place. The journey to get back there should, he felt, have been longer. Instead, it was like walking out of the cinema on a bright afternoon, blinking and readjusting to the everyday reality.

He saw a taxi moving towards him, orange sign beckoningly lit. He beckoned back. The driver eyed him sternly with a look that said, 'Aye, that'll be right', and continued along the road. It was an early reminder of his new status: ex-con. Criminal. Not to be trusted.

Still, he thought, heading for the nearest bus stop, he could hardly complain. He *was* a criminal. A career criminal, in fact. He'd broken into more places than he could remember, and just because he stole information rather than goods didn't change the fact that it was theft. Sure, there was always the excuse that it was the only way to uncover an unpleasant truth, but housebreakers probably had their self-justifications too. It's insured. I need the money more than them. They've got it a sight easier than me, they can stand me a fucking video that's probably rented anyway.

And this great search for truth, this endless crusade to unmask the evil villains – what was that *really* all about? Was the world just lucky to have such a selfless champion, toiling bravely for no greater reward than the knowledge that justice was done? Or was there, perhaps, some other motivation in it for him? Hmm, could be on to something there.

Self-aggrandisement? Self-righteousness? The plaudits of being the man who broke the story? Well, maybe, but there were easier ways to get all of those things, none of them requiring one to creep around in the dark, dressed like a particularly depressive beatnik.

He got a thrill from trespassing; that was definitely part of it. The hair-prickling buzz of being where you weren't supposed to, of finding out what others wanted kept from you. It was the sin of Adam and the crime of Prometheus, though he was fucking kidding himself if he thought he was as innocent as the former or as beneficent as the latter.

His motives were not pure, nor even merely selfish. They were malicious, envious and borne of insecurity.

He was the mediocrity who wanted to humble the mighty. He was the outsider who could only define himself by that from which he was excluded. And if he needed any more evidence, he only had to look back to the first place he'd ever broken into, and the events preceding it: the secondary school English department, after he'd been knocked back for a dance at a teenage disco. It was about making himself feel better than the things – or the people – to which he could not belong; finding secret places he could pretend he was retreating to, when really he was just disguising his loneliness.

Marriage to Sarah had been the first thing he was truly a part of, and the fact that he had happily abandoned his past ways was less down to his promise to her, than to no longer feeling such a need. It was only when something came between them – when he was once again excluded – that he returned to this glorified thumb-sucking.

Never again.

He made it back to the flat just before ten. There'd been no-one waiting for him at the prison gates, and nor was there anyone to welcome him home. Sarah's relentlessly spiteful rota kept her absent from all the significant dates on the calendar – birthdays, wedding anniversaries, Christmas – so it had been no surprise when Parlabane learned that she would be at work all day and on call all night to mark this particular milestone. He wondered whether the SPS had informed whoever made up the rota of his accelerated release date, before they informed him.

Parlabane made himself his first decent cup of coffee for six weeks, and drank it while checking his email and filling a long-fantasised warm bath. Sarah had been opening his letters and sending them to him inside, so there was no post backlog to catch up on, but his email server had been constipated with more than two hundred messages.

He scrolled down, opening the tiny few that were from recognised sources, then had a quick scan of the rest. Most of them were flames from aggrieved Catholics castigating him for attacking their religion. The reason for the volume was that one of them had appended him to a group mailing list so that he would receive every comment she and her cyber-Tim buddies exchanged on the matter.

There were also a few goodwill messages, but as they were all from subscribers to a Rangers newsgroup, they weren't congratulating him on his contribution to the secularisation of Scottish politics.

He set up a filter to auto-delete future mail from the same sources, then binned the lot, with the exception of one of the goodwill greetings, which he held on to as evidence of an unlikely anthropological phenomenon: lower primates operating electronic communications technology. The next step for Rangers fans might even be self-awareness, and what an exciting day that would be for those around to see it in 3001.

The bath was bliss. It cleared his mind while cleansing his body, so that he could emerge, naked and reborn, ready to face the challenges of the day as though the past few months had all been last night's bad dream. Unfortunately, the first challenge was the brick wall of not actually having anything to do.

Faced with the alternative of looking out and revising his CV (to which he could now append a criminal record, bound to dazzle any prospective employer), he rationalised that, despite his scepticism and well-intentioned misgivings about getting sucked in or just suckered, it couldn't hurt to make a quick phone call.

'Scoop! You're out. And all in one piece, I hear.'

'Just about, Jenny. Are you still allowed to consort with scum like me?'

'Don't you watch the telly, Jack? Coppers go drinking with villains all the time. It's how we get our best info. I take it you're dying for a pint after all that enforced temperance, and your good lady wife's ministering to the infirm?'

'The thought hadn't crossed my mind, but seeing you mentioned it.'

'I'll be in the Cask at about seven. Your round. Call it part of your debt to society.'

'I pawned half my colon to pay that debt. Me and society are square. But I will buy you a few in return for a favour.'

'Now how did I know that was coming? You're not even out of jail a full morning and you're tappin' me already. Oh well, at least I don't have to worry about prison changin' you. What do you want?'

'That shooting in Auchenlea on Wednesday night.'

'Where?'

'Auchenlea, ya east-coast ignoramus. Near Paisley.'

'Oh, the one in the quarry? Hemi-headectomy, no anaesthetic?'

'Aye.'

'What about it?'

'I just need the lowdown.'

'I can get you the name of the detective—'

'I don't think he'd be very forthcoming to *me*, even if I hadnae just got out of jail.'

'Got you. And you're not after the press-kit version, I take it. What's the angle?'

'Too crazy to admit, Jen. Let's just say I'm tryin' to rule somethin' out for peace of mind.'

'Fair enough. The less I know, the better, from my experience with you. I'll ring you back in an hour, okay?'

'I don't deserve you.'

'Probably not, Scoop. And I'm damn sure I don't deserve you.'

The phone rang after forty-five minutes. It was someone trying to sell him a conservatory. Nice as it might look sticking out a couple of flights up over East London Street, he told the guy to fuck off. Jenny called back ten minutes later.

'Don't know what you're tryin' to rule out, Scoop, but I hope it wasnae drugs, because that is very much the word. Traces of cocaine in the briefcase he was found with, and in the boot of his car. It could have been a deal that went wrong or even a deliberate double-cross. Looks like he was doing the selling: they found more than fourteen hundred in cash in the guy's flat.'

'Did he have any form for drugs?'

'Nah. Could have been an amateur learnin' the hard way. The Paisley boys think he might even have been shot personally by one of the heid-bummers, as opposed to a minion.'

'How'd they work that out?'

'They found a shell. Ballistics say it was from a large-calibre handgun – well, actually, I don't think it needed experts to work that out, given the mess it made. But the thing is, they reckon the gun must have been a bit tasty, somethin' upscale that your average ned wouldnae be able to get his paws on. Hence, they figure it might have been Mister Big's personal hand-cannon.'

'So have they got a suspect yet?'

'One or two. They're still checkin' alibis.'

'And was there anythin' at all that diverged from it bein' just a nasty wee drugs hit? I mean, the guy was in a decent job, a professional.'

'Principal cocaine demographic these days, Scoop. Lawyers, doctors, IT types: pay-day is Class-A day.'

'Sure. But that's buyin', not sellin'.'

'Aye, but maybe he figured he could cut out the middle man and start sellin' to his pals. Who knows.'

'So there's nothin' else in the frame?'

'No. Well . . . No.'

'Well what?'

'It's nothing.'

'Tell me anyway.'

'He got a phone call less than an hour before he was murdered. Cops at his flat did a 1471.'

'Who from?'

'I can't tell you, Jack, you know that. Anyway, it doesnae matter, because they checked it out and the guy had nothin' to do with it. He was a hundred miles away at the time. Aboot ten witnesses saw him an' a china gettin' pissed and fed in a hotel up in Perthshire. It's a red herring. This was just, as you say, a nasty wee drugs hit.'

'Good.'

catholic guilt

Elspeth sat back in her chair with a tired sigh and listened as the bubblejet's ink head shuttled back and forth, printing out copies of her letter of resignation. She had thought she might feel some sense of relief, but none came. Perhaps later, once it had been delivered. At this stage, there was still a chance to change her mind. At this stage, she was still a minister and an MSP, whatever her intentions.

Maybe she felt no relief because this action was not a true resolution; at best, perhaps a procrastination, and at worst, she was merely running away. But what else could she do? If she confessed all and revealed what had really happened, it would be at the cost of both her own career and her father's reputation, and she felt that only the first of those was hers to sacrifice. After everything she had gone through to protect Joseph Doyle's name, she wasn't going to let Ian Beadie or anyone else damage it now. Instead, she would just slip from notice quietly, taking her secrets with her.

What-ifs couldn't help now, but nonetheless, she couldn't stop asking herself why she hadn't bargained harder when Beadie offered his sordid little deal. Why hadn't she demanded the files and some guarantee of his silence in exchange for her part in the plot? The answer was that she'd been hit so hard at the time that she could only see what was immediately in front. Thus, Beadie had walked out with what he needed from her, and still held on to the leverage that bought it for him.

He had got exactly what he wanted – Beadie always got exactly what he wanted – and left her to discover that he'd bought her soul with ashes. She knew she shouldn't be surprised, either, as her soul hadn't so much been sold as poinded: sequestered for a warrant sale in lieu of a debt she couldn't afford to pay.

She wasn't the only one to get stiffed, not that it was any consolation. The Churches had got little more out of their deals; the only difference was that they didn't realise it. After years – decades – of dwindling influence, they'd been duped into thinking that Scottish society was paying them attention again. It wasn't. The *media* was paying them attention, but only while they were saying what the media needed them to; only while they were talking about sex.

The Churches wouldn't notice until they tried talking about something else, so perhaps the biggest tragedy was that the delusion might last forever.

Elspeth had often felt that people wrongly believed her religion to be preoccupied with sexual morality, and that this was a result of the media only ever asking for the Church's opinion on those matters. Now she was having to ask herself what had led the media to be so selective, and the answer was as logical as it was depressing. It was kind of a chicken-and-egg scenario.

Jack Parlabane's irritatingly persistent accusation had been that Cardinal Doollan and Father Francis Shelley were claiming to represent people who did not share their beliefs. Elspeth would level a worse charge: that they had misconstrued the beliefs of the people they *did* represent.

To Elspeth, her faith was a widely encompassing philosophy, a humanitarian creed that had its roots in community, in compassion, in sharing, in forgiveness, in reaching out, in togetherness. Her parish priest, Father Gilfillan, epitomised

313

that in what he preached from the pulpit, and what he practised on the ground, whether it be his work for a local drug outreach centre or just his way of finding time to talk to everyone who stopped him in the street. It was a statistical likelihood that the pair of them were not an isolated anomaly, and there was plenty of anecdotal evidence to support this. So why was it that the men at the top, whenever a microphone or tape recorder was placed under their noses, could only talk in tones of reproach and condemnation, and why, for the love of Christ, couldn't they get past the bedroom?

Hadn't it occurred to them that there were greater evils abroad in this world than two people having sex; greater evils than even, dare she whisper it, abortion? What impact might it have had, she wondered, if Cardinal Doollan had put as much effort into the issue of homelessness in Scotland as he had into the issue of the unborn. Oh sure, unquestionably he thought homelessness was dreadful, he'd give you a quote, and Shelley would elaborate upon it later if you wanted, but neither of them was organising conferences and demonstrations on *that* issue. They weren't going into schools and indoctrinating the weans into a belief that homelessness was an evil shame upon our society, and that they should dedicate themselves to *its* eradication.

But then, the unborn child was a less complicated thing to care about. An unborn child couldn't behave in a manner you disapproved of, could not hold opinions you disagreed with, and wasn't going to stand before you in the street with a cup in its hand, stale sweat and urine on its clothes and that dazed junkie look in its eyes.

In the aftermath of Moundgate, Shelley had been surfing a wave of media attention, reaffirming the Church's right – 'no, *duty*' – to have a say in shaping Scotland's morality. So what had he done with this exposure? What had been the sum of his newfound visibility? Er, highlighting the Catholic protest against the Greencross teenage advice clinics.

Nobody could presume to know the will of God, of course, but Elspeth felt sure that if Jesus had been given the same opportunity, harassing high-street pharmaceutical staff would not have been his first priority.

And the most sordid, revolting aspect was that this platform, from which Shelley was now able to lecture and pronounce, was entirely built on a lie. All of his vindication was drawn from this conveniently vivid illustration of where society's permissive morality was leading, an illustration he knew to be fake. Watching him pour forth his denunciations had therefore turned Elspeth's stomach; but rather than that, it had turned her head too.

This, she finally understood, was what people saw in *her*, what they identified her with because she'd been forthright about her faith. This was why, despite years as an impassioned campaigning reporter, her reputation was instead as a sexual-spoilsport columnist. And this, she now realised, was the real reason the Party had been shy of putting her in the spotlight. It wasn't because of what she believed, but about what the public assumed she believed. If you wore your religion on your sleeve, then you were a hostage to how that religion was reflected through the actions of men such as Doollan and Shelley. Readily – proudly – identifying yourself as a Catholic brought a baggage of public perception, and it didn't matter whether that perception was wrong: it only mattered that it was inescapable.

Was it fair, then, that she might have accomplished more in politics had she just kept her faith to herself? It didn't seem fair, but she was beginning to appreciate that it was *right*.

315

There she was, angry at Doollan and Shelley for weighing into the abortion issue rather than the issues *she* thought were more pressing. Why was that? What was it that she felt they could bring to the table? Was it that they represented the faith she felt part of? Perhaps, but only partly. In the main it was because they represented the authority of God, and let's face it, everyone wants God on their side in an argument. That was where politics and religion had an incompatibility.

Bringing your faith into a political debate was, however you tried to disguise it, an attempt to attach God's authority to your case, and that simply wasn't on. Few might argue with your fervent belief that God shared your abhorrence for homelessness, but what about the rest? Abortion? Sex education? The welfare state? Agricultural policy? Did God share your position on those things too? What, pray, was God's stance on the euro? Beef on the bone? Land reform? A proposed cut in interest rates?

Politics, even in this shallow age, was still ultimately about argument and discourse. You could not discourse – and you bloody certainly couldn't argue – with someone who claimed divine right. Elspeth then, like all politicians, was freely entitled to her religious beliefs, but there was a damn good reason why she shouldn't bring them to work.

Unfortunately, this realisation had come too late to save her career, but that was something she was going to have to live with, and in the end one of the smaller things likely to be troubling her conscience.

Whether it was ever going to dawn on the likes of Doollan and Shelley was another matter, though at least the latter was finally suffering some long-overdue remorse. He'd called her up at the weekend, the first time they'd spoken since that shameful day at Beadie's house, and he sounded a shadow of the indignant figure who'd been lambasting the unrighteous these past months.

'Elspeth?'

'Yes?'

'It's Fa— Francis Shelley. Father Shelley.'

His voice was quivering, which instantly sent ripples of anxiety through Elspeth, who assumed it could mean only one thing.

'What's happened, Father?'

'Oh, Elspeth. It's a terrible thing we've done. A wicked, wicked thing.' He sounded close to tears.

'I know, Father.'

'No, you don't. It's so much worse. I . . . Oh God.'

'Father? What's—'

'No. It's too late now. I can't talk. I shouldn't have called. I'm sorry.'

At which he hung up.

Terrified that this meant the story was out – or at least, given the Catholic predilection for confession, imminently so – she called the one man who was bound to know.

'Nothing's out,' Beadie assured her. 'You'd know a lot more about it by now if it was. And nothing's *coming* out, either. I've made damn sure of that.'

'I don't know, Ian. He sounded like a man who really needed to unburden himself. I'm only surprised it didn't happen sooner.'

'Well it didn't an' it's no' gauny happen now, either. I'll talk to him. And don't you be gettin' any cathartic impulses yourself, my dear, otherwise I might have to get a few things off my own chest.'

She knew Beadie was right. Shelley wouldn't squeal: he had too much to lose, not least his liberty. His conscience had eventually caught up with him, but like her, he would quickly realise that his penance was to go on carrying his burden, alone.

However, it was not her penance to go on living this lie in public, nor for her to be Beadie's remote-controlled political proxy, something she was sure he had in mind for the longer term. She was giving up her seats and her position, as stated on the letters now lying in her printer's out-tray. To paraphrase the classic Tory ministerial valediction, she was resigning to spend more time with her regrets.

If she drank, she knew she'd be sinking a very large one now. Instead she would have to settle for a few silent tears and a cup of tea.

She checked the clock. It was just before six. She'd wait for the morning to hand in the letters. Might as well enjoy one last night as a senior MSP in this, Scotland's first modern parliamentary administration. Then, looking at the document on her computer screen, it occurred to her that it might be more appropriate if she emailed it. That was how this whole hateful chain of events had been set in motion, so it would be her own bitter little joke to bow out the same way.

She opened her email programme and attached the resignation letter to a new message, then paused as her cursor arrow hovered over the Send command. Same as before, it was just a matter of one mouse-click: like pulling a trigger on a gun, the end result seemed massively disproportionate to the action. This time, though, it was her own decision. She pressed the mouse-button and sat back, sighing.

'Error: no server connection found.'

She clicked again.

'Error: no server connection found.'

She checked her Inbox. There had been no mail for hours. She launched her web-browser.

'Page not available in offline mode. Go online now? Yes. No.'

Y.

'Error: no server connection found.'

Bugger.

Elspeth picked up the telephone and dialled the technical help extension number, which was marked on a sticker at the side of her monitor.

'Hello, technical support, Allan speaking.'

'Yes, hello, Allan, this is Elspeth Doyle upstairs. Sorry to bother you, but would you be able to tell me why I can't send any emails just now?'

'Yes, Ms Doyle. I'm afraid one of the main servers is down over at Scotia OnLine in Glasgow. Nothing we can do about it this end, unfortunately.'

'Do you know when it's likely to be back up?'

'Eh, God, how long is a piece of string? It's been down since about lunchtime, and I think they're at sixes and sevens over there. I'd have been on to them, shoutin' the odds by now, except it might be a wee bit insensitive.'

'What do you mean?'

'Well, one of their senior engineers was killed last week. I think that's why they're a bit higgledy piggledy.'

'That's terrible. Killed? What happened to him? Was it an accident at work?'

'God, no. He was murdered. Did you not see the story? Somebody shot him. Ms Doyle? Ms Doyle?'

Elspeth hung up the call. She reached for the mouse again and set about deleting both the email and the original resignation document from her hard disc. Then she took the printed copies and ripped them to pieces, having worked out that resigning right then might lead to more than just the death of her career.

319

protestant work ethic

Beadie could taste metal in his mouth as he sucked the stinging nick on the edge of his finger. There were tiny filings scattered like glitter around his hands, held there by the sweat as he toiled through the hours in his garage. It was after three, but he wasn't sleeping much these nights, so he figured he might as well make use of the time. He felt like he was jet-lagged, as though his body clock was out of synch with everyone else's because he was still conditioned by the place he'd just visited. The strange thing was, it was night there too.

It was always night there.

He was managing to sleep a bit during the day, but that wasn't exactly a compensation, as he still had a business to run during those hours. Truth be told, he'd have sacked himself if he wasn't head of the company. Not only was he sleeping on the job, but when he was awake, he looked like death warmed up. He didn't smell too good either. No matter how many showers he took, however many times he changed his clothes, he would be stinking again within half an hour, from this sour, fevered sweat that seemed to be permanently seeping from every pore.

What sleep he was getting wasn't doing him much good, as he only had to close his eyes to return to Wednesday night. When he was conscious, he saw the incidents replay in an endless loop, like a trailer for a film with all the highlights crammed together in a frenetic montage. But that was PG-certificate stuff compared to the recurring dreams.

He was back at the Craggan Moor Hotel, having the same dinner, but his guest was not Shelley. Instead he shared the table with Sanderson, half his head missing, the blood and brains from the windscreen framed behind him on the wall as a modernist painting. Sanderson was smiling out of his half a mouth, raising a glass of Ribena in a toast as the photographer came in to take their picture together.

'Say cheese.'

Down the road, a team of divers was searching the bottom of Loch Faskally, led by the headless Mr Heron. He was in a wetsuit and flippers, oxygen tanks on his back and the mouthpiece floating where his face should have been, bubbles streaming from it and rising to the surface.

Meanwhile, back at the hotel, Sanderson was switching the bottles, taking the Ribena the waitress had brought and replacing it with a bottle from his bag. He poured two glasses of his own blood from the bottle and passed one to Beadie, who drank it. After that, Beadie ran to his room and threw up dark purple liquid flecked with shards of bone. That was when he always woke up, soaked in the reeking sweat.

It would fade, he knew, as guilt always does. He just had to be strong and tough it out. These were the hardest days, he kept telling himself. It would only get easier from here. The dreams weren't all about guilt anyway: they were as much prompted by his fear of being caught, and that would fade also.

It was in such times that people got themselves caught by doing foolish things. He'd always thought the idea of the murderer returning to the scene of the crime was bollocks, but in the past few days he'd several times felt an impulse to go back to the quarry or to the car park in search of some undefined sense of reassurance, as if he needed to check he hadn't left a business card and a note saying 'I DID IT'.

Panic, that was all it was. Instinctive fear and insecurity.

The police had bought both the angles, for God's sake. They were looking for a drug-dealer in Paisley and some gay maniac up north. There were no witnesses, other than the ones who could verify that he and Shelley got blitzed on Château Musar before staggering off to bed, and that the Lexus they arrived in hadn't moved from the car park from check-in until check-out.

The only remaining dangers were from his own behaviour and that of his partner in crime. It had therefore set Beadie's heart walloping again when Elspeth phoned to express her concern about Shelley (though thank God she didn't have a clue what was really bothering him).

As soon as he heard what she had to say, he'd immediately worked himself up into another fit of fretting, thinking that this whole business was like trying to flatten air bubbles in wallpaper: as soon as you pushed one down, another one popped up elsewhere. He had been so immersed in his own neurosis that he'd forgotten the priest would be going through it too; probably worse, given his profession. And with Jack Parlabane out of jail and looking for something to while away his unemployed hours, it would not do to have a guilt-ridden priest suffering from an urge to, as Elspeth put it, unburden himself.

Once again, though, he knew to stay focused, stay calm, let the frantic feeling pass. The reason he had got away with this so far was that his plan had not been devised in haste or hot blood, so he wasn't going to do anything rash now.

He'd waited, then, until his heart had slowed and he could see only rational facts and logical probabilities, not fears, what-ifs and maybes. Parlabane, realistically, was not a worry. The guy's main concern would be finding a new job, and it wouldn't impress any potential employers if he went sniffing around Shelley again. Quite the opposite, in fact, which had given the never-sleeping PR man in Beadie an idea.

The most pressing matter was simply to calm Shelley down. The priest hadn't left his house since Thursday, and the worst thing you could do at a time like this was sit around stewing in your own juices. On top of that, it might start to look suspicious if he didn't show up for work again soon, especially when his job was all about visibility. Fortunately, Beadie had just the suggestion to get him back in the swing.

He stretched his arms and yawned, the smell of creosote thick in the air from the garage walls. The nick had stopped bleeding, but the metal taste remained, and he could feel particles on his tongue like little hairs. His arms weighed heavy with a fatigue that he wished he could transfer to whatever part of his brain controlled his sleep.

He'd sleep after tomorrow. After tomorrow, the fear would fade, the guilt would fade and in time, his dreams would be his own again. For now, though, there was work to be done.

atheist in a foxhole

'Don't get up, Father.'

'Ian. What are you doing here? I've got this appointment in—'

'I know. Just came to lend you some support.'

'What do you mean? I don't need any support. He's the one who's apologising, remember? And what do you think you're doing, wearing a dog collar? Are you trying to take the piss, is that it?'

Bzzzzz.

'Hang on, I'd better get this.'

'Father Shelley?'

'Yes, Margaret.'

'Mr Parlabane is here to see you, downstairs.'

'Oh, right, I—'

'Tell her you'll be five minutes.'

'What?'

'Tell her you'll give her a shout when you're ready.'

'Margaret? I just need five minutes here. I'll give you a shout when I'm ready.'

'Right-o.'

'What was that all about, Beadie?'

'Just give me one second and I'll explain.'

This, Parlabane was sure, had to represent a new low. He was sitting in the archdiocese reception area, waiting – *being made to wait* – for the opportunity to go upstairs and apologise to a priest. Evidently, he had been mistaken when he assumed he'd paid his debt to society, and was more than a little miffed to have no recollection of this stipulation being made when the sheriff was passing sentence. However, part of his sentence and part of his debt it most definitely was; that much had been made clear. Just as long as he got a fucking receipt.

He'd received a phone call yesterday from a Father Grady, Shelley's assistant or bum-boy or whatever, suggesting that a show of penitence might motivate certain powerful parties to put a good word in with previous and potential employers. 'We are, after all, in the forgiveness business, Mr Parlabane.'

He had resisted asking whether their turnover had improved upon the three hundred years it took them to pardon Galileo, and in fact bit back a variety of less-than-magnanimous responses in deference to the bigger picture. He was the one who had fucked up, after all. He owed Shelley an apology as much as he'd owed one to Sarah, having effectively used the priest as a stick to beat his wife with. The guy had only been doing his job. Parlabane might not approve of his job, but there was still no question over who was in the wrong, and anything that improved his chances of being restored to gainful employment was worth a shot.

Well, that was the theory, anyway. It had seemed a lot easier yesterday than it did now in the reception area; but then, most things had felt a lot easier yesterday, as he had spent most of it in bed with his wife. Thinking about it, maybe that was the catch-22 with these guys: if they got laid once in a while, they wouldn't be so permanently hung up about sex.

Then he remembered the flaw in his equation: he was

forgetting about hypocrisy. Plenty of them were getting laid – using condoms too, the cheeky bastards – but 'Do as I say, not as I do' was very much the motto of organised religion. And when they got caught, it was pointed out that they were only human, and should not be condemned by members of the public just because they succumbed to weakness. Condemnation was for *priests* to dole out when members of the public succumbed to weakness.

Yet here he was, getting ready to apologise to one of them. Shouldn't it be the other way around? How about a wee 'sorry' for telling women in the Third World not to use contraception even when they've already got twelve starving weans. Or for propping up South American dictatorships? Or for looking the other way while the Jews, gays and gypsies were being led to the gas chambers?

Yeah, yeah, Jack. Any more clichés you'd care to troop out while you're here, or will that do? Amazing how imperative it became to dwell upon other people's wickedness when your own conscience was bothering you. Why else would Associated Newspapers still be in business?

'Mr Parlabane?' said the receptionist.

He looked up.

'You can go upstairs now. I'm sure you know the way,' she added sourly.

He walked reluctantly to the lift, where the doors slid open before he could reach for the button. A rather sweaty priest emerged from the car, heading for the exit. Parlabane thought he looked familiar, but couldn't place him.

The lift arrived at the second floor, and he made his way along the corridor, thinking there better not be a fucking photographer. He attempted to console himself with the belief that he *had* to be bottoming out here. Someone else had knobbed his wife, he'd been arrested, fired, jailed and stabbed, and now he was about to pucker up to the God Squad.

It could not possibly get any worse than this.

He knocked on Shelley's door, which was slightly ajar. There was no reply. He knocked again, still eliciting no response.

He nudged the door open a little more and had a look inside. Shelley was sitting with his back to him, like a child in the huff.

'Hello?' he called softly, walking into the office.

The priest said nothing, just sat there facing the window. Presumably he'd swivel round once Parlabane had eaten some liver.

Parlabane's eyes strayed to the papers strewn untidily about the man's desk. Maybe if he kept the bugger distracted, he could yet pochle a copy of that report he'd been looking for. But no, that was an unworthy thought. Best just to get this over with.

'Father Shelley?'

Still the priest said nothing, but Parlabane did hear a dripping sound.

He took a few steps towards one side of the desk.

'Oh fuck.'

Shelley was dead. He'd been stabbed through the left eye, the blade rammed all the way into his brain until only a short length of steel remained jutting out, along which the blood was trickling. Upon closer inspection, Parlabane was able to measure precisely how much steel was jutting out, in inches and centimetres. The blade was a tapered and sharpened ruler, similar to the one that had been used on himself.

He could hear two more sounds. One was of footsteps

approaching in the corridor. The other was the jaws of a trap snapping shut around its prey.

Beadie pulled off the dog collar and stuffed it into a bin next to where the Lexus was parked. He couldn't afford to hang on to any souvenirs, even though this one had served him very well: a disguise as simple as it had been perfect. Nobody asked who he was or where he was going; even fucking Parlabane didn't look twice at him as he came out of the lift.

He got into the car and closed the driver-side door with a reassuringly heavy clunk. Safety, at last. Then he pulled on his seatbelt and turned the ignition key, leaving the engine idling as he looked in his rear-view mirror.

It took less than ten minutes for the first police car to appear, racing around the corner behind him, lights and sirens heralding its urgency. Beadie indicated and pulled away.

He drove home, parked the Lexus in his garage, had another shower, then went to bed, where he slept dreamlessly for eighteen hours. It was the sleep of the just.

The just-got-away-with-it.

It was taking all of Parlabane's will simply to concentrate on feeling nothing, to hold on to that hollow sickness, because beyond it was a fear that threatened to consume his sanity. They were marching him, one on either flank, towards A Hall, the remand wing, along hallways echoing with taunts and vicious promises. Fear, in the past, had been of things only imagined, even unimaginable: harm and hurt he had never known. Now, the feel of a blade in his gut was as real to him as the smell of this place was unsettlingly familiar.

Fear used to be about ifs. Now it was about when. The

only if was who got to him first: some religious bampot avenging the murder of a priest, or the hired hand of whoever set him up, in accordance with the second rule of assassination. Either way, he knew he'd be lucky if he lasted the week; a miracle if he lived to stand trial.

The Glasgow polis had charged him at around 2:00 am after the mandatory sustained headgames session. With the right of silence abolished and reticence now officially established as a tacit admission of guilt, he faced down their attrition by rigidly sticking to the facts and offering no elaboration, a tactic *un*officially established as a tacit admission of guilt.

Predictably – inevitably – they informed him that there was no Father Grady. He told them, in that case, to find out who had phoned him the day before, at which they all but laughed in his face. They had no doubt whatsoever that he had done this, and who could blame them? Only the clumsily obvious semiotics of the murder weapon pointed to any other explanation, and the police traditionally tended towards a less paradoxical interpretation of such self-evident signs of guilt.

He was driven across to Saughton in the morning, where he would, theoretically at least, stay until the trial. There would be no return to the comparative comforts of E Hall, however, as the governor explained in person upon his arrival. Not only would he be placed under high security, but what privileges he *was* due might be a long time in coming, as the prison system's bureaucracy could sometimes be slow in processing these things. This last the governor had outlined in a tone intended to convey that he was personally going to ensure as much, before adding, redundantly, that he was a practising Catholic.

'Did I miss the trial?' Parlabane had asked, discovering

some remnant of defiance like a fragment of food between his teeth two hours after a meal.

'What?'

'The trial. You know, the part where they find out whether I had anythin' to do with this shit or not. It's just, you seem awfy sure. I was wonderin' if I'd slept through it or somethin'.'

'No, you've got it all to look forward to, you cheeky bastard. But I'd give you a thousand to one on the outcome.'

'A pound,' said Parlabane.

'What did you say?'

'A pound. Thousand to one, you said. I'll have some of that action. If you're so fuckin' confident, let's make it official.'

'Get him out of my sight.'

'You guys are both witnesses,' he told the screws as they led him from the room.

'I'd keep my mooth shut if I was you, pal.'

Parlabane was already wishing that he had. His chances were poor enough without him antagonising the people supposedly charged with his protection. To remind him of this, he was taken a circuitous route to A Hall, deliberately walked through a gauntlet of seething abuse before being flung into his solitary cell, where a stack of that day's newspapers was waiting on the bed.

'Compliments of the governor,' the screw explained. 'He thought you might want to read up and have a wee think aboot what you've done.'

The door slammed behind him and was locked with a reverberating clatter of metal. Parlabane sat down on the bed and angrily scattered the pile of papers to the floor, where the front pages fanned out before him like a hand of cards. Hell of a hand, right enough, seeing as they all

330

had the same face. More than that, most of them even had the same photo: Shelley, in civvies, smiling uncertainly at the camera, holding up a glass in salute.

Only *The Saltire* dissented, opting for an older shot of the priest in full God-bothering regalia, 'celebrating' mass alongside Cardinal Doollan. However, when he picked the paper up and flipped open to page three, there it bloody was, in colour, across four columns, though this time Shelley's dining companion was not cropped out.

Last supper: Fr Shelley pictured last Wednesday, having dinner at Craggan Moor Hotel with Scottish PR guru Ian Beadie.

A shudder hit Parlabane so hard that he dropped the newspaper. It landed atop the pile, page three and the rest of the section sliding away from the front folio. The two faces smiled up from the image, both raising their glasses, toasting his achievement at finally working out what the fuck was going on.

The sweaty priest in the lift. It was Ian Beadie – that was why he knew the face. He just couldn't place it at the time because it didn't normally have a dog collar underneath. It was *Ian fucking Beadie*.

Parlabane sat up and tried to put the brakes on his racing mind. He knew how desperate he was right now, and he knew how easily implausibilities could fade from sight when you really needed to believe something. This had to be rationalised.

Why would Beadie want Shelley dead? Why would he even be having dinner with the guy? Parlabane picked up the paper again and scanned the copy. 'Beadie had been working closely with Fr Shelley since being hired last

331

year in a low-key consultative capacity, to advise upon the Church's dealings with the media. The PR man said he was shocked and deeply saddened by . . .'

Hired last year in a consultative capacity. And Jesus, hadn't the Church's public profile been raised after this 'guru' came aboard, especially since . . .

Parlabane swallowed. 'Well tear off my cock and call me Rita.'

What had he told himself just three days ago? The only winners out of the Moundgate affair had been the media and the Churches. Media: Ian Beadie. Churches: Father Francis Shelley.

'Tell me you don't do conspiracies anymore.'

Logan's voice faded into Jenny's.

'He was a hundred miles away at the time. Aboot ten witnesses saw him an' a china gettin' pissed and fed in a hotel up in Perthshire.'

Craggan Moor Hotel was in Perthshire, a hundred miles from Auchenlea.

'Jesus.'

The person who phoned Sanderson less than an hour before his death had to have been either Beadie or Shelley. No, Beadie, definitely. His name would have meant nothing to Jenny, whereas if it had been Shelley, ethics or not, she would definitely have said *something*.

They had cooked up Moundgate between them. Or more likely, Beadie had cooked it up and Shelley was both willing accomplice and co-beneficiary; Shelley didn't have the savvy, and he certainly didn't have Beadie's balls. They hired Sanderson to doctor the server logs, just as Logan was claiming, and being a computer techie, he must also have been the one who found a way of installing the incriminating files on to the four MSPs' hard drives.

332

However, once the whole thing was set in motion, the stakes went through the roof, and they must have become very nervous about the price to be paid if they were caught. At that point, Sanderson would have become a major liability. Maybe he was even shaking them down, or maybe they just got jittery; whatever, they had him silenced. Had to be. They hired someone to frag him, and in the time-honoured fashion, made sure they were well out of the vicinity in the company of a whole host of witnesses. So if anybody did link them to Sanderson – as that phone call indeed had done – they could prove they were in Perthshire at the time, a long, long way from gunmen and drug-dealers. Christ, the cops would have an easier time trying link them to 'the headless cottager' than the shooting of the computer-geek, as they were only twenty miles away from *that* one.

Last Wednesday night.

In a car park near Killiecrankie, just off the A9.

Which ran between Craggan and Glasgow.

No, he thought, reining himself in. Keep the heid.

Still, stoater of a coincidence that Mr Heron should lose his, where he did, on exactly the same night.

'No, wait, I've got it,' he'd said to Logan, joking: 'they made it look like a sex-killing to disguise the true motive for the murder.'

So, as long as he was sitting in a prison cell with nothing better to do, why shouldn't he have a quick game of 'what if'? What if the pair of them weren't tucked up in their hotel last Wednesday? What if they hadn't hired a hitman to pop Sanderson? What if they were palming the wine off on the nearest pot-plant in readiness to sneak down the road in the dead of night and do it themselves? What if that required a phone call to the victim shortly beforehand, maybe to

333

arrange a late-notice meeting? What if, on the way back, they had to stop at Killiecrankie because of a puncture, or engine trouble, and there they were seen by a travelling tool salesman who could now testify that they weren't asleep up the road when they should have been? What if they panicked and shot him, like they shot Sanderson, once in the head, executioner-style? What if they then cut his head off with his own tools to disguise how he had died, adding a few latex embellishments to confuse the cops? And what if Beadie then realised that the only remaining threat to him getting away with the whole thing was his partner-in-crime ever opening his mouth?

What would all of that leave?

It would leave Jack Parlabane standing over a dead priest's corpse, set up to arrive in exactly the wrong place at exactly the wrong time. And not, he suddenly realised, for the first time, either: the reason he'd never found that fucking church attendance report was that there never was one.

'The only place you'd find a copy of it is in this office.'

They'd laid a trap for him before. Beadie, being familiar with Parlabane's reputation, had got Shelley to dangle the bait of a non-existent document, then he had walked in like a fucking mug, with his eyes half shut and his trousers round his ankles. And why had they set him up? Because he was investigating the Catholic Church at a time when the Catholic Church had a lot more to hide than the true size of its congregation.

Parlabane lay back on the bed and put a hand to his cheek, where he was surprised to find not a minor itch, but a bead of water. Tears had begun to seep from his eyes. This must have been because his ducts had received advance notice that in about another five seconds he was going to realise that he had never been so angry in his life.

He had just deduced that the biggest scandal in the history of modern Scottish politics had been a fake; that the self-righteous puritanism that had consequently tainted the nation was founded on lies; and that behind it all was a self-serving conspiracy that went to the very heart of the tabloids and the moralising religious lobby. On top of that, he had worked out who murdered both David Sanderson and Father Francis Shelley, and solved the mystery of the headless sales rep for an encore.

Unfortunately, the cops weren't going to believe a word; he had no proof of any of it; and if he actually lived that long, the first chance he'd get to look for evidence would be in about fifteen years.

the second rule of assassination

'Hello?

   'Hello. You know who this is?'

   'Naw.'

   'Good. That's how it stays.'

   'D'you know who this is?'

   'Course I know who this is. I fuckin' phoned you, didn't I?'

   'Oh aye, right enough. Whit d'ye waant?'

   'Message to your boss. Queen Street station toilets. There's a thousand in cash in a sealed plastic envelope in the cistern of the first cubicle as you go in the door. If Jack Parlabane's dead in two days, there'll be another four grand. If it's three days, it'll be three grand. Four days, two.'

   'Aye, I get the picture. Who the fuck's Jack Parlabane?'

   'He's inside. Jimmy'll know.'

Elspeth checked the names on the brass plate and rang the bell, then stood back, trying to compose herself so that it *didn't* look like her heart was punching through her ribcage. She was enduring a prolonged state of mortal terror, partially ameliorated by the rationale that she was safe as long as Beadie didn't know she suspected anything, and thoroughly re-aggravated by the knowledge that rationality had absolutely nothing to do with Beadie's current state of mind. After the shock of learning about the Scotia OnLine engineer's death, she had taken some comfort in the absurdity of her own conclusions, but that comfort had lasted roughly the same time as Francis Shelley's life. After that, she knew not only that she was right, but that Beadie would kill her next if she did anything to raise his suspicions. In fact, if she had managed to deliver those letters when she originally intended, she might be dead already: a convenient wee 'suicide' that tied into her resignation with serendipitous plausibility.

The woman who answered the door had long sandy fair hair that would no doubt be a beautifully flowing asset to her appearance when she didn't look as though she'd been recently assaulted with a Van de Graaf generator. She had the eyes of someone who had not only gone a long time without sleep, but who for the duration had been unable to think about anything other than her fears. Elspeth knew, because she saw the same eyes every time she looked in a mirror.

She peeked out at Elspeth through a gap the length of the chain that hung between the door and its frame.

'Hello? Can I help you?' she asked. Her voice sounded croaky with tears and worry. Elspeth hadn't expected an English accent, but she hardly needed to confirm that this was the right person.

'My name is Elspeth Doyle. I'm here because I know who really killed Francis Shelley.'

The woman took a moment for the words to register, as though she had just woken up and her brain was only gradually getting into gear. Then she fixed Elspeth with a stare that threatened reprisals if her intentions turned out to be less than sincere.

'That makes three of us,' the woman said. 'Four, if you count Ian Beadie.'

Elspeth gawped.

'Oh come on, I know my husband's not quite been himself lately, but he's still Jack Parlabane.' She unhooked the chain. 'Come on, you better get inside. We need to talk. I'm Sarah, by the way.'

Sarah led Elspeth to the living room, along the obligatory polished floorboards of the hallway. The flat was generally bright and attractive, in conflict with Elspeth's mental picture of chez Parlabane: a darkened lair, the walls entirely covered in newspaper cuttings interlinked by crayon-drawn arrows in an erratic scheme that made sense only inside his crazed and paranoid head. Well, she supposed he had been in prison for a while of late: time enough for the missus to redecorate.

'How do you know?' Elspeth asked.

'Jack phoned. He filled me in on what he's worked out. As ever, some of it's nuts and some of it makes perfect sense. In my experience, it's the nuttier parts that usually turn out to be the most accurate. But I think the big question here is how do *you* know?'

'That's a long story.'

Sarah folded her arms impatiently. 'Well, I've checked the paper and the telly's shit tonight, so why don't you tell me.'

'You better have a seat,' Elspeth said. 'I'll tell you what I know, you tell me what you know, then we'll see where that leaves us.'

Elspeth told her all: the parts she suspected, the parts she knew, the parts she played; from the email to the blackmail. She didn't leave many blanks, but those she did were filled by Sarah. Between them they had everything, apart from proof.

'But you've got the disc, haven't you?' Sarah asked. 'Can't you go public with that, blow the whole thing open?'

'All the disc would prove is *my* part in the affair. There's nothing but my word to say it came from Beadie. If I went public with it, you're right, it would blow the whole thing open, and it would be all too easy to imagine me being found shortly afterwards, having apparently done away with myself out of shame and remorse. It wouldn't help your husband, either.'

'What about McLeod?'

'McLeod could testify that he was at the meeting, but he wasn't told anything about the details of the plan. He might be dead too, otherwise. And none of this connects Beadie to any of the murders. They've got a red-handed suspect for Shelley, and Beadie's got probably the best alibi in the world for the others.'

'So what are we going to do?'

'I was hoping you could tell me. You've had more experience with this sort of thing, I'm led to believe.'

'Mostly vicarious. Anaesthetics is my line. The one who unravels conspiracies is indisposed.'

'I was thinking more of his reputed talent for getting into places where vital evidence might be concealed. There must be something in Ian Beadie's house that ties him to all this stuff.'

Sarah stared pensively at the floor for a moment, calculating, evaluating. When she looked up, it was with the same steely admonition she'd shown at the door.

'I'm afraid my own abilities don't stretch to housebreaking,' she said. 'But they might stretch to jailbreaking.'

'Jai— How?'

'How can wait. How isn't the problem. The problem is that Jack would need to know his part in advance, and this is hardly something I can tell him over the phone.'

'Can't you visit him?'

'Not until his paperwork clears, and the governor's made it obvious that's not going to happen any time soon. Could be another five days, by which time it could be too late.'

'Too late? Why?'

'The second rule of assassination.'

'What's that?'

'Well, the first rule of assassination is kill the assassin.'

'You mean like Ruby and Oswald.'

'The second rule is: if everyone thinks some other mug is the assassin, kill him before he can say otherwise. Also like Ruby and Oswald, depending on how you view the Warren Report.'

'I see your point. But there must be some way of getting the message to him.'

'Yeah,' said Sarah. 'There must. Of course, it would be easier if one of us was the Minister for Home Affairs.'

Elspeth smiled.

'What have you got in mind?'

'*Definitely* the best alibi in the world.'

He walked the north landing again, eyeing his target on the south corridor through the railings and mesh, waiting patiently for his moment. The daft bastard was still mopping away like a fart in a trance, lost in his thoughts as he dipped the mop in the bucket and half-heartedly slapped it about the tiled floor. Stupid prick was too utterly wrapped up in his own miserable little world to even notice that he was being watched; Christ, he could just have stood there beside him and the clown wouldn't have clocked, instead of circuiting around and back, around and back, like he'd already done three times.

On the last pass, the bucket had looked just about empty, and sure enough, when he came around level on the

340

opposite side, he saw the little arsehole lean the mop against the wall and wander lethargically away, bucket in hand. He'd be off to the storeroom for a refill and a fly fag, or maybe just a wank if he was out of snout.

It was time to make a move.

He doubled back and bounded down the stairs, emerging into the corridor below, a few yards behind Dead Man Walking. He slowed down to match his quarry's pace, feeling an involuntary tingle in his arms, running like a ripple from his shoulders to his fingers in excited anticipation. He was really going to enjoy this; even his muscles knew it.

They were nearing the storeroom. He had a quick look around to make sure no-one else was in sight, then quickened his step so that he reached the door just as Dead Man was opening it.

He bundled him inside with a heavy push and closed the door quietly behind them.

Dead Man turned around to face him, trying laughably not to look scared.

'Jack Parlabane,' he stated flatly.

'Fuck off.'

He took Dead Man by the back of his collar and drove a heavy fist into his stomach, following through as though he'd been aiming three feet further back. Dead Man doubled. He grabbed his shoulders and straightened him up, then hit him again.

'Does that name mean anything to you?' he asked.

'Fuck all,' Dead Man replied.

Mikey sent the nut in, smashing Dead Man's nose and clattering his head off the wall behind.

'Wrong answer, Burnsy. Try again.'

'Aw right, aw right,' he spluttered, holding a hand to his

bleeding face. 'He's fuckin' . . . that cunt that got stabbed doon in the fuckin' spraypainters.'

Mikey kneed him in the balls. 'I think you can be a bit more specific.'

'Aw right. I fuckin' stabbed him. So fuckin' whit?'

Mikey took hold of his collar again and slammed his face off the edge of a thick wooden shelf. Burnsy held his hands up in surrender.

'So we both know who we're talkin' about now, yeah Burnsy?'

'Aye.'

'But we're not the only ones talkin' about him. What's goin' down? What have you heard?'

'Altiyeman, I've heard fuck all. I fuckin' swear. How would I hear anythin'?'

Mikey hit him in the stomach again with all the force of the first punch, the benefit of a rigorous personal fitness regime. Then he did it twice more and let the skinny little corpse drop to the floor, gasping and choking.

'You heard enough last time to know it was worth your while puttin' a blade into him, so don't fuckin' lie to me. I could keep this up all day, you little bastard, and I'd enjoy every minute, so start talkin' or I'll break you in half.'

The corpse spluttered for a few seconds more, then regained enough breath to speak.

'I'm fu . . . I'm fuckin' . . . tellin ye man . . . I've heard fuck all aboot this cunt.'

'Well, in that case, maybe you wouldn't mind answerin' a different question.' Mikey gripped him by the collar and pulled him up to his knees. He bent over and stared into the corpse's eyes. 'Do you think I'm a fuckin' idiot?'

He walloped Burnsy's face off another shelf with a thud that shook every container in the room. Then he pulled him

342

back and tensed his muscles to repeat the action. 'Three, two . . .'

'Aw right,' Burnsy said in a half-whisper. He was starting to cry, but the tears would be hard to see amid the blood and bruising. 'Fuckinnn . . . stop hittin' us, man, fuckinn . . . I'll tell you.'

'Fuckinnnn . . . tell me then,' Mikey imitated.

'It's fuckin' Corpus, man. Jimmy Christie. Fuckin' word's oot. Wants him deid, if any cunt can get access. Fuckin' *soon as*, that's the word. Soon. As.'

'Who's on it?'

'Fuckin' open bounty, man. First come, first serve.'

'Is that right?'

'Aye.'

'So do you talk to Corpus now and again, Burnsy?'

'Fuckinnn . . . time tae time, like. How?'

'I'd like you to pass somethin' on. Just a word to the wise, really.'

'Whit?'

'In fact, you can pass it on to everybody. Whatever's on offer for doin' Parlabane, it's not worth what I'll do to them later.'

'I hear you, man. I'll fuckin' pass it on, man, fuckin' straight up.'

'No, Burnsy. Folk can misinterpret things in here. I think my meaning would be clearer if the message was illustrated.'

The corpse shrank and began sobbing.

'Aw fuck, man. Naw, man. Aw fuck, *please*. You ken how it is. That wee bit o' business wasnae personal. I fuckin' tell't him that.'

'I know it wasn't personal, mate. But this fuckin' is.'

*　　*　　*

343

Parlabane heard the door being unlocked and sprang to attention. The set-up in the spraypainters had made him terrified of further conspiratorial involvement on the part of bent screws, so since he got into the remand wing, every time they came through the door, his heart-rate shot up and so did he.

The door opened. It wasn't one of the usual screws, but the face was familiar nonetheless.

'Mr Hayes. What are you doing over here in practice-prison? Thought up some new ruler jokes for me?'

'I don't think that would be in very good taste, considering what you did to the late Father Shelley.'

'What I *allegedly* did. This is A Hall, remember. The fat lady's still doin' her vocal warm-up exercises.'

'Aye, and her closin' number'll be a wee ditty entitled "You're going down".'

'Don't bet on it. Not with the governor's book, anyway. Thousand to one on.'

'Yes,' Hayes said, smiling. 'The governor's very much lookin' forward to welcomin' you back here on a long-term basis. He is therefore very anxious that nothin' should come between you and your richly merited date with the judge. For that reason, he was very grateful to one of our inmates for the information that a wee remuneration was bein' offered in exchange for your demise.'

'Wow, that one came right out of left-field. A hit on me? Who'da thunk it. Very altruistic of the chap concerned, though. What was in it for him?'

'He asked no reward other than the opportunity for a visit with yourself, if you were agreeable. I told him I could think of few people less agreeable, but there you are. Or rather, here he is.'

Hayes stepped back out of the cell and signalled to

his left. There were heavy footsteps outside. Parlabane's pulse quickened as he imagined some berr coming in and producing a blade from up his sleeve, then slitting his throat as Hayes looked on and made cracks about what he would do with his share of the reward. Instead, Mikey Briggs's imposing form filled the doorway.

'Mikey!'

Parlabane was not the most tactile person, but he was so grateful to see a friendly face that he couldn't help hugging the guy. It was either that or bursting into tears, and quite possibly both.

'I'm not sure I want to see this,' Hayes muttered, closing the door.

'All right, mate?' Mikey asked brightly. 'Apart from . . . ?'

'Apart from, yeah. Been better, if truth be told. I mean, for one thing, the state of the floors in this hall is a fucking disgrace. Cannae get a decent buffer-pad for love nor money.'

'Maybe this'll cheer you up,' Mikey said, holding out a palm. There was a tooth in it.

'What the fuck is that?'

'It used to belong to Billy Burns.'

'Who?'

'Foo, altiyeman, fuckinnnnn.'

'Ahhh. Got you now. Thanks.'

'It was a pleasure. Believe me.'

'So how's yourself?'

'Interesting, interesting. Had a visitor today that I wasn't expecting.'

'How could you get a visitor you weren't expecting?'

'Pertinent question, but all in good time, mate. The visitor was a charming lady by the name of Sarah Slaughter.'

'Sarah—' Parlabane started loudly.

Mikey clamped a palm over Parlabane's mouth and thrust something into his hand.

'Keep it shut and listen up, all right?'

Parlabane nodded and looked at what he had been given. It was a small, clear-plastic cylinder containing a deep blue liquid.

'What's this?'

'It's called Methylene Blue. Present from your missus. Magic potion.'

'Don't suppose it could make me disappear?'

'Funny you should say that.'

'Ian?'

'Is that you, Elspeth?'

'Yes.'

'How are you keeping?'

'Not at my very best, if the truth be told. Still reeling from what happened to Father Shelley.'

'God, I know. Horrible, horrible business. It's only just sinking in for me, really. I mean, I had dinner with the man last week. Great night we had, too. He was such a great character, especially once you got him away from all the trappings, you know?'

'I didn't know him as well as you. I suppose at least they got the bastard. Jack Parlabane, I mean. I can't say I ever liked him much, but I would never have expected him to do a thing like that. Maybe it's true that prison does strange things to people; makes them harder, colder.'

'Careful, Elspeth. Mustn't let anyone hear the New Labour Home Affairs minister say a thing like that. No, seriously, though, I always thought he had a vicious streak in him. There was malice in everything he ever wrote. It must have finally bubbled over on to the surface. Ach well, he'll get what's comin' to him, you can be sure of that.'

'I damn well hope so. I could use some cheering up. I don't suppose you'd be free for a bite of dinner tonight?'

the old 'guard, I'm feeling ill' routine (a variation)

'Guard. Guard. Guard, I need help in here. Guard, I'm no' kiddin', I think somethin's well wrong. Guard. Guard.'

Guthrie put down his tea and looked across at Croft.

'Has he still no' piped doon? Who *is* that?'

'Guard. Somebody, please.'

'It's that yin that killed the priest,' Croft told him. 'Parlabane. Cell nine.'

'Well, I wish he'd shut up. I'll go in there and lamp him in a minute, gie him somethin' tae cry aboot.'

'Guard. I think I need a doctor. Guard.'

'He got stabbed himself, didn't he?' Croft said.

'Aye, so I heard.'

'He hasnae gied us any bother before. Maybe I should take a wee look in.'

'Up tae you, but I'm no' gettin' aff ma arse for the likes o' him. Does he think it's fuckin' room service?'

Croft got up and walked to the door of cell nine, where he pulled back the screen and had a look inside. The prisoner was lying in a foetal position on the bed, clutching his stomach, his face obscured by his knees. His breathing sounded laboured, punctuated with wincing intakes of breath and further calls for help.

'Guard. For Christ's sake, I'm fuckin' sufferin' in here.'

Croft unlocked the door and walked into the centre of the cell. The prisoner remained where he was, but Croft was now able to get a look at his face.

'Fuck me.'

The guy looked like he was already dead. His skin was a hideous grey colour, like a corpse several hours cold, and his lips were the deep blue of a drowning victim.

'Guard. I need medical attention.'

Croft shuddered at the sight, then took a couple of steps back and leaned out of the door. 'Graeme, you better get in here, an' fuckin' sharpish.'

'It's my stomach,' the prisoner said, with obvious difficulty. 'It's agony.'

Guthrie arrived at the door a few moments later.

'Right, whit's the big drama aw aboo— Oh Jesus fuckin' wept.'

'I told you,' Croft said. 'He says it's his stomach.'

'Well nae kiddin', Dr Finlay. You work that oot yoursel'?'

'I had surgery,' the prisoner said, in between gasps and grunts. 'I was stabbed. They had to . . . operate. I think somethin's burst inside. The surgeon said to phone him . . . aaah . . . if anythin' went wrong. He said it was really . . . ooh . . . important. I think somethin's well wrong. My . . . my fuckin' piss has turned blue.'

Croft looked to the plastic container sitting by the bed. The contents were indeed, bafflingly, blue.

'Fuck me, look at that, Graeme.'

'We better get a doctor.'

'No,' the prisoner groaned, straining to sit up. 'You have to phone the surgeon that did the operation. He said . . . aaaah . . . ffffft . . . he said *he* had to be told first if . . . aaah . . . there were any complications. I'd say . . . mortal agony and blue piss were . . . pretty fuckin' complicated, wouldn't you?'

'Right,' Guthrie ordered Croft. 'Gie him a ring.'

'His name's Mr . . . Quinn. His number is—'

349

'I thought you says he was a doctor.'

'He's a sss . . . surgeon. Surgeons get called mister. Christ, can you just fuckin' phone him?'

The prisoner gave them the number and Croft ran to the phone. The governor had made it clear that arses would be very brutally kicked if anything happened to this guy, and though this probably wasn't what he was specifically worried about, it would be the same difference if the bloke snuffed it.

Croft dialled the number. It was picked up after four rings.

'Hello?'

'Hello, is that Mr Quinn?'

'Yes. Who's speaking?'

'Mr Quinn the surgeon?'

'That's correct. Who—'

'This is Douglas Croft. I'm an officer at Saughton, in A Hall. We've got a prisoner here who says you operated on him recently, and that he was to get in touch if there were any complications.'

'What was his name?'

'Parlabane. Jack Parlabane. He'd been stabbed.'

'Oh yes, I remember that one. Sharpened steel ruler. Very messy. Big risk of infection. What's the problem?'

'He's got very bad stomach pains.'

'Stomach pains? Right. Any other symptoms?'

'He looks aboot deid, if that's a symptom.'

'Oh dear. Greyish pallor, is that what you mean?'

'Aye.'

'Damn. What about his urine?'

'Urine?'

'Yes. Has he passed any urine, man?'

'Oh Christ aye. It's turned blue.'

'Blue? Oh good God. Sounds like an anastamotic leak. You've got to get him into theatre immediately.'

'A what?'

'An anastamotic leak. He had major bowel surgery. The sutures must have burst, and there'll be all sorts of toxic matter getting into his system. Jesus. This man could be dead in two hours. I need to operate. You've got to get him to the RVI as soon as possible. Don't wait for an ambulance, just get him into whatever you've got and bring him here, *now.*'

Croft ran back to the cell, where Guthrie was standing over the piss-pot, examining the contents suspiciously.

'The surgeon said he could have had an ana— an anan— ah fuck it, some kinna leak, an whatever you caw it, it's fuckin' serious. He reckons his stitches have burst inside. Says he could be . . .' Croft remembered himself and moved closer to Guthrie, whispering in his ear. 'He says he could be deid in two hours. Says the blue piss is a really bad sign.'

'Aye, I'll bet it is,' Guthrie said, his tone far from sympathetic.

'What?'

'Did it never occur tae you that this yin might be takin' us for mugs? They're devious wee bastarts. He could have read aboot this blue piss symptom somewhere, an' noo he thinks he can get a wee holiday in the infirmary instead o' here while he's waitin' for his trial. He could have just burst a biro intae this pot here.'

'Aye, but fuckin' look at him. He looks like he's got wan foot in. The doctor said we couldnae waste any time, Graeme. Fuck's sake, mind what the governor says.'

'I mind fine. But this yin's gaun naewhere until I see fresh pish comin' oot him the same colour as that.'

'Your . . . compassion is . . . too much,' the prisoner gasped.

'Aye, save the Oscar performance for the judge. Get another container, Douglas. Somethin' clear – a plastic tumbler.'

Croft ran back to their office. He knew he had less experience in this game than Guthrie, and that you could never afford to be anything less than cynical at all times, but he also knew a sick man when he saw one, and he didn't want a death on his conscience. The only plastic tumbler he could find was an opaque purple, which he rather thought might prejudice the test, so he poured the last of Guthrie's tea down the sink and brought his mug, which was a crisp white inside. Guthrie wouldn't be pleased to have it pissed in, but Croft was confident enough of the end result to think he deserved to be taught a wee lesson.

He returned to the cell and handed the mug to the prisoner. Guthrie only noticed what the receptacle was when the prisoner knelt down and placed it on the floor in front of himself.

'Hey, what the fuck do you—'

But it was too late. The prisoner was already pissing, and the piss was quite undeniably blue.

Guthrie was looking on, open-mouthed in horrified astonishment.

'Get a fuckin' stretcher,' he ordered.

Parlabane could see Sarah as soon as they opened the prison van's doors. She was standing in scrubs at the entrance to the A&E department beside the similarly attired Ross Quinn and his wife, Yvonne, a theatre nurse. The three of them immediately moved to greet the arriving party, Quinn pushing a trolley.

'Douglas Croft?' Quinn asked.

'Aye, that's me. This is Graeme Guthrie.'

'Ross Quinn. I've got a theatre ready. There's no time to waste. Let's get him on here.'

Parlabane was helped on to the trolley, whereupon Guthrie removed one of his handcuffs and attached it to the steel frame.

'I don't think that's entirely necessary,' Quinn said. 'This man is in no condition to run away, believe me.'

Guthrie ignored this, then made a show of examining all of their photographic hospital name-badges. Prick.

Sarah and Yvonne pushed the trolley through the casualty department and on towards the lifts, Quinn walking alongside and examining Parlabane as they progressed. The two screws kept pace at the rear.

'When did the pain start?'

'Ffft . . . ooh . . . about two hours. Maybe more.'

He patted at Parlabane's middle. 'Does it hurt there?'

'It's kind of all ov— AAAH. Aw, Jesus. Aw fuckin' hell.'

'Christ, that's right over the previous incision. Let's speed this up. Come on.'

They wheeled the trolley towards the lifts at jogging pace, Sarah running ahead to summon a car. The steel doors slid open just as they got there, then all six of them climbed inside. It wasn't far to the anaesthetic room now, for which Parlabane was grateful, as he was fed up writhing and moaning.

'Can you take that handcuff off now please?' Quinn asked. 'It's going to be very difficult to work around his arm if it's attached like that.'

'The handcuff stays,' Guthrie said. 'I'm no' takin' any chances with him, especially if there's scalpels an' what-have-you lyin' aboot.'

353

'There will be no surgical implements "lying about". And he'll be under anaesthetic by the time he gets to theatre. I really can't have him chained to the trolley.'

'This is a very dangerous man you've got here. Murdered a priest. It would be more than my job's worth if he got loose. I'm sorry, but I've nae choice.'

Parlabane gave one more penalty-box writhe and clutched his stomach.

'Just . . . get me to theatre. Never mind about the handcuffs. Ooow.'

He caught Sarah's eye and gave her the minutely perceptible nod of confirmation she was looking for.

'I really must insist,' Quinn went on. 'This is abdominal surgery we're—'

'Mr Quinn,' Sarah interrupted. 'These men have orders. We'll just have to work around the handcuffs. We've done it before.'

Quinn looked at her and got much the same subtle signal.

The lift arrived on the second floor and they resumed their brisk pace until reaching the anaesthetic room.

'I'll see you in theatre,' Quinn said, then disappeared through an adjacent set of swing doors.

Yvonne took the front of the trolley and Sarah the rear as they wheeled it into the anaesthetic room. Guthrie and Croft attempted to follow, but Sarah turned around at the door and blocked their paths.

'You can't come in here. You'll have to wait outside.'

'We're not supposed to let him out of our sights,' Guthrie protested.

'Well, there's only one door out of here. You can stand there and watch that if you like, but you're not coming into my anaesthetic room, okay?'

They backed out reluctantly and Sarah closed the door with a rebuking slam.

'Arseholes,' she said, then turned to Parlabane. 'Right. Better make this look the part. Lie still and knock off the theatrics.'

'What, no kiss of life?'

'There's a window on that door, Jack. Don't want them bursting in here to save me. Let's get to work.'

Fifteen minutes later, they were wheeling him out again with a mask over his mouth and a drip tube attached to his neck, the venflon held in place with tape. There *was* a second door in the anaesthetic room, leading directly into theatre, but the plan was to let his escorts see that Parlabane was out for the count. Despite that, the screws again attempted to follow them into theatre, and again Sarah chased them.

'You're not sterile,' she explained. 'Have you never seen *ER*? Anyway, he's under enough general anaesthetic to drop a rhino, and he's going to be staying that way for a good four hours—'

'*Four hours?*'

'At least. He isn't getting his tonsils out, for God's sake. I'd suggest you both take a seat in the waiting area down the hall. There's a coffee machine and some newspapers. Make yourselves comfortable and we'll keep you posted as we go along. And we'll come and get you *before* we wake him up, okay?'

'Aye, okay.'

Yvonne stuck her head out of the swing doors and made sure the screws had done as they were told.

'All clear,' she reported.

'Right.'

Parlabane pulled the mask from his mouth and untaped

the drip, while Sarah removed a blue holdall from the cupboard where she'd left it earlier.

'What are we going to do about the handcuffs?' Quinn asked. 'I suppose I could saw them off and then say sorry later. They won't be bothered if you're still here and haven't done a bunk.'

'No, no. Leave the handcuffs to me,' Parlabane said. He looked towards Sarah. 'God, I've always wanted to say this.'

'What?'

He held out his free hand. 'Scalpel.'

Sarah rolled her eyes and handed him a scalpel from Quinn's tray.

'Tweezers.'

Those too.

'Metzenbaum scissors.'

'What for?'

'Just wanted to say that as well.'

He got to work picking the lock, holding the tweezers with his fixed left hand and working the scalpel delicately with his right.

'Where on earth did you learn to do that?' Quinn asked. 'Sorry, daft question. I suppose it's true what they say: you learn to be a more accomplished criminal in prison.'

'No, Jack was a thoroughly accomplished criminal long before he went to prison.'

'Thank you, darling.'

The cuff snapped open. Parlabane handed back the implements to Sarah and hopped off the trolley. Yvonne placed a life-size resuscitation-practice dummy on to the green mattress, attaching the ventilation mask and the drip to its plastic head with more tape. Quinn then began to cover the dummy in surgical drapes.

356

'My kind of patient,' he muttered. 'Chances of a malpractice suit? Very slim.'

Sarah opened the holdall and handed Parlabane replacements as he took off his clothes.

'Trainers, black,' she said. 'Sweatshirt, black. Jeans, black. Socks, black. It's the "in" colour this winter.'

'The new black, even.'

'Mobile phone, black. Keys to BMW, black, parked on Lauriston Place. Anything else?'

'Well, outside bet, but worth asking: you couldnae think of anywhere I might be able to lay hands on some latex surgical gloves?'

Quinn tossed him a cardboard box full of them. Parlabane removed two pairs and stuffed them into a pocket.

'I've put all your gear in the boot,' Sarah told him. 'If there's anything I've forgotten, the keys to the flat are on the ring there.'

Parlabane pulled on a set of blue theatre scrubs over his clothes and slapped a matching cap on to his head, tucking his hair under the elastic.

'You've got four hours,' Sarah stated. 'Be careful. If you don't make it back here on time, we're *all* fucked.'

'Thanks,' he told them. 'I owe all of you.'

'Just make sure you get the bastard,' Quinn replied. '*We* all owe him.'

Parlabane kissed Sarah once, then pulled a surgical mask over his nose and mouth, tying it behind his head.

'Good luck,' she said.

He walked out of theatre and headed for the lifts, passing the screws on his way. They were sitting around a table, counting their coppers for the coffee machine. Croft glanced up at him as he passed, then looked away.

He pulled off the mask and cap in the lift and walked briskly out of the building. A glance at his watch told him it was 19:55. Fuck. He had four hours to get back here, but that wasn't his only schedule. Elspeth Doyle was having dinner with Beadie in Glasgow at eight. All the screws' fannying around had cost him half an hour at least. Sarah might have left him the Beamie, but he couldn't go flooring it along the M8, as getting stopped by the cops would hose everything. He'd just have to hope the service at the Rogano of a Saturday night was as crap as he'd often heard.

He made it to the BMW in a couple of minutes. It was sitting right where she said, the road surface around it beginning to glisten with the clear March night's frost. He opened the boot first and had a look inside, finding a black canvas sports bag sitting bang in the centre like a crown on a pillow. He unzipped it and did a brief inventory, smiling at what he saw. Sarah had forgotten nothing. All the tools of his forsworn secret trade, and her blessing on top. She'd even chucked in the Jaguar night-vision scope his friend Tim Vale had given him, the old rogue scornfully sceptical of his claim that he'd put those days behind him.

Parlabane closed the boot and walked around the side of the Beamie, then unlocked the door and climbed into the driving seat. He grinned and hit the ignition.

as two men dealt amidst the chill

Elspeth swallowed a generous mouthful of her main course and threw her head back, making an appreciative growling noise as she did so. She relaxed her shoulders, as though melting with the pleasure of it, then smiled across at Beadie. She was practising the politician's most essential and ancient art: the disingenuous ability to present a relaxed and approachable face while simultaneously scheming and panicking about a millimetre beneath the surface.

'God, that is good,' she said. 'I think I'm starting to feel like a human being again.'

'Aye,' Beadie replied. 'You need wee treats like this now and then to remind you why you're knockin' your pan in the rest of the time.'

She held up her tumbler of mineral water, and Beadie chinked his wine glass against it.

'Cheers,' they both said.

'You look like you were in need of a wee bit of *la dolce vita* yourself, Ian, if you don't mind me saying.'

He nodded as he chewed a piece of steak. 'Aye,' he said, swallowing. 'Hard couple of weeks. Eh, I mean, a lot on my plate at work and then the shock, you know. It's never easy, but . . .'

'I know what you mean. Never mind a hard couple of weeks, it's been a hard few months as far as I'm concerned.'

'Tough at the top, eh?' He grinned with smug and laboured innuendo.

'I've never known pressure like it. But then, it's hardly been the quietest time in the world of politics.'

'Is there ever such a thing?'

'All things are relative. But it isn't just the pressures of the job I've had to cope with. The pressures of how I got it haven't been a breeze either.'

'Sounds like Catholic guilt talking, Elspeth. Forget it and move on. There isnae a politician in power anywhere in this world who didnae stab a few backs to get where he is. Nature of the game. Regrets and remorse are for your memoirs.'

'Oh, I'm learning that now. And make no mistake, I'm learning to be grateful for the shove you gave me, as well. But it was trial by fire earlier on.'

She had another mouthful of her meal, the pause allowing her to gauge how he was taking this. He seemed calm enough, though Beadie could play the politician's game too.

'The worst thing wasn't guilt,' she resumed. 'It was fear that it would all go belly-up.'

Elspeth spoke that bit quieter, casting an eye upon the surrounding tables. No-one was paying them any heed, despite her current profile. That was the great thing about a place like this: nobody looked at you twice because the clientele all wanted to believe they were the most important/famous/powerful person in the room.

'I was sure the evidence, as it stood, wasn't going to be enough; and if they traced it back, we both know where the trail would have led. It might have been a bit easier on me if I'd known you had a bit of back-up. How did you manage to get those server logs to corroborate?'

Beadie stopped his fork on the way to his mouth. 'I'm

sure I have absolutely no idea what you mean,' he said, smiling. 'And anyway, as someone once put it, the more you know the less the better.'

The fork completed its journey. Elspeth smiled back as conspiratorially as she could manage, trying to mask her disappointment. Still, there was plenty of steak left, plus dessert and coffee to get through yet.

'Well, I was bloody relieved about it anyway, let me tell you. You're right, though. Best if I don't know the details. I'm assuming it must have been some kind of computer-hacking job. I was only curious because I didn't know you were a "leet haxor", but I suppose if you were able to cook up that email programme, you must be pretty *au fait* with these things.'

Beadie was nodding again as he chewed. He seemed in a hurry to get the mouthful down, as he had something to say. Her gambit had worked. He'd tell her *he* wrote the programme because he didn't want to admit any link to dead computer engineers. It wouldn't be the truth, but at least it would tie him in.

Beadie swallowed, then reached for his wine just when Elspeth expected him to elaborate. He took a gulp and shuffled in his seat while he did so, as though scratching his back by rubbing it against the chair.

'Ehm, do you mind if I ask you something, Elspeth?'

'No, fire away.'

He reached down to his side with his right hand. When he brought it back up, it was holding her dictaphone, which he raised to his mouth.

'Do you think my heid buttons up the back?' he said into the mike.

Elspeth looked down to the side of her chair, where her bag should have been. He'd stuck his leg across under

the table and pulled it over to himself. That was what
the shuffling had been about.

'Don't try an' play games with me, Elspeth. I wrote the
fuckin' book.'

He pressed Stop and removed the tape, placing it in his
pocket. Then he stood up and dropped the dictaphone on
to her plate, splashing sauce all over her front.

'Dinner's on you,' he said, and walked out.

She waited until he was out of sight, then reached for her
phone, checking her watch as she did so. It was thirteen
minutes past nine.

Parlabane was on the roof of Beadie's house when his
mobile went off, its shrillness suddenly piercing the chill
silence of the night. The noise was so unexpected that he
flinched in shock, promptly lost his grip and slid down the
tiled incline until his foot jammed in the guttering, where
the bracket bent under his weight and stopped about one
degree short of snapping.

He had made it to Eaglesham in just under an hour. The
address was on a road outside the village, one of a short
row of upmarket detached villas with farmland front and
rear, the kind of neighbourhood where Tommy Sheridan
probably didn't score many votes. The spacious gardens
were separated by tall privets and, in some cases, fir trees.
Privacy was assured, and so, no doubt, was security.

He had driven past the last house in the row, intending
to park in front, when he noticed a junction with a narrow
farm-track a little further ahead, hidden from the road by
more hedges. He took the Beamie ten yards down the track
and killed the lights.

Parlabane removed the theatre scrubs and stuck them
under the passenger seat, then unlocked the boot and

opened the holdall. The first thing he took out was his 'utility bra': a canvas tabard vest equipped with myriad hooks, clips and pockets to accommodate all the toys and gadgets that had made his experiences in journalism just that bit more exciting than those of the bloke who compiled the intimations. He selected the items he needed and made sure they were secure, then strapped the vest on tight.

The hedge bordering the track looked forebodingly robust, which ruled out the option of a rear approach. Fortunately, the pavement out front wasn't a popular route for pedestrians. He made his way along it briskly, then vaulted the metal gates to Beadie's drive rather than risk any rusty squeaks by opening them.

When he reached within five yards of the building, an exterior floodlight came on, causing him to drop flat to the lightly frosted grass, where his colour scheme betrayed serious shortcomings in its camouflage capacity. He lay still, his hands and feet keeping his tensed body just above the ground like the downstroke of one long press-up. His eyes scanned up and ahead, but he saw no activity from inside. After ten seconds, the floodlight went out again. It was motion-activated, for the dual purpose of automatically illuminating the householder's approach and scaring the crap out of trespassers such as himself.

Parlabane resumed his progress stealthily and remained at ground level until he was past the flood, where he drew slowly upright next to a side window. He unhooked the Jaguar night-scope with his left hand and reached into a velcro-sealed pocket with his right, retrieving another useful gizmo that had ironically only come his way once he supposedly no longer had any use for it. It was a device to detect electrical current, given him by a bloke called Spammy Scott, who was allegedly an electronic engineer during his brief flirtations with consciousness. Spammy had designed and constructed the thing as what he considered an appropriate token of appreciation for services rendered; services which might not have been rendered quite so effectively if the person he and Parlabane had been burgling that night had remembered to turn on his security system.

He held the device in his right palm and ran it around the frame. When his hand reached the top spar, the LED lit up like a Nitshill window in late November. It was alarmed; so would be all the ground-floor windows. Either that or Beadie should sue the numpties who did his last rewire.

Parlabane closed his left eye, held the scope to his right and peered through the glass. Looked like a living room. Two settees, widescreen telly, DVD player, coffee table. What he was looking for was high up in one corner, just below the cornicing: a laser-activated motion sensor. Normally, all you'd see was a white plastic box, and chances were the first you'd even notice it was when a tiny red light blinked on because you'd just tripped the thing. With the night-scope, however, Parlabane could see the beam, cutting the room in half at forty-five degrees to the corner. There'd be more, too. A guy who made his living pissing all over other people's privacy would take every care to protect his own.

He'd have to play this one extremely canny. Going in through glass was not an option because the idea was to avoid leaving any evidence that someone had been there. Cutting off the electricity was out too, as he might need a swatch at the guy's computer. He winced at the memory of just such a fuck-up, about six years back in Van Nuys.

He walked around the back, staying close to the walls in case there were any more exterior detectors. A quick

SpammyScan™ confirmed that the ground floor was a no-no. It was going to have to be a drainpipe job. How disappointingly low-tech.

Parlabane was out of practice but not out of shape. Having found a sturdy iron drainpipe (the burglar's buddy), he was on the roof in less than a minute. The only hairy spot was getting on to the tiles from where the pipe met the gutter. The brackets had seen better days, and one of them bent almost straight as he hauled himself on to the slope above, being more used to supporting moss and dead sparrows than bodyweight.

He climbed further up the incline until he reached an encouragingly rusted skylight, and had just run the detector around it to no response when the mobile burst startlingly into life, precipitating his heart-stopping tumble.

He pulled himself back up the tiles, this time making his way to the stone base of two chimney pots. Hanging on with one hand, he contorted himself to allow the other one access to the pocket containing his still-ringing phone.

'Hello?'

'Jack?'

'Jack's kinda busy at the moment, can I take a message?'

'It's Elspeth. He's on his way home. Have you found anything yet?'

'I'm no' inside yet. Where did you go for dinner – McDonald's?'

'He walked out. He rumbled me.'

'Fuck. How long have I got?'

'Twenty minutes. Twenty five at the most.'

'I love pressure. I *live* for pressure.'

'Be careful.'

He hung up.

'I won't,' he muttered.

Returning to the skylight, he found the encouragingly unmodern rusted frame to be less encouragingly stuck fast. He had a quick look inside with the scope, seeing a jumble of boxes on top of bare floorboards. It was the attic glory-hole. No motion sensors, but nor was there a way in without taking out the pane. Chances were Beadie seldom went up there, but even so, all it would take was the heavens to open tonight and the guy would know all about it by morning. It would have to be a last resort. Parlabane checked his watch. If he hadn't found another route inside in five minutes, then he'd take his chances with the rain.

He let himself slide slowly back to the gutter, then draped his legs down until his feet found an upstairs window-ledge. Resting his weight gratefully on the stone, he took out Spammy's gizmo and gave it another whirl around the two-part frame. There was no response.

'Thank fuck.'

Trying to banish thoughts of whether the device was as reliable as its creator, Parlabane pulled from his vest a rubber suction-cup attached to a short wooden handle. He stuck it to the bottom pane and gave it a tug with both hands, at which the window stubbornly failed to slide upwards.

'Arse.'

Looked like this last hurrah would have to showcase the full repertoire, like a bloody farewell tour. He reached to another pocket and removed a miniature power-drill, its cylindrical handgrip housing the batteries, which unfortunately he could not remember changing any time recently. This could be one number that got quickly dropped from the set, he thought, pushing the On switch with his thumb.

It buzzed into life, prompting a loud sigh. He applied it to the top spar of the lower frame, driving a small hole upwards at forty-five degrees, into the centre of the locking mechanism. He then took out a tiny screwdriver and pushed it inside until it found the lock's internal screw-thread. He twisted the screwdriver until the lever on top flipped open. Ten seconds later, he was in.

He looked at his watch. Fifteen minutes, maybe twenty. He'd call it twelve. The guy owned a Lexus and no doubt drove like he owned the fucking road too. Plus you could add ten miles an hour through anger at Elspeth.

He found himself in what looked like a guest bedroom. Single bed, sparse furniture, fading paperbacks gathering dust. The sight reminded him to put on the surgical gloves. Protective clothing must be worn beyond this point.

His remit was to find something – anything – that could tie Beadie to the murders, and from Parlabane's point of view, preferably the murder of Francis Shelley. The extremely big question was what, and he'd been banking on a little more than the duration of a tea-break to answer it.

There would undoubtedly be traces of metal, matchable to the murder weapon, wherever Beadie had filed down the steel ruler; most probably his garage. The problem was, that sort of evidence was only valuable if it was the polis who found it, on the spot, and they weren't going to go knocking on the PR man's door with a search warrant until they had some other reason to suspect him.

The other murder weapon offered more potential, but only if he hadn't dropped it in a river. Weighing against that depressing possibility was the fact that Beadie was now a man who couldn't be sure how soon he might next need to kill somebody; plus he would have no urgent need to dispose of it until he became a suspect. Nonetheless, he was also a man who had gone to elaborate lengths to avoid leaving a trail, so Parlabane couldn't afford to concentrate his efforts on looking for something that only *might* be there. He'd have to look at what *was* there and hope for the best. And he'd have to do it inside eleven minutes.

Elspeth had told Sarah that Beadie's study was on the ground floor, and opined that it was the best bet to find something incriminating, as that was where he kept all his documentation. It was also where she was no doubt hoping Parlabane would find the file on the St Saviour's children's home, according to what Mikey had relayed. Well, if he came across it, fine and good, but on this schedule he couldn't really afford to go out of his way.

Parlabane opened the door and looked along the upstairs hallway with the night-scope. He could see a beam at knee-height at the far end, and closer examination revealed that its source was chest-high on the wall of the stairs, which turned ninety degrees at the top. He climbed over the banister and draped down on to the staircase, landing with a cushioned thump. There'd been a similar layout in his auntie's house when he was a kid, and he had persisted with an identical manoeuvre despite equally persistent warnings that he'd break his neck. If he ever saw her again, he could now tell her it wasn't just him being a pain in the arse: it was vital practice.

He descended the rest of the stairs on his belly, stopping on the last one before the flight met the bottom hall so that he could scope for more sensors. Just as well. There was a motion detector of the nae-kiddin' variety above the open bathroom door at the far end, facing towards the front of the house. It boasted two automated beams covering the entire length of the hall at different downward angles, rotating left to right through a narrow arc like a Wimbledon spectator's head, though without the Union-Jack 'Come on Tim' plastic hat.

'Aw, for fuck's sake.' He was wishing he'd cut the power now. There wouldn't be time to look through the bastard's computer anyway.

The opening to the staircase was about four feet from the point nearer the far end where he could safely crawl under the lower of the beams. According to Elspeth's directions, the study was to the left of the bathroom, which meant he had a chance. The beams were staggered so that they each looked in different directions at the same time, but that meant there was a gap of about half a second while the lower one was sweeping towards the opposite wall. Balling into a tight crouch on the last stair, he watched the pattern through the scope a few more times, then chose his moment. He scuttled out and dived flat to the carpet, tensing up in anticipation of alarm bells. None came. He exhaled at length, then pulled himself forward by his arms, dragging his legs lifelessly behind.

The study door was closed, which meant more careful timing. Pressing himself against it in a crouch, he took hold of the handle and waited until the beams met in the middle, then pushed it open a few degrees. When they crossed again, he pushed it further, until after three instalments it was wide enough for him to roll inside.

He had another look at his watch. Eight minutes, disallowing the possibility that Beadie was, even then, dying in an entertainingly horrific fireball after losing control of his luxury motor.

Parlabane switched on the light and was taken aback. He'd seldom seen a room like this so neat; studies, dens, bureaux or whatever – even (perhaps especially) in the most pristine houses – were normally where the last vestiges of the male's uncivilised instinct made their messy stand. This primness was testament, he supposed, to Beadie's meticulous nature, a thought that augured poorly for his chances of finding anything the anal bastard had over-looked.

The PC sat on a desk in the centre at ninety degrees to the door, the monitor's screen facing away from the curtained window. Two of the walls were lined from floor to ceiling with four rows of shelves. One small corner of the shelving housed dozens of CD-ROMs, floppies and manuals, but the rest of the space was taken up with literally hundreds of alphabetised A4 manila folders, coloured name tags on all of the top right-hand corners.

Parlabane lifted one off the shelf at random. 'BOYD, Michael', the tag said. Inside were several zoom-lens black-and-whites of a chubby, middle-aged guy in a suit, standing on the steps of a hotel with a woman half his age, probably his secretary. There were also copies of hotel and restaurant bills, and receipts for jewellery.

Parlabane returned the folder and looked again at the sheer volume of material. Jesus. If it was a reflection of *his* mind that he kept looking for corruption, then what did this lot say about Beadie? He had to have a record of just about every petty indiscretion, every unfortunate act of human weakness committed by anyone in Scotland who met the minimum public profile or income-bracket criteria.

Call Guinness, he thought. We've located the world's saddest wank.

He scanned the shelves quickly, thinking he might as well nab what Elspeth was looking for, seeing as it was all so conveniently laid out. There was nothing under Doyle, so he tried among the 'S's for Saint Saviour's. Pulling out the file, his eye caught a glimpse of another familiar name an inch along.

SANDERSON, David.

Parlabane laid the folder down on the desk. Inside was an official document written in an indecipherable script; he guessed Thai. There were also photocopies of front-and-side mugshots of the late computer geek, and a black-and-white photograph of a young oriental girl. The document, presumably an arrest report, was dated 12/8/93. It predated the sex-tourism laws that would have automatically put Sanderson on the UK paedophile register, which meant he had successfully kept it a secret back home – other than from the Sinfinder General, who had recently put it to use.

It certainly helped complete the picture, but as evidence, it was useless. Beadie was already linked to Sanderson by the phone call, a connection neutralised by his alibi for that night. And if anything, a file like this would provide a motive for Sanderson to kill Beadie, not the other way around. Also, if Parlabane removed it from the house, there was little way of proving its origin; like the metal filings he'd speculated about, the cops would have to come here and find it.

Six minutes.

He looked at the computer. Those things were like confessional diaries in the digital age; people would keep record of things on them that they'd never dream of leaving written down on paper. They'd thus served Parlabane well over the years, but only in garnering information, not evidence. Once you had removed or copied a file from a hard disc, there was no way of proving where it originally came from; no way, in fact, of proving you didn't make it up yourself. Besides, he'd be lucky if the thing had fully booted up by the time he'd need to leave.

He needed something tangible. His thoughts, once more, turned to the gun, and this was as likely a place as any for Beadie to be keeping it.

The desk had two drawers on the left-hand side. He pulled open the top one, revealing several pens and pencils, a rubber, a stapler, staples, a paper punch, post-it notes, coloured adhesive labels: just about every standard item of office stationery *other* than a steel ruler. He grabbed the handle of the drawer below. It was locked.

'Aw gie's a fuckin' brek, here.'

He checked his watch again. He'd need time to get to the staircase past the beams, then he'd have to climb back up to the banister he'd draped from to avoid the sensor at the top. Still, the timetable wasn't definite, and he'd hear the car when his unknowing host arrived home. Beadie would have to open the gates and the garage door, put the motor in and then close them all again, which ought to provide enough time to get back upstairs and out the window.

Worth a shot.

Reaching into another vest pocket, he removed his lock-picking utensils, wrapped in their own wee canvas pouch like one of those personal-grooming 'gift' kits you got three of every Christmas. He busied his fingers. The handcuffs had taken no time back at the hospital, but now that he *had* no time, the pressure was taking its toll on his touch.

Three-and-a-half minutes. The desk drawer remained closed.

Parlabane stopped what he was doing, took a breath, composed himself and resolved not to look at his watch again until either he'd popped the lock or Beadie came home.

It had the desired effect. Having steadied his hands, he could better gauge the action of the levers inside. A delicate flick of the wrist sprang the catch and the drawer rolled open.

He looked inside. Two unopened green slabs of A4 printer paper looked back.

'Jesus fuckin' wept.'

He rolled the drawer shut with a bang and wiped sweat from his eyes, frustration and a growing sense of hopelessness threatening to manifest themselves in tears. Though not meaning to, he caught another glimpse of his watch. Just under three minutes, for what it was worth. At that point it belatedly struck him that printer paper was not something one generally tended to keep under lock and key.

Parlabane pulled the drawer open again and lifted out one of the slabs, revealing a metallic carrying case underneath. He picked it up delicately and placed it on the desk in front, noticing to his enormous satisfaction the manufacturer's name etched on the metal. Jenny said the gun that killed Sanderson had been something upscale, something your average ned wouldn't be able to get his hands on. Unless Sternmeyer had very recently diversified into designer toolboxes, this was exactly what he'd been looking for.

He pressed the snib to unlatch the lid of the case. It was, of course, locked. He took a couple of long, slow breaths. It was decision time.

If Beadie's prints were on the gun, it was everything he needed. Ballistics would match it to the bullet that killed Sanderson, and while that wouldn't directly clear Parlabane for Shelley, it would certainly make the cops listen very carefully when he told them what he knew. Beadie's clever alibi would tie Shelley into the Sanderson shooting, providing a motive for him to then kill the priest, and after that the cops would search the house, where they'd find the Sanderson folder and probably some tell-tale metal filings too. *If* Beadie's prints were on the gun.

If he'd wiped it, it was catch-22 again. The cops could still tie the gun to Beadie if they found it at his house, but that wasn't going to happen while they still had no grounds to suspect him. And all of the above depended on whether the gun was even in the bloody case, and not at the bottom of the Clyde. It felt heavy enough, but not knowing what the case would feel like on its own, he couldn't be sure.

There was a dull clang of metal from outside, followed immediately by a squeak of hinges. Beadie was back.

Parlabane stayed in his seat and reached calmly for the miniature drill. He dismantled the lock in seconds, then flipped open the lid, holding his breath as he did so. It took all his nerve not to shut his eyes too. But there, lying snugly amid the carved foam rubber, flanked symmetrically by two 28mm ammunition clips, was a Sternmeyer P-35 11mm pistol, visible laser-sighting mechanism attached in front of the trigger-guard.

There was a creak from outside as the aluminium garage door was swung open.

'Welcome home, Ian.'

Parlabane picked up the Sternmeyer and slotted a magazine into the breach, then sat back in the chair and waited, having just thought up a way of making damn sure Beadie's prints were on the gun.

final card for the burning game

Parlabane sat patiently listening as Beadie came in the front door and switched off the beeping alarm system. He heard the sounds of the hall light being turned on, the door being locked, keys being thrown on a table, a coat being hung up, then footsteps on linoleum and finally a kettle being filled. Aw, bless. Poor diddums had suffered a spoiled Saturday night, all he had to look forward to was a cup of tea in front of *Sportscene* before bed, and now heartless Parlabane was going to deny him even that.

He made his way softly along the hall and stood in the doorway, waiting to be noticed. Beadie was at the sink, rinsing a mug, which he dropped and smashed as prompted by Parlabane clearing his throat. Beadie leapt back against the washing machine, hyperventilating, his fright and horror no doubt exacerbated by Parlabane's artificially deathly complexion.

'Oh my God oh Jesus Christ oh fuckin' Jesus God.'

'I didn't realise you were so religious, Ian. Must have been all that hangin' about with Francis Shelley.'

'Oh good God, they killed you,' he whimpered, shivering. 'I'm seein' a ghost. You're a ghost.'

Parlabane raised the Sternmeyer and pointed it at Beadie's head. 'You fuckin' wish.'

Beadie stopped shivering and merely stared. Parlabane could see him processing the information, working out the possible explanations, and trying to suss the odds.

'I'm warning you, Parlabane. You fuck with me and there'll be hell to pay.'

'That's all right by me, pal,' he replied, narrowing his eyes. 'I know the boss.'

Beadie put his hands in the air like a bank clerk in a cowboy picture.

'Into the study. Now. I'm sure I don't need to tell you how much damage these things can do to the human head.'

Parlabane stepped out of the doorway and allowed him to pass, training the gun on him the whole time.

'The baw's on the slates, Ian, so take a seat. We've got things to discuss.'

Beadie backed unsurely into the chair, while Parlabane stayed on the other side of the desk. He could see the PR man's eyes begin to flit back and forth. He was already looking for a way out, already running through the logic and no doubt calculating that if Parlabane was going to shoot him, he'd have done it by now. It was time to disabuse him of that notion.

'I won't fuck around playin' games like Elspeth did,' he said, keeping the laser-dot in the middle of Beadie's forehead. 'I'll just tell you the deal. We both know the situation I'm in, and we both know how that situation came about. So, the way I see it, if I just stick this gun up a wee bit closer, like, say, to here . . .'

He jammed the gun between Beadie's eyes, which were already closed tightly, his teeth clenched and his whole face screwed up in frightened anticipation.

'And blow your fuckin' brains all over the wall, then all I'd have to do after that would be to stick the pistol in your dead right hand, and my problems would be solved. Maybe I could even tap in a wee suicide note on the computer there, explainin' all the evil, nasty things you've been up to. Then again, maybe that wouldnae be necessary, because you'd have just shot yourself with the gun that killed David Sanderson, a name the polis would subsequently find on a file just a few feet from your already stinkin' corpse.'

Beadie's eyes were open again, though he didn't look much less terrified. Nonetheless, Parlabane could tell the bastard was still evaluating angles.

'You're waiting for the "but", aren't you? Well, we'll get to that, but before we do, let me just underline how much satisfaction it would give me to end it this way. I would really fucking *love* to end it this way. And let me also avail you of the knowledge that there is absolutely no question of legal retribution holdin' me back, either, because I'm not even here.'

Beadie's eyebrows arched. It was as close to a question as he was ready to manage.

'I'm under general anaesthetic right now, fifty miles away, to which I have five witnesses; two of them the fuckin' prison officers who brought me to the hospital. I've left no prints and negligible damage. It *will* look like a suicide, and as I said, it would solve all my problems.

'So without further ado, on to the but, which I can tell you're now gettin' impatient to hear. It's extremely simple, Ian. If you can come up with an alternative means of incriminatin' yourself for the murders of David Sanderson and Francis Shelley, then I'd have no further reason to kill you. Apart, that is, from my own pleasure, plus the facts that I'd be doin' the world a favour and I wouldnae get caught. So there you are.'

Parlabane cocked the hammer.

'Any suggestions?'

Beadie's expression had changed from one of terror to one of reeling daze, the look of a man who had been utterly blindsided. He looked up blankly, his mouth opening and closing like a particularly glaikit goldfish.

Parlabane picked up the telephone that was on the desk next to the computer, and dialled his home number, holding the receiver to his chest so that Beadie wouldn't hear whose voice was on the answering machine. He pressed the silence button while he spoke.

'I realise it's difficult when you're under pressure, so let me help you out. Let's start with an easy one. State your name for the benefit of the tape.'

He released the silence button.

'Ian. Ian Beadie,' the PR man said, trance-like.

Parlabane pressed the button again.

'Well done. The questions will get harder from here, though. And please bear in mind that this confession is for *your* benefit. I already know the answers, so if you tell lies . . . BANG!'

Parlabane shouted the last word, walloping the underside of the desk with his knee at the same time. Beadie shook in his chair, then began panting heavily in a mixture of shock and relief.

'So. Why don't you start things off by tellin' me somethin' only the murderer would know. Tell me, for instance, what you did with Tom Heron's head.'

Beadie looked, for the second time that night, as though he'd seen a ghost. Parlabane smiled.

'Boy, does that face tell a story. But I'm afraid your face isnae gaunny be enough – not if you want to stay alive. Talk, ya bastard.'

When he had heard everything he needed to, Parlabane replaced the receiver on its cradle and unclipped a length of climbing cord from the back of his vest.

'Place your hands on the armrests, palms up, and please don't try anything that would force me to revert to Plan A, okay?'

He tied his prisoner to the chair by his wrists, noticing as he did so that Beadie had pissed himself, probably when he'd walloped the desk.

'Now *that* is the response of a man who knows first-hand what an eleven millimeter bullet can do at close range.'

'Fuck you, Parlabane.'

'Ooh, devastating comeback. Sadowitz would be jealous.'

Parlabane picked up the St Saviour's file from the desk, preparing to leave, then put it down again. He'd almost forgotten. Tsk tsk.

'Just occurred to me. There was one other way we could have resolved our wee differences tonight. A quick game of Rochambo.'

'What?'

'It's very straightforward. What happens is we kick each other in the balls until one of us gives in. "Firsties" is, understandably, a serious advantage.'

He stomped Beadie's groin with his right foot, an act that was hugely satisfying and not quite entirely gratuitous. The prisoner doubled over in his chair, useless with pain. Parlabane flipped on the gun's safety catch with his thumb, placed the pistol in Beadie's right palm, closed his fingers over it, then quickly pulled the weapon away again.

'Right, I think that's everything. I'd better be off. Oh, and if you do manage to escape, feel free to use the rope for toppin' yourself.'

Parlabane placed the gun inside the St Saviour's file, stuck the folder under his arm and walked out of the house. When he reached the Beamie, he placed his prizes in the holdall along with his vest, minus the mobile phone, which he dialled as soon as he was in the driving seat. It was time to deliver the big news – plus an ETA.

As soon as he heard the front door close, Beadie set about putting his rage to work. His wrists were secured across the armrests of the swivel chair, the rubber-coated tubes linking the seat and its back in a closed L-shape, the cord criss-crossing in front of his damp lap. He stood up, lifting the chair off the ground, and hobbled to the hallway, where he began swinging it against the wall, summoning all his fury to the task.

Beadie had never known anger like this.

He'd emptied his bladder then spilled his guts, having no choice but to tell the bastard everything. There had been no question Parlabane would shoot otherwise: Beadie of all people knew how easy it was to kill somebody if it was the only way to stay out of jail, and that was without having been there before and getting a knife in the stomach for a souvenir.

He was aware that there had to be parts Parlabane didn't know, but equally, he had no idea which parts those were, so he'd been forced to tell the truth about the whole lot. Parlabane was obviously in cahoots with Elspeth, and Beadie couldn't be sure how much Shelley had really told her. It had been utterly fucking hopeless, so he'd had the good sense to take no chances at that stage. If some opportunity presented itself later, fine, but it was difficult to come up with a contingency plan when there was a laser-sighted dot on your forehead and your lap was full of piss.

The castored feet of the chair were the first to come away, the swinging motion having unscrewed the rotating trunk from the seat. Another few thumps and the left armrest began to wobble, and soon after that it was shaky enough to create some slack in the criss-crossed cords. He eased his left arm out first, then fully extricated himself from the shattered contraption and returned to his desk.

He picked up the phone and hit the redial button. It rang twice then connected, the recognisable static hiss telling him it was an answering machine even before the recorded announcement commenced.

'Hello, this is Sarah. Jack and I aren't available at the moment . . .'

Beadie smiled. He put down the phone and booted up his PC.

Parlabane had got lucky in finding the gun, and the wee shite had improvised the situation very effectively from there, but improvisation always leaves a margin for error. A margin wide enough, in this case, for Beadie to slip through.

He keyed the name into a database field and hit Return. The address appeared in a microsecond. Edinburgh. He would be there in an hour.

Beadie ran upstairs and quickly changed into fresh underpants, then pulled on a pair of black trousers and a brown polo-neck. After that he went to the garage, where he put a lump-hammer, a chisel and a screwdriver into a plastic bag, then threw the lot on to the Lexus' passenger seat.

The wife had to be part of this scam to get Parlabane out of the clink, so she'd still be at the hospital until he was safely back there. That meant there would be no-one home for a good couple of hours. If Beadie got hold of that tape, all bets were off. Parlabane could tell the cops where to look for Heron's head, but without the tape he had no evidence of how he knew that. Same deal with the car-hire booking. All the information was useless unless Parlabane could prove its source.

However, that still left the gun.

Logically, Parlabane couldn't hang on to it himself in his present situation, so he'd have to give it to the missus to take home. That presented an opportunity not only for retrieval, but for revenge.

Croft was getting restless. There'd been plenty of horrendous nightshifts when he'd have given anything just to be sitting on his arse, reading the papers and drinking cups of tea, but this was anything but relaxing. He'd never seen anyone look so sick before, and he'd *definitely* never seen blue piss. The surgeon said the bloke could die in hours from something like this, and they'd both sat there ignoring his cries for Christ knew how long before he finally went to investigate. On top of that had been Guthrie's insistence on seeing him pee, which had cost what might yet prove to be a crucial few more minutes.

'Will you sit at peace?' Guthrie said. 'You're like a wean needin' the lavvy. Simmer doon. It's only been a coupla hours, an' the wummin says four at least.'

'Aye, but they've no said how it's gaun. I think that must be a bad sign.'

'Ach, don't talk pish. Whit are you worried for anyway? Be aw he deserves if he dies. I mean, I'm no' even a Catholic, an' I was fuckin' disgusted by whit that bastard did.'

'Still, it's no' gaunny look good if he dies on oor shift. You heard whit the governor said aboot this guy. I need tae know *somethin'*.'

Croft got up from his chair.

'Where d'you think you're gaun?'

'Tae the theatre.'

'You heard the wummin. We're no' sterile. You cannae go in.'

'I'll chap the door.'

'Don't be a fuckin' eejit. If it's gaun badly, the last thing they'll need is some tube distractin' them.'

He sat down again.

'Read the fuckin' paper.'

Croft sighed and picked up the *Recorder* once more.

Ten seconds later he was back on his feet.

'Naw. I'm climbin' the walls here.'

Guthrie got up to go after him, but they both stopped when they saw that the nurse was already coming down the corridor towards them.

'How's he doin'?' they asked simultaneously.

'Mr Quinn has things in hand. He's repaired the problem.'

'So he's all right?'

'He will be, yes. The patient is out of danger, but Mr Quinn still has to tidy a few things up, so we'll be about another hour.'

'Grand.'

'Mr Quinn said to pass on his thanks for your swift action in bringing the patient in.'

'Just doin' our jobs,' said Guthrie, the hypocritical bastard.

'And I'm sure Mr Parlabane will also be very grateful to you both for how you've helped him out tonight.'

Beadie parked his car on East London Street and pulled on his leather gloves. Parlabane wasn't the only one who wouldn't be leaving any fingerprints tonight, though Beadie doubted he'd be able to make the same claim about negligible damage.

He'd be throwing dirt on his wife's coffin in fucking handcuffs. Let's see how smart he looks then.

There was loud music belting from a converted church at the roundabout, opposite the bottom of Broughton Street. The bass beat echoed loud into the streetlit night as he crossed the road, polythene bag of tools in his right hand. No-one saw him, but even if they had, he looked like nothing more than a bloke with a carry-out, heading purposefully for a close. Party time.

Beadie walked quietly up the stairs on the balls of his feet until he reached Parlabane's door. He could hear the sounds of a late-night movie from the flat opposite: gunshots and squealing tyres. Good. He could afford a few bangs of his own before they came to check whether they had heard something or not.

He edged the tip of the chisel into the gap where the door met its frame, holding it in place with his left hand, then drove the hammer against it with his right. It was heavy, solid wood, and it absorbed much of the sound, leaving only the clunk of metal to reverberate around the close. Beadie looked over his shoulder at the other door, feeling the sweat run down his sides, his armpits having resumed their productivity with renewed zeal since Parlabane showed up. There was no sign of a response. The chisel was now wedged in securely enough to allow him both hands on the hammer. He took a firm grip, imagined Parlabane's face, and gave it all he had.

The door opened about half an inch, barely restrained by the one screw that was still attaching part of the lock to the splintered wood of the frame. After that, he simply had to lever the bolt back with the screwdriver and he was in.

Beadie closed the door behind himself and switched on a light. There was a small table in the hallway bearing a beige plastic telephone, but no answering machine. He had a closer look, but the phone only had the standard touch-tone digits. There had to be another extension. The kitchen, most probably, or the bedroom.

There were three doors at the far end of the hall. He walked down and pushed one gently, enough to see from the towel rail and linoleum that it was the bathroom. Turning ninety degrees on one heel, he nudged another door open and looked straight ahead. Mounted on the wall, next to a fridge freezer, was a combined telephone and answering machine, its red light blinking in the kitchen's darkness to signal that there was a message to be heard.

A message that would *never* be heard.

Beadie walked immediately to the machine, not even waiting for the fluorescent tube to grudgingly light his way. He pulled open the plastic covering and reached for the tape, which was when he heard the sound of the door closing at his back.

He turned around just as the fluorescent light finally flickered on, revealing three uniformed policemen standing around the kitchen, extendible batons in hand. Directly in front of the door was a woman holding up a warrant card.

'Detective Inspector Dalziel, Lothian and Borders Police.'

Beadie gulped.

'You're fucked,' she said, smiling.

say hello to civilian

Parlabane shuffled his back a little and luxuriantly buried his shoulders in the quite magnificent arrangement of pillows he had constructed. He had a four-bedded room to himself while he 'recovered', and the nurse had acceded to his request to concentrate its entire cushionary compliment on this one spot. The only flaw in what was an otherwise quite monumental achievement in personal comfort, was that his left wrist remained cuffed to the aluminium frame, which slightly impeded the optimum newspaper-reading position. However, it could not detract from his relaxed appreciation of certain of life's simple pleasures: viz, a Sunday morning lie-in augmented by a prolonged gloat over the sports desks' palpable discomfort at having to report upon the defeats suffered the previous day by Celtic and Rangers.

Guthrie and Croft were sitting by the door, and had for the past ninety minutes been getting amusingly agitated over the failure of any relief to show up and let them go home. Guthrie had gone off and phoned at one point, returning with a frustrated expression and the unwelcome information that they had to stay put for now because there had been 'a development'.

They both got up and looked out of the door every time they heard footsteps in the corridor. Parlabane almost felt sorry for them. They'd been there all night and hadn't got a wink of sleep. The same could not be said for himself, as he had zedded blissfully since his anaesthetist came in to 'make sure he was settled for the night', quietly informing him that Beadie had shown up as expected, and that the PR man, the gun and the tape were all now in police hands.

There was yet another shuffle of feet as the two screws heard yet another approach outside. This time they backed into the room again in the company of two very serious and official-looking gentlemen in suits.

There was a brief discussion in lowered tones, interspersed with looks in Parlabane's direction, and much disgruntled incredulity from Guthrie.

One of the men approached the bed, holding up a warrant card.

'DS Williamson, Strathclyde CID,' he said. 'Mr Parlabane, I'm here to inform you that all charges against you, relating to the murder of Francis Shelley, have been dropped. You'll be free to go home whenever the doctors discharge you as fit.'

The cop turned to Guthrie.

'There's still some formalities to be completed, but I think we can take the cuffs off now.'

'Aye, that'll be right.'

The other official held up a document in front of the screw, who looked at it with obvious disgust. Shaking his head, he handed the keys to Williamson with a grunt, determined not to be the one doing the uncuffing. Guthrie then looked at Croft with a bewildered shrug and made for the door.

'Oh, before you go, Mr Guthrie,' Parlabane called out.

Guthrie turned round, already seething in anticipation.

'Whit?'

'Remind your boss he owes me a grand.'

*　　*　　*

387

Elspeth switched on the radio at a minute past the hour to hear the latest news. Jack Parlabane had been released from custody following the arrest of a new suspect for the murder of Father Francis Shelley. In a separate story, Tayside police divers were searching an area of Loch Faskally in response to new developments in the hunt for the killer of Tom Heron, who had been found decapitated in a car park near Killiecrankie ten days ago.

Elspeth knew it would not remain a separate story for long.

The printer finished running off her resignation letter. She signed the copies, put each of them in an envelope and popped them in the mail tray. Then she performed her last official act as a minister of the Scottish executive, which was to sign a document recommending the early parole of one Michael Briggs: 'a model prisoner', according to the text.

She looked at the clock again. It was just after three. This was the last time she would be here, but there was no point in hanging around any longer. What was done was done, and what was over was definitely over. Best go home and enjoy the peace while it still lasted, because there was one hell of a storm forecast for tomorrow.

Elspeth walked out of the building and into the car park, where she noticed that something had been left under one of her windscreen wipers. It was an A4 manila folder, insulated from the elements by a transparent blue plastic sheath. She removed it from the windscreen and turned it over, revealing a handwritten note under the plastic on the other side.

Dear Elspeth,

This would make a good story for someone trying to get back into campaigning journalism.

Sarah.

PTO.

She pulled the note from the covering and turned it over.

PS: This file doesn't mention your father once.

Elspeth almost tore the plastic in her haste to get the folder out of the sheath, then climbed into her car, where she could better protect it from the wind. She flicked frantically through the contents, scanning handwritten testimonies and typed documents, as the truth began to dawn. Beadie had never shown her anything with her father's name on it; he'd only flashed the files in front of her, told her a story and let her worst fears do the rest.

She put her face against the steering wheel and waited for the tears to come. They soon did, but not for long, and to her surprise the only emotion she could feel throughout was relief.

Wiping her eyes, she looked again at what it said on the front of the note, then put her key in the ignition.

'At least let me keep the night-scope. That was a gift.'

Sarah was unceremonially dumping all of Parlabane's equipment into a black bin-bag in the bedroom.

'Yeah, and so was that jumper my mother got you for your birthday, but you didn't hesitate to get rid of that.'

'Oh come on, it's valuable. It might come in handy some time.'

389

Sarah sighed. 'Okay. You can keep it. But the rest goes.'

Parlabane placed the scope on the floor then watched her close the bag and tie a knot in it. It was all going: the utility bra, the lock-picking kit, the drill, the micro-camera, the glass-cutters, the suction-pad, the works.

'Do you want to say something?' Sarah asked with gleeful derision. 'Make a commemorative speech, perhaps?'

Parlabane shook his head in an exaggerated gesture of solemnity.

'No,' he said. 'I've no regrets. I'm gettin' too old for this cairry-on. Besides, the binmen don't come until Tuesday, so—'